No

MW01092532

Thomas Hall

BRIGHTON PUBLISHING LLC
435 N. HARRIS DRIVE
MESA, AZ 85203

No Loose Ends

Thomas Hall

Brighton Publishing LLC
435 N. Harris Drive
Mesa, AZ 85203
www.BrightonPublishing.com

Copyright © 2016

ISBN: 978-1-62183-390-1

ISBN 10: 1-62183-390-9

Printed in the United States of America

First Edition

Cover Design: Tom Rodriguez

Dedication

Always Marcia

Steve,

I have great respect for you as a ballplayer, as a friend, and most importantly as a human being.

Sincerely,

Tom Hall

Chapter One

FRANKLIN COUNTY, MAINE
AUGUST 26

The call came in at 2:32 in the afternoon. It was answered before the first ring was completed.

"This is the 911 operator. What is your emergency?"

There was a slight hesitation, and then the caller's voice burst through the receiver.

"My brother... There's been an accident."

"What is your location, sir?"

"The ranch... Redemption Ranch."

"In Pendleton, you mean?"

"Yes, that's it."

"What happened?"

"I think my brother must have fallen off his horse. The horse came back to the main house. I tied him up in the barn and then got in my Jeep and went out to check on my brother. I know what trail he usually rides on. I found him, but there was a lot of blood. He must have hit his head. I tried to revive him... but... I think he's... gone."

"What's your name, sir?"

"Tom Chambers... I mean that's my brother. I'm James Chambers... JT Chambers."

"All right, Mr. Chambers. I'm going to put you on hold while I switch over to the other line to dispatch the ambulance. Don't hang up, sir; stay on the line." The operator was gone less than twenty seconds. "The closest emergency response team is in Eustis. It's probably going to take them at least fifteen minutes to get to you."

"Okay. I'll wait by the front gate to let them in."

"I'll radio that information ahead."

An ambulance and a Franklin County Sheriff's police car arrived just under twenty minutes later. They followed JT Chambers in his Jeep along a well-worn dirt road. Shortly after they passed a cluster of buildings, the Jeep left the road and headed toward what appeared to be a forest of tall pine trees. The Jeep stopped after about a quarter of a mile next to a trail that went off to the left. As JT exited his vehicle, the three emergency responders and the officer from the county sheriff's department did the same. They followed him for about 100 yards along the trail. JT stopped suddenly and pointed to a spot 30 yards in front of them, but he didn't go any farther. The emergency personnel ran past him, while the police officer remained behind.

"Mr. Chambers?"

"Yes."

"I'm Officer Scanlan with the sheriff's department."

JT nodded, but didn't say anything.

Scanlan eased his notebook out of his pocket as he addressed Chambers again. "Can you tell me what happened? Or if you need a minute...?"

JT stared at Scanlan briefly and then looked back to where the emergency responders were tending to his brother. After a few seconds, he spoke softly.

4

"It doesn't matter. I think he's gone. I don't think they can do anything."

"I'm sorry."

"I told the 911 operator I was at the main house, when... my brother... Tom's horse came back without him. I tied the horse up in the barn, got in the Jeep, and then went looking for him. I started on the trail that he usually rides on. I found him after about ten minutes. There was some blood on the rock next to where he must've fallen. I tried to revive him, but I couldn't. That's when I called 911."

Officer Scanlan was about to ask another question when he saw the female ambulance attendant approaching.

She caught JT Chambers's eye and said, "I'm sorry, Mr. Chambers. We can't make the official call; they'll have to do that at the hospital. But I'm afraid your brother is... deceased."

JT remained silent for nearly half a minute and then said, "I'd like to see him before you transport the body."

"Certainly."

As he headed toward his brother's body, JT looked over at Officer Scanlan and said, "Can we wait until later for any more questions? I want to go to the hospital with him."

"Of course."

The ambulance driver and the other attendant moved farther away to allow JT some privacy. When the driver was sure he was out of earshot, he took out his cell phone, although he was reasonably sure that he wasn't going to be able to get a signal. To his surprise, the phone quickly came to life. He tapped the hospital icon on the screen, heard the phone on the other end ring twice, and then someone picked up.

"Eustis Medical Center."

"Andrea?"

"Speaking. Who's this? Is that you, Colin? I wasn't looking at the caller ID."

"Yeah. It's me. We've got a fatality. Is anybody from the medical examiner's office on-site at the medical center?"

"I don't think so."

"Okay. Would you have someone ready to pronounce the victim DOA, and then notify the ME's office to find out who's on call?"

"Will do. Who is it anyway?"

"I think his name's Tom Chambers."

"Tom Chambers?"

"Yeah."

"And where are you?"

"In Pendleton."

"Redemption Ranch?"

"Yeah, that's what the sign out front said. What is this place anyway?"

Andrea initially ignored the question. "I think that must be JT's brother."

"I think the brother is the one who let us in. You know him?"

"Not personally... I forgot you didn't grow up around here. Most people who have lived here for a long time know about Redemption Ranch, or at least they think they do. But the people in that family have always kept to themselves. Supposedly, they take in runaways, give them some religion, and get 'em on the straight and narrow. What happened, anyway?"

"It looks like he fell off his horse and hit his head."

"Sad. Rumor was that the brother hadn't been around for a while. He ran into some trouble and came back to try to turn his life around—maybe try to find his own kind of redemption."

❦Chapter Two❦

TEN MONTHS LATER—JUNE 14
DANVERS, MASSACHUSETTS

Maddie Walker was lying in bed in a near-fetal position. It was 7:10 in the morning, and she had already been fully awake for three hours. She knew it would be a lot easier if her mother were home; she could run interference. But her mother was at a nursing conference in Philadelphia. Even her older brother might have been some help, but he was starting a summer internship before his junior year at Cornell.

Maddie's thoughts were interrupted by a familiar sound emanating from the kitchen downstairs: her father making coffee. It startled her momentarily, but then her mind returned to where it had been. She knew that she had to tell her father, but that also meant she would probably have to admit that she had lied to him. Maddie could already envision the disappointment in her father's eyes. She'd only seen it a few times in her sixteen years of existence, but it affected her much more deeply than any punishment she had ever received.

Maybe he wouldn't press her for details about what she suspected. Maybe he'd just accept what she was saying. Who was she kidding? Her father was a retired FBI agent. He knew when career criminals were holding something back; he wouldn't be able to tell with his own daughter?

This was at least the fifth time in the last two hours that those thoughts had come into Maddie's head, always with the same imagined outcome. And then, not even aware that she was going to, Maddie got out of bed, put on her robe and slippers, and headed downstairs.

As she entered the kitchen, her father looked up from the Sunday paper.

"Hi, sweetheart. What are you doing up? You have a chance to sleep in and you're not taking it?"

Maddie smiled. "No, I couldn't sleep."

"Everything all right?"

Maddie wasn't quite ready to talk about it, so she deflected her father's concern. "No, just... school stuff. Nothing serious."

Craig Walker stared at his daughter for a moment and then offered, "Okay. Want some breakfast?"

"I'll just have some orange juice for now. I'll get it."

Craig Walker continued to watch his daughter as she headed over to the refrigerator. *I'll just wait her out*, he thought, as he pretended to go back to his paper. A moment passed, and then Maddie sat down at the kitchen table directly across from her father. He glanced up periodically, but Maddie was looking off to the side; their eyes never met. After a few more minutes, the silence became awkward.

Maddie broke first. "Can I talk to you about something?"

Her father resisted the temptation to indicate that he knew what was coming and instead answered, "Sure."

"You know my friend, Sam... Samantha Daniels?"

"I've heard you talk about her. I don't think I've ever met her though."

"No, I don't think you have. Mom did when she picked me up from school one day."

There were times when Craig Walker's interrogation techniques from his days with the FBI came in handy, even when dealing with his own children. This was one of them. He simply waited for his daughter to continue. Another moment passed, and she did.

"I'm worried about Sam."

"Why? What's the matter?"

"We had a final exam last Thursday in World Cultures, and she missed it."

"Maybe she was sick. I assume you tried to call her."

"A couple of times on Thursday and then a bunch of times on Friday, but they all went to voice mail, and she didn't call me back. I tried texting too."

Maddie could see that her father was not convinced. She knew that she'd have to give him more, but that meant he'd find out that she had lied. At that point, she resigned herself to that eventuality.

"She didn't show up for the Habitat for Humanity meeting yesterday. We had both decided we were going to do that this summer to start building up community service credits. You have to have a hundred hours in before graduation."

"I remember. You mentioned that to me the other day. I can see why you might be concerned, but maybe Sam just changed her mind."

"She's not like that. I can't help but think that something's happened."

"You don't think you're jumping to conclusions?" Craig realized how patronizing the words sounded after they left his mouth, but evidently, Maddie didn't hear it that way.

She said, "There's more."

"What?"

Maddie took a deep breath. "Yesterday, when I called to tell you that I was going over my friend's house after the Habitat meeting, and that her mom would give me a ride home ... Well, I went to Sam's house instead."

"What? Why did you do that? Where does Sam live?"

"Over in Faxon Mills."

"That's ten miles from here." He paused. "So you lied to me? You didn't go to your friend's house? Then how did you get home?"

"Taxi."

"You're running around at nine o'clock at night, and you took a taxi home? What were you thinking?" Walker asked.

"You have every right to be mad," Maddie admitted. "But just listen to the rest, okay?"

"You're giving me permission to be mad. Well, thank you. I have to tell you, I'm really disappointed, Maddie. This isn't like you."

It was just as Maddie had anticipated: the look on her father's face was far more devastating than any of his words. "I know, Dad. I'm really sorry, but I was so worried about Sam."

"If you were so worried, why didn't you tell me about this last night?"

"Because I knew I'd have to tell you that I lied. And I did start to tell you... but then I just couldn't. I haven't slept much the whole night. I'm really worried."

A combination of fear for her friend and the emotion generated by her father's disappointment brought Maddie to tears.

Craig Walker took a breath and only half-jokingly wondered how long it would take Maddie's mother to fly back from Philadelphia. He felt like he was in over his head. After another minute, Craig decided to dial things back.

"All right, listen. I want you to tell me everything. I won't interrupt except to ask questions. I'm going to try to stay calm. We'll sort this out. There are going to be consequences, young lady. But if you're worried about your friend, let's see if I can help."

Maddie brushed away some of her tears. "Thanks, Dad... I'm really sorry. I thought I had to do something."

"We'll talk about that part later. Tell me what happened."

"Well, like I said, Sam missed the final in World Cultures, and she didn't return my phone calls or my texts. And then when she didn't show up for Habitat, I got really concerned. Habitat was all she talked about for the past two weeks. I've only known Sam since school started. She's a year ahead of me. We both just happened to take the same elective. That's the only class we have together. Anyway, at the Habitat for Humanity meeting, our adviser was talking about where the houses are going to be built this summer. She wanted to make sure it would be easy for some of us to get there, especially if we were too young to drive. And since our high school is a charter school, we've got kids from all over. Sam had told me that she lived in Faxon Mills, but I'd never even been there. But then I saw her address on the list our adviser had." Maddie paused. "That's when I got the idea to go to her house. Well, actually it's an apartment."

Craig Walker tried to keep his voice steady as he asked, "Does she live with her parents?"

"Not exactly."

"What does that mean?"

"I think her father's dead." Maddie paused. "And I think maybe her mother's in jail."

"What? So she lives by herself? This just keeps getting better and better." Maddie's father put up his hands. "Okay, I'm sorry. Go ahead."

"I've never heard of it before, but someone told me that Sam's considered an adult."

"By whom?"

"I forget the term, but like legally she's an adult."

"You mean emancipated minor?" he asked.

"Yeah, that's it."

Craig started to shake his head, but caught himself before it went too far. "How did you get to her apartment?"

"I found it on Google maps, and then I used the Uber app on my phone."

"You have an Uber app?"

"Yeah, mom had me download it in case I missed the bus, and she couldn't pick me up."

"I thought Uber only operated in big cities?"

"No, they..."

"Never mind," Craig interrupted. "Tell me the rest."

"It was nearly seven thirty when I got to Sam's apartment. There was no answer when I buzzed. Luckily, the building superintendent lives in one of the apartments. So I tried him."

Craig closed his eyes and shook his head again, but didn't say anything. Maddie spoke more softly.

"He said that he happened to see Sam leave Wednesday morning. On Thursday, the person in the next apartment complained that a smoke detector from Sam's apartment was beeping, like the battery was dead. The superintendent said he went into her apartment and fixed the smoke alarm, but there was no sign of her. He said it was possible he missed her, but he hadn't seen her since Wednesday." Maddie paused and let her account sink in.

After a moment passed her father said, "Is that the end of it?"

"Not quite."

"All right, go ahead."

"It's been almost four days and no one has seen Sam. I was sure something had happened to her. So I decided to go to the Faxon Mills Police Station to see if I could file a missing person's report."

Despite his pledge to hold off on passing judgment or doling out punishment, Craig exploded.

"I can't believe what you're telling me, Maddie. This is not one of your young adult novels. You're not a detective; you're a sixteen-year-old girl. Do you have any idea how dangerous all of that was? And involving the police... I can't begin to think how long you're going to be grounded."

Maddie's eyes filled again. "I don't care about that. I just want her to be all right. I don't care how long you ground me. Will you at least try to find out where she is?"

Craig could see the sincerity in his daughter's expression and hear it in her voice. Although he had already made up his mind that he would look into it, he still asked the question, "What did the Faxon Mills police say?"

"I think they knew that Sam was an... emancipated minor. I guess maybe she's supposed to register with the police in the town where she lives. But that's the problem. Legally she's not a minor, so she's not considered missing right away. And I'm not old enough to file a missing person's report anyway. The policeman I talked to said until they had more information, they wouldn't do anything. So that's why I'm so worried. Nobody's going to file a report. Who's even going to start looking for her?"

Craig stared intently at his daughter. There was no question that he was angry, but he had to admit that he felt some pride too.

"Okay, I'll see what I can find out."

Twenty minutes later, Craig closed the front door behind him, walked down the steps, and took the slate path over to the driveway. After agreeing to look into the disappearance of his daughter's friend, he had told Maddie that he needed to clear his head, so he was going out for a run.

As he did some easy stretching, he reflected back on the conversation he'd had with Maddie. Had he overreacted? Probably not. Even though what she'd done could have been dangerous, it was the lying that bothered him the most. He supposed that most sixteen-year-old girls lied to their parents about one thing or another. It was obvious that Maddie regretted doing it. And it wasn't about drugs or drinking or boys. It was about her friend. So maybe it wasn't so bad after all.

Nevertheless, he had told Maddie at the end of the conversation that while he was out running, she could *answer* the phone, but she couldn't initiate any calls or texts. She was grounded all next week except to go to school for her final exam in English on Tuesday.

"Your mother will be home from the conference on Wednesday. I'm not going to tell her about this until she gets back. Then we'll decide together what additional punishment is appropriate."

Maddie hadn't protested; she just accepted her fate. "I understand."

After a few more minutes of stretching, Craig walked to the end of the driveway, pressed the button on his stopwatch, and then headed down the street. His course varied depending on whether he was doing three, four, or five miles. Today would definitely be a five-miler.

He was sure that when he had told Maddie he needed to clear his head that she assumed it was because of her behavior. But that was only partially true. He had been retired from the FBI for a little over a year. At age fifty-one, he was far from being past his prime, which was why the Bureau had set up a special program that allowed him to take on cases when for some reason the local or state police couldn't or wouldn't. His last case as a regular agent had involved an abducted child and was very high profile. The toll it had taken on him helped him decide to retire. But then he missed the detective work, or at least some of it—certainly the part about putting the bad guys away.

And then last year after he was officially retired, Craig had again partnered up with the same detective he had worked with on the abduction case: Dave Munoz. Munoz was about as sharp as they come, and they worked very well together. But once again, the case was high profile, involving a serial killer, and it had taken an emotional toll.

Craig suspected that continuing to deal with psychopaths and sociopaths had to affect a person. So maybe it was the cumulative buildup of witnessing all that depravity. Or maybe it was just because he was getting older. But over the last several months, Craig continued to have dreams about those last two cases in particular, and they weren't pretty.

The problem was that he was still very good at what he did. That was not ego talking. It was the percentage of cases he'd closed; it was the number of commendations he'd received; it was why the Bureau had approached him about continuing to work for them even in retirement. Of course, the Bureau wasn't being totally magnanimous in the creation of the special program. Craig Walker had the reputation of giving full credit to the local law enforcement personnel with whom he worked. That was a far cry from the FBI's perceived standard operating procedure. The brass at the Bureau knew a PR coup when they saw one, and that's why the agency created the program.

The nice thing about trying to clear your head while running was that thinking took your mind off the physical exertion you were expending. Craig passed the one-mile mark and didn't even realize it. When he did glance at his stopwatch, he figured he was running at about a 6:30 pace—not bad for a guy in his fifties.

After a moment, his mind jumped back to his conversation with Maddie. He wasn't sure whether it was a good idea to get involved with another case, but he'd told his daughter that he would see what he could find out. So what choice did he have? There was no going back on that now. The best he could do was to try to convince himself that looking into Sam Daniels' disappearance was not a real case, or at least it wasn't in the same category as the two cases that continued to invade his sleep.

At that point, there was no way for him to know exactly how wrong he was.

Chapter Three

Craig finished the five miles in just over thirty-one minutes—an even faster pace than the 6:30 of his first mile. Maddie was upstairs in her room when he returned. He decided to shower, get dressed, and then check out something on the Internet before he had any further conversation with her.

Thirty minutes later, Craig was sitting on the edge of his bed with his laptop open to a website about "emancipated minors." A number of things that he read puzzled him. Unlike a few nearby states, Massachusetts did not have a formal procedure for a minor to seek emancipation. So how had Sam Daniels gotten emancipation status? Also, emancipated minors had to be able to support themselves. Sam was still in school. A part-time job wouldn't pay enough for her to rent an apartment, never mind buy food and clothing. He wondered if Maddie would be able to answer those questions.

He went to a few additional sites, but didn't find anything new. Craig closed up the laptop, left the bedroom, headed down the hall, and then knocked on Maddie's door.

"It's open."

Maddie was seated cross-legged on her bed with her Dr. Dre earbuds in. Splayed out on the bed in front of her were a number of school textbooks and a tablet. Craig decided to keep things light.

"I still don't know how you study while listening to music."

"It's just background noise, and I keep the volume down; otherwise, I wouldn't have heard you knock."

"Still seems like a distraction, but your grades say otherwise, so who am I to complain?"

Maddie removed the earbuds and raised her eyes slowly to meet her father's. "I really am sorry, Dad."

"I know you are." He paused. "But you understand why I was so upset, and how dangerous that was? You know you can always come to your mother or me, no matter what. Have we ever not listened to you?"

The tears in Maddie's eyes threatened to spill over.

"No, you both always listen."

"Is that how you really feel, or are you just saying what you think I want to hear?"

"No, I mean it."

"So why didn't you come to me this time?"

"I don't know. I don't have an answer for that."

They sat silently for a few moments, and then Maddie said, "Dad, can I have a hug?"

Her father didn't say anything. He just moved closer and opened his arms. Maddie spoke while her head was still resting on her father's chest.

"I hate that I lied to you. I know it's hard to believe, but that's the first time I've lied to you since I was a little kid."

Craig pulled away slightly and raised his daughter's chin so he could look directly at her. "How about we make it the last time?"

Maddie smiled. "Deal."

As they separated, Walker said, "I wanted to tell you what I'm planning to do about Sam."

"Okay."

"First, you have to understand that this isn't an official case at this point. So I'm just a private citizen asking some questions. If I don't get the answers I need, or the local police don't take it seriously, then maybe I can get the approval to make it an official FBI case. But I have to be careful. It can't look like I'm using FBI resources for a personal matter."

"But you'll make it an official case if you can't find Sam any other way?"

"Well, technically it's not up to me. But yes, I'm pretty sure I can promise that."

"When are you going to start?" Maddie asked.

He smiled at his daughter's impatience. "Right away. Today. The first thing I'm going to do is call Dave Munoz. You remember Dave, don't you?"

"Sure, I met him when you two worked those cases together."

"Right."

"But if this isn't an official case yet, how can he help?" Maddie asked.

"Dave is actually a detective down in Stanfield. I want to find out what he knows about emancipated minors and how they're treated by the local police. I want to have as much information as possible before I go over to the Faxon Mills Police Station."

"You're going over there today? Can I come?"

Craig just stared at his daughter; she quickly got the message.

"Sorry, Dad. I guess I'll just stay here and study."

"That's my girl." He paused. "I wanted to ask you a couple of questions. Do you know when Sam became an emancipated minor and how she supports herself?"

Maddie shook her head. "I don't know. She doesn't talk about that stuff very much. Every once in a while she'll say something, but I don't think she likes to talk about it. So I never ask her questions about her family. The only reason I know as much as I do is because I overheard her talking to her guidance counselor. She said that her father was dead and her mother was in jail. That was at the beginning of the school year. I do know that she wasn't at our school last year. I think she moved here from Connecticut."

Craig leaned over and kissed his daughter on the forehead. "Okay, back to work. I'll let you know before I head over to Faxon Mills."

"You sure you don't want me to take a ride with you? I know exactly where the police station is." She hurriedly added, "Just kidding." And then she smiled and raised her eyebrows to open her blue eyes wider.

If there was any residual anger left in Craig Walker, it was now long gone. He responded, "I would take you with me, but rumor has it that you're grounded—maybe until you're twenty-one."

As Craig headed downstairs to call Dave Munoz, he thought about the exchange with Maddie. Maybe he wasn't in over his head after all. He also thought about how much easier he and his wife had it than so many of the dysfunctional families he had dealt with over the years. It had to be more than luck though, didn't it? And then he thought about Sam Daniels. Her father was dead; her mother was in jail. She's on her own, and she's only seventeen. Maybe it wasn't an official case yet, but he was going to treat it like one.

Dave Munoz picked up after the third ring.

"Hey, Craig. It's been a while."

"Yeah, at least a couple of months. Sorry to bother you on a Sunday, Dave."

"Not a problem. I'm just hanging out until the Sox come on."

They talked for nearly ten minutes, catching up with each other's lives, and then Munoz said, "As good as it is to hear from you, Craig, I suspect this isn't strictly a social call."

"I see your skills as a detective are still as finely honed as ever."

Munoz laughed. "That's from working with you."

"All right, enough of the BS." Craig paused and then became more serious. "My daughter, Maddie, has this friend, Samantha Daniels…"

Walker spent the next ten minutes outlining everything Maddie had told him, although he did leave out the part about her amateur detective adventure and subsequent grounding. When he finished, Craig asked, "What can you tell me about emancipated minors? Any suggestions on how I approach the Faxon Mills police about this?"

"As far as I know, we don't have any emancipated minors here in Stanfield. I do think they usually are registered with the local police, however. When I worked in Boston, I know we had a number of them, and they were registered with the neighborhood stations. But the only interaction I had with any of them was if they got into trouble—drug possession, fights… stuff like that. I never remember a situation where one of them went missing. It's really like a Catch-22, isn't it? Since they're under age, you'd like to start looking for them like you would any minor. But because they're considered adults, they have the right to do as they please. It's not as if someone would be checking up on them."

"That's exactly the problem."

"Are you considering getting involved officially?" Munoz asked.

"Not yet. I want to hear what the Faxon Mills police say first."

"Why don't you call me back later and let me know what they said. I'm off for the next two weeks. I had to take the vacation time before July first or I'd lose it."

"Busman's holiday, huh?"

"When I found out I had to take the time, it was too late to make any big plans. So what else am I going to do?"

"All right, I'll tell you what. If it becomes an approved investigation, then I'd like to bring you on board. If the Faxon Mills police are willing to investigate, then I'm going to back off."

"Okay, I'll wait to hear from you."

On the ride over to Faxon Mills, Craig Walker was still trying to decide how to play it: tell them he was an FBI agent, now retired, upfront, so they'd take him seriously, or take on the role of concerned citizen with no law enforcement background. He opted for door number two.

The Faxon Mills Police Station looked more like a house than a municipal building. It made sense, however. Faxon Mills was a rural community with the feel of a small town, even though there were a number of large horse farms on its outskirts.

Craig parked out front in one of the four non-handicap parking spaces reserved for visitors. After he entered the station, he waited at the front counter for about 30 seconds before a uniformed officer glanced up from his desk and approached. He looked to Craig as if he were still in high school. Of course, everybody was starting to look that way to him. "Can I help you, sir?"

Craig responded, "I hope so." He looked at the name tag and added, "Officer Snyder, My name is Craig Walker. I actually live in Danvers." Officer Snyder looked a little surprised as Craig continued. "My daughter was here last night. It seems a friend of hers is missing, and this friend *does* live here in Faxon Mills."

"What's the friend's name?"

"Samantha Daniels."

"Doesn't ring a bell but I'm quite sure we don't have a missing persons report on anybody currently."

"My daughter was told that she couldn't file anything officially, but I would guess whoever she spoke with last night would have started a file or made some notes."

"I think Officer Crawford was on last night. Let me take a look at the logbook. I'll be right back."

Five minutes later Officer Snyder returned. "I'm sorry, sir. There's nothing in the logbook. Are you sure it was last night?"

"Positive."

"I don't know what to tell you. How old is this girl who's supposed to be missing?"

"Seventeen."

"Why haven't her parents reported her missing?"

"She's an emancipated minor." Craig could see by the look on the young policeman's face that he had no idea what that meant. Rather than embarrass him, Craig added, "As you know, her parents have to be out of the picture for her to be emancipated. That's the problem. There really isn't anyone to report her missing, because in the eyes of the law she's an adult."

"As I said, there's nothing in the logbook." Officer Snyder paused, obviously considering something. "Officer Crawford is out on patrol. I could radio him and ask him to come in."

"I'd appreciate that."

"Okay, give me a minute."

Craig took a seat and waited. Ten minutes later, a uniformed policeman who appeared to be in his forties came through the front door, barely acknowledged Craig and went behind the counter. Officer Snyder and the newly arrived officer disappeared into a room off to the side. Craig could hear someone raising his voice and assumed it was Officer Crawford who sounded none too pleased to have been called back to the station. When the two policemen emerged from behind closed doors, Snyder sat back down at his desk as the other policeman approached the front counter. He had removed his hat; he had a military type buzz cut and was graying at the temples.

Craig stood and moved toward the counter, as the policeman said, "I'm Officer Crawford. What seems to be the problem?"

Craig didn't like Crawford's tone, but he kept his cool. "I'm Craig Walker. My daughter was here last night because she believes a friend of hers is missing."

"Yeah, I remember."

Craig expected Crawford to continue. When he didn't, Walker said, "I know it's a bit complicated because the girl is an emancipated minor, but I was wondering if anything can be done to... expedite... looking for her."

"What's your concern, Mr. Walker? Why are you involved?"

Keeping his cool was getting more difficult, but Craig took a breath. "My daughter asked me to see what I could do. It's possible that her friend, Samantha Daniels, has been missing since Thursday."

"And why would she think that?"

"They go to school together, and Samantha didn't show up for her final exam on Thursday, and she missed a club meeting yesterday." Craig realized how flimsy that all must seem, so he added, "And the superintendent of her apartment building hasn't seen her since Wednesday morning."

"So, it sounds like you've already been doing some investigating, Mr. Walker. Not a good idea; you need to back off. If and when it becomes a police matter, we'll handle it."

That did it for Craig. "Really? You didn't even log in my daughter's visit. When does it become a police matter, when you find a body?"

"Watch yourself, Mr. Walker."

Craig decided he wasn't going to waste any more time talking to Crawford. "Well, thanks for your time." He threw Crawford a fake smile. "I'll be in touch."

Crawford wasn't sure what Walker meant by that, but he wanted the last word, so he offered, "I mean it, Mr. Walker. Stay out of this." He was now talking to Walker's back, as he added. "You might want to keep an eye on your *own daughter*. A young girl out by herself at nine o'clock at night—not a good idea."

Craig was steaming as he started his car and pulled away from the station. But at least one good thing had come out of the encounter with Crawford - It had made the decision much easier. If Walker had anything to say about it, this was going to become an official FBI investigation real quick.

When he got home, Craig immediately called his former FBI supervisor, who was also the one in charge of the post-retirement program, and explained the situation. The supervisor gave his approval in less than five minutes. Craig also got permission to deputize Dave Munoz. While an investigation into a seventeen-year-old girl's possible disappearance wouldn't necessarily warrant the FBI's attention, never mind bringing another investigator on board, the high-profile success of Walker and Munoz made any request to partner up the two a relative no-brainer.

Craig told Maddie the good news, and then called Munoz.

"I got the approval if you were serious about wanting to be involved."

"I'll see you tomorrow at nine o'clock, okay?"

"Sounds like a plan."

"So, I take it you didn't get too far with the Faxon Mills police?"

"That's an understatement." Walker lowered his voice, concerned that Maddie might overhear. "The cop I spoke to was a total jerk. He made it pretty clear that he was in charge and didn't like anybody questioning his decisions. I don't think there's any way he's going to look for Maddie's friend. Even if he did, I wouldn't like the odds of him finding her. I'd be surprised if he could find his ass, even if he had his hand in his back pocket."

Chapter Four

Walker sat at his dining room table with only a pad of paper and a laptop in front of him. The laptop would only get any use if he needed to Google something. Any notes he took would be handwritten. Walker was decidedly "old school" in that regard. As he sat there, he realized that in many ways, this investigation was uncharted territory for him. Most of the crimes he had investigated over the years were just that—crimes. But there was no evidence that anything criminal had occurred in this instance.

Regardless of that, however, the fundamentals of any investigation tended to be very similar: Find out as much as possible about the central figures in the case. Use whatever technological resources were available. Study the evidence gathered and see where it led you. So Craig stuck with the basics as he compiled a list of things that needed to be done.

First, he had to ask Maddie some more questions. He wrote a number of them down, knowing that some additional ones would be generated by his conversation with his daughter.

The next words he wrote down were "guidance counselor." Maddie had mentioned that she had overheard Sam talking to her guidance counselor. It was certainly possible that that person knew as much about Sam as anyone.

Walker followed up that notation with the words "telephone records and credit card statements." While in many investigations, telephone logs and financial records would usually be requested early on, in this case, Walker knew he would need a warrant and that would take time. It would be better to talk to Sam's guidance counselor first. Whatever he discovered from that interview might make getting a warrant easier or unnecessary.

The next notation he wrote down was "apartment." After he and Dave Munoz went to the school, Sam's apartment would be the next stop. While it was possible that the building superintendent would refuse to let them in without a warrant, the fact that he had already spoken with Maddie and the fact that the FBI was involved would probably gain them access without it. And if it turned out they needed a warrant, he could ask for it at the same time as he asked for the one for the telephone logs.

As he looked down at the writing in front of him, Walker acknowledged that he was really pushing things by opening up an FBI investigation to try to discover the whereabouts of Sam Daniels. On the other hand, the seventeen-year-old girl really had no one else to advocate for her. In many ways, she was like the thousands of homeless teenagers who lived on the streets. If they went missing, nobody noticed.

Walker also knew that a major part of his willingness to pursue the case was because Maddie had asked him to. Another smaller part was the pompous attitude of Officer Crawford. As Crawford's name came into his head, Walker added a few more words to his list. "Visit the Faxon Mills Police Station." He would have to give them a heads-up that there was going to be an FBI investigation in their community. In his younger days, he might have enjoyed rubbing Crawford's nose in it. But after many years on the job, Walker had come to respect the vast majority of local and state police. He believed Crawford was an exception. Walker actually hoped that Crawford wasn't there when he showed up at the station. One-upmanship wasn't anything he was really interested in at this point. His focus was exclusively on finding Sam Daniels.

He waited until Maddie came downstairs to take a break from studying before he had her join him at the dining room table.

"I need to ask you some more questions."

"Sure."

"Have you tried to call or text Sam recently?"

"Well, no. You told me I couldn't."

Walker had forgotten about that. "I actually just meant while I was gone. But why don't you go get your phone and try again. I want Sam's telephone number anyway. At some point, I'm going to try to get a warrant for her phone records."

"Okay, I'll be right back."

Maddie returned in a few minutes, already moving her thumbs in rapid speed over the keyboard. A moment later she said, "It went through. Should I call her too?"

"Yeah, why not?" Walker replied.

Maddie went back to the contacts' screen, found Sam's number, and tapped it. After five rings, it went to voice mail.

Maddie said, "Hi, Sam. It's Maddie. Call me and let me know you're okay." After she disconnected, Maddie went to her contacts again and gave the phone to her father so he could write down Sam's number. As he did that, he noticed that there were two other numbers listed for Sam.

"What are these other numbers?"

"Oh, those are old. The last one listed is the current one."

"Sam changed her phone number a couple of times since you've known her?"

"I guess."

"Do you have any idea why?"

"No clue."

Walker let that piece of information settle in for a moment, not sure if it meant anything or not. He eventually glanced down at his list of questions and asked, "Is Sam on Facebook, Twitter, anything like that?"

"Not that I know of."

"What about driving? Does she have a car?"

"I don't know if she knows how to drive, but she doesn't have a car."

Walker made a couple of notes and then continued with the questions. "Is there any chance that Sam ran away?"

Maddie looked at her father with an incredulous expression on her face.

"Really, Dad?"

"Why are you looking at me like that?"

"She has her own apartment. Legally, she's an adult, and she can come and go as she pleases. What would she be running away from?"

Walker started to defend his question, but then realized the logic of Maddie's response. "Okay, point taken." Unfortunately, he couldn't leave well enough alone, as he dug a new hole for himself. "What about a boyfriend? Does she have a boyfriend?"

Maddie looked at her father in the same way she had just a moment before. "No, she doesn't have a boyfriend. And even if she did, she's not about to go running off with someone. She. Has. Her. Own. Apartment."

Walker smiled. "All right, all right. I surrender." Walker caught his daughter's eye. "Permission to treat Maddie Walker as a hostile witness?"

Maddie sat back and chuckled. "Denied, but I'm not being hostile, just realistic. You can ask the rest of your questions, assuming they're better than those were."

Walker sat back as well and smiled more broadly. He loved these kinds of exchanges with his daughter. It was scary to think she'd be off to college in two years. He'd miss this, just as he did with her brother. His thoughts turned to Sam Daniels. Walker wondered if she had ever had moments like he and Maddie had just had.

Maddie must've been thinking something similar because the lightness in her voice disappeared. "What else do you need to know that might help, Dad?"

"Do you have a picture of Sam?"

"No."

"Not even on your phone?"

"No. Sorry"

"Okay." Walker paused as he looked down at the list in front of him. "You mentioned Sam's guidance counselor. Do you have a name?"

"Her name is Mrs. Burns—Alice Burns."

"I think Dave and I are going to go see her first thing tomorrow."

"That's a real good idea. I know Sam likes her a lot. She might be able to help."

Maddie and her father talked for another fifteen minutes, and then she went back upstairs to study. Once Walker was sure that she was out of earshot, he made a couple of calls to the hospitals in the area. The people he spoke with were somewhat reluctant to give him any information over the phone without seeing his credentials. But he was able to glean that no one by the name of Samantha Daniels, or even a Jane Doe, had been brought in.

He spent the next hour and a half reviewing what he knew and formulating questions for Mrs. Burns, but mainly wondering in what direction he would go if those first few steps didn't produce anything—a possibility that he viewed as very likely.

Dave Munoz arrived a few minutes before nine on Monday morning. Walker offered him a cup of coffee, which he accepted. The two investigators sat at the kitchen table, engaged in some small talk briefly, and then Walker said, "Maddie's not up yet. She didn't get much sleep the night before, so I'm just as glad that she's sleeping late."

"Maybe I'll get a chance to say hello when we get back later on." Munoz said. "So obviously you think there's something to her concern about this friend of hers... Samantha Daniels. Right?"

"Yeah, I do. Maddie's a pretty typical teenager, whatever the hell that means. But she seems to have good instincts about things. Of course, I'm biased, but I think she's reading this correctly."

"So what's the first step?"

"According to Maddie, Sam is pretty close to her guidance counselor, a Mrs. Burns. I think we should start with her. I'm hoping she can give us some insight."

On the ride over to the school, Walker filled Munoz in on everything else he knew at this point, which wasn't a whole lot. Munoz took it all in and jotted down a few notes. As they pulled into the school parking lot, Walker realized that the lot was only half-full.

"I forgot. This is finals week. The students only have to show up when they have exams."

Walker led the way to the front entrance where they had to sign in before going to the guidance office. The guidance office had a large counter with two desks behind it. Neither was occupied.

They waited about thirty seconds, and then Walker called out, "Hello, anybody here?"

After a few moments, a woman who appeared to be in her fifties came out from one of the offices in the back. She looked at the two men on the other side of the counter over the top of her glasses.

"Can I help you?"

Walker answered. "We're looking for Mrs. Burns."

The woman smiled. "Good news for you. You found her. I'm Alice Burns." She offered her hand. Walker extended his.

"I'm Craig Walker."

"And I'm Dave Munoz," Munoz said as he also shook Mrs. Burn's hand.

"What can I do for you gentlemen?"

Walker responded. "I tried to call earlier to set up an appointment, but there was no answer."

"Our receptionist is out sick. Sorry about that. But you're here now, and I'm not a stickler for appointments anyway. Are you a parent of one of my students? I don't recognize either name."

"My daughter, Maddie—Maddie Walker—goes here, but actually we're here about another student. Samantha Daniels."

"Sam? I'm not sure I understand. What about Sam?"

Even though Walker looked around to make sure there was no one else in the area, he nevertheless lowered his voice.

"My daughter, Maddie, is a friend of Sam's. She hasn't been able to get in touch with her. She's concerned that Sam is... missing."

"Missing? What?"

Walker continued. "We're aware that Sam is an emancipated minor. The local police are not in a position to investigate this." Walker took out his FBI credentials and showed them to Alice Burns. "My partner and I have been authorized to look into it."

"The FBI?"

"Would it be all right if we spoke some place more private?"

The guidance counselor looked stunned. "Uh... We can use the conference room, I guess," Mrs. Burns said. "Sam and the FBI?"

Walker said, "We're hoping it's nothing. But until we can verify her whereabouts, we're taking it seriously."

Alice Burns shook her head, obviously having trouble processing what Walker was telling her. Eventually she said, "The conference room is this way. Why don't you have a seat? I'll get Sam's file."

Less than five minutes later, she was seated across from Walker and Munoz.

"Are you sure she's missing?"

Walker answered. "It looks that way. Were you aware that she didn't show up for her World Cultures exam last Thursday?"

"No. I won't get notification of any absences until tomorrow afternoon after all the exams are done. Then I'll contact the students who may have missed their exams. If it's a legitimate absence, they can schedule a makeup on Wednesday or Thursday. If not, they're out of luck." She paused. "Parents are notified immediately through our automated system if their child is absent. Of course, that wouldn't matter in Sam's case, would it?" Mrs. Burns said. "There must be more to this than her missing one exam."

Walker said, "There is. A few things, actually. She's not answering her phone; she didn't show up for the Habitat for Humanity meeting, and the superintendent of her apartment building hasn't seen her since last Wednesday."

Alice Burns looked alarmed. "I have some concern about her not answering her phone and the building superintendent not seeing her, but not going to the Habitat for Humanity meeting—that gives me the most concern. She wouldn't miss that under any circumstances I can think of. She was very passionate about that."

Walker nodded his head. "That's what my daughter said."

Munoz spoke for the first time since he introduced himself. "Is there anything you can tell us about Sam that might help us figure out where she might be?"

The guidance counselor opened the file in front of her, although she didn't look at it as she spoke. "This is her first year at our school. She transferred here from Connecticut. I don't know how much Sam shared with your daughter, Agent Walker, but Sam didn't have an easy time of it the last few years. Her father died about five years ago, and her mother's in jail—according to Sam because of drug involvement."

Walker asked, "Where is her mother incarcerated?"

"Sam didn't tell me specifically, but I'm pretty sure it's Connecticut."

Munoz interjected. "And yet she left Connecticut to come here to Massachusetts?"

"Yeah, I admit it does seem odd. Although I got the sense that she was estranged from her mother. I think it's possible that Sam just wanted to get away from her old life. The thing is... I never pushed too hard with Sam. I wanted her to trust me, and I figured if I started prying, she'd shut me out. I only asked her things that I absolutely needed to know." Alice Burns paused. "I will say this—her transcript from last year is somewhat unusual. All of her classes were completed through independent study. They were certified by a high school in Bridgeport, but for at least the last several months of her sophomore year, she didn't attend that school."

Walker spoke again. "Do you know why?"

"I called the guidance department, but since Sam is an emancipated minor, legally they can't release that information without her permission."

Walker said, "Really? Not even school records?"

"No. She has all the rights of an adult. It's just like for our seniors. Once they reach eighteen, we have to send any correspondence, including report cards, directly to them. They don't have to show anything to their parents if they choose not to."

Walker was shaking his head. "Please don't tell my daughter that."

Alice Burns smiled. "Sorry, Agent Walker. Legally, we have to."

They were all quiet for a moment, and then Munoz broke the silence.

"What's Sam's attendance been like? Has she ever been absent for an extended period of time?"

"No. I think she might even have perfect attendance. At the most, she's missed one or two days the whole year."

Munoz continued. "Is there anything she talked about a lot? Any place she liked to go?"

"Habitat for Humanity." A moment passed and then a look of recognition came across the guidance counselor's face. "Come to think of it, she did mention that she wanted to go visit some horse farms this summer. She told me that she used to ride, but I think that was before she moved here."

Munoz wrote down a few notes and then asked, "Is there anything else you can think of that might help us?"

"I'm afraid not. Sam tends to be very private," Mrs. Burns said. "This is scary. It's hard for me to imagine that Sam would just leave. I think she felt comfortable here; it was a fresh start."

Walker asked, "You wouldn't happen to have a picture of Sam, would you?"

Alice Burns shuffled through the file in front of her and produced a small thumbnail photo. "I'm sorry, but this is all I have."

Walker responded. "That's okay. This is fine." He paused as he looked at the photo. "Pretty girl."

Alice Burns didn't acknowledge Walker's remark. Instead, she pulled out what appeared to be a business card from Sam Daniels's file.

"I forgot about this. This may be helpful." She handed the card to Walker.

"What is it?"

"It's a card for Sam's social worker."

"She has a social worker?"

"At the beginning of the school year, this woman came to see me. She said that she was helping Sam with the transition to her new school. She wasn't at liberty to talk about Sam's history because of the legalities involved. But she gave me her card and said I should call her if Sam ran into any trouble. I completely forgot about it. There was never any reason for me to contact her; Sam's been a model student."

The three of them talked for a few more minutes. Walker gave Alice Burns one of his cards, and he and Munoz signed out at the front entrance and left.

Once they were outside, Walker said, "I think we should follow up on the social worker, rather than head over to Sam's apartment."

Munoz nodded. "I agree," he said. "I jotted down some notes about Sam's mother and the horse farms, but neither situation would seem to explain her being gone for four days."

"That's what I was thinking too." As he said that, Walker took out his phone and punched in the number on the business card Alice Burns had given him. As he waited for the call to go through, he said, "The social worker's office is over in Lynn. That's about ten miles in the other direction, but I still think we should go there first."

"I agree. I just hope she'll talk to us."

"Only one way to find out."

ᴄᵃᵃⱽ⌐Chapter Five℣ᴰᵒ

Cassandra Jeffers, Sam Daniels's social worker, had agreed to see Walker and Munoz as soon as they could get to her office. She was waiting for them outside her cubicle when they arrived. The three shook hands; Walker and Munoz showed her their credentials, and Mrs. Jeffers invited them to sit down.

Cassandra Jeffers was a tall, slender black woman, whom Walker estimated to be in her mid-forties, but the pictures in frames labeled "grandchildren" on the shelf behind her desk suggested that she was at least ten years older than that.

Mrs. Jeffers spoke first. "I hope I can help you. But as I said on the phone, I haven't had any contact with Sam in months."

Walker asked, "Can we go back to the beginning? How did you get involved with Sam to start with?"

"I got a call from a social worker in Connecticut. Each state has its own Department of Social Services, but we also have a New England network. The woman who called me said that there was an emancipated minor moving into this area, and she might need some assistance with the transition. I was happy to do it, although I have limited experience with emancipated minors. Massachusetts doesn't even have a formal process to grant that status, but Connecticut does."

Walker interrupted. "Does the law require an emancipated minor to have a social worker?"

"No. And it's not like having a probation officer, where the client has to check in periodically. In essence, after initially getting her registered at school, I just made myself available if Sam needed something."

Munoz entered the conversation. "So how often did you see Sam?"

"In total? Probably three times. Twice when she first moved here and once as I said several months ago."

Munoz continued. "Why did she move here? Do you know?"

"I wasn't told directly, but I think it was a condition of her emancipation that she moved out of the area where she was living in Bridgeport."

Walker took over. "But why Massachusetts? And why Faxon Mills?"

"I think there were two primary reasons. One was the proximity of Massachusetts, but more importantly, the Bay State Charter School. Its curriculum specializes in government and the social sciences, along with a strong community service component. Sam was very interested in all of those things."

Walker nodded. "My daughter goes there. She's actually a friend of Sam's. That's how this investigation got started," he said. "You said there were two reasons."

"The second reason was the horse farms. Sam said that she had recently learned to ride and was hoping to take it up again. But that must've been someplace other than Bridgeport. There aren't any horse farms near there that I'm aware of."

Munoz asked, "Do you know how Sam supports herself?"

"There was some sort of trust fund. Actually, that's the reason I spoke with her the last time. Her rent is paid directly, and she gets a monthly allowance. For some reason, her allowance didn't get credited to her account, so she called me."

"Do you know what bank?" Munoz said.

Cassandra Jeffers opened the file on the desk in front of her and searched through a number of papers. "Uh... Here it is. Southern New England Financial," she said. "There's a lot I don't know about Sam's situation. She wasn't very forthcoming. But to be fair, I really didn't need to know the details in order to help her get acclimated. I did get the impression that she'd been hurt—not physically, but that's possible too, but emotionally. I suspect that's why she wouldn't open up about her past. She has trouble trusting people."

Cassandra Jeffers reached for a scrap piece of paper on her desk. "Let me write down the name and number of the social worker from Connecticut. She should have a lot more information than I do. Honestly, I would have no idea where to even begin to look for Sam. I just haven't been that involved in her life."

Walker accepted the Connecticut social worker's information and said, "But it sounds like that was her choice."

"I appreciate you saying that. But in this job, you're always second-guessing yourself... You know? Could I have done more?"

"Sounds like law enforcement."

Cassandra Jeffers smiled. "I guess that's true."

As he and Munoz got up to leave, Walker handed Cassandra Jeffers his card and asked her to call him if she remembered anything else that might help.

On the way out to the parking lot, Munoz said, "That's twice now that someone mentioned the horse farms as well as Sam's connection to Connecticut. Initially, I didn't view either one of them as very important, but now I'm not so sure. I think we need to check them both out."

Walker responded. "I agree. But let's head back and visit Sam's apartment. Then we can figure out where to go from there."

Sam's apartment building was fairly nondescript. The outside was well maintained, but the walkway and the front façade were showing some signs of age. As Walker and Munoz pulled up, they noticed a man up on a ladder working on a light fixture near the front entrance. As Walker approached, he pretended to cough, attempting to alert the man of their presence.

As they got closer, the man turned toward them, and Walker asked, "Excuse me, are you the building superintendent?"

The man started to descend the steps of the ladder. "Yes."

Walker waited until the man was off the ladder completely. "I think you spoke with my daughter yesterday. She was looking for her friend Samantha Daniels."

"Yes, that's right. But as I told her, I haven't seen Sam for several days." He looked more intently at the two men in front of him. "I'm sorry, who are you?"

As Walker produced his badge, he said, "I'm Agent Craig Walker, and this is Detective Dave Munoz."

The building superintendent looked more closely at Walker's credentials. "FBI? Why is the FBI interested in Sam? She's just a kid."

Walker offered an explanation, and the building superintendent seemed to accept it. "I'm Angelo Lentini by the way."

The three men shook hands, and then Walker followed up on the explanation he had offered. "As I said, our only interest is to find Sam. We'd like to take a look at her apartment to see if she left any clues as to where she might have gone."

Angelo Lentini hesitated. "If this was any of the other tenants, I don't think I could let you in if they weren't home. But if this might help you find Sam, okay."

The building superintendent led the two men up a flight of stairs to the second floor. He searched through a large ring of keys, found the one he was looking for, and unlocked the apartment door. "When you finish, just close the door behind you."

"Thanks," offered Walker. And then he extracted one of his cards and handed it to Angelo Lentini. "If anything occurs to you, or you see Sam, please give me a call."

The building superintendent nodded and left.

Sam's apartment was a typical one bedroom. Walker was a little surprised at how neat it was. He couldn't imagine Maddie keeping her bedroom this neat, never mind an entire apartment. Munoz took the bathroom and the bedroom, Walker the living room and the kitchenette.

After about ten minutes, Munoz called out. "Craig, come in here a minute, will you?"

Walker stopped what he was doing and headed for the bedroom. Munoz was standing next to the closet as Walker approached.

"There's a piece of luggage in here that looks brand new. I guess it's possible that she had another piece, but that seems pretty unlikely for a seventeen-year-old. So either she was traveling very light, or she wasn't planning on spending the night any place," Munoz said. "Plus there's this."

Munoz moved toward the bathroom. "As you can see, there's some makeup on the counter. You'd know better than I, but would Maddie spend the night someplace without bringing that stuff with her?"

"Maddie doesn't use a lot of makeup, but that looks like overnight stuff similar to what my wife uses. She's at a conference in Philadelphia now, and she took all her makeup with her. It's hard to imagine if you use those overnight cosmetics, you're not going to take them with you," Walker said. "Did you find anything else, like a diary, or a calendar, or a day planner? Anything like that?"

"No, nothing like that."

"I found a couple of things too. Let me show you."

Munoz followed Walker back into the kitchenette area. A couple of feet to the right of the sink was an outlet with two chargers plugged into it, but no devices attached to them.

"I would suspect those chargers are for a phone and a tablet. It looks like the one Maddie has. The school issues one to every student. If Sam was going away for any length of time, I'm sure she would have taken those with her."

"No doubt."

As he moved into the living room, Walker said, "There's also this." He pointed to the couch where there was a backpack, the contents of which had all been removed.

Walker continued, "I was going through her backpack. Nothing stood out, but then I remembered something Maddie told me. Sam missed her World Cultures final exam. Maddie's taking the same course. Some of Maddie's textbooks are electronic; she has them on her tablet. But the World Cultures' text isn't available electronically. She showed it to me because it's so big, and she was complaining about having to lug it around all the time."

Walker pointed to the contents of Sam's backpack. "The World Cultures text isn't here; there are other texts, but not that one. I think it's possible that Sam took it with her, probably planning to study," he said. "The makeup, the luggage, the chargers, and the missing text… Wherever Sam went on Wednesday, I think she expected to be back that night."

Munoz responded. "Yeah, I don't like the look of this. It seems likely that something is preventing her from coming home."

"Or someone."

"Yeah."

The two investigators sat in Walker's car for several minutes, deciding what to do next.

Walker offered the first suggestion. "I think it's time to contact one of the federal judges to try to get a warrant for Sam's phone and credit card records. It might be the only way to trace her whereabouts."

"I assume you're going to use Peter Stansky for that."

"Nobody better."

Peter Stansky was also a retired FBI agent who specialized in technology issues. He was part of the FBI's post-retirement program as well and had been instrumental in helping solve the other two cases Walker and Munoz had worked on.

Walker scrolled through his phone contacts, found the number for the judge he wanted to meet with, and placed the call.

The judge's chief clerk answered. "Judge Thompson's office."

"Darren?"

"Yes. Who's this?"

"Hi, it's Craig Walker."

"I thought you were retired."

"I am. But sometimes you just can't stay away. What's that line from the Godfather? 'Every time I think I'm out, they keep pulling me back in.'"

Darren laughed. "It's probably not the best idea to use a Mafia analogy when you want something from a judge."

"Yeah, you're probably right."

"So what can I do for you, Craig?"

"I was hoping the judge might have a few minutes this afternoon."

"I can probably squeeze you in for ten or fifteen minutes. What's this about?"

Walker gave him the abbreviated version.

"All right, let's make it for three o'clock."

"Thanks, Darren." Walker looked over at Munoz and said, "We're on for three o'clock at the federal courthouse in Boston."

A moment later, Walker searched through his phone contacts again and called the FBI field office in Boston. Once he was cleared after giving the appropriate code, he was transferred to another office. He gave the individual as much of Sam Daniels's pertinent information as he had and asked to have the application for a warrant filled out. The person he was speaking with asked where Walker wanted it faxed.

"I'll pick it up. I have to bring it over to the federal courthouse in Boston anyway."

After Walker hung up, Munoz said, "It sounded like they're going to prepare the warrant."

"Yeah, no problem."

"You probably should give Peter a call to let him know what might be coming."

"Good idea."

Once again, Walker scrolled through his contacts, found Peter Stansky's number, and tapped the screen. After several rings, it went to voice mail. Walker left a short message, and asked Stansky to call back when he got a chance.

Munoz spoke up as soon as Walker disconnected. "It's too late to head to Connecticut today, but maybe we should call and see if we can set something up with the social worker for tomorrow. Also, I know it might be a bit of a sore spot, but we should probably let the Faxon Mills police know what we're doing." Munoz smiled. "It'll give you a chance to reconnect with—what was his name— Officer Crawford?"

"Yeah. What a piece of work he is. Okay, you're right, though. Why don't you drive while I call the social worker in Connecticut? After we finish at the police station, you can pick up your car at my house, and we can drive into Boston separately. That way you'll be halfway home."

"Sounds good," Munoz said. "The only other thing is the horse farms."

"That's right, I almost forgot. Let me do a little research on that tonight and maybe we can work it in tomorrow before or after Connecticut."

Munoz offered something that they both had been thinking. "You know if this were a child we were trying to find, four days would seem like an eternity. And just because Sam Daniels is an emancipated minor doesn't make me feel a whole lot better about it. Four days is still four days."

Chapter Six

Walker dug out the piece of paper Cassandra Jeffers had given him with the Connecticut social worker's contact information on it. He punched in the number and after the third ring he heard, "Charlotte Blanchard."

"Hello, Ms. Blanchard. I got your name and number from Cassandra Jeffers from the Massachusetts Department of Social Services. My name is Craig Walker. I was hoping to talk to you about one of your former clients: Samantha Daniels." Before Charlotte Blanchard could raise any issues of confidentiality, Walker continued. "I know there are privacy concerns, but it appears that she may be missing. My partner and I are investigating her possible disappearance," Walker said. "Actually, I'm with the FBI."

"The FBI? Is this some sort of joke?"

Walker sensed that the social worker was still very wary about talking with him. "No, I assure you this isn't a joke. And I understand your reluctance to speak with me, especially over the phone. That's why I'd like to meet with you in person, and that way you can be certain that I am who I say I am."

There was a slight hesitation, and then Charlotte Blanchard responded, "You're serious. You're with the FBI?"

"Yes."

Before Walker could say anything further, she continued, "I can't ethically even acknowledge that I know the person you mentioned, but if what you're telling me is the truth, I'd be willing to meet with you. But it can't be tomorrow; I'm out of the office all day. What about Wednesday?"

"That would be fine. What time?"

"Let me just check my calendar." A moment passed, and then she said, "I have an opening at two o'clock."

"Okay, we'll see you then."

Instead of ending the call, Charlotte Blanchard said, "You are aware that individuals who are no longer Connecticut residents are ineligible to receive any services from this office?"

"Yes, I'm aware that Sam Daniels now lives in Massachusetts, but I think you probably know more about her situation than anybody else we've spoken with."

"Okay, Mr.... Walker was it? Or Agent Walker, I guess. I'll see you on Wednesday."

As Walker disconnected, he looked over at Munoz. "She can't see us until Wednesday at two o'clock. Actually, that's just as well. I don't like leaving Maddie alone if I'm going to be that far away. If need be, I could have made other arrangements, but since Cheryl's coming back Wednesday morning, that should work out fine."

"Why don't we plan to meet at the police barracks in Framingham around eleven-thirty and drive down together? We can take my car," Munoz said.

"Okay, that's a good idea."

It took about twenty-five minutes to get to the Faxon Mills Police Station. Walker was still hoping that Officer Crawford wouldn't be there. Although he probably deserved to be taken down a peg, Walker never took particular pleasure in doing that, especially to somebody in law enforcement.

As soon as Walker and Munoz entered the station, Walker spotted Officer Crawford and saw him look in their direction. Crawford stared a bit more intently and then an expression of recognition came across his face. He spoke before Walker and Munoz reached the counter.

"What are you doing back here, Mr. Walker?"

Walker took a breath. "I just wanted to let you know that if you were planning to start an investigation into the disappearance of Samantha Daniels, there's no need."

A knowing smirk crossed Officer Crawford's face. "Let me guess. She's not missing anymore."

Walker shook his head. "No, she's most definitely missing. It's just that the FBI is going to be involved."

"What are you talking about—the FBI?"

Walker removed his credentials from his pocket and showed them to Crawford. Munoz did the same. Then Walker added, "This is Detective Munoz, and it's *Agent* Walker. This is just a courtesy call to let you know what we're doing."

Crawford was obviously stunned by what he was hearing. He had trouble coming up with anything coherent to say.

Eventually he asked, "Why is the FBI involved in this, and why didn't you identify yourself before?"

"It shouldn't have been necessary, if you were doing your job. But since you aren't going to, we'll do it for you."

Crawford clenched his jaw. "Nobody ever said we wouldn't look for the girl. We were about to gather more information."

"Yeah, right. Keep telling yourself that."

Walker turned his back to the counter. "Have a nice day, Officer Crawford." After a few steps, Walker turned back around. "As I said, this is an FBI investigation now. Please stay out of it."

Once they were outside, Walker said, "I wish I hadn't let him get to me like that."

"From what you told me, and from that little exchange, I'd say he was asking for it, Craig."

"Doesn't matter. I should've been more professional."

"That's not the way I saw it. The guy makes Barney Fife look like Eliot Ness."

Walker burst out laughing. "Have you been saving that one? That was good."

They headed back to Walker's house in Danvers to pick up Munoz's car. Maddie was up by then. She had a brief conversation with her dad, said hello to Dave Munoz, and then went back upstairs to her bedroom.

Munoz offered, "It's only been about six months since I've seen her, but she seems to have grown up so much in that time."

"I know. It's scary as hell."

"I don't think you have anything to worry about. She seems to have her head on straight."

"Easy for you to say." He paused and nodded. "But I like our chances," Walker said. "Listen, I can fix us a couple of sandwiches before we head into Boston. It'll give us a chance to recap where we are."

"Sure."

Forty-five minutes later, each in his own car, Walker and Munoz were on their way to the FBI office to pick up the warrant. It was waiting for them when they got there. Walker looked it over, thanked the agent who had prepared it, and he and Munoz drove to the federal courthouse.

After showing their credentials and going through the metal detector, they took the elevator to the seventh floor. They were ushered into Judge Thompson's chambers a few minutes after three o'clock. The judge was standing in front of his desk when Walker and Munoz entered.

"Hello, Agent Walker. How have you been?"

"Fine, Judge. This is my partner, Detective Dave Munoz."

"Yes, I remember the name from the cases the two of you investigated. Excellent work, by the way."

Munoz responded, "Thank you, Your Honor."

The judge turned to Walker. "So Darren filled me in somewhat. But tell me, exactly what is it that you need?"

Before Walker could respond, the judge went and sat down behind his desk, and invited Walker and Munoz to sit also. Walker then spent the next several minutes outlining the situation and then handed the judge the warrant.

Judge Thompson looked it over for a moment and then asked, "Do you suspect this young woman of any wrongdoing, any criminal activity?"

"No, nothing like that. Nothing that I'm aware of. She just seems to have disappeared, and it doesn't make much sense."

"Okay. I don't see anything controversial here. All the stuff with the NSA has made me a bit leery. But this seems straightforward." The judge removed a pen from the holder on his desk and signed the warrant. "Well, good luck. I hope you find her, and I hope she's okay."

As Walker and Munoz exited the courthouse, Walker's phone buzzed. It was Peter Stansky.

"Hi, Peter. I was just about to call you."

"Sorry I missed you before. So what's up?"

Walker gave him the same quick summary he'd given to Judge Thompson. When he finished, Peter Stansky said, "All right, I'm going to need all of Samantha Daniels's information—phone number, address, bank, and anything else you've got—plus the warrant."

"I'm just leaving the courthouse now. I'll go back over to the FBI office and fax everything to you."

"That'll work. I doubt I'll have anything until sometime tomorrow. The phone companies are usually pretty quick, but the banks—that could take a while."

"That's fine, as soon as you can."

"Okay, one way or the other, I'll call you tomorrow."

"Thanks, Peter."

After Walker recapped the conversation for Munoz, the two went to the parking garage. They reconfirmed that they would meet at the Framingham barracks on Wednesday, and Walker said he would check out the area horse farms the next day.

"Obviously, if I get any information from Peter, or if anything else develops, I'll give you a call."

A smile formed on Munoz's lips. "Don't forget to keep Officer Crawford in the loop too."

Walker shook his head and said something under his breath. Munoz was about to ask him to repeat it, even though he had clearly heard him. But it didn't matter; Munoz wasn't about to attempt the physical contortion that Walker had suggested anyway.

Maddie had given up on trying to study anymore. She felt fully prepared for her final, but even if she hadn't, it was too hard to concentrate; she kept thinking about Sam. Maddie was now sitting in the living room anxiously waiting for her father to get back. She had wanted to ask him what was happening with the investigation earlier when Dave Munoz was there, but she felt like she would be interrupting, so she held back. But at this point, she was dying to know.

As soon as her father arrived home, Maddie jumped up off the couch to meet him at the door. "Did you find out anything?"

"Let's sit down," Walker said.

An expression of concern came across Maddie's face. "Is it something bad?"

"No, no. It's just that it's going to take a while to explain everything."

Craig Walker spent the next ten minutes telling Maddie all about talking to Sam's guidance counselor and the social worker, the visit to Sam's apartment, and the warrant to get Sam's phone records and financials.

"Dave and I are also going down to Connecticut on Wednesday to talk with Sam's original social worker," Walker said. "We're taking this very seriously, Maddie. But as of right now, honestly, we don't have much to go on."

Maddie started to get emotional. She haltingly asked, "What could have happened, Dad?"

"I don't know, honey. I'm really hoping that the phone records or her credit card purchases will tell us something. It might even be possible to track her whereabouts from her phone."

"And you'll have that information tomorrow?"

"I think so," Walker said. "I know this is hard, but we're going to do everything we can to find her."

Maddie was unable to respond; she could only nod.

Craig Walker watched his daughter fight back tears, and an idea came to him. "I take it you're finished studying?"

"Yeah, pretty much," Maddie said.

"Well maybe then you could help me out with something having to do with the investigation."

Maddie's face brightened. "Really? What do you want me to do?"

"Let me ask you something first. Did Sam ever mention anything about horseback riding?"

Maddie appeared to be searching her memory. "Actually, yeah. She talked about doing some riding this summer. She asked if I wanted to come, but as you know, that's not my thing."

"Any idea where she was thinking of going?" Walker asked.

"Not that I remember."

"Okay, here's what I want you to do. Get on the Internet and find all the horse farms in the area. Make a list with their addresses and phone numbers."

"Do you really think this is important?"

"To tell you the truth, I don't know. But I think it's worth checking out. Oh, and I only need the places that offer riding. I'm sure some of them are either just training farms or breeding farms."

"Okay, I'll do it right now. Thanks for letting me help, Dad."

Craig Walker went over and kissed his daughter on the forehead. "You're welcome. I'm going to go start supper."

A half hour later, Maddie came into the kitchen with a piece of paper in her hand. "I think I have everything you asked for."

"That was quick."

"Well, I just did the horse farms within about fifteen miles from here. There were seven of them total, but only three have actual riding. And one of them is primarily for kids with special needs. We actually heard about that one at school. The horseback riding is like some kind of therapy. Anyway, I left it on the list, just in case."

"That's great, Maddie. Let's eat first, and then I'll take a look at what you've got," Walker said. "By the way, what time is your final tomorrow?"

"Nine o'clock."

"You want me to drive you, or are you going to take the bus?"

"I'd rather you drove me, if it's okay."

"Sure. After I drop you off, I'll take a ride and visit the horse farms on your list that look promising. You'll probably have to take the bus home, though."

"That's okay."

After they finished eating, they went to sit on the couch in the living room to review Maddie's list. Walker read it over twice and said, "I think the two you highlighted—Essex County Equestrian Center and North Shore Paddocks—are the most likely. I'll try them first, and if nothing pans out at either of those, I'll try the one for special needs students." He glanced down at Maddie's list and read aloud, "Stoneledge Therapeutic Equestrian Program, Stoneledge Stables."

"Do you really think Sam might have gone to one of these places?" Maddie asked.

"It's one of the only leads we have. Two different people mentioned horseback riding, not to mention you. We need to look into it."

Maddie was just about to ask another question when her father's phone buzzed. Walker looked down at the screen. "It's your mother."

"You're not going to tell her about the other night are you?"

"I told you, not until she gets home."

"Okay, I'm going upstairs so you guys can talk."

Walker picked up the phone as his daughter left the room. "Hi, Cheryl. How're you doing? How's the conference?"

"Actually, it's pretty good. I had my doubts, but it's definitely been worthwhile. I miss you guys, though."

"Same here."

"So anything going on there? Maddie's got one more final, right?"

"Yeah, tomorrow." Walker paused. "I've taken on another case... with Dave."

"When did that happen?"

Walker told his wife all about the investigation except for Maddie's escapade. When he finished, his wife asked, "How's Maddie handling it?"

"She's having a tough time. I'd heard her talk about Sam Daniels, but I didn't realize they were so close."

"It's been fairly recent. Maddie asked me if she could invite Sam over a few times, and I said yes, but for some reason, it never worked out," Cheryl said. "I'm sure you looked into it already, but is it possible that Sam just ran away?"

Walker did his best imitation of his daughter's response to the same question when he had asked it.

Cheryl broke up. When she stopped laughing, she said the same thing her husband had said. "I guess she has a point, doesn't she?" There was a brief silence, and then Cheryl's tone changed. "You must think something serious is going on or you wouldn't have taken this on."

"I've been trying to downplay it a little bit for Maddie's sake. There is some evidence to suggest that wherever Sam went, she didn't expect to stay there very long. Now, whether she just changed her mind or something more sinister is going on, we just don't know at this point. But my gut is telling me it's not simply that she changed her mind. She's been gone for more than four days. If this were a child that was missing for that long, we'd be in panic mode, and we'd probably be searching for a body."

"And you don't have any strong leads?"

"We barely have any leads, never mind strong ones. I think the phone records may be our best bet."

"It's got to make it that much more difficult because Maddie's involved."

"You got that right."

"Well, give her a kiss for me, and tell her I'm thinking about her... and Sam," Cheryl said.

"Will do."

"I might not get a chance to call tomorrow. It's a really full day."

"Don't worry about it. I'll pick you up on Wednesday morning around nine at Logan, right?"

"Yeah, that's right. Love you."

"Love you, too."

As Walker disconnected the call, he looked to his left near the bottom of the stairs and saw Maddie standing there. She had evidently overheard everything. Maddie was visibly shaking as she moved toward her father.

"I'm so scared for her, Dad."

Walker opened his arms, up and Maddie folded herself into her father. "I know, honey." In all his years with the FBI, Walker had never promised anything he couldn't deliver, but in this instance, he couldn't help himself. "We'll find her, Maddie. I promise."

Chapter Seven

Before he started the car to drive Maddie to school for her English final, Craig Walker looked over at his daughter and asked, "With everything that's happened, are you going to be okay to take your exam?"

"Yeah, we were given the essay questions ahead of time, and we're allowed to bring in outlines. I'll be okay."

"I meant to ask you. Have you talked about Sam's disappearance with any of your other friends?"

"Not really. None of them knows Sam. She's not in our grade." Maddie paused. "So you're going to the horse farms today?"

"At least three of them anyway," Walker said.

"And then you're supposed to find out about Sam's phone records, right?"

"I hope so."

"What time will you be home?"

"It depends. But I would expect I'll be home about the same time as you are."

"So you'll let me know what happens as soon as you know?" Maddie asked.

Walker smiled. "Well, I'm not going to interrupt your exam, but as soon as you get home, I'll tell you whatever I find out."

Although Walker continued to be amazed at his daughter's ability to change topics in a nanosecond, it no longer left him totally surprised. So when Maddie uttered her next words, he was able to take the shift in subject matter, if not the content, in stride.

"I was thinking, Dad. When Mom gets home, I should be the one to tell her about what I did. It's my responsibility. You can be there if you want, so the two of you can decide what other punishment I should get. But I should have to tell Mom myself."

Walker thought of asking, "Who are you and what have you done with my daughter?" But instead, he offered, "I think that would be a very mature way to handle it."

"Okay then. That's what I'll do."

Walker reached over and gave Maddie's arm a squeeze. "Good." He glanced at his watch and said, "We better get going."

Fifteen minutes later, they were pulling up to the front of the school. As Maddie exited the car, she said, "Good luck, Dad. I'll see you at home."

"Good luck on your exam, honey."

Walker's first stop after dropping Maddie off was the Essex County Equestrian Center. There was a large, ornate sign at the front entrance to the facility, with the initials ECEC prominently displayed in script. The manager of the property was very personable and gracious, but he had never heard of Samantha Daniels and didn't recognize her picture.

Walker had a similar experience when he went to North Shore Paddocks. That visit took a little longer because the manager wasn't immediately available, and there were two additional individuals who booked riding sessions. Walker had to talk with both of them, as well as the manager. But the results were the same. No one recognized Sam's name or photograph.

Although Walker had acknowledged to himself that any kind of promising lead coming out of the visits to the horse farms was unlikely, he was still somewhat disappointed as he headed for the next facility.

Stoneledge Stables hadn't officially changed its name, but on its website, it referred to itself as the Stoneledge Therapeutic Equestrian Program (STEP), primarily because it was now exclusively what was called a hippotherapy center.

Walker parked his car in front of the main office and headed inside. There was a woman in her twenties seated at a desk and talking on the phone. She smiled at Walker and gestured for him to have a seat, which he did. There was a nameplate on the desk that read Erika Martin.

The woman disconnected the call twenty seconds later, smiled again, and introduced herself.

"Hi, I'm Erika Martin."

"Craig Walker."

"What can I do for you, Mr. Walker?"

"I'd like to speak with the person who books the horseback riding sessions."

"Well, I do some of that. But you probably want to talk with my mother, Teresa Martin. She's the general manager. Are you with an agency, or is this a personal family matter?"

"Neither, actually. I'm investigating the possible disappearance of a young woman, and I have reason to believe she might have come to one of the horse farms in the area to do some riding."

"Are you with the police?"

Walker took out his credentials. "Actually, I'm with the FBI."

Once again, Walker got the reaction he often got when he made that pronouncement.

"The FBI?" the woman asked. "We specialize in therapy for individuals with special needs. Does the person you're looking for fit into that category?"

"No, but I'm checking out all of the facilities in the area that offer horseback riding."

"As I said, it would seem doubtful that this young woman would have come here, but let me call my mother, and you can talk with her."

Five minutes later, Teresa Martin was standing next to Walker. She invited him into her office and asked, "How can I help?"

Walker outlined what he was doing there and what he was hoping to find out.

When he was done, Teresa Martin asked, "What's this young woman's name?"

"Samantha Daniels, although she goes by Sam."

"Sam Daniels... huh? For some reason that does sound familiar."

Walker extracted Sam's picture. "Does this help?"

Teresa Martin studied the picture for another moment. "Yes, actually I do remember her. She was here."

"Really? When? Can you recall?"

"A couple of months ago, I'd say. She wanted to know if she could volunteer here. She said she was a bit rusty, hadn't ridden in a while, and wondered if she could do some riding before she volunteered. As you can imagine, we couldn't do anything close to what we do here without volunteers. Some of our clients need to have three people tending to them at any given time. Anyway, I told her to come back when she got out of school for the summer, and we'd see what we could work out. I haven't seen her since though."

"She seems to have made an impression on you," Walker said.

"Now that you say that, I remember something else. Maybe that's why all of that stuck with me. All of our employees and volunteers have to have a criminal background check, but you probably know that. Anyway, when I mentioned about the background check, it seemed to bother her. I didn't push her about it. I just figured I'd wait to see if she came back, and I'd deal with it then. But I remember her reaction distinctly. That's probably why it stayed with me." Teresa Martin paused. "I don't know if I'm allowed to ask this, but is that why the FBI's involved?"

"As far as I know, she's never been involved in anything criminal. This is strictly a missing person's investigation," Walker replied. "Let me ask you something else. You said that she talked about not having ridden in a while. Did she mention where she had ridden before?"

"Now you're really taxing my memory." Teresa Martin expelled a breath before continuing. "I couldn't swear to it, but I think she said she learned to ride somewhere in Maine, but that's as much as I remember."

Walker thanked Teresa Martin, and as he had done at the other two horse farms, he left his card.

Walker arrived home shortly after eleven o'clock. He didn't expect Maddie much before noon, so he spent the next hour looking at the websites of all the horse farms in Maine. There were sixteen of them, but nothing stood out. He reminded himself that he was primarily pursuing the horse farms connection because he didn't have much else to go on.

Maddie got home around 12:10 p.m. She dropped her backpack on the couch and bounded into the kitchen where her father was sitting with his laptop open.

"Did you find out anything?"

Craig had debated with himself earlier about whether to mention Teresa Martin's observation about Sam and the background check when he spoke with his daughter. He opted not to.

"Well, one of the managers at Stoneledge did remember Sam. She was there a few months ago."

Maddie's eyes lit up. "Really? That's good, right?"

Again, Craig debated how to answer his daughter. This time he decided to paint a more realistic picture. "I don't know, maybe, maybe not. You have to remember, Maddie, it was a while ago, and we don't know if it has anything to do with why Sam's missing."

Walker could see his daughter's posture change, obviously signaling her disappointment. He pretended not to notice. "Did Sam ever mention spending any time in Maine?"

"No, I don't think so. Why?"

"The woman who recognized Sam's picture said she thought Sam had learned to ride horses in Maine."

"She didn't tell me anything about that."

The conversation moved from Sam to Maddie's English final—which she thought was pretty easy—to having some lunch. Shortly after they finished eating, Maddie went up to her bedroom to listen to music, while Walker reopened his laptop to look at the Maine horse farms' websites again. A few minutes into his search, his phone rang. It was Peter Stansky.

Walker pressed the green phone icon after the first ring.

"Hi, Peter. I could use some good news."

"I wish I had some," Peter said.

"Nothing?"

"Samantha Daniels had three different phone numbers in the past year. They were all registered to prepaid phones, so there's no way to access her phone records. Unless you have a specific carrier, none of that information is saved."

"Three prepaid phones? That seems really strange, doesn't it?"

"I don't know what to tell you. But you know as well as I do that if you're trying to hide something, your best bet is to use a prepaid," Stansky said. "Unless... Didn't you tell me this girl's only seventeen? She wouldn't be old enough to sign up for a phone."

"Normally that's true. But she's an emancipated minor. In the eyes of the law, she's an adult. She can sign a contract, just like any other adult," Walker said. "I suppose there's no way to trace her phone either?"

"I thought of that, but the prepaids she bought don't have GPS chips in them."

"How do you know that?"

"From her credit card statements. She bought all three phones at Walmart. I have the dates, how much she paid, and the model numbers. No GPS."

"Wow, I really thought this was going to provide some sort of direction for us," Walker said. "Anything else on the credit card statements that might help?"

"She didn't use her credit card all that often. The most recent purchase was online from the Massachusetts Bay Transportation Authority about ten days ago."

Walker's voice became animated. "A train ticket?"

"No, it's just a monthly pass. You can use it throughout the system for buses or trains."

"But there'd be a record of where the card was swiped. What if we got a subpoena to find out if she used it on the day she went missing?"

"I thought of that, but getting that information would probably take weeks. And even if you did get it, it's not going to help very much. It'll tell you where she got on the bus or the train, but not where she got off."

"You're right," Walker replied. "What about the rest of the financials?"

"She gets money deposited each month into her account, pays a few bills online, and withdraws money from local ATMs. That's about it."

Walker then asked, "Any credit card usage or ATM withdrawals in Maine?"

"Maine? I don't think so, but let me take a quick look." A minute later Peter Stansky said, "An online purchase from L.L. Bean, that's all. I have to say, Craig. I know this girl is only seventeen, but even at her age, you'd expect to see much more of a paper trail. There's almost nothing here. You combine that with the purchase of the prepaids, and it does raise some questions about what she might have been into, don't you think?"

"I know what you're saying, Peter. And one of the people I interviewed today expressed some concern along those lines. So I guess we can't completely rule it out, but we haven't uncovered any direct evidence so far that suggests she was involved in anything illegal."

Walker told Maddie about the first part of the conversation he had had with Peter Stansky, leaving out the possibility of Sam not being what she seemed. Although he had decided to try to be more forthcoming with his daughter about the investigation, raising that idea wouldn't serve any real purpose.

But when he called Dave Munoz to fill him in about the day's events, he did throw out the idea that Peter Stansky had posed.

"I don't know, Craig. I guess it's possible, but I'm not really buying it. She'd have to be pretty sophisticated to have planned all this. And that's certainly not the picture we have of her at this point." Munoz said. "And why would she leave all of her clothes behind? And what's she doing for money? From what you told me, there have been no recent ATM withdrawals."

"Yeah, that's what I was thinking as well, but I wanted to get your take on it. It really doesn't make sense that she disappeared intentionally, but then nothing about this case is making any sense right now."

"No argument from me," Munoz said. "Maybe the trip to Connecticut tomorrow will give us something."

"Lots of eggs in that basket."

ᚱ Chapter Eight ᚱ

C raig Walker pulled into the cell phone lot at Logan Airport shortly after 9:00 a.m. on Wednesday. His wife's flight from Philadelphia had landed ten minutes ahead of schedule, but Cheryl had at least one checked bag, so it would probably be another few minutes before she called.

Walker glanced at his watch. Once he dropped Cheryl off back home, he planned to leave by 10:15 a.m. to meet Dave Munoz at the barracks in Framingham by 11:30 a.m. for their trip to Connecticut.

A moment passed, and his thoughts turned to the case. *We better uncover something soon...* Before he could complete that thought, his phone buzzed.

As soon as the call connected, he heard, "Hi, honey, it's me. I just picked up my bag. I'm in Terminal B."

"Okay, I'll be there in five minutes."

The arrival lane for Terminal B wasn't particularly crowded. He spotted Cheryl immediately, pulled to the curb, put the car in park, but left the engine running, and exited the car.

"Hi, stranger," he said.

"Hi, yourself."

He gave his wife a quick kiss, picked up her luggage, and deposited it in the trunk. As Craig pulled away from the curb and headed for the airport exit, he asked, "How was the flight?"

"Uneventful. Just the way I like it."

"And the conference?"

"Like I said on the phone, better than I expected. There were some very practical ideas about saving time in the ER, especially with paperwork. I can use a lot of the recommendations right away."

"Speaking of that, when do you go back to work?"

"Friday."

"That's good. At least you'll have a little down time."

"Yeah, tomorrow anyway. Maybe I'll plan something with Maddie. I assume you're still going to be working on the case. How's that going, by the way?"

"Not very well. In terms of most investigations, it would still be early, but Sam Daniels has been missing for nearly a week, and there's no trace of her whatsoever," Walker said. "Dave and I are going to Connecticut later on today. I'm hoping we find out something useful; otherwise, I'm at a loss."

"Does Maddie know that it's not going well?" Cheryl asked.

"I've gone back and forth with that. As I told you the other day, I tried to downplay how serious it could be, but she overheard us talking. And she's bright enough to understand the reality of the situation. I'm walking a bit of a tightrope right now."

Walker was quiet for a few moments and then without consciously being aware he was going to, he said, "Maddie's going to want to talk with you about something."

Cheryl turned slightly in her seat with an expression of concern on her face. "What?"

"She wants to tell you herself. I'm not sure I should have said anything to begin with."

"Should I be worried?"

"No... I mean, I was upset at first... but... I shouldn't say anything else."

"You seem reasonably calm, so I'm guessing she doesn't have a nose ring or a full sleeve tattoo."

Craig laughed. "No, neither of those," he said. "Isn't it great that those were the two worst things you could come up with?"

Cheryl smiled at her husband. "Yeah, I guess it is," she replied. "So you're not going to tell me?"

"No. It'll be better if you hear it from her and react naturally."

"So now you're questioning my acting skills?"

"How did the tables get turned here so that I'm on the defensive? I'm not the one who did anything wrong."

Cheryl smiled again. "I don't know what to say. I just know it makes my life so much easier when you're on the defensive."

Craig smiled as well. "You don't play fair."

"What are you always telling our children? 'Whoever told you that life was fair?'"

"Now I'm definitely not telling you."

As it turned out, Maddie woke up only a few minutes before Craig was scheduled to leave. He said good morning to her, kissed his wife good-bye, and headed out the door. He had no doubt that Cheryl would handle everything with their daughter in a Solomon-like way. She always did.

On the ride down to Framingham, Walker was able to focus entirely on the questions he wanted to ask Charlotte Blanchard. He had written them down the night before, and they were now in his briefcase in the back seat. But he was readily able to recall each and every one. His memory for detail seemed as strong as ever. He suspected that Dave Munoz was engaged in a similar exercise as he drove up from southeastern Massachusetts toward Framingham.

At 11:15 a.m., Walker eased off of Route 9, drove a few hundred additional feet, and then stopped at the gate to the barracks. He had called the night before, so his name was on the list that the trooper at the gate had in his possession. After Walker showed his ID, he was let in and shown to an area where he could leave his car. Munoz was already there.

The ride down to Connecticut consisted of a recap of the investigation and the sharing of the questions they both had developed. The questions were virtually identical.

About midway, Munoz asked, "You don't think Peter's idea about Sam being involved in something illegal is a real possibility, do you?"

"No, I don't. I didn't want to dismiss it out of hand, though. That's why I wanted your take on it. I can see why Peter would think that way, however. He doesn't have the background that we have."

"So tell me some more about the horse farms and the possible connection to Maine," Munoz said.

"I don't know for sure that there is a connection. The woman I spoke with—Teresa Martin—was pretty sketchy on that."

Walker spent the next twenty miles elaborating on his visits to ECEC, the North Shore Paddocks, and Stoneledge Stables. And then they were in Bridgeport.

The voice on the GPS directed them south of I-95 not far from the ferry that ran between Connecticut and Long Island. Much of Bridgeport had seen better days, and the building that housed the Connecticut Social Services' offices was no different. The outside of the building could easily have been mistaken for a factory from the 1920's. Inside, however, there had been an attempt to make the lobby area more presentable with some fresh paint, some institution-type furnishings, and some plants.

Walker and Munoz stopped at the information desk and were directed upstairs to the second floor to Charlotte Blanchard's office. They were early, but she was able to see them minutes after they arrived.

She appeared to be in her fifties. She had brown hair and brown eyes, and wore an expression that radiated some wariness.

But once she verified the credentials of her two visitors, she seemed to relax and offered a smile.

"I remembered a lot of the specifics about Sam Daniels's case, but I took the file home with me last night to review it. I've been a social worker for over twenty years, and I'd be hard-pressed to recall any situation as unique as this one. It's very complicated," Ms. Blanchard said. "But, I'm getting ahead of myself, aren't I? You told me on the phone that you think Sam has disappeared. Why do you think that?"

Walker spent the next several minutes recapping where they were in the investigation. At the end, he said, "So besides giving us information on Sam's background, we were hoping you might have some idea of where she might have gone."

"Actually, right after you called, I started giving that a lot of thought. But I didn't come up with anything."

Munoz asked, "She grew up here, right? Any chance that she would've come back here?"

"I doubt it, especially since that was one of the conditions of her being emancipated—that she leave this area."

Walker spoke next. "Can you tell us about that?"

"As much as I know, sure." The social worker paused to gather her thoughts. "After her mother was arrested, Sam was scheduled to go into foster care. Her father died about five years ago, so there was nobody to take care of her. But Sam's mother told the court that there was a trust fund set up for Sam in her paternal grandfather's will. Of course, Sam couldn't access it until she turned eighteen. Sam's mother asked the judge if something could be worked out. She didn't want Sam in foster care, and Sam didn't want any part of it either. I got all of this information secondhand. I wasn't officially involved at that point; that came much later.

"Anyway, evidently, the judge interviewed Sam, found out that for the past few years while her mother was dealing drugs, Sam was basically on her own anyway. So he came up with the idea of emancipated minor status, which would allow Sam to tap into the trust fund. But as I understand it, there were conditions."

Walker said, "Like what?"

"Here's where it gets complicated. At the time all of this went down, Sam was a juvenile. All of those records are sealed. I don't have access to them. So anything I tell you from here on in is whatever I could piece together from what Sam was willing to share with me, or what other people told me, and of course from my own experience. For example, I hate to say it, but Sam must've been involved in something illegal, or there would have been no reason to seal her records. I've never heard of sealing juvenile records unless criminal activity was involved."

Walker and Munoz looked at each other and wondered if their reluctance to accept the possibility raised by Peter Stansky had been shortsighted.

Munoz then asked, "Any idea what that might have been?"

"Just a guess, but I suspect it had to do with drugs. It also fits in with what one of the court officers told me."

Munoz followed up. "What was that?"

"Again, I was told this because I wanted additional background about Sam when I was assigned to her case. As you can imagine, because her juvenile records were sealed, there was very little in the file. Anyway, the court officer heard a small portion of this in open court before the judge went back into his chambers with only Sam and a court stenographer. So who knows how accurate it is, although it does seem to make sense.

"What I was told was that the judge made a deal with Sam to give her a second chance. She had to leave Bridgeport and have no contact with anyone here. She had to go to some sort of—for lack of a better term—rehab facility for a few months and complete all her schoolwork online. If those conditions were met, the judge would seal her records, grant emancipated minor status, and allow her access to the trust fund."

Walker sat back in his chair, clearly surprised by what he had just heard. Eventually, he said, "Rehab would suggest drug involvement."

"Yes, but I don't know that for sure," Ms. Blanchard said.

"Any idea where this facility was located?" Walker asked.

"No."

"Could it have been in Maine?"

"No idea."

A few moments passed and then Munoz asked, "When did you get assigned to Sam's case, and what was your role?"

"I got involved probably shortly after Sam went to the rehab facility, although that's just a guess. I hadn't even met Sam at that point. I was told to check with the guidance office where Sam had gone to school to make sure she was submitting her schoolwork and then to make sure it was forwarded to the school in Massachusetts when it was completed. I also set up her bank accounts, and then I coordinated all that with Cassandra Jeffers in Massachusetts."

Munoz asked, "The guidance department at the local high school must know where Sam was during her... rehab."

"No, they didn't; I asked. Everything was done online. It seemed the judge was trying to give Sam a fresh start and didn't want her history to follow her."

Munoz said, "So when did you first meet Sam?"

"It must've been right after she completed rehab. She had to meet with the judge in person. Actually, Sam told me that—not the first part about rehab—she never made reference to that. But the second part about meeting the judge and being granted emancipated minor status. That's as much as she volunteered. She came back the next day as well to confirm when she was moving to Massachusetts and also to make sure everything was in order with the trust fund money."

Walker then asked, "Who arranged for her apartment and the registration at the new school?"

"It must've been the court. It wasn't me, and it wasn't Cassandra Jeffers."

"That's pretty unusual, isn't it?"

"Very. But as I said, I think the judge saw something in Sam and decided she deserved a break. Have you ever met her? She's a very impressive young woman. I could sense her determination and... resilience right away."

Walker said, "I think I know the answer to this question, but... Do you think there's any chance Sam came back here and got involved in whatever she was doing before?"

"In this job, I've learned never say 'never,' but I very much doubt it."

"What about the possibility that she came back to visit her mother? She's incarcerated close by, right?"

"Yes, she is. But that's even more unlikely. The same court officer who gave me all the other information was also there at the second appearance for Sam's mother. When she told the judge about the trust fund to keep Sam out of foster care at her initial arraignment, I don't think she knew that Sam had been the one who turned her in. I don't know why, but for some reason that came out during her second appearance."

"You weren't kidding when you said this was complicated." Charlotte Blanchard smiled as Walker continued. "One additional question—and this is coming out of left field. But over the past year or so, Sam's been using prepaid phones only. Any idea why?"

"That one I can answer. We tried to sign her up for a regular phone plan the second time I met with her, but we finally gave up. Try explaining emancipated minor status to a customer service rep, who keeps saying, 'But she's not eighteen.'"

It was Walker's turn to smile. "Well, that does help to clear that up. Thanks," he said. "One more favor. Do you have the name of the judge who oversaw Sam's case?"

"It's not in my official file, but I remember it. It's Judge Frazier, Arthur Frazier," Ms. Blanchard said. "I assume you're going to ask him to unseal Sam's records." Charlotte Blanchard didn't wait for a response. "I sincerely hope you have some other promising leads. Because, honestly, in my experience, getting juvenile records unsealed is next to impossible. I think you'd have better luck talking to the customer service rep from the phone company."

Chapter Nine

Before he and Munoz left, Walker gave Charlotte Blanchard his card and made his usual request—call if she thought of anything else. On the way out of the building, Walker suggested that they grab a late lunch at the rest stop along I-95. The suggestion was more about a relatively private place to talk rather than cuisine.

Munoz pressed the start button on his car, but before he shifted into drive, he looked over at Walker and said, "I don't have any experience with sealed records. Do you think Charlotte Blanchard was right about how difficult it is to get them unsealed?"

Walker responded, "I don't have any experience with that either, but my guess is that she knows what she's talking about."

"Even if it might help find somebody who's disappeared?"

"That I don't know. But I've got another idea." Walker took out his phone. "Let me call Peter. I'm thinking that before we even make a request, we need to find out as much as we can about Judge Frazier. I'm sure we're going to have to plead our case in person if we have any chance of getting what we want. And maybe if we play this right, we won't need the records unsealed."

Walker found Peter Stansky's number on his phone, tapped the screen, and placed the call. Stansky answered immediately.

"Hi, Craig. Okay, it's my turn to ask. Are you calling with some good news?"

"No. As usual, I need a favor."

"Not a problem, go ahead."

Walker briefly outlined the meeting with Charlotte Blanchard. At the end he said, "So if you could do a computer search and get as much information as possible on the judge. Again, his name's Arthur Frazier. My guess is that he's probably assigned to family court in the Bridgeport area."

Stansky responded, "Are you going to ask for the application to unseal the records right away?"

"No. I'm hoping that won't be necessary."

"How so?"

"At this point, maybe all we really need is where Sam Daniels went for rehab or whatever it was. The judge doesn't have to unseal any records if he's willing to give us that information. If he won't, or we need more, then we can file the application."

"All right, let me see what I can find out. I'll call you back as soon as I know something. It shouldn't take too long."

"Dave and I are just going to grab something to eat. We're still in Connecticut."

Stansky paused for a moment. "Is that your way of telling me to hurry up? Are you thinking you can visit the judge this afternoon?"

"I hadn't thought of that, but..."

"Of course you did," Stansky interrupted. "I didn't just fall off the turnip truck, you know. And I know how your mind works."

Walker let out a chuckle. "Okay, you got me."

"You're so transparent. Enjoy your lunch. I'll call you in a few."

Although Munoz had only heard Walker's side of the conversation, it was all he needed.

"That's a great idea about just asking the judge for the information."

"In theory, yeah, but we'll see."

Once inside the rest stop, they each ordered something from Boston Market, found a table far away from anyone else, and began to discuss what they had learned from Charlotte Blanchard.

Walker began. "Anything stand out for you from what we heard today?"

Munoz shook his head. "Other than the whole thing is pretty bizarre? I don't know," he said. "I was trying to figure out if the fact that Sam turned her mother in to the police could have anything to do with her disappearance. But if there's a connection, I'm not seeing it." Munoz paused. "But the main problem is that all of the information we got today is about Sam's past. It explains how she got to Massachusetts, but nothing about where she might have gone... Unless where she went is somehow tied to what we were told today. But there's no way to know that.

"I will say this. I don't think Sam came back here to Bridgeport, or that she got involved in whatever she was mixed up with before. It just doesn't make sense. We now know for sure that she wasn't using the prepaid phones because she was trying to hide something. Plus, she has access to the trust fund her grandfather set up for her. So she doesn't need money. If you put those two things together, it would seem to rule out her being involved in anything illegal," Munoz explained. "I think it's just like we said at her apartment—wherever it is she went, she wasn't intending to stay away."

Walker responded, "I'm with you on that. But you said it: we now know a lot more about her past, but none of it points us to where she might have gone. And even if the judge gives us the information we want, there's no guarantee that's going to help either."

They continued to talk for the next fifteen minutes in between bites of food. Walker was just about to suggest that they leave when his phone vibrated on the table. He glanced at the screen, looked over Munoz, and said, "It's Peter. Let's hope he's got something."

Walker picked up the phone, pressed the green icon, and said, "Hi, Peter. It only took you about twenty minutes. That might be a record."

"Maybe, but I've got to disappoint you again."

"What?"

"I was able to get the information on the judge right away. I even called in a favor and got his office number. Trouble is the judge is on vacation until after July Fourth—a cruise to Alaska."

Walker's shoulders sagged. "I should have known it wasn't going to be that easy. All right, Peter. Thanks for your efforts."

As Walker ended the call, Munoz said, "No dice, I take it?"

"The judge is on vacation. Alaska, no less."

Munoz sat back and shook his head. "So where do we go from here?"

Walker looked defeated. "If this were a regular investigation, I'd say we should start from the beginning again and review everything in the case file. But there's almost nothing in the case file. No witnesses, no trail, no forensics, not much of anything."

"What about the Maine angle?" Munoz asked.

Walker reached down next to his chair and picked up his briefcase, snapped it open, and removed a folder.

"That's probably all we've got right now. I typed up a list of the horse farms in Maine last night. There are sixteen of them. Why don't you take a picture of the list? I'll contact the first half, and you contact the second half. It might be too late by the time we get home today, so first thing in the morning then."

Munoz took out his phone, snapped the picture of the list, and checked to make sure he could read it. He then said, "You still have that photo of Sam? Let me take a picture of that too. After I call each of the horse farms, I'll follow up with an e-mail with her photo attached."

"Good idea," Walker said. "I hate to say it, but this almost seems like busy work. We really don't have any concrete evidence that Sam was in Maine, other then what Teresa Martin thinks she remembers. And even if Sam was in Maine last year, we don't know that's where she was headed for last Wednesday."

The discussion during the ride back to Framingham didn't produce any insight. Neither of them held out much hope that contacting the facilities in Maine was going to provide a lead, but they had little else to pursue.

After Walker picked up his car at the barracks and was safely on the Mass Pike, he used his hands-free device to call home. Cheryl answered on the second ring.

"Hi there."

"Hi, honey."

"I can hear it in your voice. It didn't go well, huh?"

"We got a lot of information, but nothing's coming together. I'll fill you in when I get home. Depending on traffic, I should be there by four thirty. I mainly called to find out what happened with you and Maddie. I wanted to know what I'd be walking into."

"I think it went pretty well. I suspect I wasn't as upset as you were. But I wasn't right in the middle of it when it happened, and I knew that everything worked out all right. So she's grounded for a week, except for Habitat for Humanity on Saturday. I didn't see any need to add on to what you had already decided, especially since she handled it the way she did," Cheryl said. "And now that Sam's still missing, she's going to have to deal with that too. No need to pile on."

In spite of the frustration the day had brought and the way he was feeling, Craig allowed himself to fall into a pattern of easy banter with his wife. "You know, you've got this parenting thing down pretty good."

Cheryl laughed. "Yeah, I use the flying-by-the-seat-of-my-pants method."

Craig laughed out loud. It felt good.

In contrast, several hundred miles to the north, Sam Daniels was just starting to become aware of her surroundings, and she was terrified.

Chapter Ten

I t had taken every ounce of strength that Sam possessed to keep her eyes open for more than a split second. And when she was finally able to do that, she almost wished she hadn't. The brief moment of consciousness produced a flood of images—some literally right before her eyes. But most of them were flashes of memory from as recently as a few days ago and others more distant. But none of them as yet was in focus.

Physically, she sensed that she was all right. She didn't feel any pain, only weakness. She was able to tell that she was lying on her side on a dirt floor. Her arms and legs felt as if they weighed hundreds of pounds. She wasn't sure whether she could stand, even if she wanted to.

One of her arms seemed to be stretched out, and then she saw why: her wrist was chained to a ring attached to a stone wall. As that realization hit her, her eyes threatened to close again. *It had to be drugs*, she thought. She must've been given something, but that particular memory wouldn't crystallize.

She forced her eyes open again and saw a small LED lamp about five feet away, certainly out of reach. It was providing what little light there was. And other than the immediate space around the lamp, nothing else was illuminated.

As each second passed, Sam began to piece things together in her mind. Although she couldn't see much of what was above her, the fetid quality of the air suggested that she was underground, or maybe in a cave of some sort. That probability sent her into a panic. Although her mind was still trying to process all that was happening, her deep-seated fear of not being able to breathe—something she'd had a fear of since childhood—charged to the front of her brain.

But it was even more than not having enough air; it was being trapped and not being able to open the door. The door. Why had she thought of a door? There was no door here. And then the memory came back to her—the root of her panic. Sam saw herself being locked in a closet. It happened mainly when her mother was turning tricks to feed her habit, but other times too. Sometimes when she was just dealing and wanted Sam out of the way.

Twelve-year-old Sam would feel the world closing in on her. There was no air in the closet, no room to move. The summer was the worst; it got so hot in there. Sometimes Sam would get down on the floor of the closet and try to breathe in air from the space between the bottom of the door and the floor. But the closet door was warped, so there was almost no air. And the physical exertion it took to get on the floor and to get back up made her ability to breathe even worse. She would try to take her mind elsewhere, to think of anything else. But that never worked.

Once, she started crying so hard that she became exhausted, and she finally fell asleep. That had been the only time that Sam had been able to get through the ordeal in the closet without the panic it caused staying with her for days. However, she had never been able to repeat those actions again. It was as if her mind was telling her, "I know what you're trying to do, but it won't work."

The memory she had just conjured up had at least provided a momentary distraction. But there was no way to sustain it. The terror started to wash over her again. She began to hyperventilate, making everything worse.

She forced herself to sit up, thinking that a change in position might make things more bearable; it didn't. A scream found its way to her throat, and every muscle in her body tensed as the scream escaped.

She dug her fingernails into her arm, trying to divert the emotional pain into something physical. At that moment, Sam knew that if there had been some way to end her life, she would have chosen to do so rather than continue to feel the way she was feeling. The irony was that, just like when she was locked in the closet, she felt as if she were in a coffin, unable to move and unable to breathe.

A moment passed and she unconsciously decided to lie down again. It was as if something was telling her that lying down consumed less energy, and maybe if she could somehow shut down her brain, she could fall asleep. Down deep she knew that was foolish, but it was all she had.

As she started to stretch out, her foot brushed against something. She sat up again and peered into the faint light. It appeared to be a bowl of food with a spoon in it and a bottle of water. The food looked like it could be oatmeal. The state of her drugged mind and her overwhelming fear didn't allow her to contemplate how the bowl and the water might have gotten there. As she stared at the food, additional saliva came into her mouth, and she realized how hungry she was.

It took some effort, but eventually she was able to reach the bowl and the water. Simultaneously, a thought came into her mind: *What if there are more drugs in the food or the water? Or what if they're full of poison?* Instead of fearing what the answer might be, Sam embraced the possibilities. Either way, the pain would stop.

The physical act of eating and drinking allowed her breathing to slow down, and the panic to subside slightly. She didn't try to force herself to think of anything in particular – like where she was, or how long she'd been there, or why this was happening. She just let her mind go wherever it wanted to. And where it wanted to go was only the here and now.

After several minutes, her eyes became heavy once again, and she felt herself slipping into sleep. She must have been right; there were drugs in the food or the water. As she was drifting off, Sam had a sense of déjà vu, as if she had experienced something similar to this feeling before and not just recently. But her mind wouldn't allow her to explore that notion any further.

Just before she put her head down on the damp earth and lost consciousness, an additional memory came into her head. Sam was clawing at someone's arm. Was it her own arm, as she had just done minutes before? No, it was somebody else's. It was a man—a man with a beard, and...

The man with the beard removed the bandage from the underside of his right arm. It had been almost a week, and it wasn't healing as quickly as he would've liked. Of course, the girl had dug her nails in pretty deep.

He glanced over to the other side of the room where the confrontation had taken place. Could he have handled it differently? Maybe at first, but once she figured everything out, what choice did he have? He couldn't let her leave. And since he wasn't completely sure whether anyone knew that she had come there, any other option was out of the question, at least until he knew more.

He looked down at the still oozing deep scratch the girl had inflicted on him. He decided to change the bandage, but do nothing more. It wasn't infected; it would eventually heal by itself.

His thoughts then returned to the issue of how he was going to resolve all of this. His business partner was making things difficult. Eli Peters had been born in the Ukraine to a Ukrainian father and an American mother. His name was actually Illya Petrovich, but he hated everything about his foreign origins. So as soon as he was old enough, he changed his name to Eli Peters, went to Canada, and became a citizen. His business ventures started out perfectly legal, but when the opportunity to cross the line into illegal territory presented itself, the huge profits became much too tempting. The fact that he had dual citizenship and was allowed easy travel between the United States and Canada was an added bonus. The man with the beard had met Eli more than a year ago. And just like a good marriage, they had started out as friends, had a brief business courtship, and then decided things were going so well they'd take the plunge.

That's why this new situation was especially troubling. They had a good thing going. They just needed to get past this minor problem. But he knew Eli wouldn't be happy if he called again. But what was he supposed to do? If things weren't progressing, then he'd have to change his plans, and the girl would have to be dealt with more permanently.

I don't care; I'm not waiting any longer, the man with the beard thought. He picked up his untraceable phone and punched in the code for Canada, followed by the rest of the number. He figured the caller ID would show up as "unknown number" on Eli's phone screen, but he'd know who it was.

After the third ring, Eli answered and sounded upset. The man with the beard could always tell when Eli was upset; a trace of his Russian accent would find its way into his voice.

"I've got nothing to tell you, JT. As soon as things cool down, I told you, I'd let you know."

"It's taking too long. I can hold off on the regular merchandise, but the... other situation is more pressing. I still don't see what the problem is; you were able to handle... bigger... shipments in the past."

Eli raised his voice, and his accent became more pronounced. "That was nearly a year ago, and we knew what was coming. We've had to pull back because of all the heat we've been getting. It's going to take at least another few days before we have everything in place."

"A few days? It's already been a week."

Eli pushed back, trying to remind the man with the beard who was really in charge. "This is your mess, JT. Don't forget that. I didn't ask for any of this; I'm just trying to help you out. You're the one who screwed up. If you don't like the way I'm handling it, get somebody else to clean it up."

JT wouldn't back down. "We've been doing business for nearly a year, and this is how I get treated?"

"Don't give me that no respect shit. This is a sweet deal we've got going, but don't think for a second you're the only game in town. Granted, your situation is unique, and I'd hate to lose it, but I'll go somewhere else if I have to."

JT doubled down. "No you won't, and you know it. I may just take a little trip up to Canada, bring the merchandise with me, and dump it on you."

"And what good will that do? You'd be totally screwed. You wouldn't have any place to keep the merchandise, and you wouldn't have a clue how to sell it off," Eli said. "So here's how it's going to be. I'll contact you when it's safe to move the merchandise. But if you call me again, we're done. If you don't think I'm serious, try me. I don't give a shit one way or the other. Have a nice day, JT."

JT started to throw his phone against the stone fireplace, but caught himself. He decided to try to cool off before considering what to do next. He was clearheaded enough to realize that decisions made in the throes of anger were rarely the best ones. He had learned that particular lesson the hard way.

He paced the floor for the next several minutes and then stopped in front of one of the large windows that faced to the north. He stood before it and peered out into the darkness toward the place where Sam Daniels lay asleep.

His anger had dissipated somewhat, but it still fueled his darkest thoughts, *it might be best to cut his losses and get rid of the girl before everything else with Eli blew up in his face.*

Chapter Eleven

The rush-hour traffic going through Boston was more like a Friday night than a Wednesday night. Walker had expected to be home by four thirty; instead, he walked into his house at five- fifteen.

Cheryl was waiting for him in the kitchen. She turned and smiled as he came over to her and gave her a kiss on the cheek. He was about to say something, but Maddie rushed into the room and asked, "What happened?"

Craig looked toward his daughter and responded, "And hello to you too, Maddie."

Maddie lowered her head slightly. "I'm sorry. Hi, Dad." She then went over and gave her father a hug.

When Craig released his daughter, he said, "Okay, let's sit down." He looked over at Maddie. "We were able to confirm a lot of what you told us about Sam. Her father *is* dead and her mother *is* in jail."

At that point Craig hesitated, wondering how detailed he should get. He decided to go with the PG version for Maddie's benefit.

"It appears that a family court judge thought it would be best if Sam got out of Bridgeport. That's why she was allowed to become an emancipated minor. We know that she came here last September, but we don't know where she was for the few months before that."

Maddie asked, "Is there some way to find out; that's really important, isn't it?"

Her father smiled. "Yes, it is, but it appears that only the judge knows where she went."

"Can't you ask him?"

"He's not available. He's on vacation in Alaska."

Maddie looked pensive and then said, "That's why you were asking me about Maine? You think that's where she was before, and maybe that's where she is now?"

"I honestly don't know, sweetheart. That's the best lead we have, so we're definitely going to look into it."

"Can I help?" Maddie asked.

"Sure. Let me talk to your mother for a few minutes, and then I'll tell you what you can do."

"Okay. Thanks, Dad." Before Maddie got up out of her chair, she looked at her father and, struggling to keep her emotions in check, she added. "I know you're going to find her."

As his daughter left the room, Craig had to work at keeping his own emotions in check as well. Cheryl put her hand on her husband's arm.

"It's tough to be your little girl's hero."

"Most days I don't mind, but not today."

Cheryl waited a moment and then asked, "So what else aren't you telling us?"

"That obvious, huh?"

"Well, I don't know if Maddie picked up on it, but I could tell from your body language that there was more."

"You're scary, you know that. You should be working for the FBI."

"Nah, give me the blood and guts of the ER anytime," Cheryl said.

Craig put his hand on top of his wife's hand. He left it there for a few moments and then said, "You're right. There are some other details." He paused for a moment. "Sam's juvenile records are sealed, which probably means she was involved in something illegal." Craig was quick to add, "But there's no proof of that, or that she continued doing whatever it was that she might have been involved in when she got to Massachusetts.

"She was given emancipated minor status by the judge at her mother's request. Sam's grandfather on her father's side left her money in his will. But get this. Sam was the one who turned her mother in, although it's not clear if the mother knew that."

Cheryl was shaking her head. "How do some kids even make it into adulthood?"

"Good question," Walker said. "The problem we have, like I told you on the phone, is that nothing is coming together. We have this missing piece: Where was Sam sent? Oh yeah, I forgot I left that part out. The judge told Sam she had to go to—what the social worker called—rehab. But we don't know where. Of course, even if we did, there's no way to be sure that's where she was headed to last Wednesday."

"But you think it might be in Maine?"

"That's based on what one of the managers at the horse farm thinks she remembers. Not exactly DNA evidence."

"So what are you going to have Maddie do?" Cheryl asked.

"I've got a list of sixteen stables in Maine. Dave's taking half the list, and I've got the other half. Maddie can look up my half and get as much information as possible on each one. I'll contact them tomorrow morning. Dave's going to do the same, and then we'll compare notes and see what comes out of it."

"I think it's good that you're letting Maddie help."

"I thought so too, initially. Now I'm not so sure. If things turn out badly, is she going to feel responsible somehow?" Walker asked.

Maddie jumped into her assignment with the same enthusiasm she had shown with the search for the local horse farms. Ninety minutes after she started, she had produced eight printouts off the Internet. She highlighted pertinent information and made detailed notes on each page.

Craig joked with Cheryl that maybe he had suggested that the wrong family member join the FBI. He then spent the rest of the night reviewing each of the printouts. If there was a clue to Sam's whereabouts on any of those pages, it was well hidden.

Dave Munoz had a similar experience. He had fallen asleep in a chair in his living room with printouts on his lap and others strewn out on the floor. He awoke shortly after 2:00 a.m., gathered the papers together, and went to bed, hoping fresh eyes in the morning would yield better results.

Craig got up at 7:15 on Thursday morning, made himself some coffee, and began to read over the printouts for at least the fifth time. He decided he had to wait until nine o'clock before making any phone calls. There were two facilities from his list that offered therapeutic services, although not exclusively. He decided he would start with those.

Cheryl and Maddie came downstairs within a few minutes of each other, both inquiring how things were progressing. He explained that nothing in the printouts appeared terribly promising, but the real test would come with the phone calls.

Maddie asked if there was some way she could help. Her father responded, "You've already been a big help. The phone calls are really a one-person job. If anything else comes up, I'll let you know."

On the spur of the moment, at 8:20 a.m., Craig decided that he should go for a run. He always felt better after exercise, and sometimes pushing through physical exertion freed up his mind to see something he hadn't seen before. But at the end of the three miles, nothing had come into his head that was of any value. He showered, shaved, and got dressed. He placed the first phone call at 9:07 a.m.

By 9:30 a.m., Craig had talked with someone at the first three facilities on his list. In all three cases, the managers had no recollection of anyone named Samantha Daniels.

Craig e-mailed Sam's picture and asked for a follow-up e-mail in return, confirming that it had been received, but more importantly requesting whether they remembered seeing anyone who looked like the girl in the photo. Two of the three managers responded right away. But at 10:15 a.m., Craig was still waiting for the third.

It took another hour and a half between phone calls, e-mails, return e-mails, and callbacks before Craig was able to cross off all of the horse farms on his half of the list.

He waited another half hour before he called Dave Munoz.

"Hi, Dave. I hope you had better luck than I did."

"I'm afraid it doesn't look very good, but I might have one possibility. The woman said she'd call me back; she has to check her files. I'm holding out some hope because this particular horse farm does offer hippotherapy."

"What's the name of the facility?" Walker asked.

"Caribou Equestrian Center."

"What is the woman checking for in the files?"

"She called me back after I e-mailed Sam's picture. She said she looked familiar. They had only recently switched over all their records to computers. She wanted to check out the paper copies, just in case something got missed."

"When do you expect to hear from her?"

"It should be soon... I... Wait a second, someone's beeping in. Let me call you back."

Five minutes later Walker's phone buzzed. It was Munoz.

"That was the woman from Caribou. No luck."

They both remained quiet for a moment, and then Munoz asked, "Any idea where we go from here?"

"I don't think we have a lot of options. I could try the judge's office and see if his clerk will contact him in Alaska."

"It's worth a shot, I guess."

"I'll call you back and let you know how I made out."

Twenty minutes later, Walker was back on the phone with Munoz. "The judge evidently gave strict instructions: no phone calls, unless it's an emergency. And his clerk quickly determined that our investigation doesn't qualify."

"Sounds like we're back to square one," Munoz said.

"Yeah, I'm afraid so," Walker replied. "I'm going to review my notes again, but I can't say I'm very optimistic."

"I'll do the same." Munoz paused. "If we have to shut things down, I don't envy you having to tell Maddie."

"I know. I've been trying not to think about that."

Chapter Twelve

JT continued to force himself to calm down, and eventually, any thoughts of doing something foolish left him. He hated to admit it, but Eli had been right. If he brought the girl up to Canada, he would have no idea how to contact the right people. Of course, if he had known everything was going to be delayed, he would have left the girl locked in the cabin bathroom instead of moving her. So now he would just have to wait until Eli called him back and gave the go-ahead.

JT spent the next half hour preparing food, which he laced with ketamine, one of the so-called date rape drugs. While he had never used ketamine for that purpose, in this current situation, it was perfect. It immobilized the girl and kept her docile. He preferred that to injecting her with drugs, as he had done the first few days, which forced him to be in close proximity and at risk of another attack. When he finished mixing the ketamine with the canned hash, he grabbed a couple of bottles of water and was about to leave the main house when he thought of something.

He went into one of the bedrooms in the back of the house, the one where his father had died four years earlier—where the man had been bedridden for the last two years of his life. JT went into the adjoining bathroom, found a bedpan, wiped it off, and brought it with him.

He put the food and the other items on the floor behind the driver's seat of the Mercedes SUV, started it up, and headed toward the cabin next to the one where he had kept the girl for the first few days. Prior to the girl being there, none of the cabins had been used in almost eight months, ever since the last of the girls had left, or, more precisely, had been shipped out.

JT was hoping to find some leftover clothing in one of the old dressers in the cabin. And sure enough, when he opened the bottom drawer of the second one he tried, he found a few items: a pair of shorts and a couple of T-shirts. He had no idea if they would fit the girl, *but beggars can't be choosers,* he thought.

He tossed the clothes into the back seat and drove the additional quarter mile to where he had taken the girl. He parked at least 100 yards away. Realistically, there was no way anybody could be watching him, but he decided not to tempt fate.

When he reached the hidden door, he pushed aside the brush on top of it, removed a key from his pocket, opened the lock, and lifted the panel. The door made a creaking sound as it strained against its hinges. JT picked up the items he had brought with him and carefully descended the stone steps, using a flashlight with a strong beam to guide him.

It took him nearly thirty seconds to walk the 40 yards to where the girl lay sleeping. JT saw that she had eaten almost all of the food and had drunk most of the water he had left. He removed the used items, replaced them with the ones he had brought, and left as quickly as possible.

He wanted no part of dealing with the girl while she was awake. He wasn't completely sure why he felt that way. Obviously, their first encounter had not gone well. But he was fairly certain that his aversion to interacting with the girl was more than just the physical confrontation they'd had. As that thought came into his mind, he subconsciously reached for the bandage on his arm and wondered if maybe he was having second thoughts about his plan. He really didn't know; what he did know, however, is that he wanted no part of a fully awake captive pleading with him.

Twenty minutes after JT left, Sam began to wake up. As she came to, the terror she had felt hours before began to engulf her again, but when she noticed the new items next to her, it subsided slightly. It appeared that the bearded man didn't intend to kill her, not if he was bringing her food, and clothing, and a receptacle for relieving herself.

But before she could fully process that realization, a sense of claustrophobia overtook her again. She tried closing her eyes and taking deep breaths. The first two breaths came easily, but then she couldn't force the third, and panic set in. Sam began to cry and to shake uncontrollably. After several minutes, she was totally exhausted, unable to even lift her head. But by lying completely still, she was eventually able to normalize her breathing, and her fear dialed back a notch. She then tried to will her mind elsewhere. And for a brief time, she was successful. She began to remember bits and pieces of what had happened to her.

Last Wednesday, she had taken a bus to the Liberty Tree Mall in Danvers, another bus to Salem, and then the train into Boston. Next, she'd taken a bus to Lewiston, Maine, and then... What was the sign on the next bus? Oh yeah, Western Maine Transportation Services.

When she got off that bus, it seemed as if she must've walked five miles to the ranch. Well, it was in the middle of nowhere, she acknowledged. And then she'd seen that huge gate at the entrance. The gate she remembered was nowhere near as massive as this one. She had pressed the button on the intercom, but nobody had answered. She had then looked up and seen the video camera on the pole. Had that always been there as well?

Sam had sat on the ground waiting for at least fifteen minutes. She had come a long way and didn't want to simply turn around and go home. And then she remembered the climbing rock.

The ranch was surrounded by natural rock formations— granite, she thought someone had told her—but there was one spot a few hundred feet from the entrance where you could scale the natural formation fairly easily. She had never done it when she was here before, but some of the other girls had just to sneak out for a while.

She wasn't sure what difference it would make for her to be on the other side of the gate. She hadn't come simply to visit the place; she needed to speak with JT. But she remembered thinking that maybe the intercom is broken, or the video camera is broken. Maybe JT is actually inside at the main house. She probably hadn't really believed any of that, but she was tired of just sitting there.

She had walked back and forth past the climbing rock three or four times before she finally recognized it. Sam had struggled somewhat to climb it, nearly falling twice, but eventually she reached the top and was able to shimmy down to the ground on the other side.

It had taken her several minutes walking along the dirt road inside the property before any of the buildings came into view. But unlike the front gate and the video camera on the pole, the main house, the cabins, the barn, and the chapel had all seemed very familiar.

When Sam arrived at the main house, she had knocked three or four times, but no one answered. She had tried the door, but it was locked. Eventually, she had just looked in the windows. It didn't appear that anyone was there. Even though she had spent nearly three months at the ranch, she had never been inside the main house. That was off-limits for all the girls.

She had looked around for a few more minutes and then had decided to visit the cabin where she had stayed nearly a year ago. Was it possible that any of the girls were still here? It seemed unlikely; she never remembered the ranch being as empty as it appeared to be now: no JT, no counselors. The place seemed abandoned.

When Sam had gotten closer, she could see that the cabin door was open. Once inside, it was obvious that no one had lived there for quite a while. She had wondered what could have changed. Maybe the whole trip had been unnecessary.

She had spent several more minutes in the cabin, and then she had knelt down next to the bunk where she had slept. There were no longer any mattresses covering the wooden slats on any of the bunks, so she could see through to the floor. And there carved into the wood were her initials: SD.

She had smiled at the memory. When one of the other girls in the cabin had seen her initials, she had started calling her San Diego, and it had stuck. After that, almost nobody called her Sam. While she stared at her own initials, she noticed another set next to hers: CS, which she remembered stood for Crystal Simmons, the girl she had gotten closest to during her stay at the ranch. Sam remembered often wondering what had become of her.

Something else had then dawned on her. If there were no girls at the ranch, what about the horses? She had quickly gotten to her feet and run out of the cabin, sprinting across the open field to the barn. The condition of the barn had been similar to the cabin. It was obvious that no living creature had been inside for a long time.

The same sadness Sam had felt days before when she'd found the barn empty overtook her again. And the distraction of her memory began to give way to fear. Her breathing became labored, as the reality of being trapped was all she could think of again.

Part of her wanted to try to fight through her panic, but another part of her just wanted her mind to shut down, to turn itself off so the panic would end. She eyed the food that had been left for her. It looked like some sort of hash, not something she would normally eat. She waited only another five seconds and then the desire to not have to feel the way she was feeling won out.

She devoured the food, not from any sense of hunger, but rather with the intent of getting the drugs into her system as quickly as possible. Her last fully conscious thought before she succumbed to sleep was one of despair. *No one knows I'm here; why didn't I tell someone?*

But then there was a split second realization and a flicker of hope. She had told someone, at least part of it, but…

It was now nearly three o'clock on Thursday afternoon. Walker had been pouring over the Maine horse farm printouts for several hours. But there hadn't been a word, or a phrase, or a location, or a name that had triggered even the slightest sense that it might be something worth pursuing.

Walker waited until 3:15 p.m. before he finally phoned Munoz. His partner answered immediately.

"I've been half-expecting, half-dreading your call. But I figured I'd just keep looking until I heard from you. Unfortunately, I've got nothing."

Walker sounded defeated as well. "Same here."

"Have you told Maddie yet?"

"No. I wanted to touch base with you first."

"Are you going to officially shut the case down?"

"I'll wait until tomorrow. Obviously, give me a call if something occurs to you, and I'll let you know once the investigation is officially closed."

"Sorry, Craig. I feel like I let you down. And Maddie too."

"Not your fault. Talk to you tomorrow."

Walker went into the living room and found his wife reading. Maddie was upstairs. Cheryl looked up from her book, as her husband said, "I can't justify keeping the case open any longer. We're totally out of leads. I just talked to Dave."

"Are you going to tell Maddie right away?"

"I think I should."

"Do you want me to be there?"

"No, it's all right. I'll do it myself."

"Okay. I'll be right here in case you need me."

Walker called upstairs to his daughter and then went to wait in the kitchen until she came down. He could tell by the expression on her face that she knew what was coming. He chose his words carefully and tried to put the best spin possible on it, but it didn't matter.

"I'm going to have to suspend the investigation for the time being, Maddie."

Before he could elaborate, she interrupted. "There must be something else you can do."

"I wish there was, sweetheart. But..."

"But you said you were pretty sure she went to Maine," Maddie said, unable to hold back her tears. "Can't you go up there... and... look for her?"

Walker half smiled at his daughter's naiveté. "If we had any kind of lead, I'd be up there in a heartbeat."

"I know... It's just that..." Maddie wasn't able to face the reality of what was happening. She ran out of the kitchen and up to her room.

Walker remained seated where he was; Cheryl came in thirty seconds later.

"I know she didn't take it well, but she's going to be all right; she really does understand."

"You're probably right, but it doesn't make it hurt any less."

"For her or for you?"

"Both," Walker said.

Neither of them spoke for a few moments, and then Cheryl said, "They say that sixteen-year-olds are half little girls and half grown-up women. I think we've seen it first hand in the last few days, haven't we?"

"She shouldn't have to deal with stuff like this."

"You can't protect her from everything."

"I know, but this is my job; I should have been able to do more."

They commiserated for another few minutes, and then Walker decided he would go out for a run. He came downstairs after putting on his running clothes, got a drink of water, and was about to head out when his phone buzzed on the kitchen counter and everything changed.

∾Chapter Thirteen∾

Walker picked up his phone and checked out the number on the screen, but he didn't recognize it. He pressed the green phone icon, waited a moment, and then said, "Hello."

"Agent Walker?"

"Speaking."

"Hi, Agent Walker. This is Alice Burns, the guidance counselor from the high school. We met the other day."

"Of course, yes..."

"I hope I'm not disturbing you, but I found out something that I thought might be of help to you... about Sam Daniels."

Walker had been leaning against the kitchen counter, but upon hearing Sam's name, he straightened up.

"What did you find out?"

"I think I might know where she went. I think she went to Maine, to a ranch."

Alice Burns had Walker's full attention. "Why do you think that?"

"Well, each year I require all my students who are juniors to write a draft of their college application essay before they leave for the summer. Are you familiar with what those are?"

"Yes, Maddie's not old enough, but I remember our son having to write one."

"Anyway, I started reading them this afternoon. I got to Sam's about a half hour ago. Hers was very personal and very tragic; she talked about her recent past and what happened to her. It's very compelling. Toward the end of the essay, she mentions having been sent to a ranch in Maine before she came to Massachusetts."

"Did she mention the name of the ranch?" Walker asked.

"No, she just refers to it as a ranch. But the reason I think she may have gone there is that she wrote me a note at the end of the essay saying that she felt like she had to get permission from the person who ran the ranch to include it in her application. According to Sam, every one of the girls who were at the ranch except for her were runaways, and the ranch was a stickler for protecting their privacy and the privacy of the ranch.

"Sam asked me to keep all this confidential until she got permission to use it in her application," Mrs. Burns said. "I know it's not definite that that's where she went, but I thought you should know."

"Absolutely. Can I get a copy of the essay?" Walker asked.

"I thought you might want that. I had to get permission from my principal, but he said it was okay to make one for you."

"Are you still at school?"

"Yes, I was planning to leave shortly, but I can wait until you get here."

"It shouldn't take me more than fifteen minutes."

"Okay. I'll wait by the front door to let you in. I'm not sure if anyone else is still in the building except for the custodians."

"I'm on my way, and thank you."

Walker left the kitchen, cutting through the living room on his way upstairs. Cheryl looked up from her tablet as he came into the room.

"Who was that on the phone?"

"The guidance counselor from Maddie's school. We may have just caught a break. Sam handed in a draft of her college essay to this Mrs. Burns and in it she wrote that she needed to go up to Maine to get permission to write about this ranch where she stayed. I'm heading over to the school to pick up a copy of the essay. I'm just going to throw on a pair of pants over my running shorts."

"You really think this is something?" Cheryl asked.

"It might be grasping at straws, but we don't have anything else," Walker said. "Don't say anything to Maddie until I know more."

"All right. Good luck."

Walker got to the school a few minutes before four o'clock. Alice Burns was waiting just inside the front door. As Walker got closer, she opened it up and let him inside. Walker spoke first.

"I really appreciate the phone call. This could be a real breakthrough."

The guidance counselor handed a folder to Walker with a copy of the essay inside. "I wish I had started to read the essays earlier."

"You had no way of knowing," Walker said. "Obviously, I have a copy now, but is there anything else that I should know before I leave?"

"I don't think so. It's actually pretty scary what she went through. You'll see what I mean when you read it," Mrs. Burns replied. "I wrote my cell phone number on a Post-it inside the folder. I'm taking a long weekend, but I'll be around. Call me if there's something else I can do."

Walker thanked her and headed back to his car. He sat there for the next ten minutes, reading the essay three times. Alice Burns had not exaggerated; it was truly scary what Sam Daniels had gone through. But something else struck Walker, something that gave him hope. Sam appeared to be a survivor. Assuming that she was being held against her will, that particular trait might make all the difference.

Before starting up his car and driving home, Walker took out his phone, found Peter Stansky's number, and tapped it. A moment later, Peter was on the line.

"The last time we spoke, things were not going very well. Any change?"

"Maybe."

"What do you need?"

Walker gave Stansky the abbreviated version of the new development, primarily focusing on Sam's reference to the ranch, not her other difficulties.

When Walker finished, Peter asked, "So you don't have any specific name or location for this ranch?"

"No, but what I was hoping you could do is a computer search for all the ranches in Maine. I think that would be the best approach. What I don't understand is when I did the original search for horse farms, why I didn't get any hits for ranches. You'd think there'd be some link between the two."

"That does seem strange. Okay, let me see what I can find out," Peter said. "Are you home now?"

"No, I'm still at the school. I'm heading home now."

"When you get there, e-mail me a copy of the list of horse farms you already eliminated; no sense in looking at those again. Oh, and you might as well send me a copy of the essay too, just in case."

"All right. As soon as I get home, I'm going to call Dave and let him know what's going on. I'll send you a copy of the list and the essay right after that."

"Okay," Peter said. "Keep a good thought, Craig."

Walker drove the eight miles back to his house without being aware of the distance or the time it took. All sorts of ideas were pinballing in his head. Walker pulled into his driveway and was about to exit the car then thought better of it. He decided to call his partner from the car rather than inside the house. He didn't want to take the chance of Maddie hearing any of it.

Dave Munoz answered on the second ring.

"Did you change your mind about waiting until tomorrow?"

"No. We may not have to shut the case down after all."

"Why? What happened?"

Walker gave Munoz a more detailed account of Sam's essay than the one he had offered to Peter Stansky, but he held back on any description of Sam's retelling of the horrific circumstances until the end.

"I'll scan the actual essay and e-mail a copy to you, but it's even worse than we imagined when we first started investigating."

Walker expelled a breath before he continued. "According to Sam, after her father died, her mother became so depressed that she couldn't work. She took up drugs, all the opioids including heroin; Sam was twelve at the time.

"It started to get real bad when Sam was fourteen or fifteen. Her mother turned to prostitution and would lock Sam in a closet when she had men over to the apartment. The mother eventually started dealing drugs as well, and she had Sam make some of the deliveries.

"Her mother also got Sam hooked on drugs. That was about three months before the mother was arrested. According to what she wrote, Sam was picked up making a delivery, and because her mother had told Sam that she was going to have to start *accommodating* some of the men who had been frequenting the apartment, Sam turned her mother in to the police."

There was silence on both ends of the call for a few moments, and then Munoz said, "Are you serious? How do you do that to your own child, or anybody else for that matter?" He paused. "So how does the ranch fit in?"

"It's in the essay. Evidently, this Judge Frazier met with Sam in his chambers and heard the whole story. He promised her that her juvenile record—drug possession with intent to distribute—would be sealed if she went to this ranch, got clean, and stayed in school. That's kind of where the essay ends. Sam wrote a note at the close of it indicating that if she wanted to include information about the ranch, she felt like she had to get permission because there were a lot of runaways there, and she didn't feel right talking about the place without getting permission."

Munoz said, "That all seems to fit with everything we found out earlier."

"Yeah, I think it's all true."

"No other clues about the ranch?"

"Not that I can see, but that's why I want you to take a look. I'm hoping Peter will get back to me fairly soon with the new list. We can divide it up like we did the last time."

"Hopefully with better results," Munoz said.

"Yeah. As I said earlier, I can't figure out why the original computer search didn't pull up any ranches."

"That does seem odd."

"All right, Dave. I'll send you the essay, and as soon as I hear from Peter, I'll give you a call."

Cheryl was still sitting in the living room when Craig came inside. He looked toward the stairs and asked, "Is Maddie still in her room?"

"Yeah, she hasn't come down yet."

"I'm going to use the computer in the den. I need to send out a couple of e-mails to Dave and Peter Stansky after I scan in the essay. It should only take me a few minutes. We can talk in the other room after I finish."

Five minutes later, they were seated at the kitchen table. Cheryl could tell by how animated her husband had been that the trip to the high school had borne some fruit.

Craig opened the folder that held the essay and said, "This could be the break we needed. We still have to pinpoint exactly where Sam might have gone, but now we know it was probably a ranch in Maine."

"A ranch?"

"Yeah. Remember, I mentioned that it appeared that the judge had sent her someplace for rehab? Well, evidently that was to this ranch in Maine."

"So you were right; it was rehab?" Cheryl asked.

"Yeah, but that's only half the story."

Walker spent the next ten minutes detailing the content of Sam's essay. When he finished, Cheryl shook her head and said, "She's one tough kid."

"No doubt about that," Walker said. "What I am concerned about though is that if she went to that ranch, why haven't we heard from her? From what she wrote, the ranch was like a sanctuary. She felt safe there, and she was protective of the privacy of the other girls who were there. If that's where she went, what changed?"

"It doesn't sound like you're as optimistic as I thought you were."

"I'm optimistic that this is a solid lead. I'm just not sure it's going to bring about the outcome I was hoping for."

"Are you going to tell Maddie?"

"Not about Sam's life in Bridgeport, certainly. I'm just going to tell her that we're keeping the investigation open because of the new information about the ranch."

"You should do that as soon as possible. She could probably use some good news."

As Walker climbed the stairs, he thought about exactly what to say to his daughter. He didn't want to oversell what had transpired, but he wanted her to feel hopeful; she deserved that.

He knocked on Maddie's bedroom door, and she responded quietly.

"Come in."

Craig Walker entered and closed the door behind him. He then sat on the edge of his daughter's bed.

"I'm keeping the investigation open."

"Really?"

"Yes. I got a phone call from Mrs. Burns a little while ago. Sam had written a draft of her personal essay for college, and in it, she mentioned a ranch in Maine. She said she was going to go up there at some point."

"That's what you thought, right? Did she say where it was?"

"No. So we still have some work to do to figure it out, but I think we're on the right track."

Maddie leaped up and gave her father a hug. "Thanks, Dad."

Craig Walker held on to his daughter for a full fifteen seconds, hoping that the moment would etch itself into Maddie's memory bank. *This sense of feeling protected is what all sixteen-year-old girls are entitled to,* he thought, *in contrast to the fear and abandonment that Sam Daniels must have felt.*

Ᏸ⁀Chapter Fourteen⁀Ꮗ

I t was nearly 7:30 p.m. before Peter Stansky finally called back.

"Hi, Craig, sorry it took so long, but I wanted to make sure I had expanded the search enough to include every possibility. I still don't understand why, but for some reason, Maine makes a distinction between horse farms, stables, and ranches. But none of the other New England states do that. So when I Googled 'ranches in Maine' I got a totally separate list from the search for 'horse farms and stables.' But when I tried the same thing in Massachusetts, the search included all three of them. Go figure.

"Anyway, I've already e-mailed you the list. I was surprised to find that there were twenty-nine different facilities with ranch in their title. I just hope the girl didn't just refer to it as a ranch when it really isn't called that."

Walker said, "There's no way to tell that for sure, but I didn't get that impression from the essay."

"No, I agree; I didn't either." Stansky paused. "She sure didn't have it easy, did she?"

"No, no she didn't. Listen, as always, thanks for everything, Peter."

"Glad to do it. One last thing. Of the twenty-nine ranches I listed, twenty-five have websites. I pasted the link next to each one. The other four don't have websites; they may even be out of business, but I included them anyway. After I generated the list, I refined the search to include a rehab component, but I didn't find anything."

"That doesn't surprise me; that would've been too easy."

"All right, Craig, I'll let you get to it. Good luck, and if you need anything else, just let me know."

As soon as he hung up, Walker called Munoz. "I forwarded a copy of Peter's e-mail with a list of all the ranches. Evidently, Maine makes a distinction between horse farms and ranches. That's why my original list was incomplete. Why don't you take the first fifteen on the list, and I'll take the rest."

"That sounds good," Munoz said.

"I'm sure I'll be up late, so if you find anything, don't hesitate to call. Otherwise, I'll touch base with you tomorrow."

Walker finally went to bed around midnight after spending over four hours staring at his laptop. He focused exclusively on the ten ranches that had websites. The other four that didn't would require some additional digging, and he decided that he needed fresh eyes for that. Those would have to wait until the morning.

Not surprisingly, although he was very tired, Walker had trouble falling asleep. So he decided to try to make productive use of his time. In the past, he had employed a technique in which he tried to clear his mind and not think about the case that he was investigating. And while it seemed counterintuitive to avoid thinking about the very thing you were working on while expecting to discover some new insight, there were a number of scientific and psychological studies that suggested the practice had some validity. And although Walker could personally attest to the success of this technique, it was not to be on this particular night.

As he awoke on Friday morning, and his brain kicked into conscious mode, he searched its recesses for anything meaningful relating to the investigation. Nothing came to the forefront. He stayed in bed for another few minutes and then went downstairs.

Cheryl was already in the kitchen finishing her breakfast and was about to leave for work. As her husband entered the room she said, "I was barely awake when you came to bed last night. Any luck?"

"No, not so far. I'm hoping that Dave might've found something."

Cheryl came over and gave her husband a kiss on the cheek. "I have a ten-hour shift, so I won't be home until well after six. What do you want to do about dinner?"

"I can put something together; we can wait for you," Walker said.

"Actually, why don't you and Maddie eat early? I'll fend for myself when I get home."

"You sure?"

"Yeah. Maddie likes to eat early."

"Speaking of Maddie, she's not up yet?"

Cheryl looked skeptically at her husband. "Teenage girls usually don't get up early if they don't have to. Plus, she's grounded, remember? There's not a lot of upside for her rolling out of bed before nine or ten."

Craig didn't respond immediately. Eventually, he said, "After I read Sam's essay, I had some second thoughts about having grounded Maddie."

"For an FBI agent, you're a softie. You know that?"

"Keep that to yourself, please."

"As if everybody doesn't already know," Cheryl said.

"Well, it really only applies to Maddie."

"So you're admitting it?"

"Denying it at this point seems pretty futile, don't you think?"

"I do." Cheryl moved closer to her husband. "How about this? Why don't you take her out for lunch or dinner? That way the punishment stays intact, but she gets out of the house and gets to spend some more time with her dad."

"I knew there was a reason I married you."

"I thought it was because you wanted to have someone in the medical profession close by in case of an emergency."

"Well, that too."

Walker took a quick shower and was downstairs on his laptop twenty minutes later. The first two ranches that didn't have websites appeared to have gone out of business, or to have been sold as private homes and no longer operated as working ranches.

The third ranch listed without a website was more difficult to pin down. Peter Stansky had provided two links for the facility called Redemption Ranch. The name struck Walker as being odd, but he dismissed his concern and clicked on the first link.

Redemption Ranch was not the official name of the property. It was just what the locals near Pendleton, Maine, called it. Evidently, it had been given the name because the land was owned by the Church of Universal Redemption, a small sect that could trace its origins in America back to the 1640's. Josiah Pendleton, who had emigrated from Dover, England, had claimed the land shortly after his arrival. The land consisted of some eight hundred acres, much of which was natural rock formation. The linked article went on to say that about one hundred acres in the middle of the property was suitable for farming, which was how the sect had survived the early years in the New World.

The article read like a Wikipedia entry but was actually an excerpt from a book about Maine by a Professor Randolph Mason. Nothing in the rest of the article alluded to anything current, or anything about the facility actually serving as a ranch, a rehab center, or a haven for runaways. Walker thought it was probably a dead end, but he clicked on the second link Stansky had provided.

The next article detailed the accidental death of Tom Chambers ten months before. Once again, the name Redemption Ranch was referred to only as the name the locals had given to the property, and there was no mention of any activity at the ranch related to rehab or runaways.

Before closing the link, Walker reread a portion of Sam's essay to double-check the time frame. According to what Sam had written, she was out of rehab weeks before the accident had taken place. So, even if by some chance Redemption Ranch was where she had been, she wouldn't have known anything about the accident.

Although he doubted he would find anything helpful, Walker decided to spend a few more minutes looking into Redemption Ranch. When he Googled it specifically, he found there had been a novel published with that name, but its setting was out West and had nothing to do with the Maine property. The only other two links that seemed relevant were the two Peter Stansky had already given him.

Then Walker Googled "Church of Universal Redemption." There were at least two pages of links from that search. He clicked on the first one and found a more detailed description of the establishment of the church in America. The article also indicated that during the mid-1800s, some of the sect members had moved to Ohio where they started an offshoot of the original church. There was no mention of the ranch.

Walker tried the next two links with similar results. And if someone had asked him why he hadn't stopped there, he wouldn't have been able to explain his actions. He clicked on the fourth link to find something a little bit different: a description of the sect's hierarchy. It was five years old and listed Lemuel Chambers as the head of the church. Walker knew from the article about Tom Chambers' accidental death that Lemuel Chambers, his father, was now deceased.

He was about to close down the link when he glanced at the list of church elders. Walker didn't see it at first, but then it jumped out at him. Third from the top, in alphabetical order was the name Judge Arthur Frazier.

Walker felt something like a jolt of electricity throughout his entire body as the ramifications of what he had discovered hit home. It wasn't just some bizarre coincidence; it was the missing piece of the puzzle. He was convinced that he now knew where Sam had gone.

Walker's two decades of FBI experience kicked in, and his mind automatically began to formulate the next steps he needed to take. The first thing he had to do was to get in touch with someone at Redemption Ranch. But unlike the other properties Walker had investigated that had websites, there was no contact information for Redemption Ranch.

He initially tried the traditional route—411 information for Franklin County, Maine—but there was no listing. He followed that up with a more expansive Google search but came up empty. Walker decided he had to ask Peter Stansky for help again.

Stansky had just about gotten the word "Hello" out of his mouth when Walker broke in.

"Sam Daniels was sent to a place called Redemption Ranch. I'm sure of it. The judge who ordered the rehab is an elder in the church that owns the property."

"Redemption Ranch? Was that one of facilities that didn't have a website?"

"Yes. That's why I'm calling. I need some contact information."

"Okay, let me think for a second." Stansky paused for a few moments. "I'm pretty sure I already tried the FBI database, but let me try that again. Remind me about the information I already sent you on this Redemption Ranch. A lot of those places are running together."

"One of the links you sent me was about how it was founded and the religious sect. The other one was about an accidental death on the property."

"Now I remember. Okay, let me check our database again, and then I'll contact the local police. If I get nothing there, I can try the registrar of deeds. I'll call you back in a few minutes."

Walker ended the call and immediately tapped Dave Munoz's number on his phone.

Munoz answered at the second ring. "Hi, Craig, I..."

"I know where the judge sent Sam," Walker said.

Walker spent the next several minutes explaining how he had come to that conclusion as well as his conversation with Stansky.

"As soon as I hear from him, I'll let you know."

Twenty-five minutes later, Walker was back on the phone with Stansky.

"Anything?"

"I'm afraid not much. No luck with our database. And there are no local police in Pendleton where the ranch is located. So I contacted the Franklin County Sheriff's Department. They were reluctant to give me any assistance over the phone. I couldn't blame them; they don't know who I am. Anyway, I suggested that if they couldn't give me the phone number that they could at least call the ranch and ask whoever answered to get in touch with me. The officer I spoke with still didn't like the idea, but he did it anyway. The landline is no longer in service.

"Then I tried the registrar of deeds office, and they told me that the property is owned by the Church of Universal Redemption, which we already knew; that's public information anyway. However, the woman who answered the phone did tell me that any correspondence to the ranch is sent in care of James T. Chambers. I checked out this James Chambers in our database and through 411. If he has a phone, the number is unlisted."

"Things just can't be easy, can they?" Walker asked.

"I guess not."

"It sounds like Dave and I are going to have to go up there in person."

"I don't see that you have much choice. I did find out one piece of good news. There's a new FBI training facility about twenty miles outside of Pendleton near Eustis, Maine. You and Dave can probably arrange to stay there while you're investigating."

"Good to know. Thanks Peter."

"I'll keep trying to find some way to contact this James Chambers. Maybe Facebook, Twitter, LinkedIn, something."

"I appreciate it."

As soon as he hung up, Walker called Dave Munoz and filled him in.

"Are you up for a road trip?"

"Yeah, seems like the only option."

"All right. I'm going to get in touch with somebody at the training facility to make sure we can stay there."

"Were you thinking about going up there today?" Munoz asked.

"No, let's go first thing in the morning. I want to give Peter some more time to see what he can find out."

"Okay. I took a look at the map. Pendleton is way up there, probably a little over four hours from your house."

"Yeah, that's about what I figured."

"All right. I'll plan to be at your place around seven in the morning."

"I'll see you then. Oh, and Dave, obviously, we don't know how long we're going to be there, but I'd pack for a few days at least."

Walker ended up taking Maddie out for dinner. He had decided to wait until then before he shared any of the developments from earlier in the day. He purposely left out any mention of drugs, rehab, or the rest of Sam's story. There was no need to color his daughter's impression of her friend.

Toward the end of their meal, he said, "You have Habitat tomorrow, right?

"Yes."

"You shouldn't mention anything about this to anyone. If someone asks about Sam, just answer truthfully. You haven't heard from her."

"How come?" Maddie asked.

"When people know the FBI is involved in something, it often gets blown out of proportion. We still don't know what we're dealing with; until we do, I don't want to draw any attention to the investigation."

Chapter Fifteen

Sam began to stir, but didn't fully wake up. A dream was still lingering on the periphery of her consciousness, and she didn't want to let it go. She was riding Topaz, the horse she had ridden the first time one of the counselors had given her a lesson. Topaz was so majestic looking and yet so gentle. Sam remembered being told that the horse had gotten his name from his distinctive coloring, a yellow-brown blend that easily conjured up images of the November gemstone.

The initial part of Sam's dream was all true, but then it quickly turned into a dark fantasy. Sam and Topaz were moving in a blur; the horse's hooves not touching the ground. Behind them was a storm with black clouds traveling even faster. In just a few minutes, it would surely overtake them. Sam pleaded with Topaz to go faster, to get them to safety. The horse responded with a burst of energy, but the storm clouds continued to make up ground.

Just as they were about to be swallowed up, Sam's eyes opened. Despite the relatively cool temperatures of her surroundings, she was sweating, and her breathing had quickened. She closed her eyes again, attempting to calm herself. Although the end of the dream had left her frightened, the other parts of it—particularly riding Topaz—had brought a small smile to her face.

Still, she didn't want to be fully awake; she knew what that would mean: fear and anxiety, as well as the inability to catch her breath. She kept her eyes closed, and eventually her mind drifted back to Topaz and then to her last memory before she had eaten the drug-laden food.

She was in the barn, and all the horses were gone. She remembered that she had then walked back to the main house, wishing she knew what could have possibly happened to the girls and the horses. She had sat on the front porch steps, trying to decide what to do.

After a few moments, she had opened her canvas bag and taken out her tablet. She was going to check on the bus schedule, since it appeared that she'd be heading home much earlier than she had thought. But there was no signal, and when she looked at the percentage of charge available, it was under five percent.

Sam thought that she had fully charged the tablet overnight, but she must not have pushed the connection far enough into the receptor. She had started to take out her phone to look up the schedule, but decided it didn't matter. She'd get home when she got home.

I guess I should at least leave a note, she had thought, *and ask JT to contact me.* She had rummaged through her bag, but realized she didn't have any paper. What she did have, however, was her World Cultures text.

She had extracted the book from her bag, opened it to the back, found an empty page, and carefully torn it out. *After tomorrow, I'm not going to need the book anyway*, she had thought, *and besides, the page is blank.*

Sam had been just about to start writing when she heard a noise in the distance. It sounded like a car or a truck, and then she had seen a dust cloud rising along what she believed to be the dirt road leading to the main house. She put the textbook and the page she had torn out down on the step next to her and stood up. She had then shielded her eyes from the sun as she looked toward the road.

It had taken another minute before the SUV came into view and another few seconds before the sunlight bounced off the familiar Mercedes emblem on the grill. Sam had wondered at that point whether the person driving was JT She had only seen him driving a Jeep. Of course, that was months ago.

As the SUV drew closer, Sam had remained standing, but then she bent down to return the textbook and the blank page to her bag. As she reached for the two items, she realized the torn out page had blown away. She saw it for a moment just before it disappeared between the boards of the porch floor.

Sam had quickly put her textbook away and then focused all her attention on the SUV and its occupant, as the vehicle came to a stop directly in front of her. A man with a beard, who she had thought looked like JT emerged, but stayed on the other side of the SUV and spoke across the roof.

"How did you get in here? We don't take in runaways anymore."

Sam was still staring into the sun, as she continued to use her hand to shield her eyes. "Is that you, JT? It's Sam Daniels... San Diego. Remember?"

There was a long pause before the man with the beard spoke.

"Yeah, I'm JT. Who are you, again?"

"Sam Daniels. I was here a little over a year ago."

JT hesitated again. "I'm sorry. There have been so many girls... It's hard to remember everyone."

Sam didn't take offense; she had only interacted with JT a few times. There was no reason for him to have remembered her.

"I understand."

The man's posture became more relaxed, but not much. "What is it that you want? And again, how did you get in here?"

"There's a kind of break in the rocks near the front gate. You can climb over them if you're careful. I just need to ask you something."

"About what?"

Sam was having even more trouble with the sun. "Can we sit down or something? I can barely even see you."

The man hesitated again. "We can go inside for a minute. Let me get the groceries out of the backseat, and I'll come up and open the door."

Sam moved to one side of the front door and watched as the man carried two plastic bags up the steps. As he got closer, she tried to picture him without the beard. Then she thought, *What am I doing? It's obviously JT; who else would it be?*

Once they were inside, JT said, "Why don't you have a seat... Sam? I'm just going to bring these bags into the kitchen."

Sam looked around briefly and then went over and sat in a large leather chair directly across from another that looked identical. She started to place her bag on the table between the two chairs, but then instead placed it on the floor next to her.

As JT came out of the kitchen and sat down across from Sam, he said, "What is it that you wanted to ask me?"

"Well, I'll be applying to college in a few months." Sam had anticipated some sort of congratulations at that point. When none came, she continued. "I have to write a personal essay as part of the application. I wanted to write about my time here at the ranch and the girls I met, what we all went through, things like that."

Sam could see by the expression on JT's face that he didn't like the idea, so she quickly added, "I'd also like to talk about some of the counselors, but I don't have to mention anyone by name."

JT gave a slight shake of his head. "I'm glad that you had such a good experience, but we want to keep what we do here private. We don't want people nosing around, especially the media. If something like your essay got out, who knows what could happen."

Although she really didn't, Sam said, "I understand." She paused. "Can I ask you something else?"

"Go ahead."

"When I was looking around before you came back, I didn't see anyone else, and then you said that you don't take in runaways anymore. So there's no one else here?"

"No. We made a decision a while back to turn the property into a religious retreat center. We'll be doing some renovating; we just haven't started yet."

"What happened to all the girls who were here and the counselors?"

JT's expression hardened. "The girls either went back home, or we found other facilities for them. And almost all the counselors were from our church in Ohio. Some of them will be back when we finish converting the ranch into the retreat center."

Sending the girls home or to another facility didn't seem plausible to Sam, but she decided not to pursue it. Instead, she returned to the reason she had come.

"So even though there are no more girls here, you'd still prefer that I don't talk about the ranch?"

JT appeared angry, but he spoke calmly. "As I've told you a couple of times now, the ranch is going to be turned into a retreat center. We can't be successful in doing something like that if everybody knows where we are."

Sam apologized. "I'm sorry. I shouldn't have asked again."

JT displayed little affect when he said, "That's okay. Don't worry about it." He then rose out of the chair and said, "So, I don't want you climbing back over those rocks. Why don't you let me drive you—I assume you came by bus—back to the station?"

"Thanks. I'd appreciate that," Sam said.

"Do you need to use the restroom before we go?"

"No. I'm fine."

"All right. Well, I do. I'll be right back."

Sam got out of the chair she was sitting in, and she was about to pick up her bag when she noticed a large stone fireplace with a huge portrait mounted above it on the other side of the room. She moved closer to get a better look. There were three individuals in the painting: an older man was seated behind a desk—the same desk that occupied another corner of the room—and standing behind the older man, over each shoulder, were two young men who appeared to be twins, and they both looked exactly like JT without the beard.

Just then JT reentered the room.

"Ready?" he said.

Sam gestured toward the painting. "Do you have a twin brother?"

JT hesitated. "No, not a twin. We were thirteen months apart. He's on the left. That's my brother, Tom. He was involved in an accident here at the ranch. That's another reason why I'm turning this place into a retreat center."

Sam wasn't usually so inquisitive, but her curiosity got the best of her.

"What happened?"

"He fell off his horse and hit his head."

"That's awful." Sam thought back to the empty barn. "One of the horses here?"

JT nodded. "Yes, Topaz."

"Topaz? He was riding Topaz? How is that possible?"

"What do you mean?"

"Topaz wouldn't allow *men* to ride him, only us girls. He'd buck and jump... Don't you remember when you tried?"

JT's expression changed dramatically, and the look on his face scared Sam. *Something isn't right*, she thought. Then Sam started to piece it together. JT might not remember her, but he wouldn't forget almost getting killed by a horse he was trying to ride. The man standing in front of her wasn't JT. This man must be his brother. But why?

"You know, you're right; it wasn't Topaz. I was thinking it was because after the accident, I sold all the horses, and I initially forgot to tell the new owner about Topaz and that he wouldn't allow men to ride him. I just mixed up which horse was which."

It was a feeble attempt. The man with the beard knew it, and he knew Sam knew it.

Sam tried to think of something to say to make the man think that she believed him, but nothing came quickly enough to her mind. The only thing she could come up with was, "I'm sorry. I've bothered you enough. I'll just get my bag and go. You don't have to drive me."

The man tried to smile, but it didn't work.

"At least let me take you to the gate."

Sam didn't feel that she had much choice but to say, "Okay." Then an idea came to her. "I'm just going to text my girlfriend. I told her I was coming up here, but now that I'm going to be home early, maybe we'll be able to go out later."

"There's no cell service here, and I don't have a landline," JT said. "I thought you said you hadn't mentioned the ranch to anyone?"

"I meant not specifically in the essay I was writing, but I did tell my girlfriend."

Sam could tell that the man was skeptical, but she thought she might have planted enough doubt.

"All right. I'm going to get you a bottle of water for your trip back."

"I'm okay," Sam said.

"It's no trouble."

Sam thought about making a run for it. But how far could she get? Well, no matter what, she wasn't going to drink that water. Then she thought, *Maybe it's going to be all right; maybe the man believed her about telling her girlfriend where she was going.*

As she went over to pick up her bag, her hands were shaking and her legs were wobbly. She knew that she had to sit down, even just for a moment.

The man came back into the room with a bottle of water in his left hand. The cap was still on, which Sam took as a good sign, provided it hadn't been opened, mixed with something, and then closed up again. But she felt pretty sure she'd be able to tell if that were the case. She realized too late that her focus on the bottled water had meant that she hadn't paid attention to the man's other hand, which was behind his back.

As she started to rise out of the chair, the man said, "Relax. Take a drink, and then we'll go."

As she accepted the water, the man's right hand shot out from behind his back, and for the briefest of moments, Sam saw that he was holding a white cloth. A split second later, it was across her nose and mouth.

Sam dropped the bottle of water and tried to stand, but couldn't. She then lashed out with her right hand and dug her nails into the man's arm as he held the cloth over her face. She flailed and clawed until she started to feel weak and began to lose consciousness. The last thing she remembered seeing was the blood coming from the scratches on the man's arm.

Her next semiconscious moment found her locked in the bathroom in one of the cabins. She had no idea how long she had been there; everything was an unfocused haze. And then the next time she had awakened, she found herself where she was presently: underground somewhere, or in a cave. She had no recollection of being moved.

Even the partial memory of what had happened left her physically and emotionally exhausted. But the fear she expected to feel had not materialized. Instead, she just felt numb. She lifted her head briefly and opened her eyes. The clothes that had been left for her were still there, and another bowl of food had also been provided. Sam didn't feel the need to consume the food with the drugs in it just yet, but she suspected it wouldn't be long.

The man who called himself JT was becoming increasingly impatient. He was never one to sit still. In school, they said he had ADHD or some such nonsense. Did anyone really expect kids to just sit around doing nothing?

He had moved the other merchandise closer to where it needed to be to transport it, and the girl was in position. Now all he needed was to hear from Eli. But that was the problem. Eli was taking his own sweet time, and he had made it clear that he was not to be contacted again. Well, at least not by phone.

That last thought gave the man an idea. There was nothing preventing him from going to see Eli in person. The last time he had spoken with Eli he had threatened to do just that, and bring the girl with him. But he had realized that was a mistake. But going by himself for a face-to-face meeting presented some real possibilities. He just might do that.

Chapter Sixteen

Walker and Munoz left Danvers a few minutes before seven. They stopped at the Dunkin' Donuts drive-thru, got some iced coffee, and then picked up Route 93. Saturday morning traffic heading north to New Hampshire and Maine would be a nightmare beginning the last weekend in June and throughout the summer. But on that day it wasn't so bad, at least not to start out.

Shortly after they merged onto the highway, Walker adjusted the passenger seat and reached into the back for his briefcase. He extracted some folders and then returned the case to the seat behind him.

Munoz glanced over.

"I don't know how you read in the car. I get a headache just thinking about it."

"I used to be the same way, but it doesn't bother me quite as much as I've gotten older."

"Oh good, something to look forward to," Munoz said.

Walker smiled. "Don't be a wise ass," he said. "So, as I mentioned back at the house, we're all set at the training facility for as long as we need to stay there. It's only been open for a month or two. They don't even have a full complement of agents taking the training yet, so there's plenty of room."

"Is there some sort of specialized training going on there?"

"Yes and no. I was told that they have a full forensics lab and state-of-the-art computer facilities, as well as an outdoor survival course. Evidently, that's all pretty standard for these new satellite training sites. Obviously, nothing as extensive as Quantico, though. But when I checked it out online, the original press release said the agents would also receive training in dealing with border issues. It didn't elaborate on what that means, but I suspect part of it will be how to play nice with Homeland Security, particularly the BEST units."

"BEST? What's that?" Munoz asked.

"Border Enforcement Security Task Force."

"I never heard of it."

"I hadn't either until a couple of years ago. Evidently, sixteen states have these BEST units now," Walker said.

"So obviously they're not just in the Southwest."

"No, there are just as many in the North. I think that's why the Bureau set up the facility in Maine," Walker said. "Not to be critical of our fellow agencies, but if FBI personnel are being trained to play nice, it would be great if Homeland got the same training."

Walker offered a few more details about the new training facility, and then he opened up one of the folders on his lap and shifted topics.

"I did some research on a couple of other things last night as well. I found out more information about the Church of Universal Redemption.

"It's much more secular than religious. They claim to be Christian-based, but only because they follow the moral teachings of Christ. They also claim to follow some Eastern moral principles too. And although the church was founded in Maine, its largest group of followers lives in Ohio.

"And as far as the church hierarchy goes, they have elders just like the Mormons. In fact, it sounds like both groups developed that concept around the same time in the 1800s. But it seems like the elders in the Church of Universal Redemption are all laypeople, like the judge. I wasn't able to get a clear picture of exactly what their role is.

"Another similarity with the Mormon faith is that members of the Church of Universal Redemption are expected to do some sort of missionary work, or some sort of volunteer work that fosters the church's moral principles. Again, I wasn't able to determine exactly what that entails."

Walker closed the folder containing the information about the church, shifted it to the bottom of the pile, and opened the folder now on top.

"Back when we first heard about Judge Frazier, I did a Google search, but last night I did another one combining his name with the church. I didn't find much. There's no mention of him being involved with the church in any biography or article I came across, except for the one listing him as an elder."

"That was a great catch by the way," Munoz said.

"Thanks. I'm not even sure what made me keep looking; it seemed like a dead end. But we both know, sometimes you just get lucky."

Walker opened the last of the three folders. "I found almost nothing on this James T. Chambers. Talk about staying under the radar. He's the son of the late Lemuel Chambers and the brother of the late Tom Chambers. There are no other living relatives that I could find."

Munoz nodded. "I did a search on him last night too. I didn't find anything either. I also took a look at the article by that Professor Mason. His book is actually available online through the University of Maine library. There were a few more paragraphs beyond the excerpt that was in the article, but not much we didn't already know. It's probably unlikely that we'll need to, but we should keep him in mind as a resource, just in case."

Munoz then changed the subject. "What time did you tell them we'd be arriving at the training facility?"

"Around eleven fifteen, give or take a few minutes."

"That should be about right."

After a decent night's sleep, the man who called himself JT had definitely decided to head up to Canada to talk to Eli, which meant he would probably be away for a couple of days. The girl wasn't going anywhere, but he would have to prepare some food for her. He didn't want the merchandise looking emaciated.

He debated whether to mix the ketamine in with the hash, as he had done the last several days. He decided not to; continuing to drug the girl had already cut into his profit margin. Besides, he wasn't going to be around and wouldn't have to deal with her being fully awake. When he got back, he'd find a way to inject her with something as he'd done before, or he'd just add some fast-acting drug to one of the water bottles.

Once he finished getting the food ready, he went back into his bedroom and threw some clothes into his backpack. He then put the three days' worth of food and water into a cooler and took everything out to the SUV. He drove to the same spot he had driven to before—about one hundred yards from where he was keeping the girl.

He left the keys in the SUV, got the cooler out of the hatchback, and carried it to the door in the ground. He then realized that he would have to leave the door exposed. There was no way to lock it or cover it over with brush because he wouldn't be immediately coming back that way. He didn't have a choice, so he convinced himself that it wouldn't be a problem

When he reached the girl, he could see that she was sleeping soundly. All of the food he had left had been consumed, as well as most of the water. But the girl hadn't changed into the clothes he had left for her.

Her choice, he thought. *What do I care?*

He placed the cooler within her reach, looked around to make sure he hadn't forgotten anything, and then turned on his phone to use as a flashlight. But instead of going back the way he had come, he continued on into the darkness. He estimated it was about a half mile to the end of the tunnel. He certainly wasn't a big fan of being underground for that length of time, but it was the quickest way to get to Eli.

A few minutes later, he passed the boxes of ketamine and fentanyl he had moved closer to the end of the tunnel a couple of days before. He knew that he was close now. Less than thirty seconds later, he arrived at the ladder. He carefully climbed the five steps and gently pushed upward against the wooden door. A ray of sunlight caused him to squint as he applied more force to the door. Ten seconds later, the door fell open, and the man who called himself JT was looking at the Canadian sky.

He still had at least a three-mile walk ahead of him to reach "civilization," but at least the first mile or so was all level ground. It was as if the glacier that had deposited the granite in this area hundreds of millions of years ago had purposefully left a clear path connecting the future national borders, but then decided to make the path beyond that nearly inaccessible. After the first mile, there were uneven rock formations as far as the eye could see.

Technically, the Canadian government owned the land JT would be crossing, although no one in an official capacity ever patrolled it; it was considered barren and uninhabitable. But that didn't mean people like Eli Peters couldn't find a way to exploit the lack of oversight.

Once Eli hooked up with JT Chambers and found out about the tunnel connecting Maine and Canada, his criminal ingenuity kicked in. He ordered a couple of custom-made, all-terrain vehicles with large cargo bins in the back and balloon tires. And as he suspected, they were more than equal to the task they were designed for.

JT saw the oddly shaped roof of his initial destination—the Frontier Water Park—around ten o'clock in the morning. The park had been built on the site of a former conservation camp. When the park had first been proposed, people living in the area thought the developers were crazy. It was just too far out of the way. There was nothing else around. But families evidently didn't mind the thirty- or forty-mile drive, most of which was on traffic-less highways.

And while it was true that nothing else was around, that was the point. When people went to Frontier Water Park, they tended to stay the whole day. Because, in fact, there literally was nowhere else to go. The road ended at the park. But it had become so popular that the owners had added a huge building that housed several indoor rides, which allowed them to stay open pretty much year round. The success of the park had also necessitated some alternate transportation options, particularly for teenagers and young adults. So buses that ran approximately every hour and a half were added.

JT walked up to the ticket window, paid his $39.95 adult price admission in American dollars (which the park readily accepted, and actually preferred because of the exchange rate), and went inside. The fact that he wasn't dressed for a day at the water park, raised a few eyebrows, but other than that, he attracted little attention.

He got some coffee and a donut, and waited for the next bus. It arrived at 10:25 a.m., disgorged about forty people, and headed back out ten minutes later with only two passengers on board. It arrived in the community of Sanglais in Quebec Province about thirty-five minutes later.

JT took a cab and was dropped off two blocks from Eli's house: an eight-thousand-square-foot estate with a gate, security camera, and intercom system identical to those at Redemption Ranch. Thirty seconds after JT pressed the intercom, Eli himself answered.

"What the hell are you doing here?"

"I'm alone," JT said.

"That doesn't answer my question."

"I need to talk to you."

There was no response, but the front gate began to swing open. Eli met JT at the front door.

"This better be good. What the hell is so urgent?"

"I'm getting really nervous about this delay. We've got to move the girl."

"And I told you, it's too dangerous right now. It looks like I've got some government people watching one of our warehouses. It's a legitimate business, but sometimes we store some of the product there before it gets shipped out. We can't take any chances," Eli said. "And what are you so nervous about, anyway?"

"I told you. The girl figured out that I'm not JT I've got to get her out of there. I can't be sure who she told she was coming to the ranch. If someone starts looking for her..."

"None of this is news."

"I know, and I considered... getting rid of her, but it's not that easy."

Even though Eli's accent became more pronounced as he became more agitated, his use of American idioms made it less noticeable.

"Are you shitting me? You've got a thousand acres of property. You can't figure out someplace to bury her?"

"They've got all sorts of special equipment now to locate bodies. If someone figures out she came to the ranch, I'd be screwed. No, she's got to be moved."

Eli didn't like JT's tone, but he also recognized his desperation. And despite what Eli had said a few days before, he didn't want to try to find another partner. The arrangement he had with JT was as close to foolproof as it got.

Another moment passed, and Eli looked as if he were considering something; he expelled a mouthful of air, shook his head slightly, and said, "All right, maybe we can do something

Monday. But just the girl, not the other merchandise. That way we only need to use one of the ATVs; two of them would draw too much attention." He paused for a few seconds, and when he continued, Eli seemed to be talking to himself. "That might work; the ATVs aren't stored at the warehouse, so whoever our friends are who are watching us should be none the wiser."

"I really appreciate this, Eli," JT said.

Eli ignored the thank you. "Okay, let's plan on Monday. You can stay here tonight if you want, and then go back tomorrow. How did you get here by the way?"

"I used the tunnel. It's faster, and I don't like using the passport if I can help it. I don't think the picture really looks like me."

"You think those guys at the border crossings pay much attention to that? Plus, you and your brother look... looked... exactly alike," Eli said. "I can have one of my men drive you up to the water park tomorrow. The rest you'll have to do on your own."

"Not a problem."

"Where's the girl, anyway?"

"In the tunnel. She's secure."

"You'll have her drugged for Monday, right?"

"Yeah."

"I probably don't have to tell you this, but just like with the other girls, make sure you clean up everything. We can make her disappear, but there shouldn't be any trace of her."

"I already got rid of all her stuff. I burned most of it, and the rest I dumped down the abandoned well, the same place I used for the other girls' stuff. And I wiped down some other areas too, but I'm not really worried about DNA or anything like that. The girl's been to the ranch before, so if somebody got suspicious and for some reason took samples that would easily explain it."

"Sounds like you've got it covered."

"I think so."

Eli was quiet for a moment, debating whether to do something he rarely did: apologize. Eventually, he decided it made business sense to offer an olive branch.

"Listen, JT, I'm sorry about being a little rough on you the other day. I'm just uptight about being watched." Eli offered his hand. "Are we good?"

"Yeah, we're good."

Eli noticed the bandage on JT's arm as they were shaking hands.

"What happened?"

"The girl scratched me," JT said.

"Really? If that had been me, everything would've been over right then and there."

c∕◦Chapter Seventeen◦∖つ

The Northeast Border Training Complex was located on federal land a few miles east of Eustis, Maine. The supervising special agent in charge was a twenty-year veteran of the FBI named Chuck Dalton. He personally greeted Walker and Munoz when they arrived around 11:30 on Saturday morning.

After handshakes all around, Dalton said, "It's a pleasure, Agent Walker; your reputation precedes you."

Walker looked surprised as Dalton continued. "Your last two cases were pretty high profile, especially within the Bureau."

Walker tried to deflect the compliment. "Please call me Craig, and a lot of people deserve the credit on those cases, including Dave here."

"Understood." Dalton turned to Munoz. "I didn't mean to leave you out. No offense."

Munoz shook his head. "None taken."

There was a moment of awkward silence, and then Dalton offered, "If you want to follow me, I'll show you where your rooms are."

After Dalton gave them a five-minute tour of the dormitory-like rooms in the barracks, Walker and Munoz dropped off their bags and returned to Dalton's office in the main building.

"My assistant filled me in from his conversation with you, but is there anything else you need, anything we can help you with?" Dalton asked.

Walker responded, "Not that I can think of. We're going to head right out. We're anxious to follow up on something." Walker paused. "Have you ever heard of a place called Redemption Ranch?"

"I don't think so. Is it around here?"

"About twenty miles west of here in Franklin County."

"I didn't think there was anything located twenty miles west of here except trees and rocks."

"It's that desolate, huh?"

"Pretty much."

"Okay, we're going to head out. I'm not sure when we'll be back," Walker said.

"Doesn't matter. There's an agent at the gate twenty-four seven. Just show your ID."

It was nearly 12:30 when Walker and Munoz drove up to the gate outside of Redemption Ranch. They exited the car and looked around briefly.

"It looks more like a fortress than a religious compound and not exactly welcoming," Munoz said.

Walker nodded. "You have to wonder who they're trying to keep out. There's nobody around here for miles."

Walker's eyes fell on the intercom system and then a moment later on the security camera. He pointed to them both, as he continued. "Those look pretty sophisticated." He took out his phone and took a picture.

Munoz asked, "Why'd you do that?"

"Well, hopefully everything goes all right once we're inside, but just in case, it can't hurt to have a picture of the equipment to send to Peter."

Walker put his phone away and approached the intercom. He pushed the button and waited about twenty seconds before trying it again. He pushed two more times, a half a minute apart, but no one responded.

Munoz asked, "Now what?"

"I don't know. I wasn't necessarily expecting this." After a moment, Walker took out his phone again. "I wonder if it's possible that the ranch has an alarm system. If so, they'd have to have either a private company or local law enforcement set up to respond. A private company seems unlikely out here. I put the sheriff's department number in my contact list. I'm going to try them again. I know Peter already spoke to someone there, but… maybe they weren't thinking in terms of an alarm response."

A minute went by and then Walker said, "You're kidding me; no signal. You want to try yours, Dave?"

"Sure." After another minute, Munoz shook his head. "Nothing."

"The guy doesn't have a landline, and there's no signal. How the hell does he communicate with anyone?" Walker asked. "I don't like this. We've got to figure out a way to get in touch with this guy."

Munoz waited a moment and then offered, "We could start to head back to the barracks, and you could keep trying until you get a signal."

"Not much choice, I guess."

They had to drive nearly eight miles before Walker got anything resembling a signal. He punched in the sheriff's department number again and waited fifteen seconds before he heard ringing.

"Sheriff's department, Officer Scanlan speaking."

Walker identified himself and explained the basics of the problem.

"One of my colleagues already spoke with someone there."

"Yes, I'm aware of that. The Sheriff told us to cooperate any way we could, but I'm sorry we don't have an alarm response list. That's handled by the local police. If there are no local police, the property owner has to make other arrangements. We don't have any way to contact the ranch. In fact, as far as I know, I might have been the last person from the department to be out there, and that was nearly a year ago."

Walker's mind flashed back to the article he had read. "That was the accidental death?" he asked.

"Yeah… uh… Tom Chambers. How did you know about that?"

"I researched everything I could about the ranch, but there wasn't much, other than an article about the accident," Walker said. "Well, thank you for your time, Officer Scanlan."

Walker disconnected the call and said, "That was a dead end. Any other ideas?"

"Maybe," Munoz said.

"What?"

"I saw a few helicopters at the training facility. Maybe they could do a flyover. If we can't get inside, we might be able to see something from the air."

"It's worth a shot. Let's go back. We need to ask in person."

Fifteen minutes later, they were back in Dalton's office. Walker laid out Munoz's idea.

"Obviously, it's not as good as getting inside, but short of camping out next to the gate waiting for someone to show up, it's the next best thing."

Dalton leaned forward. "I'd like to help, but I'm not sure I can."

"Why not?"

"How close is the ranch to the Canadian border?"

Munoz responded, "When I looked at the map, probably not more than three or four miles, maybe less."

"That's the problem. We can't fly within five miles of the border without getting special permission from Homeland Security."

"Why's that?" asked Walker.

"It's really more for out West where they had a major problem with heroin smuggling. It's relatively easy for small aircraft to go undetected, you know under the radar. But Homeland decided to extend the ban all along the eastern border as well."

Walker looked incredulous. "But it's government aircraft."

"True, but the thought was if they restrict government aircraft, then they know anything else flying that close isn't supposed to be there."

Walker looked over at Munoz. "Only one thing left to try, right?"

Munoz was thinking the same thing. "You mean a search warrant?"

"A search warrant."

Munoz shook his head. "I think that's going to be a tough sell."

"I know, and I'd prefer to just talk to this James Chambers. But if we have no way to contact him … I'm not sure what else we're supposed to do."

Walker turned toward Dalton. "I know you've only been here a short time, but have you had any interaction with any judges in the area?"

Dalton shook his head. "No, we've had no reason for anything like that," he said. "It's been a long time since I had to apply for a search warrant, but I assume things haven't changed that much. I suspect it's going to be difficult to get one on a weekend."

Walker responded, "You've got that right."

The two investigators left Dalton's office and went back to Walker's room in the barracks.

Munoz asked, "You know anybody who might have some connections up here?"

"No, not really. I'm going to give Peter a call; maybe he knows somebody. In the meantime, we can e-mail the information we have to the Boston office and ask someone to prepare a warrant. This is a training facility; I don't think anyone here does that sort of thing."

While Munoz worked on his tablet inputting the information, Walker called Stansky.

"Hey, Peter."

"Hi, Craig. Any luck?"

"Yeah, all bad!"

"Sorry to hear that."

Walker spent the next several minutes describing what the morning had been like and then asked Peter to find a judge.

Stansky didn't respond immediately. Eventually, he said, "I'm not even sure where to begin… maybe with the federal judges. The problem is though, they'll be more sympathetic, but they're less likely to be available. All right, let me see what I can do." Stansky paused. "You say that you took a photo of the security camera?"

"Yeah, I did," Walker said.

"Send me a copy. It's probably not going to tell me anything, but you never know."

For the next forty-five minutes, Walker and Munoz gathered as much information as they had to pass on to the FBI office in Boston. Walker called to let them know it was coming and what they needed.

Ten minutes later, Peter Stansky called back and sounded upbeat.

"I think I've got a possibility for you, Craig. There's a naturalization ceremony today in Bangor at three o'clock. First District Federal Judge Marion Lister is swearing in a hundred and eight new citizens. If you show up, you might be able to get a word with her."

"That's terrific, Peter, thanks. In Bangor, you say?"

"Yeah, the federal court building on Harlow Street. You better get a move on if you're going to get there in time."

"Right," Walker said. "Damn it."

"What's the matter?"

"We don't have the warrant application. We just sent the information to Boston a few minutes ago"

"I wouldn't worry about that now. Call Boston and tell them to put a rush on it and then e-mail it to you. The judge should be in a good mood because of the ceremony. She'll probably be willing to work with you."

"Do those rose-colored glasses ever get dirty?" Walker asked.

Stansky laughed. "You sound like my wife."

"She's a smart woman."

"Except when she decided to marry me."

Walker chuckled. "Okay, all the judge can say is 'no,'" he said. "Seriously Peter, thanks again. Dave and I are going to leave right now."

Walker and Munoz arrived about three-quarters of the way through the ceremony. A Maine state trooper met them at the door. They showed their credentials, and then Walker explained that they wanted a few minutes of the judge's time after the ceremony was concluded.

The trooper asked, "This is not an emergency, right?"

"No, it's not."

"I'll pass on the message, but I can't guarantee anything."

"I understand."

The last of the new citizens took the oath thirty-five minutes later. The judge posed for a number of photos with those who had earned their citizenship and then started to wend her way through the crowd toward the side door. The trooper caught up to her just before she reached for the door handle, spoke a few words, and then pointed to Walker and Munoz in the back of the room.

The judge remained where she was as the trooper made his way back to Walker and Munoz. When he got close enough, he spoke softly.

"The judge wants to know why this can't wait until Monday. I told her you said it wasn't an emergency."

Walker knew he had to phrase his answer in such a way that he conveyed urgency, but didn't overstate his case. He decided instead to go another way.

"We only need five minutes of the judge's time. If she can't help us, we'll leave and go see somebody else on Monday. Five minutes, that's all."

The trooper walked back to where the judge was waiting. Walker saw her nod her head, but then she exited the room.

When the trooper returned he said, "The judge told me to escort you to the side hallway. She'll meet you there, but she requested that I stay."

Walker said, "That's not a problem."

"She wants to see your credentials also."

"Again, not a problem."

Both Walker and Munoz had their badges in hand as they approached the judge. Once they were within a few feet, she took out a pair of glasses, put them on, and bent over to view the credentials more closely. She read aloud, "Special Agent Craig Walker." The judge turned to her right and again read aloud, "Detective Dave Munoz."

She removed her glasses and asked, "Not with the FBI?"

"Actually, yes I am, Your Honor, on temporary assignment. I have a card to that effect if you want to see it."

"That won't be necessary," the judge said. "Does this have anything to do with today's ceremony, with any of our new citizens?"

Walker answered. "No, no, Your Honor, nothing to do with them."

The judge visibly relaxed. "That makes me feel better."

Walker spoke sincerely. "I've never been to a naturalization ceremony before. It was quite impressive."

The judge smiled. "I've been on the bench for ten years. I haven't missed one in all that time," she said, obviously considering something. She looked toward the trooper. "Thank you, officer, I'll take it from here."

The trooper hesitated. "You sure, Your Honor?"

"Yes, it's fine. Thank you." As the trooper walked away, the judge said, "Let's go back into my chambers, gentlemen; we'll be more comfortable there."

Less than a minute later, Walker and Munoz were seated in an expansive office in front of a large desk. The judge removed her robe, hung it up, and then sat down.

"What's on your mind?" she asked.

Walker outlined everything from the beginning with Munoz interjecting occasionally. It took double the five minutes they had been allotted, but the judge didn't seem to mind.

Walker finished up by saying, "We wouldn't even be asking for the search warrant if we could get a hold of this James Chambers."

"I understand that," the judge said. "And you say you don't actually have a copy of the application?"

Munoz answered, "No, Your Honor. We did get an e-mail while we were on our way here with the application attached. I could send it to your account, and we could print it up."

"Not exactly by the book, is it?" the judge said.

Neither Walker nor Munoz replied, not sure that anything either of them said would help their cause at this point.

Judge Lister glanced over at the computer on her desk. She then took a pen out of its holder on the desk, scribbled some words on a Post-it note and handed it to Munoz.

"That's my e-mail address; send me the application. I'll read it on the screen. If I decide to sign it, we can print it up."

Munoz took out his phone, punched in the judge's e-mail address, and forwarded the e-mail and the attachment to her account.

The two investigators sat in silence as the judge read the application, periodically writing some notes on a scratch pad in front of her. Eventually, she replaced the pen in its holder, took a breath, and sat forward in her chair.

"I'm afraid I can't sign it—at least not yet. There are a couple of things that are bothering me. First of all, the property is owned by a church. There's not a lot of precedent for executing a search warrant on property owned by a religious organization, especially when there's no suspicion that any kind of crime has been committed.

"The second thing is the warrant is too broad. You want to search the entire property for signs that the girl was there. You don't even list the buildings that you're talking about. Is there a church on the property? Do you want to search that? Tomorrow's Sunday; what if there are services going on?"

Walker kept his voice calm. "From all the information I have, there's no local congregation."

"But it's still church-owned property?"

"Yes."

"All right, gentlemen, here's what I'm willing to do. I want to talk with a couple of local judges, get a feel for how they would handle this. I have their home numbers. I'll call them tonight and have an answer for you tomorrow. Do you have a card, Agent Walker, with your cell number on it?"

Walker found a card in his wallet and handed it to the judge as she said, "Please understand, I'm not totally unsympathetic, but that's the best I can do."

Walker felt that there was nothing he could say that would change the judge's mind, so he didn't try.

"Thank you, Your Honor. We appreciate your time."

As Walker and Munoz rose out of their chairs, the judge said, "And I appreciate the way you conducted yourselves. Maybe, because I'm used to dealing with lawyers who push things to the limit... I don't know. I will say this, you're certainly not stereotypical FBI agents, that's for sure. In my courtroom, you get a lot more with sugar than vinegar. If there's some way I can make this work for you, I will."

Chapter Eighteen

This was the part of his job that Walker hated the most: waiting. It was even worse with this investigation because the case file was so thin. There was no evidence to scrutinize again, no one to re-interview, nothing to do but wait until the judge made her decision. And what if she wouldn't sign the warrant? Then what? Walker didn't want to entertain that thought.

He had spent the last three plus hours doing Internet searches just to occupy his time. He glanced at the bottom of the screen of his laptop and noticed the time: 9:18 p.m. - not too late to call home.

He picked up his phone, pressed the "home" icon, and waited for the call to connect. He was surprised to hear Maddie's voice on the other end. She rarely answered the landline, but then he realized she must've been watching TV and saw his number come up.

"Hi, Dad. Did you find out anything?"

"Not yet, Maddie."

He spent the next several minutes explaining to his daughter the events of the day. He finished by saying, "I think there's a good chance the judge will grant the search warrant, and we'll be able to get inside and look around."

"Why wouldn't she just sign it to begin with?" Maddie asked.

Craig Walker hesitated. "I know I've been saying this a lot lately, and I don't mean to sound... patronizing. But it's complicated, Maddie, primarily because the church owns the property."

For whatever reason, that explanation seemed to satisfy her. "Will you call me tomorrow and let me know what happened?"

"I will. I promise," Walker said. "You had Habitat tonight, right? How'd that go?"

"Good. Our adviser didn't ask about Sam. I was kind of glad. I didn't want to talk about it. I was afraid I'd say something wrong," Maddie said. "So the two houses I'm going to be working on are in Lynn. I can take a bus, so you and mom don't have to drive me."

"It would've been fine either way. Speaking of your mom, is she there?"

Maddie didn't answer; she just called out. "Mom, it's Dad. He wants to talk to you."

Cheryl came to the phone less than a minute later.

"Hi, there. I was wondering if I was going to hear from you tonight."

"I knew that right after work you were taking Maddie to Habitat, and then I got thinking about the case... and, well anyway..." His voice trailed off.

"So I take it you haven't made a lot of progress?"

"Not really." He gave the same explanation to Cheryl that he had given to Maddie.

"What do you think your chances are with the judge?" Cheryl asked.

"Her last comment makes me think she's going to find a way to sign it, but who knows."

There was silence for a few moments, and then Cheryl said, "Oh yeah, I finally heard from Mark."

"That's good. And what did our son have to say?"

"Well, he didn't *say* anything; he sent me a text. I think he likes the idea of limiting his communication to a hundred and sixty characters. Heaven forbid if he had to actually speak to me for a few minutes."

Walker laughed. "Isn't he coming home over Fourth of July weekend? He'll have to talk to you then; he'll want you to do his laundry."

"Fat chance of that."

"So, what did the text say?" Walker asked.

"He likes the internship, he likes the people, and it's not just busy work."

"That sounds like he still had a few characters left."

"Actually, I'm embellishing. The real text said like job, like people, doing actual work."

"He did not."

"Well, it felt like that. Are you sure we didn't somehow restrict his monthly data plan?" Cheryl asked.

Walker laughed again. "Just stop it."

Cheryl turned serious. "Listen, good luck tomorrow. Love you."

"Thanks honey. Love you, too."

After Walker disconnected the call, he continued to think about his family. And then his mind turned once again to Sam Daniels and the fact that she had probably never been part of a *real* family, certainly not after her twelfth birthday. And that led to thinking about what would happen if the judge refused to sign the warrant. Both of those thoughts were front and center as he drifted off to sleep.

Saturday had just turned into Sunday—although Sam had no way of knowing that—as she started to open her eyes. Although she couldn't recall the specifics, the dream she had been having must have been a pleasant one, because she awoke with a sense of serenity. And then a moment later, the reality of her situation assaulted her: the chain on her wrist, the darkness beyond the small lamp, the claustrophobia, and something new—the smell of her own waste. She felt like a caged animal.

As her eyes adjusted to the semi-darkness, Sam saw the red cooler off to the side. She dragged herself over to it, opened the top, and saw the food and water. It was more than she had been left before, probably a few days' worth, she realized.

Why did he do that? She wondered. *Maybe the man who said he was JT doesn't want to have to come back here every day.* As Sam was contemplating all this, she began to feel the fear creeping back into her consciousness. She attempted to build a mental wall to keep it out, but as fast as the wall was being constructed, it started to crumble, piece by piece.

Panic began to overtake her again. She knew that she had to do something, anything. She then noticed the shorts and T-shirts that had been left for her. If nothing else, she would at least feel cleaner if she changed. She removed her pants and placed them over the pile of waste she had dumped out of the bedpan. It seemed to lessen the odor.

She then tried to take off her top, but was unable to get one of the sleeves past the chain binding her to the wall. Her entire body tensed, as frustration and anger replaced the panic. She ripped wildly at the seams of the fabric; a moment later, they gave way and the top fell to the dirt floor.

Although there was no one else there, her near-nakedness brought on a sense of embarrassment. She quickly reached for the clean pair of shorts, and with her one free hand eventually managed to get them on. Sam then grabbed one of the T-shirts, but as she started to pull it over her head, realized the chain attached to her wrist would not allow her to put it on properly. Fortunately, it was much too large, and for the most part, Sam was able to cover herself. For the briefest of moments, that small victory made her feel better. But then the mental wall started to crumble again.

The simple state of being awake became unbearable.

She acknowledged to herself for the second time since the ordeal had started that if there had been some way to end her life, she would have done it. As her pulse increased and her breathing accelerated, Sam looked toward the cooler. She had to stop the horror again. She took the cover off the cooler, removed a plate of food, and shoveled it into her mouth.

Twenty minutes later, she was still waiting for the drugs to kick in. And ten minutes after that, she was still waiting. The realization that there were probably no drugs in the food—or certainly not enough to induce sleep—brought forth a guttural scream that shook her entire body.

A few moments passed. Sam sat up and started to bang her head against the wall she was chained to. She increased the intensity in a misguided attempt to render herself unconscious—anything to make the emotional terror stop.

And then she heard something: a rumbling sound.

And then she felt something.

Or was it simply the pounding in her brain? No, something was happening. The rumbling intensified and then there was a crash. It wasn't real close, but it wasn't too far away. A moment later, Sam could feel a cool breeze coming from her right and then some dust, and then some more. It became so thick that it threatened to prevent her from breathing.

Whatever fear and panic Sam had experienced before was nothing compared to this. But in that split second, she realized that despite what she had felt before, she really didn't want to die. She wasn't ready to give up. Her next thoughts were only of self-preservation.

She instinctively reached for the other T-shirt on the ground, opened the cooler, and took out a bottle of water. She poured the water onto the T-shirt and covered her mouth. It allowed her to breathe more easily, and it kept the dust out of her lungs. Thirty seconds later, most of the dust had settled to the dirt floor.

Whatever had caused all of this seemed to be over. The spectrum of Sam's emotions—from wishing she would die, to believing that it was actually going to happen—brought on physical pain in the pit of her stomach. As best she could, Sam crossed her arms at her midsection and began to hug herself as she rocked back and forth.

Several minutes later, exhaustion borne of the panic she had experienced overtook her. It was a true deep sleep, not the drug-induced stupor that she had been subjected to over the last several days.

The New England Seismic Network reported that a 2.6 magnitude earthquake with its epicenter located in northwest Franklin County Maine had been detected at 12:47 a.m. on Sunday morning. It was only detected because of the sophisticated equipment that was available to monitor such activity. No residents had reported anything unusual at that time. In fact, it was doubtful that anyone had even felt it.

But under just the right circumstances, even such a relatively small quake was strong enough to cause the partial collapse of a tunnel, especially one that had been constructed more than 150 years ago.

Chapter Nineteen

Walker and Munoz were up by 6:30 on Sunday morning, although they weren't necessarily expecting to hear from the judge until closer to noon. By 7:15 a.m., they were sitting in the training facility's dining hall having breakfast.

In between mouthfuls of scrambled eggs, Walker said, "How'd you sleep?"

"Terrible. I'm lucky if I got four hours. You try telling your brain that there's nothing you can do until the morning, but it still won't shut down. I did some more Internet searches, but the same links we've seen ten times already kept showing up."

"Sounds exactly like what I did," Munoz said.

They continued to discuss the case for the next half hour, interspersed periodically with "chit-chat," although neither one of them was very good at it. A few minutes before eight o'clock, Munoz volunteered to take the trays up to the dishwashing area. Before he had gotten more than a couple of steps in that direction, Walker's phone buzzed. Munoz heard it and quickly returned with the trays and sat down.

Walker looked at the screen, saw the judge's name, and nodded at Munoz as he said, "Good morning, Your Honor."

"Good morning, Agent Walker. I hope I'm not calling too early."

"Not at all. I've been up for a while."

"I suspected as much. Well, I've got some potentially good news." The judge didn't wait for Walker to say anything; she just continued. "I spoke with some of my colleagues, and I'm willing to sign off on the warrant. But... there will have to be some parameters, several of which you may not care for, but I'm not going to sign it without them in place."

Walker was about to say something, but Judge Lister kept going. "I'm sorry to insist on this, but I'm afraid you're going to have to come to Bangor to go over this in person. I also want you here because you're going to have to rewrite part of the warrant. It would be inappropriate for me to be the one to make the physical changes. As it is, I'm on questionable grounds just by offering some of these suggestions. And I have to tell you that if there were any suspicion that a crime had been committed, I wouldn't be anywhere near this. Any defense attorney would have a field day with that information."

Walker hesitated a moment to be sure the judge had finished before he spoke. "I appreciate your willingness to work with us, Your Honor. It's not a problem for us to come to Bangor."

"You're very diplomatic, Agent Walker. I'm sure driving to Bangor is the last thing you want to do, but as I said, I believe it's absolutely necessary."

Walker didn't respond directly. Instead, he asked, "Do you want us to meet you at the courthouse?"

"Yes. Obviously, it isn't open on Sundays, but being a federal judge does have its advantages. Why don't we say around ten o'clock?"

"That will be fine, Your Honor. We'll see you at ten."

Munoz was able to piece together most of what was said by hearing Walker's side of the conversation. "It sounded like she wants us to go to Bangor, but she's willing to sign the warrant?"

"Yeah. But she said there were 'parameters.' I'm not sure what that means; I guess she'll tell us."

Munoz pressed a little more. "Are you okay with that?"

"Of course I won't know until I hear what they are. But I can't imagine we're not going to have some access to the property; otherwise, she would have just refused to sign the warrant and that would have been the end of it."

It took a little over an hour and a half to get to Bangor from the training facility. As Munoz drove down Harlow Street, he saw signs indicating that there was no parking in front of the courthouse, except on Sundays. He pulled in behind a large SUV.

As he and Walker emerged from the car, the two front doors of the SUV opened, and the judge and a younger man appeared.

The judge introduced the younger man as her clerk and then offered, "Chris here is going above and beyond today. It's certainly not in his job description to be chauffeuring a judge around on Sunday morning."

Both Walker and Munoz smiled at the young man.

The judge patted her briefcase and said, "I've got everything I need in here. Let's head upstairs."

Five minutes later, they were all seated in the judge's chambers. The judge opened her briefcase and removed a manila folder and said, "Before we make any changes to the warrant, let me outline what I have in mind, and you can tell me if you can live with it. Does that sound okay?"

Both Walker and Munoz answered, "Yes."

The judge kept the folder in front of her closed, as she began. "As I told you, one of my main concerns about signing the warrant was the fact that the property is owned by a church. So, to satisfy my concern, there are a few restrictions I'm going to insist upon." At that point, the judge opened the folder and glanced at the paper inside.

"First of all, you have to make every attempt to try to contact this James Chambers."

Before Walker could say anything, Judge Lister raised her hands as if to ward off any objections. "I know. You've done that.

I'm talking about making that effort again before you enter the property. If there continues to be no response, then you can proceed." The judge paused. "However, once you're inside, if you should encounter anyone, you may not immediately execute the warrant the way you normally would... by beginning a search. You need to ascertain whether you can get the required information without the search. Is that acceptable?"

Walker looked toward Munoz before he answered, "Yes. The main objective has always been to talk to James Chambers. We just haven't been able to do that."

The judge nodded. "Okay. Secondly, from your description of the entrance to the ranch, you're going to have to break in somehow, correct?"

Walker wasn't sure where the judge was going with that question, but he answered in the affirmative. "Correct."

"It will be in your best interest to keep the damage to a minimum. The FBI will have to reimburse the church for all repairs, not only to the gate, but anything else that gets damaged."

Even though Walker hadn't thought to clear anything like that with his supervisor, he answered as if he had.

"That won't be a problem."

"Good. Thirdly, you have to limit the number of agents or local law enforcement entering the property to no more than a handful. I'm not going to have dozens of agents swarming all over the grounds. Which brings me to my next point - The search is limited to wherever the security camera receivers are located. That should be your starting point anyway, shouldn't it? I believe you told me that the gate appears to be the only way in or out. So if the girl came there, she should show up on those tapes or whatever they use nowadays to record. I assume you have someone who would be able to figure out how to access the security footage."

Walker looked over at Munoz again before he spoke. "We do have a tech person who would be able to do that, but we have no way of knowing where the receivers are located."

"I understand that. I'm just saying, you can't be breaking down doors and running roughshod over the whole place. I would suspect that once you're inside the gate, it should be pretty evident which one is the main building. That's probably where the footage is stored."

Munoz asked, "Can we assume that when we're looking for the receivers, we can still gather any evidence that's... in plain sight?"

The judge paused and studied Munoz for a moment. "That's the standard, detective, even without a warrant, so yes. But I've known more than one investigator who must have had x-ray vision to have gathered some of the evidence he came up with. So plain sight means plain sight. No opening drawers, closets... cabinets— anything like that. Are we clear?"

"Yes, Your Honor," Munoz said.

The judge looked down again at the piece of paper in the manila folder. "Well, then it sounds to me like we have a deal, unless you have any other concerns."

Walker answered for both of them. "No, I don't believe so."

"Okay, Agent Walker. You can use the computer on the table over there to amend the warrant. The online version should come right up on the screen. Just hit any key."

The judge then removed the paper from the folder and handed it to Walker. "Here's an outline of the points we just discussed." The judge paused momentarily and then offered, "I know I haven't made this easy for you, but if you do find evidence of the girl having been there, I'm more than willing to expand the warrant. In that case, you'll pretty much have carte blanche. Just don't try to cut corners before you have that evidence. I don't like anyone playing fast and loose with judicial rulings, especially mine."

It took Walker twenty minutes to insert the new language in all the appropriate places in the warrant. When he was finished, the judge printed it out, read it over, and signed it.

"Good luck, gentlemen. I sincerely mean it. And as I said before, if you do find some evidence that the girl was there, I'll definitely give you permission to do a broader search. In fact, I'd be willing to issue a telephonic warrant. I'll make sure my phone is on all day."

Walker didn't want to appear ungrateful, so he remained silent about the fact that there was no cell service in the vicinity of the ranch. He simply thanked the judge again, and he and Munoz headed out to the car.

Munoz had sensed that Walker hadn't wanted to muddy the waters by bringing up the absence of cell service, so he had remained quiet as well, but he nevertheless decided to confirm it with Walker.

"I take it you didn't mention the problem about the cell service intentionally?"

"Right. I didn't want to take a chance that she'd decide to change anything else on the warrant. We need to get moving on this. And if we find something that indicates Sam was there, we'll just have to do what we did before: drive a few miles east until we get a signal. That's a problem I wouldn't mind having."

"What about using walkie-talkies? If we found something, we could radio ahead to the training facility and have someone there call the judge."

"Not enough range. Maybe it would work with a shortwave radio, but I don't think anyone uses those anymore. I doubt they'd even have them at the training site."

Once they were inside the car, Walker said, "We need to get Peter up here as quickly as possible." Walker pulled out his phone, tapped Stansky's number, and waited about fifteen seconds.

"Hi, Craig. What's going on?"

"We got the warrant, but it's got some restrictions. The good news is that it allows us access to the ranch's security camera footage," Walker said. "Is there any way you can get up here this afternoon?"

"Uh… yeah, sure. It's going to take me a few hours to drive up though," Peter said.

"What about taking a copter out of the Air Force Base at Hanscom? You're not too far from there, are you?"

"No, I'm not. That might work. Let me call the Boston office and see if they can arrange something on short notice."

"Okay, Peter. Let me know as soon as you find out."

As soon as Walker disconnected the call, he looked over at Munoz and said, "I'm going to call Dalton. We're probably going to need someone to open the gate at the ranch for us. I'm thinking they might need something like an acetylene torch. Plus, we're going to need evidence kits. I should give him a heads-up."

"So who's going in? Just you, me, and Peter?" Munoz asked.

Walker finished placing the call and then answered Munoz. "At this point, yeah. I don't think it'd be a good idea to push things with the judge. Let's see what happens once we're inside."

Dalton was more than accommodating. "I'm not sure exactly what equipment we have on hand that could be used to open the gate. But let me check with Milo; he's one of the civilian mechanics who works here. He'll know what to do. And the evidence kits are no problem. So as soon as you get back, meet me in my office. I'll make sure everything is ready to go."

Peter Stansky called back fifteen minutes later.

"I'm all set. I'm scheduled to land at the training facility around twelve thirty."

Walker said, "That's great, Peter. I just hope it's not a wasted trip."

Chapter Twenty

Eli Peters looked across the table at the man who called himself JT.

"I can't get a hold of my contact—the one who has to move the girl. I haven't used his services for quite a while. Actually, the last time was when you needed those other girls taken care of. I'm sure he must've gotten a new phone number since then."

Eli cocked his head to the side and looked away, obviously considering something. A moment later, he spoke as if he were responding to JT's unexpressed concern.

"But not to worry. Unless he's changed his habits, I know where I can find him. On Sundays, his whole family goes to church at nine thirty and then back home for brunch. Got to keep up appearances, I guess."

Before he continued, Eli took a sip of coffee. "You remember Josef? I introduced you to him when you first got here; I'm going to have him drive me to the contact's house. You can wait here. Once I confirm that everything is in place for tomorrow, I'll come back, and Josef can take you back to the water park. Let's see; it's nine fifteen now. I'll leave in about ten minutes... I should be back by ten thirty—eleven at the latest."

"Okay," JT said.

Eli threw out the next question with a total lack of sincerity. "Is there anything else you need?"

"No, I'm fine."

"Good. I'll see you in an hour or so."

Even though Eli employed Josef primarily as a chauffeur, he didn't treat him that way, believing that familiarity bred loyalty much more than it bred contempt. So Eli always sat in the front seat of the Lexus and made sure to engage Josef in conversation.

In this instance, that might not have been the best decision. If Eli had been sitting in the back seat, Josef would undoubtedly have made eye contact periodically by looking in the rearview mirror and probably would have noticed the dark-blue SUV following them.

Eli had been correct that there were government officials watching one of his warehouses, but he was unaware that they had also started watching his house. They were provincial members of the Royal Canadian Mounted Police, and they had strict orders to photograph anyone coming or going at Eli Peters' residence and to follow anyone who ventured outside the gate.

They had been fortunate to capture a photo of JT the day before. The SUV had to remain a safe distance away from the Peters' house so as not to be detected. And up to that point, nobody had simply walked up to the front gate. But with the help of a telephoto lens, one of the officers had been able to snap a three-quarters view of JT's face, which he had immediately downloaded and forwarded to the provincial RCMP Command Center. They in turn sent it along to their BEST counterparts in the United States.

Drug smuggling between the United States and Canada had become so widespread that it was not only an economic concern but also a security concern. If large shipments of heroin, fentanyl, oxycodone, and even prescription drugs were going undetected, what was to prevent chemical or biological weapons from coming in? That was why the Canadian Security and Intelligence Service was also monitoring the efforts of the RCMP and BEST. So JT's photo was now being run through facial recognition software in both countries, but so far there had been no hits.

Josef pulled the Lexus up in front of a house half the size of Eli Peters'. There was no security gate, no intercom system, not even a fence. Just before he exited the car, Eli looked over at Josef and said, "My friend here believes in hiding in plain sight. I wish I had his confidence."

The driver parked the dark-blue SUV a few hundred feet away. One of the officers calculated the address by adding six numbers to the number of houses between them and where the Lexus had parked. He called the address into the Command Center. Twenty-five minutes later, Eli Peters emerged from the house, got into his car, and left. A few seconds after that, the SUV followed.

At 10:35 a.m., Eli was back inside his house. JT was waiting for him in the living room.

"How did it go?"

"It's all set. Have the girl on the Canadian side at noon. One of my men will have the ATV there. Help get her into the bin in the back, and then you're done. Go back to the ranch and wait to hear from me about the other merchandise."

"Where's the girl going to be taken? The same place as the others?"

Eli stared intently at JT "Why do you care?" he asked.

"Just curious."

Eli shook his head. "Jesus... What is it with you? I'm taking care of it; that's all you need to know."

JT looked contrite. "You're right. I'm sorry."

Eli ignored the apology. "Whenever you're ready, Josef can take you."

"I'll just get my backpack."

When JT came downstairs, he shook hands with Eli, but could sense Eli's reluctance; evidently, he was still upset about the questions JT had posed before.

As JT headed for the front door, Eli said, "Sit right up front with Josef; don't ride in the back."

JT was about to ask why, but thought better of it. His curiosity had already pissed off Eli once, any more was asking for trouble.

The SUV stayed five or six car lengths behind the Lexus. The RCMP officer in the passenger seat took out his camera with the telephoto attachment and focused it on the car they were tailing.

"I don't think that's Eli Peters in the front seat. I think it might be the guy from yesterday."

Twenty minutes later, both cars were on a highway heading west. The SUV had to stay much farther back than it normally would because there was almost no traffic. A few minutes went by, and it became obvious where the Lexus was headed.

The officer holding the camera said, "It looks like they're going to the water park. Are you serious? What the hell is going on?"

The driver responded, "I don't know, but I better pull back some more." He slowed down to increase the distance between the two cars. And for several miles, it was fine. But then a fog bank settled in over the area, and maintaining visual contact became a problem. As soon as the Lexus put on its lights, however, the driver of the SUV did the same, and oddly enough, the fog actually made it easier to keep the lead car in view. All the SUV driver had to do was follow the red taillights.

But when the Lexus arrived at the water park and entered the vast parking lot, neither occupant of the SUV could see where the car they were following had gone. The driver started going up and down each aisle, but still couldn't find it.

About ninety seconds later, the officer in the passenger seat exclaimed, "There they are, near the front entrance."

A number of vehicles were discharging passengers, so there was a bit of a backup. As the SUV got closer, despite the fog, it was obvious that there was now only one person in the Lexus. The passenger turned toward the driver.

"So the guy gets *dropped off* here. That doesn't make any sense. Now what are we supposed to do?"

The driver responded, "My guess is that we stay with the Lexus, but why don't you call in and find out what they want us to do."

A few minutes later they got the official word: "Stay with the Lexus."

JT had no idea anyone had been following him, but nevertheless he waited several minutes before leaving the water park. It took nearly forty minutes to cover the two miles of uneven terrain, especially because the fog had left a thin coating of moisture everywhere he stepped. The last mile proved to be much easier; it only took another twelve minutes, and then he was at the trapdoor.

He glanced south toward the ranch. The Canadian side was much higher than the American side, but the fog prevented him from seeing anything beyond twenty or thirty yards. He then climbed down the steps into the tunnel, turned on his phone to light the way, and walked carefully straight ahead. Thirty seconds later, he came face-to-face with a mound of earth blocking his path.

"What the...?"

For a brief moment, JT thought there might have been a slight turn in the tunnel, and he had simply missed it. But it quickly became apparent to him that part of the tunnel must have collapsed. He could even see a small sliver of sunlight through the fog shining down on the dirt floor.

And a moment later, the ramifications of the collapse began to register: The girl was on the other side... and so was the ketamine and the fentanyl. There was no way to get to the girl or the drugs, at least not from here.

He would have to get back into the United States, but how was he going to do that? He had no passport with him. And even if he did, there would be no stamp indicating the date he had crossed into Canada. And then something more pressing struck him: the rest of the tunnel... it might be unstable. He looked around for a moment, and then rushed back to the ladder as quickly as he could, climbed the steps, pushed the hatch open, and stood up next to the tunnel entrance.

Now what was he going to do?

He thought about calling Eli if he could possibly get a signal, but then decided not to. Better to get back to the water park and think things through. By the time JT was at the window buying his admission ticket, the sun had burned off most of the fog and was starting its early afternoon descent.

The trip from the tunnel to the water park had given him an opportunity to formulate a plan, but he wanted to sit calmly for a few minutes and make sure he had thought of everything. Obviously, he had to tell Eli, but he was going to downplay how serious the blockage in the tunnel actually was. If Eli thought it couldn't be easily repaired, their business relationship would probably be over. And maybe the problem in the tunnel *was* easily fixed; he hadn't stayed around long enough to make that assessment. He'd have to do that from the other side once he got back to the ranch.

But getting back into the United States could very well be a huge problem. He then remembered that he did have his driver's license with him. Maybe he could go to one of the lesser-used border crossings, claim he lost his passport, and ask for a temporary card to get back into the States. The only tricky part about that plan was if they checked to see where he had supposedly entered Canada. Although, in actuality, the border agents were much more concerned with people coming into the United States rather than when and where they had left. JT decided he wasn't going to call Eli; he'd take the bus as he had done on Saturday. He wanted to take extra time to consider every contingency before springing the news on Eli.

It was nearly 1:30 p.m. when JT turned the corner and headed down Eli's street. The two officials in the dark-blue SUV couldn't believe their eyes when they spotted him. There was no scenario they could come up with that even remotely began to explain what they had just observed over the last couple of hours. Still, the officer in the passenger seat took out the camera with the telephoto lens and shot a number of additional photos.

One of them showed JT pressing the intercom button. But it couldn't capture the expression of apprehension on his face as he did it, or the effect on him as Eli let loose with an irrational tirade. Eventually, the gate swung open, and JT entered the property.

Once inside the house, JT tried to offer a low-key version of what had happened and what he planned to do about it. But Eli barely heard anything he said. It didn't seem to matter that what had transpired at the tunnel wasn't JT's fault. Eli was as angry as JT had ever seen him.

JT continued to try to defuse things. "It's really not that bad, Eli. It's just that I wasn't about to try to dig my way through it with my bare hands."

Eli was shouting. "How do you know how bad it was? The whole tunnel could've collapsed."

JT decided to lie. "No. When I came back out, I looked toward the ranch. The only area that was sunken in was where I had been."

Eli was still shouting, but not as loudly. "How could you see that far?"

"It's pretty flat there. I just hadn't paid any attention when I first went in."

It was obvious that Eli wasn't close to being convinced. He looked away briefly, took a breath, and evidently decided not to challenge JT any further on that point. Instead, in a quieter voice he asked, "So how are you proposing... you're going to fix this?"

JT had anticipated this question and had practiced his response, which he delivered as calmly as he could. "Once I get back, I'll see if I can take care of things by myself. If not, I'll use the people who set up the front gate security system and the computer room."

"What are you talking about? The tech people I sent you don't know anything about tunnels."

"Not them. I meant the people that I hired to build the computer room. They know how to keep their mouths shut. Plus, I pay them well."

Eli stared skeptically at JT. "And you think they'd know how to fix the tunnel?"

JT had no idea, but he quickly answered, "Yes."

Although the shouting was over, Eli's words remained threatening.

"You've screwed this up royally." Eli clenched his jaw and continued. "You've got a week to make this right. If it's not taken care of by then, we're done, understand?"

JT knew there was no point in arguing, so he simply replied, "Yeah."

A small smile appeared to form on Eli's face. "And you do know that you'll have to get rid of the girl on your own now?"

JT hadn't thought of that. "Why?"

Eli's anger flared again. "Because I've got to cancel the arrangement I just made, and we have no idea when, or if, we can use the tunnel again. I'm not willing to have anything to do with this now. Also, before you bring anyone else in to do any work, get the drugs out of there. If need be, I'll figure out another way of getting them here. But there's no alternate plan for the girl. Just do what you should have done to begin with."

Once again, JT wasn't in a position to object. "Okay."

"Tell me again, what's your plan to get back into the States?"

"I'm just going to say I lost my passport." He then appealed to Eli's vanity by quickly adding, "You said it yourself: the border guards couldn't care less. They're not going to be checking on when or where I came into Canada."

The last statement served to calm Eli somewhat. "Probably not. But it's not that easy to get a temporary card, and it's going to draw attention to you. I've got a better idea. I know a guy who makes fake passports. I'll take a picture of you with my phone, and send it off to him. He can stamp it to make it look like you came into Canada a week ago. But I'm sure it's going to take him a few days to do it."

JT knew that Eli was in his element when he was coming up with solutions to problems. He suspected that was another reason why Eli's anger had subsided. But then Eli's mood shifted and another smile formed on his lips.

"There's an added bonus of waiting a few days before you go back home. The girl might be dead by then. And I suspect disposing of a body is a lot easier than actually killing someone, although I've never had to do either. How about you, JT? You ever kill anybody?"

JT remained silent.

❦Chapter Twenty-One❦

The helicopter transporting Peter Stansky touched down at the training facility at 12:35 p.m. on Sunday afternoon. He was brought to the barracks, where he dropped off his bag in the room he had been assigned and then met up with Walker and Munoz in a conference room near Chuck Dalton's office.

"Thanks for doing this, Peter," said Walker.

"Glad to. I just hope I can help."

"I think we'll probably get underway around one o'clock. We were trying to anticipate everything we'd need, and they don't have all of it here. I'm not sure too many FBI operations have to send someone to Home Depot before they head out, but that's what we're waiting on," Walker said. "It is what it is."

Stansky looked puzzled. "What kind of equipment are you talking about?"

"They've got lock busters and battering rams that they use for training here on-site, but some of the other stuff we might need like hacksaws and bolt cutters—even chains to secure the gate after we're finished—they didn't have any of those things. And the problem is that if we forget anything, we can't just make a call to have someone bring it to us—there's no cell service at the ranch."

Stansky nodded. "Oh, right. So what's the plan? You mentioned something about the warrant having restrictions."

"Yeah, it does. First off, the judge insisted that we make every effort to contact this James Chambers again. I'm not sure what else we can possibly do, but we'll give it a go. The good news is that if we can't get a hold of him, then we can force the gate open. One of the civilian mechanics is going with us. I imagine he'll have to use some sort of metal-cutting torch. Once the gate's open, we're limited on the number of people allowed inside. To start with, it'll just be you, Dave, and me."

"Where does the security camera feed go to?"

"We don't know yet. The judge seemed to think it will be obvious once we're inside."

"Maybe, maybe not," Peter said.

"I hope we can figure it out early on; the judge made it pretty clear that she doesn't want us traipsing all over the property unless we have some evidence that Sam was there."

They talked for another fifteen minutes, and then Chuck Dalton joined them. After he was introduced to Stansky and they shook hands, Dalton said, "Milo just got back and everything's being loaded into one of our vans. I recruited two agents from here like you asked: Joe Travis and Brian Morelli. I'll introduce you when we go outside. I've briefed them to some degree, but you can give them whatever additional instructions you need to. They can ride with Milo and follow you to the ranch. Everyone's ready to go whenever you are."

The two vehicles left the training facility at 1:10 p.m. and arrived at Redemption Ranch thirty minutes later. Agents Travis and Morelli stayed in the van with Milo, as Walker, Munoz, and Stansky exited their car. Walker went through the same routine with the intercom as he had done the day before and with the same results. He tried three more times and then signaled to Milo to back the van in next to the gate.

Travis and Morelli joined Walker, Munoz, and Stansky at a safe distance away, as Milo got the torch going. He waited a moment as he tried to decide the best place to attack the gate. Initially, Milo thought removing the locking mechanism might be the easiest approach, but he changed his mind and went to the plate shielding the large bolt that clicked into place to secure the gate.

It appeared that that decision was the right one, because he was able to push the gate open after less than ten minutes.

Walker thanked Milo and then turned to Travis and Morelli.

"We have no idea what we're going to find in there. For the time being, I'd like you to stay out here. Since we won't be able to communicate, if we need you for some reason, we'll either drive back out or we'll hit the car horn with three long blasts. Okay?"

Morelli answered for both agents. "That's fine. Obviously, if something changes out here, we'll do the same: three long blasts on the horn."

"Great."

Munoz opened the driver's side door and got inside. Walker returned to the passenger seat and Stansky to the back seat. A few seconds later, Munoz drove ahead slowly, not only because they were on an uneven dirt road but also in order to take in their surroundings. Although neither Walker nor Munoz was anticipating any sort of confrontation once they were inside, they both had strapped on their service weapons, just in case.

For the first minute or so, there was very little to see except huge rocks on either side and large pine trees, some off in the distance and some directly in front of them. But then the road turned, and the trees that they had thought were straight ahead were actually off to the side and had been obscuring a number of buildings.

The first structure that came into view was directly in front of them and appeared to be larger than the others, with the exception of a taller building a few hundred yards behind it, which was easily identified, even from that distance, as a barn. Munoz pointed straight ahead.

"If I had to guess, I'd say those are the living quarters. Other than the barn, those other buildings seem smaller; they almost look like cabins or something like that."

"Yeah, it looks that way to me too," said Walker.

Stansky sat forward and added, "I was keeping my eye out for a satellite dish or something similar on the roof. I didn't see anything, though. I don't even see any wires. Of course, way up here they may be using generators."

Walker responded. "I think it's possible that everything is underground."

"You may be right. I remember that we found out that they did have a landline on the property, but it was out of service."

Munoz looked over at Walker. "So I take it you want to try the main building first?"

"Yeah, let's do that."

Munoz parked the car directly in front of the porch. Before he opened his door, Walker said to Munoz, "Pop the trunk, will you? I'll get one of the lock busters out. It doesn't look like we're going to need the battering ram or the bolt cutters. Can you grab a couple of the evidence kits?"

Munoz hit the button to open the trunk, and the three agents exited the car. A half a minute later, Walker led the way up the steps. He placed the lock buster on the floor of the porch, and just before he knocked on the door, he unsnapped the top of his gun holster.

He then called out, "James Chambers. FBI. We need to talk to you."

No answer.

Walker knocked again and repeated the request.

Still no answer.

Walker bent down, picked up the lock buster, and got to work. Despite what was depicted on TV and in the movies, the FBI rarely used a battering ram to break down a door unless it was fortified in some way. The truth was the simple lock buster device worked just as well in 95 percent of the situations they came across, especially the military-grade ones the FBI used. The device had a tightly compressed spring mechanism that exerted a tremendous amount of force in a concentrated area. Its only downside was that it wouldn't work against reinforced steel deadbolts. But fortunately, that was not the case here, and Walker had the door open in less than five minutes.

As he pushed it inward, he called out, "Anybody here? James Chambers?"

He waited ten more seconds and then looked back at Munoz and Stansky.

"Okay, let's take it slow. Just get a sense of the layout first."

The room they were looking at was quite large, easily forty feet by forty feet. At the front of it, there were hallways visible on both the left and the right side which seemed to lead to the back of the building. On the left side of the room was a fireplace with a large portrait above it. Also on the left side in one corner was a huge desk with a number of bookshelves behind it.

In the middle of the room there were three leather couches arranged as three sides of a square. Approximately fifteen feet from the open side of the square and mounted on the wall was an oversized flat screen TV. To the left of the TV was an open doorway through which kitchen appliances could easily be seen. And to the right of the TV was a closed door. From across the large room, it wasn't obvious that the door was composed of a different material than the dark wood that dominated the rest of the space.

The wall on the right side of the room featured three enormous windows and little else, except for a small sitting area with two leather chairs facing each other and a table in between them. The relative lack of furniture on that side of the room made the whole space appear lopsided, as if the daylight coming through the windows had pushed everything to the other side.

After a few moments, Walker said, "This area is pretty open. I don't see anything that would suggest a security camera feed is coming in. You, Peter?

"No, not that I can see."

"All right, let's put on some gloves and check out the other parts of the building. I'll take the hallway on the left. Dave, you take the one on the right. Peter, you take the kitchen."

Walker's hallway had two doors off of it, both closed. The first one on the right opened up into a bathroom and the second into a bedroom. Munoz's hallway also had two doors off of it, but both were open, and they were both bedrooms. Stansky didn't find anything related to video surveillance in the kitchen area either.

Walker spent a little extra time in the second room he had entered, observing that it contained a hospital bed as well as other medical equipment that would suggest its inhabitant might have been bedridden.

He glanced quickly into the adjoining bathroom and was just about to leave when he heard Munoz call out, "Craig, I may have found something."

Walker hurriedly left the bedroom and joined Munoz and Stansky in the main room.

Munoz said, "Once I finished checking out the hallway— there are two bedrooms down there, by the way—I came back out here and decided to see what was behind this door, but it's locked. Why lock this door and none of the others? It doesn't seem that substantial, but you still may need the lock buster."

As it turned out, the door was a lot more substantial than Munoz had thought. Repeated attempts to smash the lock were unsuccessful. Walker looked more closely at where some of the reinforced material had begun to give way.

"I see the problem. It's a deadbolt, but it looks like it's brass, not steel. I think a couple more tries might do it."

And they did.

Walker eased the door open. The room was only about five by eight, but it was full of electronic equipment. There were at least two computers as well as some other devices Walker wasn't familiar with. But the most prominent piece of equipment was a TV monitor, and it was showing Milo, Travis, and Morelli standing next to the FBI van.

Walker turned toward Stansky. "I'd say this is just what we were looking for, Peter."

Stansky stepped forward. "Okay, let me get in there and see what we've got."

The tech expert looked around the small room and then said, "This is state-of-the-art equipment, something you'd expect to see at a large corporation headquarters, museums—places like that."

Walker asked, "Can you access what we need?"

"I think so; there are a lot of bells and whistles, but the basics are all the same. It may take me a while, but I should be able to get in."

"All right, Dave and I are going to do some more looking around. Let us know when you've got something."

"Will do."

"Where do you think we should start?" asked Munoz when he and Walker moved back into the main room.

Walker responded, "I'd say let's stay in this room for the time being, although even that might be pushing the judge's ruling, since it looks like we've already found the place where the security camera feed comes in... But as long as it's all in plain sight..." His voice trailed off. "I have to say right from the beginning when I first got the door open, nothing seemed out of place here. And I didn't notice anything that could have belonged to Sam—no phone or purse, anything like that."

"No, me neither," Munoz said.

Walker said, "Okay, we might as well get started. I know it could be a waste of time, but I think we should begin by dusting some of the common areas and see what prints we can lift. Where are the evidence kits?"

"I left them over there by the door."

Walker went over to retrieve them.

"I'll take the left side of the room, you can take the right."

About ten minutes later, Munoz called out. "This is weird."

Walker responded as he headed over to the other side of the room. "What?"

"This table's been wiped clean... no prints. And the same with this leather chair. But the other leather chair has prints on. I guess it's possible someone was cleaning and only did the table and one chair, but it does seem odd, don't you think?"

"Yeah, it does. I guess just see what you're able to get off the one chair. And then why don't we each do one more surface? If there's anything here, that should be enough."

As they were finishing up, Stansky called out. "I think I've got something."

Walker and Munoz rushed to the small room and squeezed in behind Stansky who was seated in front of the monitor.

"It's all digital; there are no tapes. The system looks like it's set to record for thirty days, and then those images are deleted to make way for the next month. But look at this."

Stansky manipulated some switches, moved a computer mouse across a pad, and then clicked. "This is the feed from Wednesday, June eleventh through Saturday the fourteenth."

Walker and Munoz watched the monitor for ten seconds and then Walker said, "Is there a problem? It's not showing anything."

"Exactly. The images have been deleted. Someone overrode the system."

"How can you be sure?"

"Well, I can't be a hundred percent sure, but June first through June tenth is all there. And June fifteenth through today is all there. But the feed from the very day or so that the girl, Sam, disappeared, there just happened to be a system malfunction? I don't think so."

For the first time in a while, Walker's pulse quickened. This was too much of a coincidence. Sam had to have been here. But the bad news was that somebody didn't want anyone else to know that.

Munoz was thinking along the same lines.

"Do you think this will be enough for the judge to let us search the rest of the property?"

"I don't know. I think it's probably fifty-fifty. But since we can't call her anyway, let's keep looking around."

Stansky said, "I'm going to stay in here and make sure I didn't miss anything."

ᴄ✑Chapter Twenty-Two✑ᴄ

Walker and Munoz secured each of the evidence kits containing the fingerprints they had gathered and began another inspection of the main room, but nothing stood out. Ten more minutes went by and Walker made a suggestion.

"We should try the other rooms. I know we've already found where the security camera feed comes in, and technically the other rooms could be considered beyond the scope of the warrant. But if this were a criminal case, isn't it possible that the deleted video might constitute probable cause?"

Munoz smiled. "You've been watching too many *Law and Order* reruns."

Walker smiled back. "Maybe, but it's just that some piece of evidence could be sitting right in the next room. I only gave the other rooms a once-over; I didn't look that closely, did you?"

"No, not really. Same as you, I was just looking for the security camera feeds. Okay, I'm game if you are."

"I was hoping you'd say that. I'll take the same hallway I was in before, and you can take the one you were in. We can check out the kitchen area together."

Both Walker and Munoz decided to keep to the spirit of the judge's restrictions, if not to the letter of them: they wouldn't be looking in any drawers, cabinets, or closets.

After Munoz finished going through one of the bedrooms, he opened the door to the other one and realized it had an attached bathroom. He poked his head in and looked around. But once again, nothing stood out as anything but ordinary.

He was about to close the door when he spotted a small wastepaper basket next to the vanity. He moved closer and looked into the container. There was only one item inside, stuck to the bottom: a gauze pad with what appeared to be blood on it.

He was still wearing gloves, but he nevertheless gripped the pad by its corner and carried it out into the main room. He found a Ziploc bag in one of the evidence kits and deposited the gauze pad inside and sealed it. Then he called out to Walker.

"Craig, come here a minute. Let me show you what I found."

As Walker left the bedroom he was searching and came into the main room, he said, "What?"

Munoz held up the Ziploc bag. "It looks like a bandage of some sort with blood on."

"Really? Where'd you find it?"

"In the bathroom adjacent to one of the bedrooms," Munoz said. "Didn't you tell me that the training facility has a forensics lab?"

"Yeah, that's what I was told."

"I wonder how quickly they could do an analysis of this."

"You mean for DNA? I don't know. Can you even get a large enough blood sample off of something like that?"

"I'm not sure," Munoz replied. "Of course, even if you could, if you're trying to find a match, the person would have to be in the system. And if by some chance it is Sam's blood, she wouldn't be in the criminal database, would she?"

"She might be. It would depend on whether she was entered into the system before her juvenile record was sealed."

"That's true," Munoz agreed. "Let's ask Peter if he knows if this is a large enough sample."

Just then, as if on cue, Stansky came out of the small room.

"Ask me what?"

Munoz held up the Ziploc bag. "I found this bandage in a basket in one of the bathrooms. Do you know if you can get a large enough sample from this, especially since it's dried up?"

Stansky reached for the Ziploc bag.

"Let me see." He studied it for a few seconds. "It's not strictly my area of expertise, but I don't think it'll be a problem."

Walker asked, "How long would it take to isolate the DNA and then run it through the FBI databases?"

"I think you could probably get it done in a couple of hours. The main holdup is usually the backlog, not the process itself. In my experience, there are always three or four people ahead of you."

Walker responded, "The training facility has a forensics lab. I'm sure it must be linked to the FBI databases. And I've got to believe there'd be nobody ahead of us."

Stansky nodded. "If that's true, then I think you could have the results back by late this afternoon or early tonight."

"It's still probably a long shot," said Walker. "But I'm going to take this out to Travis and Morelli, and ask one of them to drive it back to the training facility."

"Just hold on for a second, Craig," said Stansky. "I want to try something."

Stansky walked back to the small room, and Walker and Munoz followed but remained in the doorway. After another minute went by, Stansky said, "Craig, do you have your phone with you?"

"Yeah, but there's no signal here, remember?"

"Humor me. Give it a try."

Walker looked skeptically at Stansky, but he removed his phone from his pocket and turned it on. A moment later, the screen lit up. He tapped the Google icon and five seconds after that he was connected to the Internet.

"What the...? What happened?"

Stansky looked at Munoz. "Dave, have you got your phone?"

"Yeah, actually I left it on."

"Try calling Craig."

Munoz found Walker's number and tapped the screen. A few seconds later, Walker's phone buzzed.

Walker looked at Stansky and asked, "How did you do that?"

"I wasn't sure if I was seeing what I thought I was. Let me show you." Walker and Munoz moved into the room as Peter pointed to a small black box to the side of the console holding the video feed equipment. "That's a jamming device. They're actually illegal. Well, it's illegal to buy or sell them. Whether they're illegal if you use them on your own property, I don't know. All I did was push in the red button, and you were able to get a signal. So there's got to be some kind of router here, either that or a cell tower some place on the property. That's the only way the phones would work."

Walker was shaking his head. "I can't figure out what the hell is going on. From what we just found out about the security video, it seems very likely that Sam was here. But it's hard to imagine that this place was just a ranch for runaways or some sort of rehab center, not when there's state-of-the-art security equipment and a jamming device."

Munoz appeared to be debating whether to say something, and then he just came out with it. "I totally agree with you, Craig, but... I'm wondering if it's possible that Sam might have gone somewhere willingly with James Chambers. I'm not even suggesting anything inappropriate, just..."

"I know," Walker interrupted. "The same idea crossed my mind too. And I guess it's a possibility. But that would mean Sam blew off a final exam and a couple of Habitat meetings—something that her guidance counselor and Maddie say she'd never do. That's why that scenario doesn't add up for me."

Everyone was silent for a few moments, and then Peter Stansky changed the subject.

"Now that we have phone service, do you want to call the judge?"

"Not quite yet," said Walker. "First I'd like to get the ball rolling on the fingerprints and the bandage. I want to contact Chuck Dalton to let him know what we've got."

Walker moved toward the doorway leading back into the main room. Munoz and Stansky followed. Walker's phone was still in his hand; he located Dalton's number and tapped it. A few seconds later, he heard it ringing.

"Craig? What's going on?"

"Hi, Chuck. Peter Stansky figured out that there's a jamming device here at the ranch; that's why we couldn't get a signal before. Obviously, he shut it down; that's why I'm able to call out."

"Any luck finding any trace of the girl?"

"It's possible." Walker told him about the deleted security footage. "At the very least, it's suspicious, but I don't know if it's going to be enough to convince the judge. Listen, Chuck, I need a couple of favors."

"Whatever I can do."

"Thanks. We lifted some fingerprints off of a number of surfaces in the main house, and we also found a bandage with dried blood on it. I know you've got a forensics lab on-site. How long would it take to run the prints and whatever DNA the blood from the bandage yields?"

"My guess is a few hours. We haven't done much of that in the few months we've been open. Actually, the prints might take longer than the blood sample. There are a lot more fingerprints in the database than DNA samples."

"I didn't think of that," Walker said. "Anyway, if you could call either Travis or Morelli—I don't have their numbers—and let them know one of us will be bringing out the evidence kits. And then ask if one of them could drive it back to the training site, I'd appreciate it."

"As soon as we hang up," Dalton said.

"Great. Thanks. I know it's going to take some time, but as soon as you know anything about the prints or the blood, give me a call."

"You got it."

As the conversation between Walker and Dalton was winding down, Munoz picked up the two evidence kits. When Walker disconnected the call, Munoz said, "I'll drive these out to the front gate; I overheard what you said to Dalton."

"Good. Thanks," Walker said. "I guess it's time to call the judge."

Stansky said, "While you're doing that, I'm going to check out what's on the desktops of the two computers in the other room. Technically, the icons are in plain sight, so as long as I don't do any hacking, I don't think I'm violating any rules."

Walker raised his eyebrows, but didn't challenge Stansky.

Two minutes later, Walker was talking to Judge Lister.

"Good afternoon, Agent Walker. Any luck contacting James Chambers?" the judge asked.

"No."

"What about evidence that the girl was at the ranch?"

Walker wanted to play things carefully, so he responded, "I'd say yes, but I guess that's up to you, Your Honor."

"I'm listening."

Walker outlined much of what had transpired over the last hour, leaving out anything that could be construed as violating the restrictions she had imposed.

He closed by saying, "I know the deleted video isn't conclusive, but when you add in the security precautions and the jamming device, it seems fairly certain that something else is going on here. And at the very least, I think you'd agree that it's surely not a typical religious facility."

"I *would* agree, but that was true before you found all that security equipment and the jamming device. I don't think anything has changed in that regard. Church-owned property is still church-owned property. If the church chooses to be more... vigilant than other sects and denominations, that's their right," the judge said. "You seem to be implying that there may be some sort of illegal activity going on there. I have to say, that's a bit of a Catch-22, Agent Walker. If I allow you to search the entire property, and you do find evidence of something illegal, but not related to the girl, it would be inadmissible, and the authorities might lose any chance of prosecuting."

Walker didn't have an answer for that argument, so he repeated his initial plea.

"Don't you think the missing security footage from the exact date that Sam Daniels disappeared is suspicious?"

"Of course it is. But you said it yourself: it's not conclusive. At best, it's circumstantial. I have to have more than that. Call me back when you get the results from either the fingerprints or the blood sample."

"That's going to be hours from now," Walker replied.

There was silence for a moment, and then the judge said, "I told you before, I'm not unsympathetic to what you're trying to do. So I'm going to give you a little more leeway. I'll allow you to search the rest of the building you're in. But the same restrictions apply, only things in plain sight."

All Walker could manage was, "Thank you, Your Honor."

Munoz arrived back just as Walker disconnected the call. Walker's face said it all.

"So no dice, huh?"

"Well, she's going to expand the warrant to include all the other rooms in this building."

"Really? I assume you didn't tell her that we've already been doing some of that," Munoz said.

"No, I didn't. I'm still trying to stay on her good side," Walker answered. "Well, we've got a lot of time to kill before we get any results back, so we might as well give the whole place another once-over. The kitchen's right here; let's start there."

Chapter Twenty-Three

It took Walker and Munoz less than ten minutes to check out the kitchen and the bedrooms in the back of the building. Since they weren't allowed to open drawers or closets, there wasn't a whole lot of investigating they could do. They returned to the main room within a few seconds of each other and found Peter Stansky over near the stone fireplace.

Walker asked, "Any luck on your end, Peter?"

"No, all the titles of the folders seemed pretty innocuous. But the fact that both computers are locked up in that room suggests to me that this Chambers guy is trying to hide something. But I'm sure whatever it is, it's probably buried in the bowels of the computer, and it's either password-protected or encrypted. It would take me a while to get at it... even if I was permitted to try."

Walker nodded. "I know it's frustrating. I feel the same way. Part of me would just like to do a normal search and not have to tiptoe around everything."

Stansky shifted topics, as he gestured at the portrait above the fireplace. "I assume that's the father sitting behind the desk and his two sons on either side. They look like twins, don't they?"

Munoz responded, "They do, but I don't think they are. James Chambers' brother was killed in an accident. Tom was his name, I think. The article we read didn't mention anything about him being a twin."

Walker joined in. "No, I don't think they were twins either. Plus, you've got to remember, it's only an oil painting." He paused.

"I'm wondering if we should just go back to the training facility and wait. I don't think there's anything else we can do here, and frankly, I don't want to be tempted to violate the judge's orders. What do you think, Dave?"

"About violating the judge's orders or going back to the training site?"

Walker let out a laugh. "Thanks, I needed that." A moment went by, and then he said, "Why don't we at least take a break and go get something to eat."

"Actually, that sounds like a good idea," Munoz agreed. "It'll give us a chance to clear our heads."

Stansky nodded. "Give me a couple of minutes to make sure everything's reset properly on the video feed. I'll be right back."

As Stansky headed over to the room that held all the electronics, Walker said, "I promised I'd give Maddie a call. Even though I don't have all that much to tell her, she's probably anxious. I'd just as soon not wait until later tonight."

Munoz moved to the other side of the room to give Walker some privacy. As he did that, his eyes landed on the large wooden desk in the corner as well as the bookcases behind it. He headed in that direction and began reading the titles on each of the shelves. Two minutes later, one of the titles grabbed his attention: *A True History of Maine* by Randolph Mason. Why did he know that title? And then it came to him. There was an excerpt from that book in one of the links about the ranch.

Munoz extracted the book from the shelf and opened it to the title page, but his focus quickly shifted to an inscription on the inside cover:

To my dear friend Lemuel,

As you know, this book should be at least a few chapters longer, or maybe there should be a second volume.

I will continue to respect your wishes, but I hope you will reconsider.

With great fondness,

Randolph Mason

Munoz let this discovery sink in for a moment, and then he rushed over to where Walker was just finishing up his call.

"As soon as I know anything more, Maddie, I'll let you know. But it probably won't be until tomorrow. Okay, I'll talk to you then." As Walker disconnected the call, he looked in Munoz's direction and saw the excited look on his face.

"What?"

Munoz handed the open book to Walker and said, "You've got to see this."

Walker took the book in his hands and began to read the inscription. A few seconds later, he looked over at Munoz, and said, "This is the same professor who wrote the article we read, right? So he was a friend of Lemuel Chambers, James Chambers' father?"

"It seems like it."

"Any idea what he's talking about with the inscription?"

"No, but at the very least I think we should contact him. It's possible that he might know how to get in touch with James Chambers."

Walker called over to Stansky. "Peter, can you come out here?"

"I'm just finishing up; I'll be right there."

Thirty seconds later, Stansky was back in the main room. He pointed at the book in Walker's hand.

What's that?"

"Do you remember that article about the history of Maine and the ranch?" Walker asked.

"Vaguely."

"Well, this is a copy of the book it was taken from. And there's an inscription that seems to suggest that the professor who wrote it was a friend of Lemuel Chambers'. Dave was thinking that this professor might have an idea how to contact James Chambers. Do you think you can get a phone number for this professor?"

"I would think so. It shouldn't be that hard." Stansky moved toward the front door. "I left my laptop in the car. I didn't think I'd be able to use it with no signal up here, but I brought it anyway. I'd rather not use either of the computers in the other room. It might look like I was doing something I shouldn't have. Also, I've got more sophisticated software on my laptop."

Stansky was back in less than three minutes; five minutes after that, he had a phone number for Randolph Mason. Walker looked at Stansky and said, "You're almost too fast. I haven't figured out what I'm going to say to him yet."

Walker *did* take a couple of minutes to put together the best way to explain the reason for his call. He then punched in the number Stansky had found. After the third ring, Walker heard, "Randolph Mason."

Walker responded with a measured tone. "Professor Mason, hello. My name is Craig Walker. My colleagues and I are investigating the disappearance of a young woman who we believe may have traveled to Redemption Ranch."

"The ranch?" Mason said. "Excuse me, but how did you get this number? Are you with the sheriff's department?"

Walker hadn't intended to jump right into it, but he didn't have a choice. "Actually, no, I'm with the FBI."

Walker was used to what came next. "The FBI? Why is the FBI involved with the ranch? There hasn't been anything about this on the news."

Walker proceeded to give the professor a condensed version of why the FBI was involved. He avoided anything told to him in confidence, but did share the limitations the judge had placed on the search warrant. As it turned out, the professor was not a hard sell, especially once he heard that a young woman was missing.

"So we were hoping that you can help us get in touch with James Chambers," said Walker.

"JT? He's not at the ranch?"

"No, and we haven't been able to reach him."

"It's been a couple of years since I've seen him. I don't believe I have an up-to-date phone number, except for the ranch. Other than that, I wouldn't have any idea how to contact him."

"What about anyone else that the family might have been close to? Other friends?"

"They kept to themselves pretty much. Frankly, my link to the family was primarily through Lemuel, the father. After he passed, I had very little occasion to interact with them."

Walker persisted. "I mentioned to you earlier that the reason we knew you had a connection to the family was because of the inscription you wrote in the front of your book. If you don't mind me asking, what does it mean, the part about you asking the father to reconsider something?"

Randolph Mason didn't respond immediately. Eventually he said, "Although Lemuel has passed on, I'm still somewhat protective of his privacy. And from what you told me earlier about looking for this girl, I can't see any way that the two things are related."

Walker made sure to keep his tone even. "You'd be surprised, Professor. Sometimes what appears irrelevant can break a case wide open."

"I don't watch a lot of TV... Agent... Walker, but I've seen enough to suspect investigators say that all the time."

Walker chuckled. "Guilty as charged. But it's nevertheless true."

Randolph Mason hesitated. "Well, I'm really going to have to give that some thought. I'm certainly not prepared to talk about it right now over the phone."

Walker's instincts were telling him that he needed to keep pumping Randolph Mason for information, regardless of whether he was going to share the story behind the inscription.

"Would it be possible for us to meet, Professor? If you feel as if you can't talk about... certain things, I can respect that." In Walker's experience very few individuals were immune to flattery, even academic types, so he added, "But it's been very difficult to find out much of anything about the Chambers family or Redemption Ranch. You seem to know a lot about both. We could certainly use your assistance."

Walker sensed that Randolph Mason was starting to come around.

"I understand. And I do want to help," Mason replied. "No promises on what I can tell you, but I'd be willing to meet with you. Unfortunately, I have guests coming over around six o'clock; otherwise, I'd be willing to come to the ranch. Actually, it would be nice to see it again; I haven't been there in a while."

"That's okay. We can come to you. Where do you live?"

The professor gave him the address.

"It's about twenty-five miles south of the ranch; it shouldn't take you more than a half an hour. That'll give me time to look through my correspondence. I doubt it, but there could be something in there relating to JT."

"I appreciate that, Professor. Thank you. We'll see you in about thirty minutes."

Munoz was able to glean the gist of the conversation. "Sounds like we're heading out."

"Yeah, it probably beats going back to the training facility and sitting around waiting for the DNA and fingerprint results. And even if nothing comes of it, we haven't lost anything."

"True."

A few minutes later, the three investigators were in the car on the dirt road heading out to the gate. Walker explained the situation to Morelli. Travis hadn't returned as yet from dropping off the evidence kits, and Milo had gone with him. Walker asked Morelli to keep the site secure in case there was some reason for them to return. But if he hadn't heard from Walker by five-thirty, he should head back to the training site.

The trip to Randolph Mason's house took twenty-nine minutes. Stansky used part of the time to fill in Walker and Munoz about the professor from his online search. He was seventy-three years old, retired from the University of Maine, and had written four books—all of which dealt with the history of Maine.

Randolph Mason's house was a well-maintained, brownish-red Victorian that had probably been built in the beginning of the twentieth century. The professor greeted them at the front door before they even knocked. He looked fifteen years younger than his actual age, due in part to the fact that he maintained a trim physique and still had all his hair.

After introductions, he led the three investigators into what could only be described as a parlor. The professor offered them coffee, tea, and water, but they declined.

Walker began. "Thank you for seeing us." He gestured to his colleagues. "I apologize if it seems like we're ganging up on you. We don't usually operate with three agents."

The professor nodded and smiled. "I appreciate that, Agent Walker. But I mainly taught freshmen, so even *three* FBI agents are not as intimidating as a two-hundred-seat lecture hall filled with eighteen-year-olds."

Walker returned the smile. "I suppose not," he said. "Were you able to find out anything when you looked through your... correspondence?"

"No, I'm sorry. Lemuel and I mainly used... what do they call it now? Snail mail? Although the last few years before he died, we did use e-mail. I looked in both places, but there wasn't anything about JT... James, as you call him."

Walker decided to ease into things in hopes of fostering some trust and eventually getting the professor to divulge the "private" matter between him and Lemuel Chambers.

"Instead of us asking you questions, would you mind telling us about the ranch?" Walker said.

"How far back do you want me to go?"

Walker really only wanted to hear about the last several years, but he didn't feel as if he could say that. "Whatever you want."

"Now it definitely feels like I'm back in front of a freshman lecture hall."

Chapter Twenty-Four

Whether it was because he had written about the specific topic or more likely because he had given numerous lectures about it, Randolph Mason didn't require any notes to deliver a detailed history of the beginnings of the Church of Universal Redemption.

"Josiah Pendleton came here in 1640 from Dover, England. And like so many of those who traveled to the New World around that time, he was seeking religious freedom. But unlike many of his fellow pilgrims, he was not impoverished. In fact, he was extremely well-off.

"His father and grandfather before him were very successful merchants who were also part owners of a shipping concern. To some degree, Josiah was probably a disappointment to the older Pendletons because he eschewed the business world in favor of devoting his life to religion, or at least to religion as he saw it.

"He had no desire to follow the tenants of the Church of England. In fact, he believed its very founding had been immoral: Henry the Eighth wanted his marriage annulled, and since the Pope wouldn't grant it, the king simply decided to break away from the Catholic Church and start one of his own.

"Initially, the Church of Universal Redemption was less an organized religion than it was a philosophy—one that espoused that all of its followers should aspire to be the most moral individuals they could possibly be. It didn't require the formal worship of a deity, because Josiah believed that being a good person was all that was necessary to honor God. But Josiah was also a practical man.

So many of his beliefs didn't get written down or ritualized until after his father died, and he had inherited his vast wealth. That was in 1635.

"The next five years saw some growth in the church with its followers numbering somewhere in the hundreds. But the church members were often ostracized—certainly much more than they were persecuted. Nevertheless, Josiah, his wife, their three children, and forty of the church's most devout congregants set sail for Boston.

"They stayed in the Boston area for several weeks and then made their way north where they claimed about eight hundred acres in the northwest corner of what is now Maine. And that became Redemption Ranch, although it probably wasn't called that until sometime in the 1900's."

Professor Mason took a breath and shook his head. "I'm sorry, gentlemen. Old habits die hard. I guess once a teacher always a teacher."

Walker started to say something, but the professor put up his hand to fend off the comment. "I know you were about to tell me that it's okay. You're very accommodating, Agent Walker, but I'm sure you're interested in more recent events."

Walker remained silent as Professor Mason continued. "As I mentioned to you on the phone, I haven't been to the ranch in several years. The last time was shortly after Lemuel died. I just came to see how JT was doing. He had decided to follow up on what his father had started. The property had been turned into—for lack of a better term—a compound for troubled girls. Most of them came from Ohio. That's where the largest number of church followers now live. A splinter group left Maine in the 1850's and moved there. These were their descendants."

Munoz interrupted. "So most of the girls weren't runaways?"

"No, as I said, I believe the initial idea was to help out the group from Ohio that was having difficulties with some of their teenagers, but then I think they took in other girls. What was unique about the situation, however, was that the Ohio group sent adults along to act as counselors. It was in keeping with the church's philosophy and mission of volunteering and providing service to the community."

Munoz asked another question. "When did the ranch stop being a compound for troubled girls and runaways?"

"I don't know that it has," The professor said.

Walker entered the conversation. "As I told you, we haven't been able to search the entire property. We've only been inside the main living quarters, but the rest of the place seems deserted."

"Really? I suppose things could've changed after Tom died." He paused. "That was a terrible thing."

"Yes, we're aware of what happened," said Walker.

"I didn't find out about it until long afterward, and just by accident. JT didn't call me, which was a little strange. But as I said, the family tended to keep to themselves, and my connection was primarily with Lemuel."

There was a gap in the conversation, and then Professor Mason said, "You asked me over the phone about the inscription I wrote in the book. I had decided to see how this played out. Although I can't see how it's relevant, and I would still ask for your discretion, I'm willing to tell you about it."

"Thank you," responded Walker.

The professor gathered himself before he spoke. "About twenty years ago, shortly after I met Lemuel, he called me and asked if I'd come to see him; he said he wanted to show me something. It turned out to be a diary of some sort from the eighteen fifties and sixties. Evidently, during those years the property was part of the Underground Railroad."

Walker asked, "You mean for getting slaves out of the United States and into Canada?"

"Yes. Lemuel was well aware that having grown up in Maine, I've always been fascinated by the Underground Railroad, even starting back when I was a little boy. But what was particularly interesting about the contents of the diary was that up to that point, all the Underground Railroad sites that had been discovered were in the eastern part of the state. For an historian like me, this was tremendously exciting, and it potentially opened up a whole new area to research," the professor said. "But as Lemuel continued to talk, I began to sense that he was having reservations, not necessarily about confiding in me, but about going public with the diary."

Munoz asked, "Why do you say that?"

"The ranch had been in his family for over three hundred and fifty years. He was afraid the state would declare the property a historical site and seize it through eminent domain. I tried to convince him that that was highly unlikely, but he wasn't willing to take the chance."

Professor Mason paused for a moment, seemingly contemplating something. Eventually he said, "There was also another reason. According to Lemuel, the diary entries made it clear that some of the church's members did not want the church involved in helping slaves flee to Canada. That was the group that left for Ohio. Ironic, isn't it? The church was built on a doctrine akin to the Golden Rule, and yet those members evidently decided that none of that applied to slaves.

"It was obvious that Lemuel was embarrassed. He didn't want any of that getting out. He swore me to secrecy, and I've kept my promise."

"Where's the diary now?" Munoz asked.

"I don't know. So even if I wanted to bring this discovery to light, I don't have the documentation. I only saw the diary briefly, but I was never permitted to read it."

Munoz followed up. "After Lemuel died, did you ask James … JT about it?"

"I did. He said that he knew about the diary. His father had told him about it, but he hadn't gone through all of his father's things at that point and didn't know where it was. This was not too long after his father had died, so I didn't feel right pressing him. He said when he found it, he'd let me know. But he never did. I left it alone for a couple of years, and then when I thought about it again, it was shortly after JT's brother died. As much as I would have loved to get my hands on that diary, it's like it wasn't meant to be. If I were to do anything now, it would feel as if I was betraying Lemuel."

The professor paused for a moment and then asked, "Do you see why I didn't believe the information about the Underground Railroad was relevant to finding the girl? Don't misunderstand. I'm not sorry I told you. I trust that you won't repeat it. It's just that I don't see any way that the two things have anything to do with one another."

Walker responded, "I would tend to agree; it certainly doesn't seem like it." Walker started to get up. "Well, Professor, thank you for your time. I know you have guests coming, so we'll be on our way."

Walker reached into his pocket, extracted a cardholder, and handed one of his cards to the professor. "If you think of anything else, please give me a call."

The professor accepted Walker's card, glanced at it, and then said, "I don't know if you'd consider this, but I'd still like to help you somehow if I could. I was thinking. What if I come to the ranch tomorrow? It's possible that I might see something that would jog my memory—something in the house that could lead you to JT."

Walker looked at Munoz and Stansky and then said, "I think that would be okay. It couldn't hurt, certainly. We're waiting on some forensic results, although I don't necessarily expect that's going to change anything. But regardless, we're planning on taking another run at the main house tomorrow morning, so sure. We're going to get there fairly early; why don't you come by around nine? I'll alert the agents on the gate to let you in."

"The gate? What gate?"

"There's a security gate at the front entrance as well as a surveillance camera."

"At the ranch?"

"Yes."

"That seems odd." The professor seemed to be speaking more to himself that anyone else when he said, "Why would JT have something like that installed?"

The ride back to the training facility took nearly an hour, providing the three investigators an opportunity to review what they knew and to lament the fact that they didn't have enough to convince the judge to let them search the rest of the property. They also used the time to engage in "what if's"—some related to the information Professor Mason had given them, but most in anticipation of the DNA and fingerprint results.

Stansky continued to try to use his laptop in hopes of finding something that would lead them to James Chambers, but the Wi-Fi signal was spotty, and even when it worked, the searches were fruitless.

Once they were back on-site, they headed for the dining hall. Other than breakfast, none of them had eaten anything all day. Over dinner they continued to discuss the investigation, but by 6:30 p.m., they were all talked out.

And then Walker's phone buzzed. It was Chuck Dalton.

"Where are you, Craig? Back in your room?"

"No, the three of us are still in the dining hall."

"I'll come right over. I've got the results for you."

"The blood sample?" Walker asked.

"Yeah, and the fingerprints too. They came back almost simultaneously. I'll be right there."

Dalton arrived less than five minutes later. He was carrying a handful of papers, which he placed on the table in front of him as he sat down. He started right in.

"There were only two sets of prints: James Chambers' and Tom Chambers'."

Munoz jumped in. "Tom Chambers? He's been dead for nearly a year. How is that possible?"

Dalton nodded. "When I agreed to take this job, one of the requirements was that I have at least some rudimentary training in forensics. I'm not an expert by any stretch of the imagination, but I remember being told that latent prints, especially those taken from porous material, like paper or leather, can easily last a year or more."

"Really? I wouldn't have guessed that," said Munoz.

Walker entered the conversation. "So does that mean that *both* brothers were in the criminal database?"

"No, James Chambers was fingerprinted a number of years ago. Evidently, he was going to volunteer with some organization, and they required a criminal background check, which meant he had to be fingerprinted."

"What about Tom Chambers?" asked Walker.

"He's a different story. He was arrested multiple times and served three years out West for possession of a controlled substance with intent to distribute."

Walker looked surprised. "He only got three years for that, even after multiple arrests?"

"Yeah, I don't know what the story is there."

At that point, Stansky opened his laptop and said, "Let me see what I can find out."

Munoz brought them back on track. "What about the blood on the bandage. Does it belong to Sam Daniels?"

Dalton shook his head. "No. It's Tom Chambers' blood."

Walker looked stunned. "*Tom* Chambers. Don't tell me you can get DNA from dried blood after a year's time."

Chuck Dalton hesitated briefly and then exclaimed, "Technically, it's possible. But there's no way that bandage is a year old, and neither is the bloodstain."

Sam Daniels' eyes had been open for several hours, but it would be incorrect to say that she was awake. Psychologists define this state of consciousness as dissociative fugue. It's characterized by amnesia, confusion regarding one's personal identity and surroundings. It's usually triggered by extreme physical and emotional trauma, especially when the precipitating event is similar to an event from the victim's past.

There is no scientific evidence to support the notion that individuals can force themselves into a fugue state. And even if that were possible, Sam Daniels couldn't have intentionally done it to herself. She had never even heard of dissociative fugue.

But somewhere in the deep recesses of her mind, it felt like a blessing.

Given a choice, Sam would have certainly opted for this zombie-like state as opposed to the anxiety and panic that had overtaken every neuron of her being for the last several days.

But whatever memories Sam had of the events that had brought her to this place were gone, at least for the time being. The chain that bound her to the wall, the cooler, the bedpan—she just accepted them as part of her current reality, and she didn't question anything about them.

For the first time in days, Sam was at peace. But this state of relative serenity came at a price. She was as much a prisoner of her own mind as she was a physical prisoner chained to a wall. And for as long as she was trapped in this fugue state, the outside world would cease to exist.

Chapter Twenty-Five

It took a few moments for Chuck Dalton's revelation to sink in, and then Walker asked, "Are you saying what I think you're saying?"

Dalton nodded. "There's no doubt in my mind; Tom Chambers is definitely still alive."

Nobody said anything for a minute, and then Munoz looked over at Walker. "So do you think that means it was actually *James* Chambers who got killed in the accident... and then his brother took over his identity?"

Walker didn't respond immediately, seeming to mull over Munoz's idea. Then then he offered, "That would certainly make sense."

Stansky looked up from his laptop. "Especially from Tom Chambers' point of view." Stansky turned toward Dalton. "I just found the link to the same information you told us about, Chuck. Tom Chambers has at least four prior arrests, but his brother is squeaky clean," Peter said. "And we saw the painting; the brothers look like twins. It wouldn't have taken much for Tom Chambers to pretend to be his brother, especially after the accident with nobody to challenge it."

"I agree," said Walker. "That's probably what happened." Walker's face displayed a troubled expression as he continued. "But again, I'm not seeing how any of this directly connects to Sam Daniels' disappearance? Unless..."

Munoz asked, "What?"

"I've got an idea, but I'm not sure… Listen, why don't we get all the files then head back to the conference room and see what we can piece together?" He turned to look at Dalton. "Is that okay, Chuck?"

"Of course."

"And thanks for all your efforts with the forensics."

"Glad to help, but it sounds like all I've actually done is complicate things."

Walker smiled. "This investigation has been strange from the beginning. Nothing's been easy. We've just got to figure out how everything's connected. We'll get there."

Twenty minutes later, every piece of paper related to the case was spread out across the conference room table. Stansky had gone directly to the conference room from the dining hall and had been using his laptop to try to get more information about Tom Chambers. Nothing he found contradicted the theory that Tom Chambers had assumed his brother's identity.

At Walker's urging, Stansky recapped his database search.

"Tom Chambers lived out in the Seattle area for a number of years. He was arrested four times, all for possession. He pleaded down to misdemeanors on the first three, but the fourth one involved intent to distribute, just like Chuck Dalton told us.

"He served three years, and then it looks like he was paroled because his brother stepped in and vouched for him. As the proprietor of the Church of Universal Redemption, James Chambers probably had enough status to pull that off. So Tom Chambers was paroled about a year ago. There's no record of any trouble with the law after his parole, and then he's listed as deceased in August of last year."

"Which we now know isn't true," said Walker. "As we've been thinking, with his brother dead, it would've been easy for him to assume his identity."

Munoz appeared pensive and then offered, "I wonder what we're dealing with here. I realize Tom Chambers is no Boy Scout, but... his brother vouches for him, takes him in, and then when the brother gets killed, he takes over his identity in a heartbeat. Maybe he's just an opportunist, but..." Munoz's didn't finish the sentence.

Walker spoke again. "I'm not sure we'll actually know what happened until we find this guy—whoever he is. What's got me concerned now is what I started to talk about in the dining hall and also what you just said, Dave. If we assume Sam was at the ranch, which I believe she was, and she came face-to-face with Tom Chambers and realized he wasn't JT—and Tom Chambers could have easily picked up on that—what would he have done in order to protect his secret?"

The ramifications of Walker's possible scenario hung in the air for a few moments. Nobody was willing to postulate on what it might mean for Sam Daniels.

Eventually, Walker said, "We've got to figure out a way to get the judge to allow us to do a full search of the property."

"I agree," offered Munoz. "But I'm not sure the way to do that is to tell the judge about the identity switch. That definitely constitutes a crime, and she's liable to order us off the property entirely."

"You could be right," Walker agreed. "But then where does that leave us?"

"Right where we were I'm afraid," said Munoz.

Walker looked over toward Stansky. "Any ideas, Peter?"

"No, I'm sorry. Obviously, there's nothing on Tom Chambers after he was declared deceased. I can keep looking, but at this point, I'm not even sure what I'm looking for."

"All right," said Walker, clearly frustrated. "Let's hang in here for a while and see if anything comes to us. If not, we'll start fresh in the morning at the ranch. We'll have to give it another shot."

"What about Professor Mason?" asked Munoz.

"I forgot about that," Walker said. "I don't think it'll hurt to have him there. Maybe he'll find something. But I'm not going to tell him about the DNA results. Sam's got to be our number-one priority. We can notify whoever we need to about the identity issue later on."

None of the three investigators slept particularly well. They were all in the dining hall before 7:00 a.m. and on the road by 7:30. Although Milo, Morelli, and Travis were basically doing little more than guard duty at the front gate of the ranch, they all volunteered to help out again.

At 8:15, Walker, Munoz, and Stansky started another search of the main house, but by 8:35, they were repeating everything they'd already done twice before.

Walker's phone buzzed at 8:45. It was Morelli. "The professor just showed up. Do you want me to bring him in, or do you want to come get him?"

"You can bring him in, thanks."

All three of the investigators were waiting on the porch as Morelli pulled up with Professor Mason. As he exited the car, the professor said, "Good morning, gentlemen." He looked around and added. "This brings back some memories."

They all shook hands and then went inside. After a moment, Walker asked, "Where would you like to begin, Professor?"

"Maybe in the corner over there to the left, and then I'll go clockwise. I tend to be methodical about things."

Walker responded, "That's fine, and there's no rush. So just take your time."

Professor Mason didn't say very much for the first few minutes until he found himself in front of the fireplace. He gestured to the portrait above it and smiled.

"This was a favorite of Lemuel's. I think it was done six or seven years ago, maybe for his sixtieth birthday. The boys would have been in their late twenties, early thirties. That looks about right, don't you think?"

It was obvious that it was a rhetorical question so none of the three investigators responded. A moment later, Professor Mason continued. "It's a good likeness of them all. In person, the boys do look very much alike, although I didn't see Tom all that often."

Walker stole a glance at Munoz but didn't say anything. A moment later, the professor looked more intently at the portrait and then turned and headed back toward the desk in the corner. After a minute he returned and said, "That's strange. Where's the rock?"

"What rock?" asked Walker.

The professor pointed at the portrait again. "See the white rock on the desk in front of Lemuel?"

Walker moved closer, as did Munoz and Stansky, although there was no need. The rock was clearly visible, even from a distance.

The professor continued, "That rock is actually limestone from Dover, England. You know, from the White Cliffs of Dover. Supposedly, Josiah Pendleton brought it with him in 1640. Lemuel always kept it on his desk. I suppose it's possible JT could have put it away after Lemuel died, but that seems doubtful. He knew how much it meant to his father." The professor looked toward Walker. "And you didn't find it anywhere when you were searching?"

"No, but we haven't been able to do a complete search. We've had to limit ourselves to what's in plain sight. So if he put it away someplace, we wouldn't necessarily know."

"Still, it does seem strange," the professor repeated.

For the next twenty minutes, the professor's travels around the large room didn't provide anything of substance. And then he reached the room that held the electronic equipment.

"What's this?" he asked.

Peter Stansky explained about the surveillance feed, the jamming device, and the computers.

The professor shook his head. "First the limestone rock is missing and now this. Lemuel certainly wouldn't have approved."

Walker was about to ask what the professor meant, but he continued. "This used to be a meditation room. Lemuel wanted a quiet space with no windows and no distractions. And now it's been turned into a place to... spy on people." He paused. "I have to tell you, this is all very surprising. I wouldn't expect anything like this from JT. It's totally out of character."

Walker again looked at Munoz and gave a nearly imperceptible shake of his head. The three investigators had thoroughly discussed whether to tell anyone about the DNA results and agreed that at this point it wouldn't further the investigation to do so. Nevertheless, it was difficult not to explain to the professor what they believed was going on.

Several minutes later, Professor Mason was standing in front of the large floor-to-ceiling windows on the far right side of the room. And while it was impossible to see any of the other buildings from that vantage point, the expansive view did help the professor to recall what else was on the property.

"There are four cabins about a quarter of a mile away over to the left. As I mentioned to you yesterday, those were used for the girls who came from Ohio. I doubt they needed them all at the same time, but maybe. They're heated, and they have bathrooms and showers. Given the rural setting here, they were actually fairly modern."

Munoz interjected, "Were you ever here when the girls were here, or later when the runaways came?"

"No, or at least I don't think so. Lemuel wouldn't have permitted anyone to interact with the girls other than church members or his own family, and that pretty much meant only JT."

After a few more questions from Walker and Munoz, the professor went on to describe the other buildings on the property.

"There's a chapel that dates back to the 1650's about a hundred yards or so from the cabins. Of course, it's been renovated a number of times, but some of the foundation is the original stone. And in a small section in the back, there are a couple of original pews. I tried to sit in them once, but I could barely fit. They were built for men and women who were much smaller. The average height for a man back then was five-three or five-four.

"Anyway, although Lemuel still called it a chapel, it was really more like a meditation center, just like that room over there. To my knowledge, they never held any religious services in the chapel.

"There's also a cemetery next to the chapel. Josiah Pendleton is buried there, as well as his whole family and most of the congregants who came here in 1640. Lemuel's also buried there. All of them have very simple stones; nothing about the Pendleton or the Chambers families has ever been ostentatious."

Walker then asked, "What about Tom Chambers? Is he buried there?"

"I don't know for sure, but I don't think so. As I mentioned to you yesterday, I didn't find out about Tom's death until long after the accident, so I never went to the service. But as I recall, I was told that he was cremated. Come to think of it, that surprised me as well. Lemuel didn't believe in cremation. I would've thought JT would have respected his father's beliefs in that regard." He paused. "But a lot of things JT seems to have done over the past year strike me as odd."

Another moment passed and then the professor spoke again. "As we were driving in, I could see the roof of the barn. I believe that's the only other building on the ranch property. I never had much occasion to be in there. I think they've always kept horses." He smiled. "Which I guess is to be expected, given that it's a ranch, even if it's located in Maine. But I don't ride myself.

"I think actually the only time I was in the barn was when Lemuel offered to take me to look at the rest of the property. They used part of the barn as a garage. He had an all-wheel-drive Jeep as I recall. I remember thinking that he was going to open up some more about the Underground Railroad, maybe even show me some of the places where the slaves crossed into Canada. But if that was his intention, he must've changed his mind, because we only ventured a few hundred yards away from the barn. We did get out of the Jeep, and we talked for a while, but he didn't show me anything else."

All three of the investigators found the professor's descriptions interesting, but none of them could see how they provided any information that would get them closer to finding Sam Daniels.

Fifteen minutes later, after the professor had looked at the bedrooms in the back of the main house and came up empty, it was time to leave.

Munoz offered to drive the professor back to the front gate, and the four men stepped out onto the porch.

As the professor reached the bottom of the steps, he turned and said, "I wish I could've been of more assistance, Agent Walker. But there wasn't anything inside that made a connection for me."

"We appreciate your willingness to help," said Walker.

"What will you do now?"

"That's a good question. I'm not sure."

The professor nodded with a resigned expression on his face. As he reached for the passenger side door handle, a gust of wind swirled around the porch area, and he had to shield his face. As he looked down, he saw that a piece of paper had blown up against his lower leg. He bent over and picked it up. It was blank except for the type at the bottom.

"Well, isn't this a coincidence. I wonder where this came from. I used to use this text in one of my freshman courses. I think they use it in high schools now." The professor then read the words on the bottom of the page out loud. "The Global Community."

Walker's eyes grew wide. "What did you say?"

"This page is from a textbook I used to use."

"Can I see it?" asked Walker.

The professor handed it to him. As soon as Walker looked at the page, he knew where he had seen it before. It was from the textbook that was used in Maddie's World Cultures course. The same course Sam Daniels was taking.

Chapter Twenty-Six

Walker stared at the textbook page in his hand. The word "coincidence" the professor had just used echoed in Walker's head. Was that all this was - a huge coincidence? As quickly as that thought entered his mind, Walker dismissed it. The page he was holding had come from Sam Daniels' textbook. He was sure of it.

Walker started to ask himself how it had come to be torn out. What were the circumstances...and why? But those questions faded in an instant, replaced with a more critical one: Would this be enough to convince the judge?

Munoz interrupted Walker's thoughts. "Are you thinking that's from the same textbook you were telling me about back at Sam's apartment?"

Walker looked up from the page and answered definitively. "Yes."

Munoz read Walker's mind. "So you don't think there's any chance it's just a coincidence?"

"No, I don't." He extracted his phone from his pocket and added, "Let's hope the judge agrees."

The professor looked puzzled. "I don't understand. What's so significant about that piece of paper?"

As Walker was finding the judge's number, he gestured to Munoz to explain things to Mason.

"The girl we're looking for is Samantha Daniels; she goes by the nickname Sam. She's taking a course, World Cultures, with Agent Walker's daughter. That's what triggered this whole thing. She missed her final exam, which we came to find out was very much out of character for her. Anyway, when we searched her apartment, some of her textbooks were there, but not the one for World Cultures. We think she probably brought it with her to study for the exam that was scheduled for the next day—the one that she didn't show up for."

The professor still didn't seem to have put it all together, but he said, "As I said, they do use that textbook in high schools now. So I guess it's possible that it belonged to that girl... Sam you said?" The professor hesitated for a moment and then continued. "Why do you...?"

Before he could finish asking the question, he could see that Walker's call had connected; the professor went silent. Munoz moved closer to Walker.

"Hello, Agent Walker. How did you make out with the fingerprints and the DNA?"

It took a moment for Walker to respond. He wasn't ready to go down that road just yet unless he had to.

"Actually, we have another development that may be more critical."

"What's that?" the judge asked.

Walker explained about the page from the textbook and concluded with, "This is just too big a coincidence for it not to mean that Sam Daniels was on the property here."

The judge was quiet for a few moments. Eventually, she said, "You don't strike me as the type of person who would fabricate evidence, Agent Walker. But you must admit that this is very strange, not to mention convenient."

"I wouldn't argue with that. But I'm not the one who found the page."

"Who was it? Don't tell me it was Detective Munoz."

Walker was starting to take offense at the judge's implication, but he knew any indignation in his voice would not serve him well. He calmly responded, "No, it was actually someone who knows the Chambers family. We contacted him to see if he knew how to get in touch with... James Chambers."

"Who is this person?"

"A Professor Mason..."

"Randolph Mason?" Judge Lister interrupted.

"You know him?"

"Yes, we've been on a number of committees together. And he's the one who found the page?"

Walker liked where this was going. "Yes, and he's right here."

"You mean he's there with you?"

"Yes."

"Put him on, please," the judge said.

Professor Mason's distance from Walker had prevented him from hearing anything other than Walker's side of the conversation. Walker approached the professor and held out the phone.

"It's Judge Lister. She wants to talk to you."

The professor accepted the phone, put it to his ear, and said, "Marion is that you? It's Randolph Mason." The professor and the judge spent about a minute catching up, and then he answered a number of her questions. Five minutes later, she asked to speak to Walker again.

Walker took the phone back and just as he brought it up to the side of his head he heard, "You've got your telephonic warrant, Agent Walker. Do whatever you need to do. And good luck." Before he could thank her, the judge disconnected the call.

Walker stood motionless for the briefest of moments and closed his eyes as he expelled a quick breath. Munoz knew what was coming; he had seen it a number of times before, but it never ceased to amaze him. Walker's focus became laser-like. He barked out commands with a combination of authority and precision that left little doubt about who was in charge. But the commands had a logic and a sense of purpose to them. So much so that no one on the receiving end thought about calling them into question.

"Professor, for the time being, I'd like you to go back inside and wait until we coordinate our next steps." Walker turned to Stansky. "Peter, whatever you couldn't do with the computers and the surveillance system is now fair game. Do whatever you need to."

Walker still had his phone in his hand. He found the number he was looking for and called out to the front gate.

"Agent Morelli, its Craig Walker. We just got all the restrictions on the warrant lifted to do a full search of the property. I'd like you and Agent Travis to come up to the main house. I'll fill you in on what I want you to do as soon as you get here. Have Milo remain out there at the gate. Tell him that if anyone shows up to give us a call."

Five minutes later, Morelli and Travis arrived at the main house. Walker didn't waste any time.

"We've already searched everything that's in plain sight. I'd like the two of you to look inside all the closets, drawers—any place where something could be hidden. I assume you still have a couple of evidence kits in the trunk, right?"

They both replied, "Yeah."

"Good. Bag anything that might belong to the girl who's missing—cell phone, purse, travel bag, anything like that. Also, we're still trying to locate this Chambers guy. So anything with an address or phone number on it, bag it too. Dave and I are going to check out the rest of the property. If you come across something you think is important, call me immediately."

Morelli nodded, and said, "Okay. We'll get started right away."

Walker turned to the professor who was sitting on one of the leather couches. "Professor, if you're up to it, I'd like you to come with us. You know the property better than anyone. But I'm not sure what we're going to find out there, and although I don't think you'd be in any danger, it's still up to you."

"I'd very much like to help, Agent Walker."

"Excellent." Walker caught Munoz's eye. "All set, Dave?"

"Let's go."

Munoz drove with Walker in the passenger seat and the professor in the back. They stayed on the dirt road as the professor directed them where to go. The road wound around some trees, and then the first of the cabins came into view.

Walker had the professor remain in the car until he and Munoz were sure it was safe to go inside. The cabin smelled musty, and it was obvious that no one had used it in months, if not longer. There was a layer of dust throughout, which had not been disturbed. The six wooden bed frames had no mattresses on them, and the three dressers looked to be in disrepair. Walker and Munoz checked out the bathroom and shower areas, but there was nothing to see of any importance. After a few more minutes, they decided to move on to the second cabin.

Walker and Munoz repeated the procedure of going in first and then calling the professor to join them. At first glance, the inside of the second cabin looked exactly like the first one, but then Munoz noticed something.

"Look at that, Craig. That bed has been moved. You can see where the front of it was dragged through the dust."

Munoz moved closer. Walker and the professor followed. Munoz bent down to get a closer look, and then he saw something.

"There are some letters here carved into the floor; they look like initials. I think it's an 'S' and a 'D.'" Munoz turned his head upward to face Walker. "Sam Daniels."

Walker got on his knees to take a look. "Those initials have been there a while. They're not fresh."

"Probably not, but we know Sam was here a year ago. It would make sense that if she came back she'd come to the place where she had stayed. Maybe it's a reach, but..."

"No," said Walker. "I don't think it is. But it still begs the question: If she was here, where did she go?"

No one had an answer for that.

After a moment Munoz asked, "Do you want me to get an evidence kit out of the car and try to lift some prints?"

Walker responded, "No, I'd rather finish the search of the rest of the property first. If need be, we can do that later."

The third cabin closely resembled the first one; it looked as if no one had been inside for a long time. And initially, Walker and Munoz thought the same was true for the fourth, but then they went into the bathroom area. There were signs that someone had recently been in there. There were what appeared to be footprints in the dust, although they weren't sufficiently defined for Walker and Munoz to be certain that's what they were. There also appeared to be scraps of food and drops of water next to a pipe that had perceptible scratches on it.

After taking in the entire scene, Walker said, "I'm not sure what all this means. I think it's very likely that Sam was in the other cabin where we discovered her initials, but then why come to this one?"

Again, no one had an answer.

Walker looked over at the professor. "Where to now?"

"The chapel is the closest."

"Okay, let's head there."

If the cabins had remained unoccupied for the past several months, it was obvious that the chapel had not been used even longer than that. It took Walker and Munoz less than ten minutes to search the entire building. And they found nothing of consequence.

Although the barn was clearly visible directly across what could best be described as a meadow, the dirt road that led there made a semicircle around the large expanse.

Shortly after they returned to the car, the professor said, "Do you want to go to the main part of the barn where the horses are kept, or the back of the barn where they keep the cars?"

Walker answered, "Where the horses are kept."

"Okay, then we can stay left on this road. The right fork goes around back."

There may have been a time when horses occupied stalls in the barn, but it wasn't any time in the recent past. Walker and Munoz were in and out in less than ten minutes. Then they drove around back to look at what the Chambers family used as their garage.

Instead of an overhead garage door that would be found on most houses, the top of the door of this structure slid along a track fifteen feet off the ground. As they had done before entering each building, Walker and Munoz gave a quick scan to make sure there was no danger before they signaled to the professor that he could exit the car and come inside.

Again, however, there was very little to see. There were no cars inside, although it was clear that the barn had been used quite recently.

Walker continued to glance at the interior, and then he said, "It probably makes sense that there's no car inside here. We've suspected for the last few days that... Mr. Chambers wasn't here at the ranch."

The professor looked puzzled by Walker's use of the term "Mr. Chambers," but didn't say anything. After another moment, however, he did ask, "What would you like to do now, Agent Walker?"

"I guess we should take a look at the rest of the property, but there are no more buildings, right?"

"That's correct."

"Okay, let's head out, but I don't think we should spend a lot of time out there, unless we find something useful. If not, we'll go back to the two cabins with the evidence kits and bag whatever we can," Walker said. "I'm hoping that Morelli and Travis found something, or maybe Peter."

The dirt road was much bumpier on this part of the ranch, and once again as they headed north, Munoz had to steer the car around a copse of very tall pine trees. He continued to drive very slowly so that both he and Walker could scan both sides of the road. Just before they passed the last of the pine trees, Munoz slowed the car even more and then brought it to complete stop. He opened his window and pointed skyward.

"Is that what I think it is?"

Walker strained to see what he was pointing at, as Munoz continued. "It looks like a cell tower blending in with the trees."

Munoz and Walker got out of the car, and Munoz again pointed to the same spot. This time Walker could see it clearly.

"I think you're right. I only see two dishes, though."

"It's probably just for the ranch. Didn't Peter say something about there had to be one of these close by?"

"Yes, he did." Walker spoke to the professor through the driver's side window. "Did you know that was there, Professor?"

"No, I don't think Lemuel even had a cell phone. As far as I know, he always used a landline. That's probably new."

"All right," said Walker. "Let's take a look at the rest of the property."

It was less than a minute after they started driving again that an SUV came into view. Walker saw it first.

"Look at that!"

Munoz slowed to a stop. "I don't see anybody inside, but I think it might have privacy glass."

"No, I can't see anybody either, but you might be right about the glass," Walker said. "Ease up next to it."

Munoz drove forward slowly and brought the car to a stop once they were alongside the SUV.

Walker turned to the professor and asked, "Do you know whose car that is?"

"It's not the one Lemuel had. That was a Jeep. I don't know what kind of car JT drives."

"Okay, Dave and I are going to get out and look around. I don't want you getting out of the car until we have a chance to secure the area. Crack open a window, but I want all the doors to stay locked. If you see anything, or need us for some reason, beep the horn. You can reach it from there, right?"

"Yes. I can get to it between the seats."

"Are you okay with everything I've said?" Walker asked.

"Yes, I understand."

A minute later, Walker and Munoz were checking out the Mercedes SUV. They announced themselves, but there was no response. They couldn't see into the front seat, but none of the doors were locked. Munoz carefully opened the driver's side door and found the keys still in the ignition. He reached in and removed them, expelled a mouthful of air, and closed his eyes for a second. He strained to see into the rear of the SUV.

Walker read Munoz's mind as he moved to the back of the vehicle. He paused for a moment before he double clicked the button to open the rear hatch. Neither one of them took a breath as the hatch slowly opened. A few seconds later, it became obvious that there was nothing inside the storage area.

Walker took a moment to get his equilibrium back and then said, "What's this car doing out here anyway? It's like it's been abandoned."

Munoz shook his head.

"All right, let's spread out. I'm going to go off to the left; you go off to the right. I'm not sure what we're looking for. Hopefully, we'll know it when we see it."

The professor watched the two investigators intently as they searched the SUV and then when they headed out away from where the two vehicles were parked. He tried to remember what the rest of the ranch looked like when Lemuel had brought him out here, but he couldn't, although he felt certain that this was almost the exact spot where Lemuel had stopped the Jeep and gotten out.

He squinted to see if he could make out anything that looked familiar, some landmark, but nothing he saw jogged his memory. A few seconds passed and then off to the left beyond where Walker was, the professor noticed something—something he had definitely seen before. But not here, not at the ranch. But then where? A moment later it came to him.

He hesitated, trying to decide whether it was relevant to what was going on. A few seconds later he concluded that Walker and Munoz should make that determination. Professor Mason pushed himself forward and slammed his hand down on the horn and then again.

Walker and Munoz both stopped in their tracks, turned, and ran back to the car.

The sound of the horn echoed through the pine trees, and the reverberation found its way into the tunnel. Although Sam remained in a fugue state, unaware of anything happening around her, at the sound of the second horn blast, her eyes had fluttered briefly. It hadn't awakened her, but something in her brain had shifted.

Now parts of her brain were at war. One part wanted to protect itself, to protect her, and stay in a virtually unconscious state. But the other part, the self-preservation part, understood that the sound it heard might be a chance to be rescued.

The self-preservation part of Sam's brain won out.

Not even aware of what she was doing or why, Sam reached for the metal bedpan, turned it over, and began to hit it with the chain attached to her wrist. It was a rhythmic banging, not a haphazard one. After a few minutes it exhausted her, but she didn't stop; she continued hitting the chain against the bedpan like some sort of metallic mantra.

The professor stayed inside the car until Walker and Munoz got within a few yards. As he opened the back door to get out, he heard Walker yell, "What happened? What's the matter?"

"There's a tunnel there. I'm sure of it."

"What are you talking about?" asked Walker.

The professor was now out of the car and pointing. "See the raised topography, the mound going straight out right past where you were? I've seen the exact same thing in Brunswick and Topsham. They dug tunnels there to smuggle the slaves into Canada. This is the same spot Lemuel brought me to. I don't know why he changed his mind, but I think he probably intended to at least tell me about the tunnel, if not show me."

The professor looked temporarily embarrassed. "I'm sorry; I got so excited about the tunnel... I just thought you should know, but... It probably doesn't mean anything."

Walker was about to respond when Munoz said, "You hear that?"

Everyone got quiet, and then Walker said, "Like a banging? Yeah, I do. Where's it coming from?"

"I'm not sure."

The professor joined in. "My ears probably aren't as good as yours, but I think it's coming from over to the left near where you were looking, Agent Walker."

All three kept listening, and then Walker asked, "These tunnels that you've seen in Brunswick—and where else did you say?"

"Topsham."

"Topsham. How do you get inside?"

"There was some sort of trapdoor or hatch, something like that," the professor said.

Walker looked over at Munoz. "We've got an abandoned SUV here. I'm wondering if Chambers left it here and used the tunnel."

"Makes sense." Munoz turned toward the professor. "If these tunnels were constructed before the Civil War, that's over a hundred and fifty years ago. Are they safe?"

"The ones in Brunswick and Topsham have been refurbished and preserved, but they were well built to begin with."

Walker said, "Let's see if we can find the entrance. That sound could be some kind of machine or something, but I'll bet it's coming from inside the tunnel."

Munoz asked, "Do you think Sam could have gone with Chambers into the tunnel, maybe heading into Canada?"

"I don't know what to think."

Over the next several minutes, the banging became more intermittent, making it more difficult for Walker and Munoz to pinpoint the sound's exact location. But eventually they spotted the wooden door that led to the tunnel. Walker lifted it and listened intently. A few seconds later, the banging resumed louder than before.

As the sound began to emanate from the open door, so did a pungent odor, which to both Walker and Munoz smelled like decay. Neither man acknowledged his thoughts to the other, not wanting to contemplate what that might mean.

Before descending into the tunnel, Walker took out his phone and turned it on to help navigate the steps as he climbed down. Munoz followed.

At the bottom of the steps as Walker looked into the darkness, he could make out a faint light in the distance. He waited until Munoz was next to him and then they moved forward very slowly, hunching over in the cramped space. The banging wasn't as rhythmic now, and it had slowed to every nine or ten seconds. But it was obvious that they were getting closer to the source.

Walker debated whether to call out, but decided against it.

Another two minutes went by as they half-walked, half-shuffled toward the faint light. By the time they had almost reached it, the banging had ceased. But a split second later, it started up again, and Walker and Munoz looked to their right. At first they couldn't be sure what they were seeing. But as their eyes adjusted, they could make out a human form smashing a chain against some other metal object.

Although neither Walker nor Munoz could see her face, they had no doubt that they had found Samantha Daniels. And she was alive.

Chapter Twenty-Seven

Walker put his phone away and picked up the LED lamp. He moved cautiously toward the huddled human form that was half-lying, half-sitting against the opposite wall, and whispered quietly, "Sam. Sam."

The form raised its head just enough so that the light from the lamp illuminated a girl's face, and Walker and Munoz could confirm that it was indeed Sam Daniels. Walker took another small step, not sure if Sam was in shock, and not wanting her to mistake him for her captor.

"Sam, are you all right? Can you talk?"

There was no response.

Walker then shone the light on the red cooler and the metal bedpan that Sam had dropped, and which was now lying next to her.

"What do you make of that?" Walker asked.

Munoz shook his head. "I have no idea."

Walker then turned the light toward the ring attached to the wall and moved it along the chain to the manacle around Sam's wrist.

"My God, who does something like this to another human being?" He looked over at Munoz. "I'm going to stay with her. You go get the bolt cutters. But as soon as you get out of the tunnel, call 911. Get an ambulance out here as quickly as you can."

Munoz took out his phone and turned it on to help guide him out of the tunnel. As he was just about to leave, Sam grunted something, although neither he nor Walker could make out what it was. Sam repeated it, this time a little louder, and then a third time, louder still. Munoz thought he understood.

"I think she's saying 'Not JT. Not JT.'"

"I think you're right," Walker said.

"Okay, I'm going."

All the way out of the tunnel, Munoz could hear Sam's chant getting louder and louder: "Not JT. Not JT." She had replaced the metallic mantra with this new one.

As soon as Munoz emerged from the tunnel, he held up his phone, checked for a signal, and then hit 911. After two rings, the dispatcher picked up.

"This is the 911 operator. What is your emergency?"

Munoz led with what he believed would get the quickest response. "This is the FBI. We're out at Redemption Ranch, and we've got a seventeen-year-old female who needs medical attention. I don't know what her condition is."

"The FBI?"

"Yes. I'm deputized Agent Dave Munoz. The Special Agent in Charge is Craig Walker."

There was a brief hesitation on the dispatcher's end, and then she said, "All right, I'll send an ambulance immediately. It's going to take ten or fifteen minutes to get to you."

"As soon as possible."

Munoz disconnected the call and ran back to where his car and the Mercedes SUV were parked. The professor got out of the car as Munoz approached.

"What's the matter?"

"We found her."

"What? Is she all right?"

"We don't know. I called for an ambulance. They're on their way."

Munoz headed to the back of the car, clicked the key fob button twice and the trunk opened. He found the bolt cutters, removed them, and shut the trunk.

"What are those for?" asked the professor.

"She's chained to the wall."

The professor's hand shot up to cover his mouth as he closed his eyes and shook his head.

"You don't think JT did this?"

Munoz answered truthfully without explanation. "No, I don't." Then he said, "Listen, Professor, here's what I need you to do." Munoz handed over his keys. "Take the car and drive back to the main house. Tell the agents there what I just told you and have them call out to the main gate to let Milo know the ambulance is coming."

"Okay, anything else?"

"Bring the car back as soon as you're done, and drive it up close to the tunnel entrance. Did you see where I came from?"

"Yes, approximately."

"That's fine. Just get as close as you can."

Munoz had a firm grip on the bolt cutters as he ran back to the tunnel entrance. He left his phone in his pocket as he maneuvered down the steps. Once he reached the bottom, he removed his phone again and used it to find his way back to Walker.

As Munoz moved closer, he could hear Sam continuing to chant, "Not JT. Not JT." It took him less than two minutes to get there, even carrying both the phone and the bolt cutters.

Walker looked up just as Munoz arrived.

"I'm not sure how badly she's hurt," said Walker. "If possible, I'd like to get her at least to the entrance, depending on whether she can walk or not. But we might have to carry her." Walker shook his head. "She's not responding to anything I say; I told her that we knew it wasn't JT who did this to her, but it was like she didn't hear me. She just kept repeating that phrase."

Munoz thought for a second. "What about if you mention Maddie?"

"It's worth a shot."

Walker hesitated for a moment, trying to figure out exactly how to approach it. After a few more seconds he said, "Sam. Sam, listen to me." He raised his voice slightly and stretched out his daughter's name. "M-a-d-d-i-e W-a-l-k-e-r sent us to find you."

A faint sign of recognition appeared on Sam's face, and she raised her head slightly to look at Walker, and then she stopped chanting.

A few seconds later she said, "Maddie?"

Walker considered moving closer, but decided to wait. "Yes, Sam. Maddie. Maddie Walker. Would you like to see her?"

Sam stared at Walker for a full ten seconds and then spoke barely above a whisper. "Yes."

"Good, Sam. That's good. I'm going to come closer to cut off those chains, all right?"

"All right."

Munoz handed Walker the bolt cutters, but he kept them behind his back, like a dentist before he administers a shot of Novocain. Sam didn't move as Walker clipped the chain first at the ring attached to the wall, and then at the wrist manacle. He thought he might have been able to cut the manacle off as well, but he wasn't sure, and he didn't want to take the chance of hurting her.

As he laid the chain down, Sam instinctively reached for the top of her shirt to cover herself. Walker then asked, "Are you okay? Can you stand up? Can you walk?"

Sam ignored the first two questions and said haltingly, "I think I can walk."

It took some effort, but ten seconds later, Sam was on her feet. Walker thought that she still appeared to be in a daze, so he kept his comments and instructions simple.

"I'm going to lead the way out, Sam. You can hold onto my shirt." Walker moved slightly to the side. "Then this other man will follow you to make sure you don't fall. Do you understand?"

Sam looked past Walker and stared at Munoz, appearing not to have been aware of his presence before. She then looked back into Walker's eyes. She appeared to be searching for something to ensure her that she could trust him.

She must have found it because she nodded her head and said, "Okay."

The LED lamp was much brighter than the light from the phones Walker and Munoz had been using. So as they moved slowly through the tunnel, the details of its construction were much more evident. The walls were made of brick for the most part, although parts of them were natural rock. And there were rings on one wall spaced about twenty feet apart. Walker wondered briefly what they could possibly be for, but his thoughts quickly moved on. The ceiling of the tunnel was arched, and in this section it was actually higher than Walker had realized. He was able to stand erect as he inched his way forward.

Initially, Sam's grip on Walker's shirt was like a vice, but eventually she loosened it. Nobody said anything until they were about ten yards from the steps leading out.

"We're almost there," assured Walker. "Do you think you can climb up the stairs?"

Sam tightened her grip on Walker's shirt as she answered. "Yes." After another five yards she asked, "Is Maddie here?"

"Soon, Sam. Soon."

The professor was waiting next to the open door as Walker emerged. He put the LED lamp down and said, "I need you to move over to the side, Professor. I don't want anything to spook the girl."

Walker then knelt down and extended his arms into the hatch door opening. Thirty seconds later, he was gently pulling Sam out of the tunnel. At that point, he was able to get a closer look at the wrist manacle, which he now saw was held in place with a small padlock. He considered trying to cut it off once Munoz brought the bolt cutters to the surface, but decided he'd have to wait to see how Sam was reacting to everything.

Once Sam was free of the tunnel opening, she stood unsteadily where she was for a moment and lifted her right hand to shield her eyes from the sun. Walker propped her up as he guided her away from the hatch door so that Munoz could get out also.

Walker was about to ask Sam a question about the wrist manacle, but he sensed that she was totally disoriented. Instead, he gently grasped one of her elbows and gestured to Munoz to do the same. Sam didn't question what was happening as Walker and Munoz eased her toward the car the professor had driven up to the tunnel's entrance.

Walker opened the back door. "Sam, why don't you lie down on the back seat, okay?"

Again, Sam didn't speak. But she followed Walker's instructions. Once she was inside, she curled up into a fetal position and closed her eyes. Munoz quietly opened the back door on the other side, sensing that a closed door might make her feel claustrophobic. Less than five minutes later, they heard sirens in the distance. If Sam heard them, she didn't react.

The professor had moved closer once Sam was in the back seat. He looked at Walker and asked, "Do you know what happened?"

"No, other than she was chained to a wall down there. She's barely coherent. We couldn't ask her much of anything."

"Detective Munoz seems to feel that JT wasn't responsible for this. Is that right?"

Walker looked over at Munoz and realized how he must've parsed his statement to the professor. Walker followed suit. "No, I don't think he was."

At that point, Munoz spoke up, but not about JT Chambers. "Maybe I should go down past the pine trees so I can show the ambulance how to get here."

Walker nodded. "Good idea."

Shortly after Munoz left, the professor asked, "Is she going to be all right?"

"I didn't see any obvious injuries, but I don't know. Certainly she's traumatized..." Walker's voice trailed off.

"Of course."

There was no more conversation between the two men for several minutes. The professor realized that anything else he might ask would probably be something Walker couldn't or wouldn't answer. And Walker had no desire to mislead the professor any further. At some point in the future, Walker would share what he knew—if possible. The professor deserved that. If it hadn't been for him, they might not have found Sam.

The sirens were much closer now, but then they stopped. Walker interpreted that to mean that the ambulance had arrived at the front gate. A few minutes later, Walker could see Munoz in the distance directing the emergency vehicle toward them.

As soon as the ambulance arrived, a young man exited from the passenger seat. Walker rushed over.

"I'm Special Agent Craig Walker with the FBI. The girl's name is Samantha Daniels; she's seventeen." Walker then pointed to his right. "She's lying down in the back of that car. I'm not sure whether she's in shock or not, but she seems disoriented. Physically, she doesn't appear to have any injuries, but I'm not sure."

The young man standing in front of Walker responded confidently. "Thank you, Agent Walker. We can handle it from here. We'll take good care of her."

Walker wasn't used to being on the sidelines, but he backed away and went to stand next to the professor in order let the emergency personnel do their jobs.

Munoz showed up a few minutes later and joined the professor and Walker. Munoz started to say something, but stopped when he spotted a sheriff's department vehicle approaching.

A male officer from the sheriff's department got out of the car, had a brief word with the ambulance driver, and then came over to where Walker, Munoz, and the professor were standing. "I'm Officer Scanlan with the Franklin County Sheriff's Department."

Walker stepped forward and offered his hand. "Agent Craig Walker with the FBI." After shaking hands, he turned slightly. "This is deputized Agent Dave Munoz and Professor Randolph Mason."

Officer Scanlan shook hands with Munoz and the professor, and then he addressed Walker again. "Didn't we speak on the phone a few days ago?"

"Yes I think we did."

"You were looking for James Chambers, right, or at least a way to contact him?"

"That's correct. We still haven't been able to do that." Walker paused, trying to decide what he should offer in the way of explanation. He went with a shortened version of the truth. "We wanted access to the ranch because we were looking for a missing girl." Walker gestured toward the car where the first responders were easing Sam Daniels out of the backseat. "Fortunately, we found her."

Officer Scanlan eyed Walker for a moment. "Should I assume that the FBI will be doing follow-up, or should the sheriff's department become involved?"

"We're not exactly sure what we're dealing with, but preliminarily, we'll take the lead on this. We'll contact you if we need your assistance. Would that be all right?"

Again, Officer Scanlan eyed Walker. "Of course," he said. "I'll just see if the emergency personnel need anything else."

"Thank you, Officer Scanlan." Walker paused. "Where will they be taking her?"

"The Eustis Medical Center. It's about ten or twelve miles from here."

As Walker looked over, he saw that Sam was now strapped to a gurney and was being loaded into the back of the ambulance. He rushed over before the doors were closed and spoke to the same attendant he had spoken to before.

"I know the straps are a necessary precaution, but she's been... restrained." Walker pointed to the wrist manacle. "Actually chained to a wall for probably the last few days. She may react to being strapped in. I just wanted you to be aware of that."

"Okay, thanks for letting me know. I'll be riding in the back with her. I can loosen the straps somewhat if it becomes necessary."

At the sound of Walker's voice, Sam turned her head. Her eyes were half closed, but she seemed to recognize Walker. She whispered, "Maddie."

Walker repeated what he had said before. "Soon, Sam... soon."

Chapter Twenty-Eight

After the ambulance and the sheriff's department vehicle pulled away, Walker returned to where Munoz and the professor were standing.

"How did she seem?" asked Munoz.

"She's still pretty nonresponsive, although I think she did recognize my voice again." Walker turned toward Professor Mason. "The fact that we found Sam Daniels in the condition that she was in changes things. The ranch is now a crime scene. I'm going to ask Detective Munoz to drive you back to the front gate to your car. You've been incredibly helpful. I don't know if we would have found Sam without your assistance, certainly not as quickly." Walker paused. "I promise I'll update you with whatever information I'm able to share, but as I said, given that this is a crime scene..."

"You don't have to say another word," the professor interrupted. "I understand completely."

"Thank you; I appreciate that." Walker then spoke to Munoz. "Why don't you drop me off at the main house before you drive the professor up to the front gate?"

"Sure," said Munoz as he moved toward the car.

The drive to the main house took only a few minutes, and as Walker was getting out of the car, the professor asked, "It's probably one of the things you can't talk about, but... if you don't think that JT was responsible for... imprisoning the girl, who do you suspect?"

"I'm afraid you're right; that isn't something I can talk about." Walker paused and then added, "At this point, Professor, we need to keep our investigation under the radar. So please don't mention any of what's gone on today to anybody else."

"Of course," the professor said. "Good-bye, Agent Walker."

"Good-bye, Professor. And I meant what I said. I'll contact you when I can."

Morelli, Travis, and Stansky heard the car pull up and were waiting anxiously just inside the door. Walker spent the next ten minutes explaining in detail everything that had transpired out at the tunnel.

"It's really unbelievable," said Travis. "Is the girl going to be all right?"

"I did see some positive signs, but it's hard to tell what kind of an impact an ordeal like that will have on her." Walker thought back to what he knew about Sam's history. "I do know this: she's a fighter. She's already been through a lot even before this."

Just as Walker finished, Munoz arrived back and entered the room.

"The professor get off okay?" asked Walker.

"Yeah, no problem."

"Good." Walker then turned back to Morelli, Travis, and Stansky. "So, any luck here?"

Morelli answered first. "Not really. Nothing stood out. We didn't find any personal items. There was no wallet, no keys, nothing like that."

Walker responded. "I guess that's not surprising. We've been assuming all along that Chambers had left the property, and obviously he'd take all those things with him. Of course, once we found the SUV with the car keys still in it, we thought he might still be here. But now it seems more likely that he drove the car out to the tunnel, left it there, and then used the tunnel to cross into

Canada. Of course, that begs the question: Why did he go to Canada in the first place, and why did he leave Sam behind?"

There was silence for a few moments, and then Walker looked over at Stansky. "How about you, Peter? Anything?"

"Actually, yes. Not as far as the computers go. There wasn't enough time for me to search through the files. If need be, I can just remove the hard drives and take them back to the training facility." Stansky's eyes lit up as he threw out the next sentence. "But... believe it or not, just before you got here I found something else in the room: a safe. It's recessed into the floor."

"A safe? How did we miss that? Show me," said Walker.

The electronics room was too small to accommodate everyone, so only Stansky and Walker went inside. Munoz stood in the doorway with Travis and Morelli right behind him.

The wheeled chair that Stansky had used to sit in front of the monitors had been moved to the side, and the plastic mat and area rug beneath it were pulled back to reveal the front door of a safe.

Walker asked, "How did you find that?"

"It was the strangest thing. One of the wheels on the chair got stuck in some sort of an indentation. It must've been either where the combination dial or the handle from the safe are recessed. When I had trouble moving the chair, I lifted up the mat and the carpet, and there it was. I didn't try to open it. I wanted to wait for you."

"Dave, can you get me a pair of gloves? I'm going see if I can open it," Walker said.

Munoz was back in under a minute and handed over the gloves. A few seconds later Walker tried the handle, but nothing happened.

"Not really a surprise." As he removed the gloves, he said, "Maybe now that we're all up to speed and with this new

232

development we should try to figure out where we go from here. Let's go back into the other room."

They all filed into the main room and sat on the leather sofas. It was obvious from their expressions that neither Travis nor Morelli were used to the agent in charge seeking this kind of input from other agents. Munoz and Stansky took it in stride, having worked with Walker before.

"It seems to me that we have a number of objectives that we need to focus on," said Walker. "Number one is finding Tom Chambers. I think we should search the rest of the property just to make sure he's not still here. I'm going to give Chuck Dalton a call and ask for some more volunteers; it's a big ranch. After the search, assuming that we don't find him, we'll send out an APB, but limit it to the Bureau... and Homeland Security in case he did go into Canada. They can keep an eye on the border crossings if he tries to come back."

Morelli looked around, seemingly hesitant to speak up. But after a moment, he asked, "What about sending the APB out to the local authorities as well, just to cover all the bases?"

"Under normal circumstances I would agree with that. But in this situation it's probably better if fewer agencies are involved. There's less chance of the media getting a hold of it. As of now, Tom Chambers doesn't know we're looking for him. If he finds out, he's liable to go into hiding, and we may never find him, especially if he's out of the country."

Morelli nodded his understanding, as Walker continued. "The second thing we need to focus on is gathering evidence and building a case against Tom Chambers. It's possible that Sam Daniels can give us most of what we need in terms of that, but at this point, we don't know if, or when, she'll be able to tell us anything. So when we search the rest of the property, we should bring evidence kits, especially for the tunnel. Speaking of which, I think that presents a bit of a problem. It was built before the Civil War. I just don't know how secure it is."

Walker looked at Morelli and Travis. "Any idea if there are any agents at the training facility with engineering backgrounds?"

Before Travis answered, he glanced at Morelli, who shook his head. "I don't have any idea. You'll have to talk to Agent Dalton."

"Okay." Walker paused. "What about opening the safe? Is there anybody who has expertise in something like that?"

Travis answered again. "I don't know, but—I realize Milo's a civilian employee—but the guy's a genius when it comes to anything mechanical. I wouldn't be surprised if he could get it open."

"Good thought. I'll run that by Chuck also."

The specific logistics of a plan were starting to come together for Walker, but before he could articulate it, Munoz asked, "Do you think you should contact the judge?"

Walker thought for a second. "Why? We don't need a warrant for anything we're intending to do; we certainly have probable cause."

"I agree, but do you think Judge Lister is going to see it that way? And not only that, but we should probably apply for a search warrant for JT Chambers' financials. If he's in the wind, he might have used a credit card or withdrawn money from someplace recently."

"That's a good point. All right, let me get her on the phone."

Walker moved to the other side of the room and tried to think about how he was going to finesse his conversation with Marion Lister. He knew that sometimes he was better off just winging it. He hoped this was one of those times. The judge answered on the third ring.

"Agent Walker, do you have some news?"

Walker got right to it. "We found the girl."

"If she all right?"

"She was chained underground for probably a week."

"Oh my God! Chained?"

"Yeah. She's on her way to the Eustis Medical Center. I'm going there shortly to check on her."

"I have to say, I admire your perseverance, Agent Walker. That girl may owe you her life."

Walker didn't bother to respond to the compliment. Instead, he seized on the opening it provided. "Obviously, since we now know that a crime has been committed, we have probable cause to expand the search even further." Walker didn't wait for an acknowledgment. "We have reason to believe that Tom Chambers, James' brother, is the actual perpetrator, and that after his brother died, he assumed his identity." Walker purposely left out the fact that he suspected that was the case even prior to his last conversation with the judge. "So, we're going to be requesting a warrant to access James Chambers' financial records."

"James Chambers or Tom Chambers?" the judge asked.

"James Chambers. As far as the law is concerned, Tom Chambers is deceased."

"What makes you think... never mind, I guess it doesn't matter." The judge paused. "All right, Agent Walker, have someone prepare the warrant, and get it to me as soon as possible. I'll sign it." The judge paused again. "I realize I haven't made things very easy for you, but hopefully the girl's going to be okay, and you'll be able to find whoever did this."

"Thank you, Your Honor."

Walker rejoined the group and began to lay out his plan.

"The judge said she'll sign the warrant for the financials. I'll call the Boston office and get the ball rolling on that." He turned to Munoz. "I'm going to use the car, Dave, to go up to the medical center. Obviously, I want to find out how Sam's doing, but I also need to explain to the hospital personnel that she's an emancipated minor. I don't know how that impacts on any medical procedures they need to perform. Plus, if she's coherent enough, I want to question her."

Walker looked over at Stansky. "Peter, can you work on the computers here for a while?"

"Sure, that's no problem."

"Good."

"While I'm in the car, I'm going to call Chuck Dalton and clear everything I need to with him. Dave, I want you to stay here and coordinate everything in case I don't get back in time."

Walker then turned to Morelli and Travis. "I'd like the two of you to go out to the main gate. One of you stay there and the other one bring Milo back here. Have him take a look at the safe and see if he thinks he can open it. If need be, one of you can drive him back to the training facility to get whatever equipment he needs. But hold off doing that until you get the okay from me. If I give you the okay, and by some chance Milo gets the safe open before I get back, bag everything carefully."

Walker paused and surveyed the faces of the other agents. "Any questions? Have I forgotten anything?" They all shook their heads. "All right then, let's get to it."

Walker was on the road less than ten minutes later. He punched in the location of the Eustis Medical Center on the car's GPS before he left and was now on the phone with the Boston office explaining about the financial warrant. They said it would be faxed to Judge Lister within an hour or two.

At about the halfway point of the trip, Walker was on the phone with Chuck Dalton, recapping everything: the tunnel, finding Sam, and the expanded warrant. He answered a few questions from Dalton, and then Walker asked about getting more volunteers and finally about utilizing Milo to open the safe.

Dalton didn't hesitate. "As soon as I hang up, I'll call Morelli and tell him to give Milo the go-ahead. And I'm sure it won't be a problem to recruit a couple more agents to help with the search."

Walker thanked him and was about to disconnect when he remembered something else.

"We could probably use someone with an engineering background as well. The tunnel seems pretty well put together, but it has to be over a hundred and fifty years old. It might be better to have someone evaluate it before anyone goes back inside."

Ten minutes later Walker was pulling into the medical center parking lot. He started to get out of the car when his phone chirped. It was Chuck Dalton again.

"Hi, Craig. We're all set. Two additional agents will be out at the ranch at two o'clock."

"That's great. Thanks, Chuck."

"Unfortunately, I wasn't able to find anyone with an engineering background."

Walker thought for a moment. "That's okay. We can hold off on the tunnel for the time being and just do the rest of the property. Listen, can you call Travis and Morelli and let them know about the additional agents coming at two and have them pass everything along to Dave Munoz?"

"Sure. How's the girl?"

"I'm just going inside now."

Walker was well aware that emergency rooms are notoriously crowded on Mondays. People bear whatever they can over the weekend before succumbing to the inevitable. And although mornings tended to be a lot worse than afternoons, he was still anticipating standing room only. To his surprise, however, the waiting area at the Eustis Medical Center was only about three-quarters full. And the intake nurse had no one standing in front of her desk.

Walker approached and waited several seconds until the nurse finished writing something and looked up.

"Can I help you?"

"There was a young woman brought in a little while ago. Her name is Samantha Daniels. I'd like to talk to whoever is treating her."

"Are you family?"

"No." Before the nurse could give her standard speech, Walker took out his credentials and said, "This is part of an FBI investigation."

The nurse stared at Walker's badge briefly, looked as if she wanted to ask a question, but didn't. Instead she offered, "Please wait here… Agent Walker. I'll be right back."

Five minutes later, the nurse returned. "Dr. Cosgrove will be out to talk with you shortly. Would you like to have a seat?"

"I'm fine here, thank you," Walker said.

It was close to ten minutes before Dr. Cosgrove appeared. He headed directly toward the intake nurse's desk, and as he got within earshot asked quietly, "Excuse me, are you Agent Walker?"

Walker had been turned around, glancing at CNN, which was on one of the TVs in the waiting room. He turned back. "Yes. Dr. Cosgrove?"

"Yes. Follow me, please. There's a small conference room back here."

Dr. Cosgrove took a seat. Walker did the same.

"May I see your credentials, please?" asked the doctor.

"Certainly."

Walker removed them and showed them to the doctor, who nodded. "This is about Samantha Daniels?"

"Yes. How is she?"

"All her vital signs are good." The doctor paused. "The ambulance attendant who brought her in said that they cut off a metal wrist manacle and that the girl had been chained. Is that correct?"

Walker wasn't sure why the doctor was asking, or why he needed to know that information, but Walker decided to go with the truth.

"That's accurate."

"The reason I ask is that she had difficulty communicating with us. It's nothing I haven't seen before: a patient goes through some traumatic event, and the body's defenses kick in and shut everything down. We have her sedated right now. Her brain needs to rest."

"I understand." Walker paused. "What's your professional opinion? Is she going to be all right?"

"Physically, aside from some raw skin in the wrist area and some dehydration, she seems in pretty good shape. We hooked her up to an IV; that's how we got the sedative into her system. Emotionally, however, it's really too early to tell." The doctor eyed Walker. "I assume, besides a genuine concern for the girl's well-being, you're asking me because you'd like to question her."

"That's true, but only when she's up to it. I know she's been through a lot."

"I wish I could give you a specific timetable, but I can't," the doctor said.

Walker took out one of his cards and handed it to the doctor.

"My cell number is there. If anything changes, please call me day or night."

"Of course."

Walker was about to leave when he thought of something. "There's a somewhat unusual circumstance involving Sam...

Samantha. She's an emancipated minor. Are you familiar with what that is?"

"Actually, I am." Dr. Cosgrove seemed to anticipate where Walker was going with this. "Are you concerned about her health insurance or permission to do medical procedures?"

"Both, I guess, although I hadn't really thought about the insurance aspect."

"Just mention the girl's emancipated minor status to JoAnne, the intake nurse. We've dealt with this before; it'll be fine."

Walker stood, shook hands with the doctor, and said, "Thank you, Dr. Cosgrove. I'll check in periodically to see how she's doing. And as I said, please call if anything changes."

"I will."

As they headed out of the conference room, the doctor said, "I just remembered something. It may not mean anything, but as I told you, Samantha didn't really say anything when she first came in. But as I started to treat her, a couple of times it sounded like she said a name. It sounded like 'Maddie.' Does that mean anything to you?"

Walker smiled. "Actually, it does." He decided not to elaborate, and the doctor didn't ask.

Hearing Maddie's name made Walker realize that he should probably let his daughter know what was going on. He left the emergency room area and headed out to the parking lot. As soon as he got into the car, he took out his phone, but hesitated punching in a number. A few moments passed, and then he decided to call his wife. He knew that she was at work and might not be able to answer, but he tried anyway.

The phone rang five times, and Walker was sure it was about to go to voice mail when Cheryl picked up.

"Hi. Sorry I didn't answer right away; I was getting lunch in the cafeteria, and I was just in the middle of paying. How're things going?"

Walker told Cheryl everything, something he had rarely done in his twenty years with the Bureau. But this case had touched his family; it had blurred the lines between his personal emotions and his professional responsibility.

After Cheryl asked a number of questions and Walker answered them, he said, "I have to get back up to the ranch. I called you because I was hoping that you'd talk to Maddie for me. You're better at that than I am anyway. Obviously, I wouldn't mention anything about Sam being chained up. I guess just tell her that I called and that we found Sam and she seems to be okay. Say she was taken to the hospital to be checked out and that you don't know any more details than that. Oh... and that she can't tell anybody about this."

"Wow, you don't ask for much, do you? Okay, I'll try, but I'm not very good at lying to Maddie. She sees right through me," Cheryl said.

For only the second time today, Walker was able to smile. "You think she sees through you? Don't you remember that she stopped believing in Santa Claus when she was four because she asked me if he was real, and I told her 'Yes?' "

Chapter Twenty-Nine

I t was Monday afternoon, and JT Chambers was sitting in a chair in a guest bedroom in Eli Peters' house. But JT felt less like a guest than a prisoner. Eli Peters was dictating everything that JT could and couldn't do: no leaving the house, no asking any more questions about the business, and, most disturbing of all, make sure you get rid of the girl when you get back. Eli had never stopped reminding JT that he was to blame for what had happened.

"You screwed up. You're lucky I'm bailing you out of this mess. And I told you, get it squared away quickly or we're done."

JT thought it was probably an idle threat, but he couldn't be sure. On the other hand, as lucrative as the arrangement had been, maybe it was time to move on. He was tired of dealing with Eli's drama. He was tired of being pushed around.

Of course, if he was not able to get the tunnel fixed, he wouldn't have much to offer a new partner. Before JT could continue pondering his future, he heard Eli's voice coming from the bottom of the stairs.

"Hey, JT Come down here."

JT stayed where he was for a few seconds—a brief defiance of Eli's summoning. But a moment later he was reluctantly out of the chair and heading downstairs.

Eli was waiting in the living room.

"Good news. I heard from the guy who does the passports. It'll be ready on Wednesday. I'll go pick it up, and then once I get back, Josef can drive you to the border crossing."

JT tried to make himself sound grateful. "Okay, that sounds good."

Eli looked as if he were about to make a comment about JT's tepid response, but he didn't. JT decided to follow up so that Eli didn't have a chance.

"So Josef's going to take me to Saint Aurelie?"

"No, I've been thinking about that. You're probably better off going to the Jackman-Armstrong Crossing. They get a lot more traffic there; you'll be less conspicuous. If you tried to cross at Saint Aurelie, you'd probably be the only one there; it's almost always deserted. The guards have nothing better to do than to scrutinize everybody who comes through."

This is the exact opposite of what we talked about, thought JT. *Eli was probably looking to pick a fight.* JT decided not to take the bait.

"Whatever you think is best."

"Good. Then it's settled. Before you go back on Wednesday, I'll go over everything we talked about to make sure there's no... confusion about what has to be done."

It's going to be a long forty-eight hours, thought JT.

It was 1:51 p.m. when Walker pulled out of the Eustis Medical Center parking lot. He debated calling the Boston office about getting someone with an engineering background to take a look at the tunnel, but decided to hold off until after they finished searching the property.

He was going just above the speed limit and estimated he'd be at the ranch by 2:15. He called Munoz.

"Hi, Dave. I'm on my way. I should be there in twenty, twenty-five minutes."

"How's Sam doing?"

"Not much change. They've got her sedated, but the doctor seems optimistic, at least about her physical condition. I'll keep checking in with him periodically. What's going on there?"

"The other two agents haven't arrived yet, but we're expecting them any minute," Munoz said.

"I was going to say go ahead without me, but why don't you wait? As I said, I'm not that far away."

"Will do."

"How did Milo make out with the safe?"

"He's still in the electronics room checking it out. I'm not sure. I told him to be honest with us. If he doesn't think he can open it, it's all right. We'll find someone."

"Okay. What about Peter?"

"He hasn't been able to get near the computers while Milo's been in there. So I don't think he's made very much headway."

"All right, I'll see you in a bit."

Walker was just about to disconnect when he heard Munoz say, "Oh yeah, Craig, I wasn't sure if it was necessary or not, but I dusted the safe for fingerprints just in case."

"Can't hurt, although I'm sure they'll come back as belonging to Tom Chambers."

Walker pulled up to the main gate at 2:14. Milo was there. Walker exited the car and walked over to him.

When he got within a few yards Milo said, "Sorry, Agent Walker. I'm pretty good with mechanical things, but I don't have any experience opening a safe."

Walker interrupted as he attempted to put Milo at ease.

"Actually, that's probably a good thing considering that you're employed by the FBI."

Milo let out a small laugh. "I guess that's true. I think I might have been able to get it open, but I didn't want to mess things up for anybody else."

"Don't worry about it, Milo. We'll call someone in from Boston." Walker paused. "Do you mind staying out here at the gate, or would you rather have someone relieve you?"

"No, I'm fine. I have to say, I'm enjoying this—doing something different."

"Well, we appreciate it," Walker said. "Did the other agents show up yet?"

"Yes, they're inside."

As Walker came through the front door of the main house, he saw Munoz and the other agents sitting on the leather couches. They had all started to get up when they heard the door open.

Munoz called over, "Hi, Craig. Come on over and join us. I was just bringing everyone up to speed."

As Walker got closer, Munoz turned slightly to his left and said, "This is Agent Dennis Chang and Agent Justin Porter."

After handshakes all around, Walker said, "Don't let me interrupt. Continue what you were doing."

"Actually we just finished. We were waiting for you."

Walker had thought everything through on the ride back to the ranch, so his words came out easily.

"All right, let's get started then. Dave, why don't you and Agent Morelli take another look at the other buildings? I know we've already searched them, but I want to make sure we didn't miss anything. You should grab a couple of evidence kits and get whatever you can from cabins two and four."

Walker turned to Morelli. "We're pretty sure that Sam was in both of those cabins recently." Walker looked back at Munoz.

"I'd just do the basics as far as the evidence is concerned. It's not as if we don't know who did this. It's more about locking everything down."

Walker turned back to the larger group. "Agents Travis, Chang, and Porter, why don't you come with me? We're going out to the tunnel area. We need to check out the rest of the property and see what else is out there. We're not going into the tunnel itself. I'm going to call the Boston office to get somebody up here to evaluate it before anyone else goes in. I'll do that after we finish the search. I'll ask about getting the safe open too."

Peter Stansky emerged from the electronics room just as Walker finished. Walker looked over and said, "Hi, Peter. I assume you'd prefer to stay here?"

"Yeah, I think I found some files that might prove interesting, but they're encrypted. It's going to take a while. I'll need some uninterrupted time."

"Okay, you got it."

As Walker pulled up next to the Mercedes SUV, he spoke to the other three agents in the car.

"Before we start the search, let's process whatever evidence we can from the inside of the SUV."

With the four of them working, it only took ten minutes to get what they needed. Walker then led the way out to the tunnel entrance.

"As you can see, at least from here, it seems pretty well built. Dave and I felt the same when we were inside, but I don't want to take any chances.

"So here's what I'm thinking: The four of us should form a line across, about twenty yards apart. Then we should walk straight ahead until we reach the end of the property, probably a half mile or so. At that point, we'll turn around and cover the area over to the right on the way back."

"We're looking for signs that someone has been here recently: footprints, trash, tire tracks—anything like that. Call out if you find something. I'll start here on the far left; Agent Travis, you're next to me; Agent Chang, next and then Agent Porter you go to the far right. Again, about twenty yards apart."

They moved through the high grass very slowly; the first quarter-mile took nearly ten minutes. Unfortunately, their thoroughness didn't yield anything. In fact, there was nothing to indicate that any living thing had ever been on this part of the ranch.

Another five minutes passed, and then Walker noticed something that drew his attention. He had been following along next to the arched mound which he was reasonably sure was the top of the tunnel. And then about forty yards ahead of him, the mound seemed to disappear. He picked up his pace, and once he was within several yards, instead of the mound, there was a concave area where the mound should have been. He came closer, and then his eyes took in the space beyond where he was standing, and he saw that the arched mound continued again.

It took a moment, but then he realized what he was looking at: part of the tunnel had collapsed. He called to the other agents, who hurried over.

"This is just what I was concerned about." He pointed to the area in front of him. "I think part of the tunnel collapsed here. Who knows how long ago?" Walker paused and looked back toward the tunnel opening. "I'm sure it's well beyond the spot where we found the girl."

Travis asked, "How far is it to the border? Any idea?"

Walker shook his head, "No, but it can't be all that far." He pointed up ahead. "That looks like a solid wall of rock up there. I don't see how anybody could climb over that. But there must be some kind of break; otherwise, how could the tunnel go all the way across the border?" Walker paused "All right, let's finish up searching the rest of the property. If we don't find anything, I'm going to call about getting somebody up here. We've got to get back into the tunnel. For all we know Tom Chambers could have been inside when it collapsed; he could be lying in there right now."

Walker and the other three agents reached the end of the ranch property within a few seconds of each other. It was now even more obvious that the solid rock formation they had seen from a distance did in fact form a natural boundary, except for a small uphill area where the mound had diminished in size and had become flush with the ground. The four of them turned around, moved over to the left, and repeated the search procedure back to the tunnel entrance. But they didn't find anything.

Munoz and Morelli were already back inside the main house when Walker and the three other agents pulled up to the front porch. As they entered, Walker saw that Peter Stansky had joined them. And although Munoz was halfway across the room, Walker could see that he was holding something. As he got closer, he saw that it was a pair of manacles, similar to the one that had been attached to Sam Daniels' wrist.

"Where'd you find those?" asked Walker.

"In the barn," said Munoz, "in a canvas bag. It was stuffed in a corner. I didn't notice it when we were in there before."

Walker got quiet; he then closed his eyes and shook his head slightly. Before he could say anything, Munoz added, "Yeah, I know. I was thinking the same thing. It probably means that Sam Daniels wasn't the first. Nobody has these just lying around."

Everyone was silent for the next few moments, and then Walker asked, "Did you find anything else?"

Munoz answered, "No, we just lifted some prints from the two cabins we talked about. How did you make out?"

"It looks like part of the tunnel collapsed."

"Really? Where?" Munoz asked.

"Probably a little more than a hundred yards or so from where we found Sam." Walker said. "Obviously, I have no idea when it happened, but I'm certainly glad we didn't go back in."

Munoz asked, "So what are you thinking we ought to do next?"

"I was going to put out an APB on Tom Chambers, but now I want to wait until we can check out the rest of the tunnel. I—" Walker was interrupted by his phone ringing. He took it out of his pocket and saw that it was Chuck Dalton.

"It's Chuck; I'm going to take this."

Although Walker gestured that it wasn't necessary, all the other agents moved to the other side of the room to give him privacy.

"Hi, Chuck. What's up?"

"I was giving some more thought to the issue of the tunnel. You know, trying to find somebody with an engineering background."

"Funny you should bring that up," Walker interrupted. He went on to explain about the partial tunnel collapse.

After Dalton asked some additional questions, he said, "Actually, what I'm about to suggest may make even more sense, given what you just told me."

"What's that?"

"Well, as I think you're aware, one of the reasons the Bureau set up this training complex was to bring various agencies together to work more closely. We're scheduled to have some joint training with Homeland Security and some of the BEST units, even the DEA. Homeland is taking the lead on the training.

"I've had several conversations with a Commander Broadhurst from Homeland. I'm thinking that I should give him a call. I have no doubt he'd know somebody who can evaluate the tunnel. And honestly, they should probably be part of this. Especially if there have been any border breaches."

Walker knew that Chuck Dalton was right, but his gut was telling him that this wasn't necessarily a good idea. He tried to come up with some rationale to oppose it, but couldn't. He tried not to allow his misgivings to enter his voice as he responded. "That probably makes sense."

"I'm glad you see it that way. I'm going to have to work with these guys. If they found out I didn't involve them in this, it could put a strain on things right from the beginning. As soon as I hang up, I'll give Broadhurst a call. I'll get back to you after I speak with him." Dalton paused. "Oh, and Agent Morelli called and told me that Milo wasn't sure about trying to open the safe. Do you want me to ask Broadhurst about that too?"

"No, that's okay. I'm going to call the Boston office."

"Are you sure? It's no trouble."

"No, it's fine."

Walker made the call to Boston and then came back over to where the group was standing. Munoz could read Walker well enough to know that the telephone call hadn't been good news. But he didn't ask and Walker didn't offer any information, other than to say, "Chuck Dalton is trying to get someone to assess the tunnel, and I just called Boston about the safe. They're going to get back to me." Walker paused. "So I'm not sure there's anything more that we can do here today. We might as well go back to the training facility."

Walker then turned to Stansky. "Why don't you take out the hard drives and bring them with you? I assume there's nothing on the financials yet?"

"No, I wouldn't expect anything before the morning."

"Okay."

Before Stansky started to move toward the electronics room, Walker turned and addressed the four agents Chuck Dalton had provided.

"Things may be shifting in terms of the investigation," he said. "I just wanted to let you know how much we appreciate your help."

Morelli responded for the group. "We were glad to do it. If you need us for anything else, just holler."

"We will. Thanks again." Walker paused. "On the way out, tell Milo thank you as well. He can head out with you. We'll chain the gate when we leave."

ᐸᐧ❀Chapter Thirty❀ᐳ

I t took Stansky less than five minutes to remove the hard drives. He then double-checked the settings on the security camera and then the three agents drove out to the main gate.

After Walker secured it and returned to the passenger seat of the car, Munoz said, "I assume the *shift* in the investigation had to do with Chuck Dalton's phone call."

"Yeah, it did. He wants to involve Homeland Security, which probably also means BEST, and probably the DEA."

Stansky spoke up from the back seat. "Obviously I know what the DEA is, but what's BEST?"

"It stands for Border Enforcement Security Task Force. There are a number of those units around the country. They work closely with similar units in Mexico and Canada."

"It sounds like you're not thrilled with the idea of involving them," said Stansky.

"Not really, no. I think it's a distinct possibility we'll be squeezed out," Walker said. "But I understand Chuck Dalton's thinking. He has to work with all those agencies. He can't be perceived as shutting them out of something like this. This is exactly the kind of possible border situation they're trained to investigate. And, to be fair, they may be better equipped to find Chambers than we are, especially if he's fled to Canada."

Munoz glanced over at Walker. "So what's the problem then?"

Walker hesitated before responding. "Maybe there is none. I'd just like to be able to see this through to the end, even if it means taking a backseat. I just don't want to be on the outside looking in."

"You really think that's likely?" asked Munoz.

"Who knows? But you know as well as I do that Homeland has the same reputation as the Bureau: once they become involved, they take over."

Munoz looked over at Walker again and smiled. "Well, not everyone in the Bureau acts like that; maybe that's true of Homeland too."

"I wouldn't bet the mortgage," Walker replied.

"So what are you going to do?"

"Until we're told differently, I think we should continue to do everything we were planning to do. At this point, it's still our investigation." Walker turned his head slightly. "A lot of that falls on you, Peter—the hard drives, going over the financials once they come in, and processing whatever we find in the safe. When I called Boston, I asked for them to send someone up here early tomorrow. I want to get a head start first thing in the morning. Hopefully, before this Commander Broadhurst shows up."

"Who's he?" asked Munoz.

"He's from Homeland. According to what Chuck Dalton told me, he's going to be taking the lead on the investigation. That's another reason why I'm concerned about what's going to happen. This guy evidently refers to himself as *commander*, but there's no such official position like that in Homeland Security. Someone with that kind of an ego doesn't strike me as an individual willing to share much of anything. But I guess we'll find out."

There was silence in the car for the next several miles, and then Munoz said, "Can I make a suggestion?"

Walker looked over and smiled. "Don't bother; I know what you're going to say. I just needed to vent. I'm not about to let Chambers get away because of some pissing contest or because we neglected to do something," Walker said. "I know that apprehending Chambers has to be the first priority. So when we get back, we can start to put together a summary of everything we've done so far, including recommendations about what to do next. That way, even if we get pushed aside, Broadhurst and his team will have all the information they need." Walker looked over at Munoz and smiled. "Of course, none of that precludes us from getting up early tomorrow morning and continuing to investigate."

Munoz turned toward Walker. "You're doing the right thing, you know. Can I remind you of something you said to me the first time we worked together? 'You can get a lot accomplished if you don't care who gets the credit for it.'"

"You actually pay attention to what I say, huh?"

"Sometimes," Munoz said.

It was nearly four o'clock when Munoz drove up to the security gate at the training facility. The guard peered into the car and spoke to Walker. "Agent Walker, Supervising Agent Dalton left word that he'd like to see you in his office when you returned."

"Thank you. You can call and tell him I'm on my way."

After the second security gate opened to let their car pass, Walker said, "You guys can go back to your rooms if you want. I'll give you a call when I'm finished talking to Dalton. I'd like to meet up in the dining hall and start in on the investigation summary sometime later on."

"I'd just as soon go to the computer lab and continue to work on the hard drives. Just give me a call when you're ready to do the summary," said Stansky.

"That's fine. I'll call you later on."

Five minutes after that, Walker was knocking on Chuck Dalton's office door.

"Hi, Craig, come on in; sit down."

Dalton waited a moment until Walker was settled in before he spoke again. "I'm feeling badly about inviting Broadhurst in. I didn't know..."

Walker put up his hands. "Don't worry about it. I admit, it threw me off initially, but it was the right call," Walker said. "I'd still like to be part of the investigation in some capacity, but I guess that'll be up to Broadhurst."

"Yeah, it will. But thank you for saying what you did," Dalton said. "I've been feeling like a one-armed juggler. But I may have figured out a way I can help you. Were you able to get somebody from Boston to work on the safe?"

"I think so, but they haven't gotten back to me yet to confirm it."

"I didn't tell Broadhurst anything about the safe, only the tunnel. And I suggested that he not show up at the ranch until ten o'clock. That should give you enough time to get the safe open. That way when Broadhurst and his team show up, you might have something new to brief them on. It would seem the more he has to rely on your intel, the more likely it is that he'll allow you to remain involved."

Walker smiled and nodded his head. "I don't know if this is a case of great minds thinking alike; certainly I wouldn't put myself in that category. But I did ask Boston to have the safe specialist show up early so we could get a jump on things." Walker paused. "But regardless, I'll make sure we put together a summary of the investigation for Broadhurst's benefit... although, I would suspect he'll still need us to fill in some of the details."

Dalton returned the smile. "That sounds like a good plan."

There was silence for a moment, and then Walker said, "Let me ask you something. What's the story with the *commander* title?"

"I wondered about that myself, so I did a little digging. Evidently, Broadhurst was in the Navy. That's where it comes from. It's possible that it's just a holdover from that."

"That makes me feel a little better," Walker said.

Shortly after Walker left Chuck Dalton's office, he called both Munoz said Stansky and suggested that they all meet up in the dining hall around 5:30. Walker explained that he had some phone calls to make.

As soon as he was back in his room, Walker took out his phone and called the Boston office. It took a few minutes to get through, but he was eventually connected to the supervising agent he had spoken with earlier.

"Were you able to find somebody who can open the safe?" Walker asked.

"Yes. His name is Paul Rizzo. He's only been with the Bureau for two years, but he comes highly recommended. He's driving up tomorrow morning. He should be at the ranch by nine o'clock."

"That's terrific. Thank you."

Walker's next call was to the medical center. He had to wait almost ten minutes before Dr. Cosgrove came on the line.

"Hello, Agent Walker. I was just thinking about calling you. Sam woke up about fifteen minutes ago. She seems much more lucid. We're attempting to engage her in conversation, nothing overly specific, just an attempt to normalize things. I think I may have her try to sleep tonight without the sedatives."

"Thank you, Doctor. That's good news."

"My shift doesn't start until eleven o'clock tomorrow morning. I expect we'll know a lot more by then. Why don't you give me a call sometime after that tomorrow?"

"I will. Thank you again."

Walker disconnected the call, but kept the phone in his hand. He debated with himself about whether to make one more call. The debate only lasted about fifteen seconds, and then he pressed the icon for his daughter's number.

Maddie answered right away. "Hi, Dad. Did you talk to Sam? How is she? What happened?"

"Hi Sweetheart. I just spoke with the doctor. Sam's doing pretty well."

"What happened to her?"

"I can't really talk about it."

"Why not? I won't tell anybody," Maddie said.

"I know you won't." Walker hesitated, wondering if calling Maddie had been a mistake. Technically, there was nothing preventing him from telling her the truth, except the trauma it might cause her. But that was exactly what he didn't want to do and certainly not over the phone.

"I'm sorry, Maddie, I just can't. You'll have to trust me on this." He paused. "The most important thing is that it looks like Sam's going to be all right."

"I know." There was silence for a moment and then Maddie added, "I love you, Dad."

"I love you too," Walker said. "Okay, sweetheart, I have to go."

After the line went dead, Walker didn't move for another few minutes while he reflected on his conversation with his daughter. Was his need to stay involved in the investigation because of the personal connection to Maddie? He tossed that around for several minutes but couldn't come to any conclusion. He then went over to the bed, stretched out, and tried to put everything out of his head.

Before he knew it, it was 5:20 p.m. Walker went into the bathroom, splashed some water on his face, picked up his briefcase, and headed out to the dining hall.

Munoz and Stansky were already there when he arrived. The three agents found a quiet spot in the corner, although the dining hall wasn't very crowded. Walker filled them in on his conversations with Dalton, the Boston office, and Dr. Cosgrove. He left out his conversation with Maddie.

257

Stansky indicated that he thought he was getting close to figuring out the encryption.

Walker asked, "Would you rather keep working on it? Dave and I can handle the summary."

"No, I need to take a break. I'll get back to it later."

After a quick dinner, the three of them got to work on the summary. It took a couple of hours, but it was very thorough. So much so that Walker suspected anybody reading it would not require any additional input from anybody else

He acknowledged to himself that he was actually all right with that.

Chapter Thirty-One

Peter Stansky had thought he was close to getting into the encrypted files, but it was now well past midnight, and he was having trouble keeping his eyes open. He decided to try one more idea before calling it quits.

He typed in eight characters and paused for a moment with his finger above the enter button. Two seconds after his finger made contact, the laptop screen came alive, displaying dates, numbers, and even some names. As he scrolled through the file, he saw that it contained a total of ten pages, one for each month, beginning with the previous September and ending with the current month: June.

Every month had a series of dates and numbers, but only October had names. He decided to print out the entire file, preferring to study the physical pages rather than continuing to strain his eyes by staring at the laptop screen.

He shuffled through the pages until he found October. He moved his eyes down to the names he had seen. There were eight names in total, all of them seemingly those of girls or women. The date next to the names was the fourteenth, followed by the notation 3kea.

Stansky had no idea what any of that could mean. He then went back to the beginning and studied each page, but he couldn't find any pattern or notation that gave him a clue as to what he was looking at. After nearly an hour, he decided to print out two more copies of everything to give to Walker and Munoz. Maybe they'd have better luck deciphering what it meant.

Before heading back to his room, Stansky did a search in the FBI database. He pulled up Tom Chambers' history. Whoever had encrypted the files would have to have had more than a passing acquaintance with computers. This was not the work of an amateur. There was definitely a level of sophistication that the average person just didn't possess, and Tom Chambers hadn't even graduated from high school.

It took Stansky another fifteen minutes, but then he found something: Tom Chambers had been incarcerated in a penitentiary in Oregon that was known to be very progressive. Inmates were encouraged to take college-level courses that were taught by volunteer instructors from the local university. Tom Chambers had completed a computer class at the prison. And although it seemed highly unlikely to Stansky that encrypting files would be part of an introductory computer course, it may have provided Tom Chambers with enough knowledge to at least ask the right questions of someone who *was* an expert.

Stansky then thought back to the first time he had seen the surveillance equipment at the ranch, and the fact that some of the images had been deleted. Although that wouldn't require the same degree of expertise as encrypting computer files, it was still not something you picked up from reading the user's manual. It seemed certain that Tom Chambers must have had some help with both things.

It was now after 2:00 a.m. Stansky didn't know if he'd be able to sleep, but he decided he'd have to try. He did manage to get in about four hours, after which he showered and shaved; he was back in the dining hall before seven. Breakfast wouldn't be available for a while yet, but there was plenty of coffee.

Walker and Munoz showed up at 7:15. Walker saw the piles of papers on the table in front of Stansky.

"Are those the financials?"

"No, they haven't shown up yet. But I was able to get into the hard drives," Peter said.

"Anything worthwhile?"

"I'm not sure. I made copies for both you and Dave. Maybe you'll see something I missed." Stansky handed them over as he continued talking. "As you can see, each page represents a different month, but I'm not sure what the entries next to each date mean. What did strike me is the month of October." Stansky gave them a moment to find the right page. "It's the only month with anything different: a list of names. I didn't make the connection last night; I was probably too tired. But as I was sitting here this morning, it occurred to me that those might be the names of some of the runaways who were at the ranch. I don't know. What do you think?"

Neither Walker nor Munoz responded immediately; they were both still reading the list of names.

Eventually, Walker said, "You could be right about that, although even if that's true, I'm not sure what significance it has. What do you make of the 3kea next to the list?"

"I have no idea. The letters 'k,' 'f,' and 'o' appear on the other pages, but this is the only place where I found the letters 'e' and 'a.' I was thinking it's possible that the numbers on the other pages might represent dollars, but that's just a guess. I will tell you this, whatever this all means, Chambers went through a lot of trouble to hide it, and he must have had help. There's no way he did this on his own."

The three agents left for the ranch at 8 o'clock to make sure they arrived in plenty of time to meet Agent Rizzo. When they got there, Walker unlocked the chain on the gate and swung it open. As he got back in the passenger seat, Stansky's laptop chirped.

A moment later Stansky said, "This looks like the financials."

Once the three agents were inside the main house, Stansky went over to the leather couches, sat down, and began analyzing the data he had just received. Walker and Munoz went into the electronics room and moved everything out of the way so that Agent Rizzo would have easy access to the safe. They also checked to make sure the surveillance feed from the front gate was coming through. Walker had left the gate open, but it was possible that

Agent Rizzo and later Commander Broadhurst would still use the intercom. Walker wanted to be sure that he could see whom he was talking to.

As Walker and Munoz came back out into the main room, Stansky said, "Nothing stands out so far; everything seems pretty routine. But let me print out some copies in the electronics room. That way all three of us can have a look."

Five minutes later, they each had a copy in their hands.

"As you can see," Stansky began, "on the first page, there's about twelve thousand dollars in a checking account, and most of the transactions seem typical: electric bill, oil bill, credit card bill. But that's just the tip of the iceberg as far as the money goes. Take a look at page four; that's where the bulk of it is—just over a million dollars, mostly in CD accounts, with a small amount in savings."

Walker interjected. "The church has a million dollars in cash?"

Stansky responded, "Technically, I don't think it belongs to the church. I think it belongs to the Chambers family."

"But given that the ranch doesn't generate any income, where did all that money come from? I know the professor told us that when the Pendleton family came here, they were pretty well-off, but still," Walker said. "Although come to think of it, I do remember him saying something about a shipping company. I guess that could have continued to be profitable over the years."

"Most likely," said Stansky. "But also, ten or fifteen thousand dollars back then would easily translate into a million dollars today." Stansky paused. "I can tell you this; other than accrued interest postings, the only account activity over the past several years involved moving the money from a trust fund into CD's. That happened right after the supposed death of Tom Chambers." Stansky paused. "There are no deposits. If Chambers is involved in something illegal, then where's the money?"

"Good question," said Walker. "All right, let's keep looking and see if we see find anything else."

After nearly ten minutes, Munoz said, "I noticed that there aren't any tax payments. Is that because this is church-owned land?"

Walker answered, "Yeah, I would think so. Although that seems hard to justify - there's no congregation; they don't hold any services here, not to mention that the current occupant of the property is a criminal." Walker paused. "You know what else is missing? Car payments. That Mercedes SUV is almost new. That's got to go for sixty grand or so. If Chambers paid cash, then where did the money come from? There's no withdrawal like that."

For the next fifteen minutes, they continued to discuss the financial pages. Two more interesting entries came to light: There was a check in the amount of $7,000 made out to the Church of Universal Redemption from the Down East Ranch; it was deposited in early September. There was also a check for several hundred dollars made out to Northeast Appraisals. But it wasn't clear whether either one had anything to do with what they were investigating.

At 8:45 a.m. Walker said, "I think I'll go up to the gate and wait for Agent Rizzo."

He didn't have to wait long; Rizzo showed up at 8:50. After a "Thanks for coming," and a handshake, Walker led the way back to the main house. Rizzo was introduced to Munoz and Stansky. He asked a few questions, was shown the safe, and got to work.

Fifteen minutes later he called out, "I've just about got it open, if you want to come in." Realizing that there wasn't going to be enough room, Rizzo added, "I'll open it up, and then get out of your way."

Walker and Munoz put on rubber gloves and headed into the electronics room. Stansky stayed in the doorway.

There was sufficient overhead light so that Walker could see the outline of the objects inside the safe, but not exactly what they were. The first object he extracted was a passport. Walker opened it up and saw the face of JT Chambers staring back at him. Walker noted that the passport was current.

"If Tom Chambers, posing as his brother, crossed into Canada, it would seem that he didn't do it the conventional way. This makes his use of the tunnel even more likely."

Munoz took the passport, put it in an evidence bag, and passed it out to Peter Stansky.

The next item Walker pulled out appeared to be some sort of official document. As it cleared the open door of the safe and the light shone on it, Walker saw the heading on the front page: The Last Will and Testament of Lemuel Chambers.

"It's the father's will. Let's just bag it for now. We can take a look at it afterwards," Walker said as he handed it to Munoz.

The third item was a book. Before Walker opened it, he was reasonably sure that he knew what it was: the diary from the 1800s the professor had talked about. Inside the front cover was a letter from Northeast Appraisals estimating the diary's value to be in excess of $10,000. Walker relayed all that information loud enough for Stansky to hear it as well.

The last item in the safe was actually multiple items: bundles of cash—some in Canadian currency, some in US currency. At first glance, all of it appeared to be in $100 denominations.

"I'd say we found out how Chambers paid for the SUV. If the bills in these bundles are strictly hundreds, there's got to be seventy or eighty thousand dollars here, maybe more," offered Walker. As he turned over the bundles, he noticed what appeared to be a date on each one. It didn't mean anything to him at that moment, but he stored it in his memory bank. He then checked the inside of the safe again to make sure he hadn't missed anything.

As Walker and Munoz emerged from the electronics room, Walker caught Paul Rizzo's eye. "Thanks for everything, Agent Rizzo. You were a tremendous help."

"Glad to do it," he said. "Listen, I'm happy to stick around if you need me, if there's anything else I can do. But I'd like to get back, if I can." Rizzo paused and said sheepishly, "My daughter's got an end-of-the-year concert this afternoon. I'd rather not miss it."

Walker smiled and looked sympathetic. "I know the feeling. It's not a problem. You go ahead. We're all set here."

They all shook hands and Rizzo left. Just as the door closed behind him, Walker glanced at his watch and said, "We've got about a half hour before Homeland shows up. Dave, why don't you take a picture of each page of the father's will, just in case Broadhurst decides to grab up all the evidence. Oh, and take a picture of the passport too."

"What about the diary? I won't have enough time to do the whole thing, but..."

"No, don't worry about that. It seems somewhat fragile. I wouldn't want to take a chance. Take a picture of the appraisal letter though."

Munoz took out his phone and got to work.

Stansky looked over at Walker. "What do you want me to do?"

"I'm going to start counting the bundles of money. Something just occurred to me. It's probably a long shot, but I wonder if the amounts and the dates on each bundle might line up with the numbers and the dates from the computer files. They certainly aren't going to match up with anything from the financials."

"That's a good idea."

Twenty minutes later, Walker had counted out two bundles of Canadian hundred dollar bills: one with $24,000 and one with $20,000. There were fifteen bundles of US dollars totaling nearly $160,000. Walker's initial estimate had been way off. Stansky made notations of all the information from each bundle and booted up his laptop to compare the numbers to the computer files.

It was now nearly ten o'clock. Homeland would be there any minute.

Walker called over to Munoz. "Are you all set, Dave? Did you get everything?"

"Yeah, I got it."

"Good. I hope I'm just being paranoid, but if Broadhurst takes over, at least by doing this, we can still work the case unofficially. I just want to make sure there are no slipups."

Just before Walker left, Stansky said, "It looks like you were right. The bundle with the twenty-four thousand Canadian is labeled ten fourteen. That's the same number listed next to October fourteenth on the page in the computer file."

"Okay, check the rest of them." Walker took another few steps and then stopped. "Wasn't October the month with the eight names?"

"Yeah, why?"

"And the three K ea?" Walker didn't wait for a reply. "Three K is another way to indicate three thousand, and 'ea' means 'each.' Three thousand each... times eight is twenty-four thousand dollars." Walker's jaw tightened. "Shit." He then shook his head. "Stay with it, Peter. I gotta go."

On the ride out to the gate, Walker tried not to think about the eight girls and the $24,000. Had he jumped to conclusions? He wasn't sure. Maybe he'd have a better idea once Peter finished making the comparisons. But right now he had to deal with Homeland showing up. Everything else was going to have to wait.

At 10:01 a.m. Walker heard a car approaching and then another and another. As they came into view, Walker thought he was looking at a commercial for Cadillac Escalades. There were six of them, all black.

The lead car pulled up next to Walker, and the passenger side door opened. Despite the relatively warm June weather, the man who emerged was wearing a blue windbreaker emblazoned with the Homeland Security emblem. He stood about 5' 8" and had dark-brown hair that appeared, even to Walker's unsophisticated eye, to be a bad dye job.

As the man approached Walker, he held out his hand and said, "Agent Walker, nice to meet you. I'm Commander Jack Broadhurst."

Even though Broadhurst had used his first name when he introduced himself, Walker decided not to. "Good to meet you as well, Commander Broadhurst."

Broadhurst noticed Walker eyeing the other Escalades. "As you can see, I'm taking this very seriously. I've got eleven Homeland agents with me, eight BEST agents, and four from the DEA. I think it's important to try to include everyone whenever I can."

Most people would have taken Broadhurst's last comment as a positive sign. Walker didn't.

He didn't believe "everyone" necessarily meant the FBI.

Chapter Thirty-Two

Broadhurst directed two of the Homeland agents who had been riding with him in the lead car to remain at the front gate. He then climbed back into the Escalade and told his driver to follow Walker. The rest of the SUVs fell into line behind them.

When they reached the main house, all the agents exited their vehicles, but at Broadhurst's direction, they remained outside. Broadhurst saw Walker's expression, which reflected some surprise.

"I prefer that our conversation be one-on-one. I process things better that way, when there's nobody else interrupting."

Walker introduced Broadhurst to Munoz and Stansky. Everyone shook hands, and then Walker said, "I'm going to brief Commander Broadhurst on our investigation. The other members of his team are waiting outside until we're done." Munoz and Stansky remained stoic, but Walker could see questions forming in their eyes. Before they could say anything, Walker continued, "I was going to suggest that while the Commander and I talk, Dave, why don't you give Peter a hand?"

Munoz responded, "Sure, no problem."

Walker grabbed his briefcase and moved toward the leather couches; Broadhurst followed. Walker took some papers out of the briefcase and handed them over.

"This is a summary of the investigation so far, although it doesn't include a couple of developments from this morning."

Broadhurst accepted the report and placed it on the cushion next to him. "Thank you, but I'd rather have you tell me everything directly."

Walker was again surprised, but he was able to avoid showing it. "Okay." He pointed to the report. "It's all in there, if I happen to forget something."

"I'm sure you won't."

Walker spent the next ten minutes outlining the case history up to the point when he and Munoz found Sam. He expounded on his theory of what had probably happened, but acknowledged that he hadn't been able to verify any of it with her. Walker minimized the personal connection he had to the case, keeping his remarks as dispassionate as possible. He was about to talk about Sam's condition when Broadhurst interrupted.

"Tell me more about the tunnel. Are you certain it goes all the way into Canada?"

"I think so, but once we saw that part of it had collapsed, we didn't want to go back in."

"Understandable. We'll check it out."

"We don't have any idea when the tunnel collapsed. I guess it's even possible that Tom Chambers could have been in there when it happened."

Broadhurst ignored Walker's speculation. "Okay, so you've got this Tom Chambers taking over his brother's identity and holding the girl against her will, but you can't confirm either one of those things as yet, correct?"

"Technically that's correct; it's just circumstantial, but there doesn't seem to be any other logical explanation."

"You may be right, but it seems to me that if we have a tunnel that crosses into Canada, something that would certainly suggest some sort of smuggling, that has to be our focus. We can build a much stronger case off of that," Broadhurst said.

"Stronger than kidnapping?"

"You told me the girl isn't talking yet; isn't it possible that she never will?"

Walker was having trouble keeping his anger in check. He forced himself to calm down, but before he could say anything, Broadhurst continued, "You mentioned something about new developments this morning. What else did you find out?"

Walker responded through gritted teeth. "We got Chambers' financial records, and Peter Stansky was able to get into some encrypted files. Also, we were able to open the safe in the other room." Walker paused, expecting Broadhurst to say something at that point. When he didn't, Walker added, "There were no red flags in the financials, but the Church of Universal Redemption account has over a million dollars in it, mainly in CDs. But there have been no large deposits or withdrawals any time recently."

Walker made a quick decision to hold back somewhat on the computer files. "The encrypted files are divided into months. Each one has numbers and dates, but Peter is still working on that to see if he can figure out what it all means. The safe is a different story. We found a passport, bundles of cash, the father's will, and a diary dating back to the mid-eighteen hundreds."

"How much cash?"

"Around sixty-four thousand dollars Canadian and over one hundred and fifty thousand dollars US," Walker replied.

"That certainly sounds like drug money to me."

Walker wanted to say, "*Isn't that just as circumstantial as the kidnapping situation?*" But instead, he begrudgingly agreed with Broadhurst's assessment. "Could very well be."

"And the passport?" Broadhurst asked.

"It belongs to JT… James Chambers."

"Is it current?"

"Yes."

"You have to wonder why Tom Chambers didn't use it then, if he actually did go into Canada and his trip was an innocent one," Broadhurst said.

Since the same thought had crossed Walker's mind earlier, his response was more sincere. "That was our conclusion as well."

Broadhurst stood up and offered his hand. "Thank you, Agent Walker. You've been very helpful. My first priority at this point is to get back into that tunnel. I've got two agents who have experience in that sort of thing. They should be able to do a quick evaluation. While they're doing that, I'm going to have the other agents search the rest of the property. I know you already did a lot of that, but a second pair of eyes never hurt, right? In the meantime, I'd like you to box up and label the contents of the safe. And I'll need the financials and the computer files as well as the hard drives. I just want to be able to move on everything if we find what I think we're going to."

Walker stood motionless for a moment. He had anticipated that Homeland might take over the case, but nothing could have prepared him for being thrown to the side like this. But his twenty plus years of being a professional kicked in and saved him from saying or doing anything he'd regret.

He was able to convince himself that it really didn't matter how Broadhurst was operating, as long as he got results and caught Tom Chambers. Walker decided that he should go one step further and make it clear to Broadhurst that he was onboard with what he was doing.

"Commander, can I make a suggestion? Why don't I drive out and show your men where the hatch door is to the tunnel and where the partial collapse occurred?"

Broadhurst didn't respond immediately. Eventually, he nodded and said, "If you really think that's necessary." He then headed for the front door.

Walker went over to the electronics room to let Munoz and Stansky know that he was leaving. They both looked up as he got to the doorway.

271

Munoz quietly said, "We overheard most of that. Just what you were afraid of."

"Yeah, I don't think there's much we can do though. I'll be back in a while."

Walker came outside on the porch as Broadhurst was addressing the entire team of agents, all of whom were standing next to their vehicles.

"Cars one and two, we'll go out to the tunnel; three and four, you do reconnaissance on the rest of the property; cars five and six, you search the other buildings."

Walker was about to indicate that much of that wasn't necessary; it had already been done, but he decided not to contradict Broadhurst in front of his own men.

Broadhurst turned and spoke to Walker. "Agent Walker, where are the buildings located from here?"

"On the way out to the tunnel, they'll be on the left."

"Did everybody here that? Cars five and six, you'll head over to the left once the buildings come into view," Broadhurst said. "Does everybody have their walkie-talkies set to the right channel?" All the agents nodded. "Good, let's head out."

Although Walker had expected to be introduced to the other agents, given Broadhurst's demeanor so far, it hadn't come as a big surprise that he wasn't.

A few minutes into the trip, cars five and six veered off and headed for the cabins and the other buildings. Several minutes after that, Walker pulled his car within twenty yards of the hatch door. He got out and waited for the agents in cars one and two to do the same.

Once everyone was gathered around, Walker said, "I'm Special Agent Craig Walker with the FBI." Walker took a quick glance at Broadhurst who remained expressionless. "This is the only entrance to the tunnel that I'm aware of. Another agent and I went inside yesterday, probably forty yards or so. It seemed very substantial, but as I believe Commander Broadhurst told you, there's been a partial collapse further along. I'll take you there now, unless you have any questions."

There were none, which didn't surprise Walker. He sensed that Broadhurst would have frowned on any questions being asked by anyone but him. And the rest of the agents were most likely well aware of that.

They got out to the site of the partial collapse less than five minutes later. Walker kept his remarks very brief. "We discovered this yesterday as well. I have no idea if it's been like this for a while, or just happened."

This time Broadhurst did speak up. "Thank you, Agent Walker, I'll take it from here."

Walker nodded, got back in the car, and returned to the main house.

Munoz and Stansky were seated on the leather couches with the contents of the safe on the table in front of them when Walker came through the door. He headed over to join them.

Stansky spoke first. "We overheard Broadhurst say he wanted everything boxed up, but we figured we had some time before he came back."

"Yeah, I'm sure we do." Walker paused. "What do you think about what I said before—the eight girls and the twenty-four thousand dollars?"

Stansky replied somberly. "Dave and I were discussing that after you left. Unfortunately, we think you're right."

Everyone was quiet for a few moments, and then Munoz said, "It didn't sound like you shared any of that with Broadhurst."

"No, I didn't. I'm not exactly sure why," Walker said. "So did you find anything else?"

"Actually, we did," said Stansky. "The date and the amount on the bundle with the other Canadian currency in it matched up with a date and number in November. But only a few of the bundles with the US currency matched up. It looks like there's about seventy-two thousand dollars missing compared to the numbers in the computer files. Like you said, it could be how Chambers paid for the SUV with a little spending money left over."

They continued talking for nearly thirty minutes about everything they knew and didn't know about the case. But the main focus was on what to do if Broadhurst cut them out entirely—something that appeared to be inevitable.

Munoz echoed what Walker had been saying. "I'm not sure we have much choice. We have to give him everything he's asking for, and then we just have to wait to see what he does with it. The problem I see though is that he's not going to communicate with us. So how are we supposed to know what's going on?" Munoz looked at Walker. "Do you think he'll be talking to Chuck Dalton?"

"I think that's our best shot," said Walker. "Of course, it's all a moot point if they don't find Chambers." Walker glanced at his watch. It was nearly 11:20. "Would you and Peter start getting everything together for Broadhurst? I want to call the medical center again."

Several minutes later, Walker was speaking to Dr. Cosgrove.

"She had a great night. I had the nurses check on her periodically, and it looks like she slept straight through. There's no question that she's much more lucid this morning. We're still not pushing her to talk about what happened. What I am considering is having our staff psychologist do an informal evaluation. She's very good; I think her assessment would give us some direction. My best sense right now, however, is that we have to take things slowly and wait until Sam's ready."

"I understand," said Walker.

No one said anything for a moment, and then Dr. Cosgrove offered, "Sam asked for Maddie again, but this time she added a last name Walker." Dr. Cosgrove paused. "So I take it this is personal as well as professional?"

"It started out that way. Well... I guess that part never stopped. It just got more complicated."

"I'm sorry, Agent Walker; I didn't mean to imply anything."

"I didn't take it that way," Walker said. "Thank you, Doctor. I'll give you a call later on."

At 11:45 a.m. the sound of the six Cadillac Escalade's returning could be heard in the main room.

"Sounds like they're coming back," said Munoz.

This time when Broadhurst entered the room, he didn't pull Walker aside. Instead he announced what they had found.

"Our engineers gave us the go-ahead to go in. They said the collapse was recent, but not a result of a structural problem. We found a cooler and a bedpan about fifty yards in, which we took as evidence.

"Then further on, just before the collapsed area..." Broadhurst paused for what could only be described as dramatic effect, "We found boxes of what appear to be drugs. The DEA agents are removing everything now. They think it's most likely fentanyl and something else.

"There was no sign of Chambers. And we couldn't get into the tunnel beyond where the drugs were, but there's little doubt that it leads to the Canadian border.

"So... did you box up everything?" Broadhurst didn't wait for an answer. "I'm going to need it all, and I'm afraid you're going to have to leave. We'll be securing the entire property. I sent an official Homeland alert to all the border crossings and to our Canadian counterparts to be on the lookout for James Chambers or Thomas Chambers."

Broadhurst looked over at Walker. "You did the right thing by having Dalton call us in on this. We're going to get this guy for you."

Fifteen minutes later, Walker, Munoz, and Stansky were on the road heading back to the training facility. Stansky spoke up from the back seat.

"I remember a few years ago, there was a bomb scare, and we had to evacuate the building we were in. I think they gave us more time to get out than Broadhurst just did."

"Not the best people skills I've ever seen, that's for sure," said Munoz.

"He's a jerk. There's no two ways about that. But if they do find Chambers..." Walker's voice trailed off.

"I know," said Munoz, "but he seems more concerned with the tunnel and the border crossing than anything that has to do with the identity theft and Sam's kidnapping. A conviction on kidnapping charges carries a much longer prison sentence than drug running, even if it involves another country."

Walker responded, "That's got me worried too. If need be though, I'll speak up about the eight girls and the twenty-four thousand dollars. That's human trafficking." Walker paused. "The only problem is it's only a theory—circumstantial, as Broadhurst would call it."

Once they were back at the training complex, they went to the dining hall, not necessarily to eat, but rather to decompress. The agent at the main gate had informed Chuck Dalton that that they had all returned, and he joined them a few minutes later. Walker filled him in on the morning's events.

"So, Broadhurst didn't call and let you know about any of this?" Walker asked.

"No, nothing," Dalton said.

"That's what I was afraid of. Well, going forward I certainly don't want you to violate any confidences, but if Broadhurst does talk to you, I'd appreciate knowing whatever you're comfortable sharing with me." Walker paused. "Of course, that may be long distance."

"What are you talking about?"

"I think we've got to consider going back to Massachusetts. There's not much more for us to do here."

"Are you talking about tonight?" Dalton asked.

"No, no. We'll stay here until the morning anyway."

The three agents did grab something to eat, although none of them was particularly hungry. They talked for another half hour, and then Walker decided to check in with the medical center again.

"Hi, Dr. Cosgrove. I had a couple of minutes; how's she doing?"

"Good. At least that's how it seems. The psychologist got Sam talking, not about the ordeal, but about other things in her life. She mentioned Habitat for Humanity..."

"Yeah, she and my daughter were planning to do that this summer," Walker said.

"She also mentioned your daughter again." The doctor paused. "I don't know if it would be possible, but when I was speaking with the psychologist she said that in her opinion, Sam doesn't feel entirely safe yet. She's not going to be able to talk about what happened until she does. One of the things that might help is being around things or people that are familiar. Do you think your daughter would be willing to come up here to see Sam?"

Walker thought for a moment. "I'll need to discuss it with my wife, but off the top of my head, I don't see why not." What Walker was thinking, but didn't say was, *At this point I don't have anything else to do anyway.*

Walker called Cheryl and told her everything that had happened, and asked her opinion about Maddie coming up. She said she'd discuss it with her, but agreed that it seemed like a good idea.

Walker got a call an hour later. Cheryl had to get somebody to cover her shift, but she and Maddie would drive up the next day.

ᴄ⌐ᴏChapter Thirty-Threeᴇ᷎ᴑ

The Canadian Security and Intelligence Services (CSIS) working in conjunction with the provincial Royal Canadian Mounted Police (RCMP) and the Canadian BEST units had ramped up the surveillance on Eli Peters. There were now two-person teams watching his home and business locations 24/7.

The team currently on stakeout duty down the street from Peters' house—the same agents who had been involved in the initial surveillance—had come on duty at 9:00 a.m. Wednesday morning. Everything had been quiet for the first hour, so the agent in the passenger seat had spent part of the time checking his phone for updates and alerts. There were eleven in total, none of which seemed particularly relevant to their assignment, so he didn't give them more than a cursory glance. And then a few minutes after ten o'clock, the large gate in front of Eli Peters' house swung open and the owner's Lexus headed out. The RCMP agents followed in a nondescript green sedan, having traded in the dark-blue SUV they had used before.

After several miles, the Lexus got on the highway heading east. The agent in the passenger seat of the trail car took out his telephoto lens and trained it on the occupants of the Lexus.

"At least they're not going back to the water park. We still don't know what the hell that was all about, do we?" The driver shook his head, but didn't respond as the other agent continued. "I think that's Peters in the car; it's not the water park guy anyway."

Twenty minutes later, the Lexus left the highway, took a couple of turns on the local surface roads, and then pulled into a neighborhood of well-to-do homes. The RCMP agents remained a good distance back and waited for the Lexus to park. Once it did, and Eli Peters got out, they called in the street address to the Command Center.

A quarter hour later, Eli Peters exited the house and got back in the Lexus. His driver retraced the route he had taken on the surface roads and the highway and made his way back to Eli Peters' house. The RCMP agent in the passenger seat put aside the telephoto lens and phoned the Command Center, inquiring whether the address Eli Peters had visited had raised any alarms. It hadn't.

His partner parked the car in the same spot he'd used before, a half block down from the Peters' house. The two agents began to settle into what they assumed would be a slow day, but a few minutes later, the front gate swung open, and the Lexus was on the move again.

The agent in the passenger seat raised the telephoto lens again and saw that it wasn't Eli Peters this time.

"I think it's the water park guy. We still don't have an ID on him, do we?"

"No, not that I know of. I'm sure the Command Center would have sent us something if they had it."

Nearly half an hour later, the passenger seat agent's phone started to buzz. The call lasted about five minutes, after which he recapped everything for his partner.

"They did finally get a hit from the photo we sent of the water park guy. His name is—or should I say was—Thomas Chambers. He's listed as deceased. He sure doesn't look dead to me."

"What do they want us to do?"

"They just said to keep following him."

Another thirty minutes into the trip, the agent who had taken the phone call remembered something. He scrolled through the alert messages and was about to close out his e-mail, thinking he had been mistaken, when the last alert caught his eye. He read it silently and then sat up in his seat and read it out loud.

"Listen to this. It's from US Homeland Security. 'Be on the lookout for an individual using the name James Chambers or Thomas Chambers. He may be attempting to reenter the United States from Eastern Canada.' That's our guy, right? It doesn't seem like anyone else has put this together?"

"Probably not. Call it in," his partner said.

The Command Center took down all the information and called back fifteen minutes later.

"Do you have a definitive destination for the Lexus?"

"No, but we've been traveling for over an hour. Right after I called you, I checked for the closest border crossings. If that's what he was intending to do, he should've cut off the highway twenty miles back. He'd already be at the Saint Aurielie crossing by now."

"All right. Stay on him. What's the next crossing? Do you know?"

"I think it's probably Jackman-Armstrong. We're about thirty-five miles away from there."

"Okay. We're coordinating with the US Department of Homeland Security. I don't know who this guy Chambers is, but whoever he is, he's obviously a priority for them. And the fact that he was at Eli Peters' house, makes him a priority for us. I'm still not sure how this is going to shake out—who's going to have jurisdiction. So I need you to check in immediately if anything changes."

Despite no longer having an official role in the investigation, Walker, Munoz, and Stansky were all up early on

Wednesday morning, hoping to glean some information from Chuck Dalton. But he didn't have anything to share, and he wasn't sure whether Broadhurst was simply being closed mouth, or that nothing of significance had occurred.

Munoz and Stansky stayed behind at the complex while Walker took the car and drove the twenty-five miles to the medical center. He arrived just before ten o'clock. Cheryl and Maddie had shown up a few minutes earlier and were waiting for him in the parking lot. As he exited the car, Maddie ran up to him, threw her arms around her father, and said, "Thank you, Dad. She's going to be okay, right?"

"It looks that way." Walker hesitated and tempered what he said next. "We're not exactly sure what Sam's been through. She may not want to talk about it, and I don't think you should ask. She just needs you to be her friend right now." Walker kissed the top of his daughter's head and added, "I'm sure the doctor will talk to you before you go in to see her."

Maddie responded with, "Okay," as she moved out of her father's embrace.

Cheryl arrived a moment later. She gave her husband a hug. "Not too shabby for a retired FBI agent."

"Those are the best kind, didn't you know?"

She smiled at him. "I agree, and let's keep it that way. Despite how it might appear, I do like having you home most of the time."

Walker smiled back. "Good to know."

Walker introduced Dr. Cosgrove to Cheryl and Maddie. The doctor offered a straightforward assessment of Sam's physical condition and prognosis. He didn't talk down to Maddie, but rather gave her similar advice to what her father had offered.

"Take your cues from Sam. Let her do most of the talking. The psychologist suggested that Sam needs to feel... normal and having you here should help her do that. Any questions, Maddie?"

NO LOOSE ENDS ~ THOMAS HALL

"What do I say to start out with?"

"What do you think you should say?"

"I guess I want to know how she's feeling," Maddie said.

"Then start with that. That's a very natural thing to ask, and it's open-ended enough that Sam can elaborate if she wants to."

Dr. Cosgrove turned to Maddie's parents. "I think it's best if the two of you wait here."

"Of course," said Cheryl.

Dr. Cosgrove looked at Maddie. "Okay, all set?"

Shortly after Maddie left with Dr. Cosgrove, Walker summarized the latest developments in the investigation for Cheryl. Toward the end he offered, "There's really not much else we can do up here except wait. After I bring the car back, I'll talk it over with Dave and Peter. But... I think we may be heading home this afternoon."

Cheryl asked, "Would you feel differently if Sam opens up about what happened to her?"

"Maybe. But I'm certainly not about to pressure her, especially since it probably wouldn't make any difference to Broadhurst."

Dr. Cosgrove escorted Maddie back into the waiting room over an hour after she had first gone in to see Sam. Walker and Cheryl looked toward the doctor, who smiled and said, "From all accounts, it went very well. But I'll let your daughter tell you about it."

Maddie was beaming as she began. "Sam seems really good. It was like how we always talk. She didn't say anything specific about what happened, but... she asked about Habitat and..." Maddie continued to fill them in for the next ten minutes. As she was finishing up, she said, "Sam started to get tired; that's why I left. But I told her I'd come back this afternoon. I think she really wants me to. Is that okay?"

Cheryl smiled. "Sure. We'll have plenty of time to get back home after that."

"Thanks, Mom." Maddie paused. "I probably should have asked you guys first, but I kind of told Sam that she could stay with us for a while once she gets out of here. I could tell that she doesn't want to stay by herself, and Mark's still up at Cornell for another two weeks. She could use his room."

Cheryl looked over at her husband. "What do you think?"

"If I was still on the case, it probably wouldn't be a good idea. At the very least, it could be perceived as inappropriate having a witness stay with the investigator. But since I'm no longer part of the investigation, it should be fine." Walker looked over at his daughter, expecting to see her filled with excitement, but instead she looked upset. "Maddie, what's the matter?"

"It's just that when I talked to Sam about staying with us, she asked if you guys would mind. I said I was sure that you wouldn't, especially since you were the one who found her, Dad. I didn't mean to say anything; it just kind of slipped out. I don't think she realized who you were. She said she wants to talk with you, but... What you just said... Does that mean she can't stay with us?"

"No, it doesn't mean that, Maddie," Walker said. "Tell me exactly what she said."

"That she wanted to thank you. And I'm not even sure about the rest. I'm sorry; I didn't mean to mess things up."

"You didn't. It'll be fine. We'll figure it out."

Everyone was quiet for a moment, and then Cheryl said, "Why don't we go have some lunch and talk this over?"

Walker glanced at his watch. It was 11:45. "That sounds like a good idea; let me call Dave to make sure nothing's going on."

Munoz assured him that everything was quiet and to take his time getting back.

It was now becoming quite apparent that the Lexus carrying Tom Chambers was heading for Jackman-Armstrong. The RCMP agent in the passenger seat phoned in the update.

"There's nothing else out here. They've got to be going to the border crossing. What do you want us to do?"

"How much farther is it?"

"Fifteen, twenty miles at the most."

"Okay. I'll call you right back."

Seven minutes later, the Command Center supervisor was back on the line.

"The orders from CSIS are to continue to monitor everything. Do not approach the suspect or attempt to detain him in any way."

"So we're just going to let him cross back into the States?"

"Evidently. I'm being told that US Homeland Security is going to arrest him as soon as he enters the country. This is all coming from CSIS."

"All right."

"Keep this line open. We need real-time updates to pass along."

There was no communication for the next several minutes, and then the RCMP agent said, "It looks like the Lexus is pulling over to the side of the road. If he stayed where he was, he would have gotten in the car lane going across the border."

Thirty seconds passed, and then he added, "The passenger just got out." The agent raised the telephoto lens and took a closer look. "It's definitely the same guy we followed to the water park— beard and all. It looks like he's heading toward the building where they process the people who walk across. The Lexus is turning around and leaving. I assume you want us to just let it go."

"Yeah, keep watching Chambers. I need confirmation that he went into the building and isn't coming back out."

"Okay, I'm on it."

Fifteen minutes later, the Command Center supervisor reported that Chambers was being detained by US authorities and the RCMP agents should return to Eli Peters' house and wait for further instructions.

Despite some initial reservations about Sam Daniels coming to stay with them for a while, Walker didn't put up much of a fight, especially when Cheryl sided with Maddie. And since any ethical issues had become nonexistent now that Walker wasn't involved in the investigation, keeping the peace at home trumped everything else. Once that was settled, Walker asked Maddie if she was sure Sam wanted to talk with him. She assured him that that was the case.

They arrived back at the medical center around 1:20 p.m. This time Cheryl and Maddie stayed in the waiting room while Walker went to visit Sam.

If he hadn't seen her name on the sign next to the door, Walker would have thought he was in the wrong room. Sam Daniels appeared to be a different person. In the tunnel she had seemed so tiny, like a small, untrusting feral animal trapped with no way out. But the young woman lying in the hospital bed in front of him had been transformed, at least physically. And when she saw him, her face radiated an expression of gratitude that Walker had rarely seen in his lifetime.

Sam had tears in her eyes and was not able to speak immediately. Walker pulled up a chair next to the bed, pretending not to notice. As he settled in he said, "Hi, Sam. Uh... Dr. Cosgrove and Maddie said you seem to be doing okay."

Sam didn't respond to Walker's statement. Instead, she offered in a quiet voice, "Thank you for finding me."

Walker didn't know how else to respond, other than to say, "You're welcome."

"I didn't know you were Maddie's father."

"I know."

"I guess that was lucky too that you used to work for the FBI." Sam paused, and her expression changed slightly as she added, "I guess I'm getting better at choosing my friends."

Walker smiled, realizing Sam was attempting to make their meeting less awkward. There was silence for a few moments, and then Sam asked, "How did you find me?"

"Maddie. She knew something was wrong when you missed your final, but mainly when you didn't show up for Habitat. And Mrs. Burns, your guidance counselor, helped too."

"My college essay?"

"Yes."

"I thought about that... when I was... at the ranch. It kind of gave me some hope."

Tears started to form in Sam's eyes. Walker wasn't sure what to do, so he just waited. Eventually, Sam spoke again.

"Are you sure that it's okay if I stay with you for a few days?"

"Absolutely."

"Thank you. That means a lot to me."

It was obvious to Walker that Sam wasn't quite ready to fill in any details about her ordeal, so he didn't say anything that could be interpreted as pushing her in that direction. He also sensed that she was at a loss as to what they could talk about other than that. He decided to make it easy for her.

"I know Maddie's anxious to see you again. Why don't I go get her?"

"Okay... and... Thank you again," Sam said.

Walker found Cheryl and Maddie in the waiting room and told them what had transpired with Sam. He finished by saying,

"She certainly looks a lot better than what I had expected. She didn't talk directly about what happened, just kind of skirted around it. But that's okay. She'll do it in her own time."

"I'm going to go in to see her with Maddie," said Cheryl. "And then I think we're going to head home."

"I might not be too far behind you. I'll call and let you know for sure."

Walker was on the road five minutes later. Five minutes after that, his phone rang. It was Munoz.

"Hi, Dave. I'm just on my way back. What's up?"

"Dalton came looking for you. They got Chambers. He's in custody an hour or so from here. I don't have any more details than that."

"I'll be there in twenty minutes."

ᑕᔑ Chapter Thirty-Four ᘉᑐ

The agent at the main gate of the training complex waved Walker through shortly before 2:30 p.m. Walker found Munoz and Stansky in the dining hall.

"Any more information about the arrest?" asked Walker.

Munoz shook his head. "No, nothing. Dalton said that if he found out anything else, he'd let us know." Munoz paused. "How's Sam doing?"

"Physically, she seems to be doing well. But she still hasn't said very much about what happened to her. I think it's possible that she might open up to Maddie before she opens up to me. Speaking of which, I've got a bit of a dilemma." Walker went on to tell them about Sam coming to stay with his family.

Munoz appeared sympathetic. "I think it's okay. You're about to shut down the investigation, right? So where's the conflict of interest?"

"I'm not sure everyone would see it that way."

"You mean Broadhurst? Why would he have an issue with that, unless he's going to bring charges against Chambers related to what he did to Sam? Then he might need her testimony. But from what you told us, he's not even considering that."

"No, I don't think he is," Walker said. "Are you guys all right holding off going back to Massachusetts, at least until we find out exactly what Chambers is going to be charged with?"

Munoz said, "I'm in no hurry. Peter?"

"That's fine."

They talked for several more minutes, and then Chuck Dalton showed up.

"I just got off the phone with Broadhurst. He rushed up to the border crossing as soon as he heard that they had grabbed Chambers. He was only able to interrogate him for about fifteen minutes before he requested an attorney. Broadhurst asked the federal court in Bangor for an expedited ruling. The attorney just got assigned a little while ago. He's on his way here."

"Why is Chambers entitled to a court-appointed attorney? And why is he coming here?" asked Walker.

"Evidently, the attorney was appointed temporarily until they sort out the identity issue. Technically, Tom Chambers is legally deceased and therefore has no assets. Broadhurst asked me if it was all right to have Chambers transferred here. We've got a couple of holding cells, so it shouldn't be a problem. Frankly, I think the fact that he was asking for a favor is the only reason he shared everything with me."

Walker nodded knowingly. "I'm sure that's true. So when do you expect everyone to show up?"

"Probably not until sometime after six."

"Thanks, Chuck. I appreciate you letting us know."

"As I told you, I'll do whatever I can. I feel responsible for getting you taken off the case," Dalton said.

"I don't blame you for that; that was all Broadhurst." Walker continued, attempting to remain positive, "And the main thing is that Chambers is in custody."

After Dalton left, Walker said, "Given what we just found out, I think I'd like to stick around here until tomorrow. I want to try to talk to Broadhurst later on, if he'll see me. I want to tell him about what we found in the computer files in case his people didn't pick up on it. He's probably not going to care, but I'll feel better if I at least let him know." Walker paused. "So what have you guys been up to?"

Peter Stansky answered, "I downloaded all the images off of Dave's phone—the passport and the will." Stansky handed Walker a folder. "I made copies for you."

"Thanks." Walker opened the file and glanced at the contents. "Anything interesting in the will?"

"Well, there are a lot of stipulations and contingencies," said Munoz. "James Chambers was to inherit most of the estate. However, there was a trust fund in the amount of four hundred thousand dollars set up for Tom Chambers. But he only got the money if he lived on the ranch continuously for a five-year period."

Stansky added, "It would seem that the father was trying to bring the prodigal son home by enticing him with the trust fund. He also seemed to figure that since he wasn't going to be around, his older son could keep an eye on the younger one." Stansky paused. "I suppose you can understand what motivated someone like Tom Chambers to switch identities with his brother: six hundred thousand dollars versus four hundred thousand dollars. Not to mention that he'd have to wait five years before he saw any of it. And the added bonus: with Tom's death, James Chambers got the trust fund too."

"What did the will say if James died first?" asked Walker.

"Other than the trust fund, all the money went to charity," replied Munoz.

"What about the ranch?"

Stansky answered. "That's another one of the contingencies. The property is technically owned by the Church of Universal Redemption, but Lemuel Chambers and his heirs are legally designated as caretakers, meaning that they can live on the property rent free for the rest of their lives."

Munoz said, "There is one piece of good news, at least for Professor Mason. Lemuel Chambers willed the diary to him, although it's stipulated that he can't take possession of it until five years after Lemuel Chambers' death."

"It sounds like Lemuel must have had a major change of heart. From what the professor told us, Lemuel was very reluctant to have the diary made public," Walker said. "That reminds me; I promised the professor I'd give him a call. I'll probably wait until the morning. Maybe finding out that he was willed the diary will soften the blow of hearing about Tom Chambers."

The three investigators talked for another fifteen minutes, and then Walker excused himself to call his wife.

"Hi, there. How did things go with Sam?"

Cheryl hesitated. "Mainly good."

"What do you mean?"

"Maddie and I just left her. It's funny you should call now. Maddie's gone to the ladies room. As soon as she gets back, we're going to head home. I'll talk fast; I don't want her to overhear me. So when we first went in, everything was fine. Sam mentioned her conversation with you, but mainly she talked about wanting to get out of the hospital and back to Massachusetts. She said that she'd like to go to Habitat on Saturday with Maddie, if possible. And then a short while later, Dr. Cosgrove came in. Sam told him that she was hoping that she could be discharged soon. He said that if she had another good night tonight, she'd be able to go home tomorrow afternoon."

Walker interrupted. "I know you have to work tomorrow. But I can arrange something, if that's what you're worried about. I'll just..."

"No, no that's not it," Cheryl said. "I already switched my shift again. That wasn't a problem. No, what happened was, I said to Sam that I'd pick up some new clothes for her to wear when she got discharged, or if she preferred, I could go to her apartment and get something. As soon as I mentioned her apartment, she got very emotional. She said that she didn't have her key, or her phone, or her purse and that the man who had chained her to the wall must have taken them. She was barely coherent. And then she buried her face in her pillow and just started sobbing.

"Maddie looked over at me; she must have been wondering what Sam was talking about. I wasn't going to try to explain it right then; I told her that I'd tell her about it later. After a couple of minutes, Sam calmed down. She apologized, and said not to worry about getting clothes from her apartment, but that she'd appreciate it if I could buy a few things for her to wear over the next several days. At that point, she seemed more worried about telling me that she'd be sure to pay me back rather than what had upset her to begin with. That was just a few minutes ago. She seemed exhausted after that, so Maddie and I left."

"That must have been really difficult," Walker said.

"Yeah, it was. I didn't know what to say to Sam or to Maddie."

It was quiet for a few moments, and then Cheryl asked, "Are you still there?"

"Yeah, I'm here," Walker said. "I have some news too. I was trying to figure out what to do with it as far as Sam is concerned."

"Why? What happened?"

"They arrested Chambers. He tried to get back into the States an hour or two ago. He's being transferred here to the training facility. I want to find out more before I head home. So I think I may wait until tomorrow morning." Walker paused. "Are you okay with that? It means you're going to have to explain everything to Maddie and answer all of her questions."

"That's okay. I'm not going to be able to put her off until you get back anyway. I'll figure something out. At least now I can tell her that they caught the guy." Cheryl didn't say anything for a moment, and then she asked, "What about Sam? Should I tell her? I could go back into her room now, or should I wait until tomorrow?"

"That's what I was just struggling with. I don't think you should go back in; you said that she was exhausted. And as far as tomorrow goes, I guess if she refers to Chambers again, then I would tell her. But if not, I wouldn't bring it up," Walker said. "Has Dr. Cosgrove mentioned anything to you about Sam getting counseling after she's released?"

"No, but I would think that's a given, isn't it?" Cheryl said.

"You would think so. Let's make sure we talk to Sam about arranging something after she settles in with us."

"That's a good idea... Oh, I see Maddie coming back."

"All right. I'll call you later after you get home to see how you made out with her."

"Okay, I'll talk to you then."

Dalton called Walker at 6:35 p.m. to let him know that Broadhurst had arrived back at the training complex and that Chambers was there also, meeting with his lawyer.

"Chuck, can you do me a favor? I need five minutes with Broadhurst. Would you ask him if he'd be willing to see me?"

"I'll give it a shot."

Ten minutes later Dalton called back. "Seven o'clock in the conference room near my office, just the two of you."

"Thanks, Chuck. I appreciate it."

Broadhurst was already in the conference room when Walker arrived. Walker decided to start with an ego stroke.

"Congratulations, Commander. That was quick work."

Broadhurst generated a small smile and responded with a failed attempt at humility. "Sometimes everything just falls into place," he said. "So what can I do for you, Agent Walker?"

"I saw Sam Daniels today. She's doing pretty well."

"Glad to hear that," Broadhurst interrupted.

Walker continued, "She hasn't spoken in detail about what happened, but she has made some reference to it, so I suspect it might not be too long. From what you said before, I know you're probably not going to charge Chambers with kidnapping or anything similar, at least not initially. What I'm asking is whether those charges can be added later on, once we get Sam Daniels' statement?"

Broadhurst didn't answer right away. Eventually, he offered. "I don't believe that'll be necessary."

"I know it's not necessary, but I don't think Chambers should just get off scot-free for what he did to her."

"That might complicate things; I might be going in a different direction."

Walker stared at Broadhurst. "What does that mean?"

"I can't really discuss it at this point."

Walker could feel his anger rising up. It was one thing to be shut out of the investigation, but now Broadhurst was bolting the door and throwing away the key. Walker calmed himself as much as he could and shifted gears.

"Did your people look at the computer files?"

"I assume so. I haven't spoken to them about it as yet," Broadhurst said.

Walker's anger kicked in again, pushing him to overstate his point.

"Well, there's a very interesting entry for the month of October. It appears that Chambers was paid twenty-four thousand dollars, three thousand dollars each for *selling* eight girls, most likely to someone in Canada. The names of the girls are listed in the file. We think that they were runaways staying at the ranch." Walker paused. "He was probably going to do the same thing with Sam Daniels."

Broadhurst's expression didn't change. "I'll have my people look into it," he said. "Is there anything else I can do for you, Agent Walker?" Broadhurst glanced at his watch and added, "I'm scheduled to meet with Chambers and his lawyer shortly."

Walker was still fuming when he returned to his room. A couple of minutes later, he found Munoz and Stansky and filled them in on his conversation with Broadhurst.

"That cinches it. He's not listening to anything I say. There's nothing more for us to do here," Walker said.

"Do you have any idea what Broadhurst meant by 'a different direction?'" asked Munoz.

"No. I'm hoping that he just said that because he hasn't had a lot of time to interrogate Chambers, but I doubt it. Whatever he meant, I'm sure I'm not going to like it. But then I'm not exactly objective when it comes to Broadhurst."

An hour later, Walker called Cheryl. "Can you talk?"

"Yeah, Maddie's upstairs."

"How did it go?" Walker asked.

"Actually, it was easier than I expected. I think sometimes we, or at least I, forget how bright she is."

"You can say 'we.' I'm guilty of that too."

Cheryl laughed softly. "Okay, 'we.' Anyway, it was obvious that Maddie had figured out that Sam had been held against her will, but the first thing she brought up was about her being chained to a wall; that freaked Maddie out," Cheryl said. "She asked me if the man had done anything else to Sam. I'm sure she was thinking of rape. I told her the truth: I didn't know."

"I don't know either. And we may never know, unless Sam decides to tell us."

"So if anything like that did happen, but Sam is not willing to talk about it, then this Chambers guy is just going to be charged with kidnapping?"

Walker hesitated. "Probably not even that."

"What do you mean?"

Walker told her about his discussions with Broadhurst, and then he added, "I hate the expression 'my hands are tied,' but in this case, it happens to be accurate. I don't see what else I can do, and Broadhurst doesn't seem to care," Walker said. "So it looks like I'll definitely be heading home tomorrow."

"Do you want me to pick you up, rather than have Dave drive you?"

"I thought about that, but maybe it would be better if it were just you, Maddie, and Sam. Sam might feel more comfortable with it being just the three of you."

"That's fine. Okay, I'll talk to you tomorrow."

Chapter Thirty-Five

Walker woke up early on Thursday morning. Surprisingly, he had slept reasonably well. There had been no tossing and turning in spite of his confrontation with Broadhurst. But now that he was fully awake, his mind continued to replay the events of the night before and wouldn't let them go. It didn't take long, however, for Walker to realize that there was a remedy readily at hand for getting rid of the endless loop playing in his head: going for a run.

When he'd packed for the trip to Maine, Walker had anticipated that he might need his running gear, and now he was glad that he had thought ahead. Before he set out, he called Munoz and Stansky and told them he was skipping breakfast to do a workout. He did some light stretching in front of the dorm-like structure where he was staying and then headed out to the quarter-mile composition track that was part of the training complex's outdoor survival and fitness course.

Although Walker preferred running on the roads because of the change in scenery it afforded, the composition track was much more forgiving on his knees, not to mention the softer landing his feet experienced as he completed each stride. He finished the five miles in under thirty-one minutes—the fastest time he had run for that distance in the last five years. More importantly, however, the ease with which he had completed the run allowed his brain to relegate the confrontation with Broadhurst to an afterthought.

As he was cooling down, Walker mentally outlined what he was going to say to the professor when he called him later. Those thoughts triggered the realization that he had another call to make even before that one. His former supervisor, the same individual who had authorized the investigation to begin with, needed to be informed that it was being shut down.

Walker took his time getting back to his room. Then he took a long shower, shaved, and around 9:15 a.m. he placed the first call. The respite from thoughts of Broadhurst that his run had provided quickly disappeared once he began to tell his supervisor everything that had happened: from the first time he and Munoz had come to Redemption Ranch, to finding Sam, and now to having to end the investigation because it had been taken away from him.

Walker attempted to keep his tone neutral, especially when he mentioned Broadhurst, but the supervisor picked up on the animus.

"It sounds like this Broadhurst character came in with guns blazing and shoved everybody else out of the way."

"That's an apt description," Walker said.

The supervisor was quiet for a moment and then offered, "I know you, Craig. So I know that it's got to be eating you up that you weren't able to follow this through to the end. But that girl is alive because of you. That's what you have to focus on."

"I know. You're right. And I know whatever happens from here on is out of my control. I'll eventually be able to let it go, but right now the idea that Broadhurst's not even considering charging Chambers with what he did to Sam Daniels and possibly others…" Walker didn't finish the sentence.

"Are you still running?" asked the supervisor. "You used to tell me that running helped clear your head."

"Yeah, actually I went for a run this morning just before I called you." Walker paused and decided to lighten the moment. "In this situation, five miles was probably not far enough. Maybe if I had run to Cleveland…"

After Walker ended the call, he allowed himself a little while to decompress before he phoned Professor Mason. The professor answered on the second ring.

"Hello, Agent Walker. I was hoping I'd hear from you. How's the girl ... Sam ... doing?"

"Pretty well. She's scheduled to be discharged this afternoon."

"That's wonderful news," the professor said. "Have you been able to apprehend the individual responsible?"

"He's been taken into custody, yes." Walker hesitated before continuing. "I'm afraid this is going to be difficult to hear, Professor. It's Tom Chambers."

"*Tom* Chambers? I don't understand."

Walker explained everything that seemed relevant to the professor's concern, leaving out some of the more disturbing details that had been uncovered about Tom Chambers' activities.

Walker closed by saying, "I'm sure this is a terrible shock"

"And you're certain it's him?" the professor asked.

"Yes, there's no doubt."

"I suppose it does explain some things. I had trouble imagining JT behaving the way he seemed to be. Do you have any idea what possessed Tom to do such a thing?"

"I suspect it was the money. By assuming James'... JT's identity, Tom got control of over a million dollars."

"I had no idea there was that much money involved," the professor said.

There was a brief silence, and then Walker said, "There is something else." Walker proceeded to tell the professor about the diary. "It's being held by Homeland Security currently, but according to the will, it should be turned over to you in about a year or so."

"I'm not sure how I feel about that. I certainly appreciate Lemuel's gesture, but... it feels tainted somehow, what with Tom's actions. It's probably best that I have a year to decide what I want to do." The professor paused. "Well, thank you for everything, Agent Walker. And I'm so pleased that the girl is doing well."

"And thank you, Professor. You were a big part of her rescue."

"That's nice of you to say. It makes an old man feel good."

Walker responded, "I don't think of you as an old man."

"Well then, I'd recommend that you have your eyes checked, but thank you, nevertheless," the professor said.

Walker laughed and said good-bye. He had barely put the phone down when another call came in. It was Munoz.

"Hi, Craig. I just wanted to find out what time you were thinking about leaving."

"Maybe an hour or so—eleven, eleven fifteen."

"That sounds good. I'll tell Peter."

"I just got off the phone with Professor Mason."

"How did that go?" Munoz asked.

"As well as could be expected, I guess. He was really taken aback about Tom Chambers."

"That's understandable. What did he say about the diary?"

"Actually, he had some trepidation about it."

"Really?"

"Yeah, I think the academic side of him is excited, but the personal side… I think he's struggling with what happened and that Tom Chambers is responsible."

They spoke for a few more minutes and then agreed to meet in the dining hall at 11:15.

Walker packed up his belongings, straightened up the room, and shortly before eleven o'clock, called his wife.

"Hi, there. Are you on your way to the medical center?"

"Actually, we're already here. I didn't want Sam to have to wait in case she got discharged early. Dr. Cosgrove said he'd start the paper work in about a half hour. We should be on our way by noontime. We'll probably stop and get something to eat along the way. So we should be home around two thirty or so."

"I think we'll be leaving shortly too. I might even beat you home."

"Okay, I'll see you later."

The three agents were all in the dining hall by 11:10. Walker indicated that he wanted to stop by Chuck Dalton's office to thank him before they left. As he started to get up, his phone rang.

"Hi, Craig. It's Chuck. Can you come by my office?"

"I was just about to do that. We were planning on leaving in a few minutes. I just wanted to thank you and say good-bye."

"After you hear what I have to tell you, you may want to stick around for a while."

"Okay. I'll be right there."

Five minutes later Walker was standing in Chuck Dalton's office. They shook hands, sat down, and then Dalton began.

"Broadhurst's been in with Chambers and his lawyer since eight o'clock this morning. A few minutes ago he called me to say that they were finalizing a plea deal."

"A plea deal? Just like that?" Walker asked.

"That's what he told me. He also asked me to arrange a meeting with you for around noon. Are you okay staying around till then?"

Walker wasn't able to hide his surprise. "Yeah... I guess. I just can't imagine why he wants to meet with me again. It certainly didn't go all that well last night."

"I don't know what to tell you. He didn't elaborate."

"Okay, it can't hurt to find out what he wants. Where are we meeting?"

"You can use the conference room down the hall here," Dalton said.

"All right. I'll be back at noon."

Broadhurst showed up at 12:10, offered a halfhearted apology for being late, and sat down.

"Did Supervising Agent Dalton fill you in?"

"He mentioned something about finalizing a plea deal," Walker said.

"Yes, that's correct. It's still subject to the judge's approval, but I don't believe that's going to be a problem, especially because I was under the gun here, and the judge knows that. The timing had to be just right; I had to coordinate everything with the Canadian authorities. That's why I couldn't share anything with you last night. It all had to be kept confidential, but I was finally able to get everything I wanted this morning."

Walker nodded, but didn't respond.

Broadhurst continued. "I thought, given that you were part of the case, at least at the very beginning, that you deserved to hear how it's going to play out."

Walker wasn't buying what Broadhurst was selling; he still couldn't figure out what he was doing there.

Broadhurst leaned forward and forced the corners of his mouth up slightly.

"Chambers has agreed to testify against a man named Eli Peters; he's one of the main distributors of illegal drugs in all of Canada. This Peters has already been taken into custody." Broadhurst paused. "Chambers has given us his supplier, so there's something in it for the United States as well. This will be a major disruption to the illegal drug trade between the two countries."

Walker had trouble displaying any enthusiasm, partly because he had no way of knowing whether this was as big a deal as Broadhurst was making it out to be. He also recognized that his lack of enthusiasm was due to his supposition that any charges related to Sam Daniels were probably not part of the plea deal. He decided to find out for sure.

"So what exactly did Chambers plead to?"

"You're wondering about the girl? I threatened him with that, but eventually I had to drop it. At the end of the day, the charges that carried the most weight were drug trafficking, identity theft, and attempting to enter the United States illegally—crimes that we have evidence for. The last charge has taken on greater significance over the last several years, as I'm sure you're aware. It could have carried a very stiff sentence if he wasn't willing to cooperate."

Walker thought back to Broadhurst's "confidential" comment. "So if you're able to tell me, what exactly is in the agreement? How much time is Chambers going to get?"

Broadhurst appeared uncomfortable and had trouble maintaining eye contact. "He'll be in *federal* prison... for three years."

Walker was stunned, and he couldn't hide it. "Three years? That's it?"

Broadhurst got defensive. "I wanted to give you the courtesy of hearing this directly from me, but it appears that you don't understand what goes into something like this, Agent Walker. There's always a fine line you have to walk in negotiations. I saved a lot of lives today. That's what really matters, not whether one individual—who will be on our watch list for the rest of his life, by the way—gets out a year or two earlier than he might have. I had to weigh all of that, and in my position, I can't worry about being second-guessed."

Walker thought the only second-guessing going on was in Broadhurst's own mind—and rightly so. Walker was quiet for a moment, still trying to figure out why Broadhurst felt the need to tell him about the plea deal, especially since he must have known what Walker's reaction would be. Walker sensed that anything he said at this point would be met with further recriminations. He decided it would be best if he just left.

"Thanks for letting me know what happened. I hope it works out the way you're expecting it to."

Munoz and Stansky were waiting for Walker in the dining hall when he finished. As he approached them, he shook his head.

"You won't believe it. I'll fill you in in the car."

Munoz and Stansky were just as shocked as Walker had been when they heard about the agreement.

"You've got to be kidding me!" said Munoz. "Three years, and he gets immunity on kidnapping and human trafficking? That's ridiculous."

"I didn't see the actual document, but that's the essence of what Broadhurst told me. He claims that this Peters guy is one of the biggest drug dealers in all of Canada, and that's why he made the deal," said Walker.

"I don't care. It still seems like Chambers got off with next to nothing," protested Munoz.

"I don't disagree," said Walker.

Stansky entered the conversation. "You know what's even more disturbing? Think about this: once Chambers gets out of prison, he gets to go live on the ranch, and after five years, he gets the four-hundred-thousand dollar trust fund."

Walker looked back at Stansky. "That can't be right."

"I'm no lawyer, but it seems to me, unless there's something in the plea deal negating it, I think the will stands as written."

Walker was shaking his head. "This just keeps on getting better and better."

Munoz asked, "Do you think it's worthwhile giving Broadhurst a call and finding out?"

"He made it pretty clear that he doesn't like people second-guessing him. And honestly, there's a part of me that doesn't want to know."

✧Chapter Thirty-Six✧

Cheryl was already back with Maddie and Sam when Munoz dropped Walker off at his house in Danvers. As soon as Cheryl heard the front door open, she went out to greet her husband.

"Hey. I was surprised that you weren't here already when I got home. Is everything all right?"

"Not exactly. Where are the girls?"

"Upstairs in Maddie's room. I set up Sam in Mark's bedroom for the time being. If she still wants to stay here after he gets back in a couple of weeks, we'll have to figure out something with the spare bedroom you're using for an office."

"That's fine," Walker said. "Why don't we go into the kitchen? I want to be out of earshot."

Walker spent the next several minutes telling Cheryl about the meeting with Broadhurst. He ended by saying, "I'm still not sure why he asked to see me. He had to have known that I'd be critical of the deal."

"And you're sure there was nothing else to it?" asked Cheryl. "I mean, even I can see that Chambers got off with practically nothing."

"If there had been something else, I'm sure Broadhurst would've told me. I didn't really hide how I felt about it," Walker said. "Anyway, that's why I was late getting back. So how was the ride home?"

"It was fine, other than I felt a little bit like a chauffeur; Maddie and Sam sat in the back the whole time, but it wasn't as if they were trying to hide anything. I could hear pretty much everything they said. Sam didn't bring up anything about the ranch, at least not that I heard."

"Well, it probably doesn't matter now, anyway," Walker said. "Did you plan anything for supper?"

"I'll figure out something," Cheryl replied.

"I was thinking, why don't I go out and pick up Chinese, or maybe a pizza?"

"That's okay with me. We could let Sam choose."

"Good idea."

Cheryl started to head out of the kitchen, but then she stopped and turned back. "I just wanted to remind you that I had to switch work, so I'm scheduled to go in tomorrow, Saturday, and Sunday. That means you'll have to take Maddie and Sam to Habitat on Saturday."

"That's not a problem. Are you sure Sam still wants to go?"

"Yeah, she does. I heard her talking to Maddie about it. Plus, I think it'll be good for her; she needs to get back into a normal routine."

"After what she's been through, I've got to think almost anything's going to seem normal."

Cheryl had already left for work when Walker came downstairs shortly after seven on Friday morning; Sam came into the kitchen about a half hour later.

"Good morning, Sam. Did you sleep okay?"

"Pretty well."

"Good. Do you want some juice… or coffee?"

"Just some juice for now. I can get it."

"No, you're a guest. Take a seat; I'll get some for you."

"Thanks. Maddie's not up yet?" Sam asked.

"No, we may not see her for a couple more hours."

A small smile formed on Sam's lips. "I can't really do that—sleep late, I mean. I never could. I don't know why."

"I can't either," said Walker as he handed Sam a small glass of orange juice.

There was silence for a few moments, and then Sam asked, "Can I talk to you about something?"

"Sure."

"Maddie and I were planning to go to Habitat tomorrow. But I'm just wondering what I should say... you know... about why I haven't been there and where I was."

"I hadn't thought about that. That's a good question," Walker said. "I think the simplest explanation would probably be best. What about saying that you had to go to Maine for a few days? If you say it that way, I don't think anybody's going to press you on it. And if they do, you can just say it's personal."

Sam nodded. "I like that idea. I think I'd be comfortable saying that. Thank you." Sam took a sip of juice before she continued.

"Can I use the phone later? I'd like to call Mrs. Burns at school. I want to thank her and ask her what I should do about missing the World Cultures final."

Walker offered a gentle smile. "I think it's a great idea to call Mrs. Burns, at least to let her know you're all right. As far as missing the final, I wouldn't worry about that for now. I'm sure the school will make allowances, considering what happened."

"But I don't know whether I'm ready to talk about it," Sam said.

"From what I know of Mrs. Burns, if you tell her you're not ready to explain everything yet, I'm sure she'll be able to work something out," Walker said. "Or, if you'd like, I could call her, tell her that you're okay, and that you'll contact her soon. That'll buy you some more time."

"Would you mind?" Sam asked.

"Not at all."

It was shortly before one o'clock when Walker finished leaving a message for Alice Burns on her voice mail. He had barely put his phone down when it buzzed. He glanced at the screen before he answered. It was Chuck Dalton.

"Hi, Chuck. I didn't expect to hear from you. What's going on?"

Dalton didn't even say hello. "I just found out that Broadhurst is going to hold a press conference tomorrow night. He's going to announce the capture of Tom Chambers and the arrest of Eli Peters, the drug dealer in Canada."

"A press conference? That's a little unusual, isn't it, even for Homeland?"

"That's what I thought too, so I called a few people to find out what was going on. Evidently, there's going to be a preliminary announcement before the press conference. Broadhurst is going to be named Director of Northern Border Enforcement. He'll be in charge of the entire northern United States."

"You're not serious?"

"Absolutely. I was told this has been in the works for a while now, and then when Broadhurst finalized the deal with Chambers, that more or less cinched it," Dalton said.

"I don't get it. Why would that cinch it?"

"Homeland wants additional cooperation from Canada. So the Canadians were asked for their input as to who should fill the new position. When Broadhurst delivered this Peters guy, he became the obvious choice."

"So you're telling me the plea deal was all about politics?" Walker asked.

"It would appear so."

"If I wasn't already retired, this would have made me file my papers."

"Don't say that. I've still got five more years," Dalton said.

"Good luck with that."

"Oh yeah, and I found out why Broadhurst asked for that meeting with you. He wanted to show the powers that be that he could work collaboratively with other agencies."

"What?"

"Yeah, he put in his report that he met with you twice before the plea deal was approved to make sure you were kept apprised of what was happening."

"That's unbelievable. That was a done deal before he even spoke with me. What a piece of work."

"Sorry to be the bearer of bad tidings."

"No. I appreciate the call," Walker said. "So what time is this press conference? Is it going to be televised?"

"Six thirty, and yeah it looks like it's going to be right in time for the nightly news."

"I doubt I'm going to watch, but maybe I'll DVR it in case I feel masochistic sometime in the future."

Dalton laughed. "Well, one thing's for sure. Broadhurst has a real dilemma on his hands."

"Why's that?"

"He's got to decide whether he wants to be called director or commander?"

Walker returned the laugh. "Knowing him, he'll probably go with both. Director Commander Broadhurst. That's got a nice ring to it, don't you think?"

As Walker hung up, he realized that despite the lighthearted end to his conversation with Dalton, there was a potentially serious side to what he had been told. Up to this point, there had been no media coverage of the activities at Redemption Ranch, but that was about to change.

It seemed unlikely that Broadhurst would mention anything having to do with Sam, but there was no way to tell for sure. Broadhurst might decide that taking credit for bringing a suspected kidnapper to justice would play extremely well in the media, even though Chambers hadn't been charged with that particular crime.

Walker's instincts told him that Sam needed to be told about the press conference, but he decided it might be better to wait until the next day after the girls got back from Habitat. That would give him time to run it by Cheryl to get her input, and it would also give him time to prepare how he was going to approach it with Sam.

Walker mulled things over for several more minutes and then decided to reach out to Dave Munoz to see what he thought. He summarized Chuck Dalton's phone call and then added, "Evidently, they're announcing Broadhurst's appointment at the beginning of the press conference."

"I guess we shouldn't be all that surprised," said Munoz. "We figured there had to be something else behind the plea deal."

"My main concern now is Sam. I haven't told her yet, but I think I have to. Who knows what Broadhurst is liable to say?"

"I think you're right; you definitely have to tell her. We just have to hope that he keeps her out of it," Munoz said. "Listen, I don't know what it could be, but if there's anything I can do to help, let me know."

"I can't think of anything right now, but why don't you give me a call after the press conference? I'd like to get your take on it."

"Okay, will do. I'll talk to you tomorrow night."

As soon as Cheryl got home from work, Walker was able to steal her away for a few minutes. He told her about Broadhurst's new appointment and the upcoming press conference. Cheryl reacted just as Dave Munoz had.

"I don't think you have any choice; you have to let her know. At this point, she trusts us. If Broadhurst exposes her, and she finds out we knew it was coming, she's going to feel betrayed. She's still fragile, Craig."

"Do you think waiting until after she gets back from Habitat is the right thing to do?"

"Off the top my head, I'd say yes. If you tell her tonight, she's got almost twenty-four hours to worry about it."

"That's what I've been thinking," Walker said. "She already asked me about what to say to the people at Habitat tomorrow." Walker went on to tell Cheryl about his conversation with Sam.

"That was good advice, but I still think she's got enough on her plate. I'd definitely wait until after Habitat. Of course, that's easy for me to say; I won't be here." She closed the distance between them and put her arms around her husband. "But you'll do fine; you certainly have so far."

"Yeah, counseling teenage girls has always been my strong suit."

Walker dropped Maddie and Sam off shortly before nine o'clock in Lynn where the new Habitat house was being built. He came home, went for a run, showered, shaved, and read the newspaper. By then it was nearly time to pick up the girls.

He had been an FBI agent for twenty years, but the knot he had in his stomach this morning came close to matching anything he had experienced over much of his career. As Maddie and Sam piled into the back seat, Walker threw out the standard parental question.

"How did everything go?"

To his surprise, Sam answered first. "Really good. Nobody asked me anything, and all our adviser said was, 'We missed you.' I told her just what we talked about—that I had to be up in Maine, and she didn't ask anything else. I guess I was worrying for nothing."

Walker was thinking, *I hope that's the case for me too.*

Before he could say anything, Maddie jumped in. "And then we got right to work. It was really a lot of fun. Some college guys asked us to help them put up sheetrock. You know what that is, right?"

Walker smiled to himself. "Yeah, I know what that is."

"Anyway, these college guys put in a few nails to keep the sheet rock in place, and then Sam and I got to nail the rest of it. We did that the whole time. We finished two whole rooms."

"Well, that's impressive," Walker said. He decided to push Maddie's buttons. "College guys, huh?"

Maddie shook her head. "Daaad." Once again, his daughter had displayed the uncanny ability to turn a single-syllable word into one with multiple syllables and at the same time make him regret that he had asked the question in the first place. Walker looked in the rearview mirror and saw Sam smiling. It was one of the few times he had seen her smile since she had come to stay with them.

They arrived back at the house in Danvers around 12:30 p.m. They all had some lunch, and then the girls went upstairs. Walker waited until 1:30 and then went and knocked on Maddie's door.

"Come on in, Dad."

As Walker entered the room, both girls turned their attention toward him. He hesitated for a moment, and then said, "Sam, I was wondering if I could speak with you for a minute, downstairs."

Maddie responded before Sam did. "Just Sam?"

"Yes, honey."

Sam appeared somewhat nervous. "Is everything all right?"

"Yes. I just need to talk with you for a minute."

"Okay."

Five minutes later, the two of them were seated at the kitchen table. Walker tried to ease into the conversation.

"I hope you know, Sam that we've tried to respect the fact that you're not ready to talk about what happened, but there's been a development that I think you need to know about."

"What?" Sam asked warily.

"First of all, the man from the ranch has been arrested," Walker said.

Sam closed her eyes but didn't say anything.

Walker continued. "His name is Tom Chambers. Did you know that?"

"I sort of figured it out."

Walker decided not to press the point. "Anyway, the reason I'm telling you this is that the person who coordinated the arrest is holding a press conference tonight. And it's probably going to be on TV." Sam's eyes opened wider. Walker quickly added, "I don't think you'll be mentioned, certainly not by name. But I thought you should know just in case."

Sam didn't respond immediately. A few seconds later she asked, "If they're not going to say anything about the ranch, what are they going to talk about? What was he arrested for?"

"He was using the tunnel to smuggle drugs into Canada."

"Oh," Sam said. "Do you think that's where he was planning to take me?"

Walker was surprised by the question. "I don't know. Did he mention anything like that to you?"

"After he drugged me, he hardly spoke to me at all," Sam said. "You said the press conference is tonight?"

"Yes. It's scheduled for six thirty."

"I'm not sure I want to watch it." Sam looked away for a second, and then back at Walker. "Habitat was great this morning; it took my mind off of what happened. And I am feeling better about things, but…"

"I understand," Walker said.

"Could you watch it for me and tell me about it afterward?"

"If that's what you'd like."

Chapter Thirty-Seven

At 6:30 on Saturday night, Walker was sitting in his home office in front of the TV, waiting for the press conference to start. He decided to record it just in case Sam changed her mind and wanted to watch it, although he doubted that was very likely. It was only being carried live on one of the "off" channels that served the New England area, but Walker suspected it was possible that several minutes of footage would be shown on the major outlets later that night.

The undersecretary of the Department of Homeland Security strode to the podium at 6:31 p.m. She spent the first five minutes lauding the agency she helped oversee before turning her attention to Broadhurst. She gave a laundry list of his accomplishments and ended the introduction by saying, "Commander Broadhurst has only been with Homeland Security a relatively short period of time, but he distinguished himself very quickly and has been on the short list for a promotion even before this latest investigation was concluded. It is an honor for me to introduce to you the new *Director* of Northern Border Enforcement. Jack Broadhurst."

What followed was exactly what Walker had witnessed firsthand in all his dealings with Broadhurst: egomania run amok. In just the first few sentences Broadhurst uttered, he made it seem as if he had single-handedly captured Tom Chambers, excavated the tunnel, arrested Eli Peters, and saved the United States from terrorists streaming across the border from Canada.

But as Broadhurst droned on, it became evident to Walker that the press corps wasn't warming to the new director, or his self-serving dog and pony show. Broadhurst had raised the specter of terrorists, but that was in the abstract; he hadn't actually captured or arrested any. And while drug trafficking was abhorrent, it was not something the reporters could sink their journalistic teeth into. As the camera panned periodically to the room full of correspondents, the expressions on their faces and their body language said it all: there was no major story here; mainly it was just a photo op.

Broadhurst must have sensed the same thing that Walker had, because ten minutes further into his remarks, he stopped looking down at his prepared speech and shifted gears. Walker couldn't believe what he was hearing.

"It may seem strange to say, but sometimes those of us who protect our country's borders can get caught up in what we refer to as the big picture and overlook the personal, individual tragedies that are often part of investigations like this. As soon as I knew that I had been selected for this new position, I made a vow that I was not going to let that happen on my watch."

Broadhurst paused and surveyed the crowd before he continued.

"The reason we found out about the tunnel at Redemption Ranch was because a young teenage girl was being held captive there. Once my Homeland team was brought in, we painstakingly searched the property for any more victims. When it became apparent that there weren't any, we turned our attention to the tunnel. And that's where we found evidence of drug smuggling and a potential terrorist entry point.

"I'm very proud of my team for its efforts in that regard, but more importantly, on the personal, human level, we caught a... sexual predator and prevented him from hurting any other young girls. In some ways, that's the most satisfying part of what my team was able to accomplish here."

Walker was holding the remote control in his hand, and it took all of his constraint not to throw it at the TV.

"You son of a bitch."

Once Broadhurst finished his statement and opened up the press conference to questions, they came fast and furiously.

"Can you give us the young girl's name?"

"Where is she from?"

"Is she all right?"

"How long was she held captive?"

The questions went on and on. Mercifully, Broadhurst didn't give out any details, *probably*, thought Walker, *because he didn't know any of them, including Sam's name.*

The press conference ended at 7:05 a.m. Munoz called at 7:06.

"If I hadn't heard it with my own ears, I wouldn't have believed it. What a jerk. At first I thought it was just going to be typical Broadhurst, nearly breaking his arm from patting himself on the back so much. But then when he made himself out to be this knight in shining armor, as if he found Sam... and then the sexual predator remark. Where did that come from?"

Walker's anger was palpable even over the phone. "I don't know. But what's got me even more pissed off is that Broadhurst's probably put a target on Sam's back. The press isn't going to let this go. They're going to dig until they find out who she is."

They talked for another fifteen minutes, and then Walker said, "I think I better go. I've got to figure out what to tell Sam."

Walker waited a few minutes and then went downstairs to find Cheryl. She had made herself some tea and was sitting in the kitchen.

"How was the press conference?"

"It couldn't have been worse," Walker said.

"What do you mean?"

Walker went on to explain. After he finished, Cheryl asked, "Why would he do something like that?"

"I think Broadhurst could tell that the press conference wasn't going anywhere. He's got a huge ego, and evidently the promotion wasn't enough. Everything's always got to be about him and what he's done. He knew the reporters would eat up the story of a young girl being held captive, and then he threw in the sex angle for good measure," Walker said. "Dave called me right afterward. He agrees with me; they're going to be looking for Sam. Somebody will figure out who she is, and then she'll become a victim all over again."

"What are you going to do?"

"I know she didn't want to watch the press conference, but now I think she should. I recorded it just in case. I could try to explain it to her, but I think it's better if she sees it for herself."

"I can offer to watch it with her, if you'd prefer not to," Cheryl said.

"Let me broach it with her and see what she's comfortable with," Walker said. "She told me that she was just starting to feel better about everything, and then Broadhurst does this."

"Are you going to talk to her right away?"

"No. I think I'll wait until she asks me about it."

"I was going to go upstairs and read for a while, but if you'd rather I stay…"

"No, no, go ahead. I'll call you if I need you." Walker glanced at the kitchen clock. "The Red Sox are on. I'm going to go inside and watch them for a while."

Just before the seventh inning started around nine o'clock, Sam came down the stairs and into the living room.

"Did you watch the press conference?"

"Yes, I did," Walker said. "Why don't you come in and sit down. I need to talk to you about it."

Sam's shoulders tensed as she took a seat. "Did they mention my name?"

"No, but they talked about the ranch and the tunnel... and that a teenage girl had been held captive," Walker said.

Sam closed her eyes. "But they didn't mention my name?"

"No, but there's more to it."

"What?"

"It might be better if you see for yourself. I recorded it. If you're up to watching it..." Walker's voice trailed off.

Sam didn't answer right away and then with some obvious hesitancy she said, "Okay, if you really think I should."

"I do."

Sam nodded. "All right."

Walker hit the DVR button on the remote, found the press conference on the list of saved programs, and clicked start.

"I'm going to fast-forward through the beginning."

Walker found the spot right after Broadhurst was introduced and hit play.

Sam sat silently as she listened to Broadhurst's remarks. She barely showed any emotion until she heard the words "We caught a sexual predator." Then the expression on her face turned to one of horror.

"Oh, my God, why did he say that? It's not true; that man never touched me like that!" Sam looked at Walker and repeated herself "Why would he say that?"

Although he believed he did know why, Walker wasn't about to get into it at that point. He hit the pause button and turned toward Sam.

"I don't know what he was thinking."

"But nothing like that happened. How can he just make something like that up? Is this because I didn't tell anybody what happened right away?"

"No, Sam. You can't think like that. None of this is your fault."

Walker could sense that Sam was trying to come to grips with something. Eventually, she said, "I think I'd like to tell you everything that happened, so you'll know that it wasn't like that."

"You don't have to do that, Sam. I believe you."

"I know you do. But... I want to."

Sam started at the very beginning when she had first arrived at Redemption Ranch and had climbed over the break in the rock formation. She told Walker about being surprised that nobody was there, that even the horses were gone. Walker wanted to interrupt to ask a question at that point, but he didn't want to break Sam's train of thought. He did make a mental note, however.

She went on to explain that seeing the man she thought was JT with a beard had thrown her at first, but then she had accepted it. Once again, after Sam explained about Topaz, the accident, and how she figured out the man wasn't JT, Walker wanted to press her for details, but he didn't. He simply made another mental note.

Sam told him that she didn't remember being moved into the tunnel, and despite how afraid she was, she didn't believe the man was going to kill her, and he certainly didn't touch her in a sexual way. As she explained about her time in the tunnel, Walker thought she was going to break down. She described it as claustrophobic, but Walker, remembering what she looked like when he first came upon her, suspected it went far beyond that.

As Sam was coming to the end, Walker spoke for the first time, explaining that the shaking sensation Sam had experienced was actually a small earthquake that had partially collapsed the tunnel.

When she finished, Sam sat back in the chair, appearing emotionally and physically spent, as if she had experienced a portion of her ordeal all over again. A couple of minutes went by before either of them spoke.

Eventually, Sam said, "Thank you for listening."

"You don't need to thank me."

Another few moments passed, and then Sam asked, "You paused the recording. Is there more?"

"A little bit." Walker pressed play again, and the screen came to life. He stopped it immediately after the section with the reporters' questions and Broadhurst's answers.

Sam looked over at Walker. "It's good that he didn't tell them anything, right?"

"It is, but what I'm concerned about is that I think the press is going to try to find out who you are. The way they reacted, I think they believe your story is more interesting."

"But how will they find me? They don't even know my name," Sam said.

"I hope I'm wrong about it. But they're reporters; they have a lot of resources."

Sam didn't say anything for a few moments and then asked, "If they really are going to come looking for me, would it be all right if I stayed here for a while longer?"

"As long as you like," Walker said.

Sam rose out of her chair. "I think I'm going to go up to bed now." She was about to leave the living room when she stopped and turned around. She had tears in her eyes. "Thank you for everything, Mr. Walker, especially for being so patient with me."

It appeared to Walker that she wanted to say more but couldn't.

Walker stayed where he was until the Red Sox game was over, although his mind was elsewhere the whole time. When he went upstairs to bed, he told Cheryl everything that Sam had said, but he left out the mental notes that he had made as she was relating her story. He needed more time to sort out why his brain had wanted to know more.

Sunday morning started off the same way that Saturday morning had. Cheryl was already at work when Walker came downstairs to make himself some breakfast. Sam showed up twenty minutes later.

"Good morning," said Walker.

"Good morning."

Walker attempted to put Sam at ease after what she had been through the previous night.

"Feels like déjà vu. Didn't we just do this yesterday morning? Do you want some juice?" Walker asked.

Sam managed a small smile. "Not right now." There was a brief silence, and then Sam said, "I talked to Maddie last night. I told her the whole story. She knew some of it already, but I felt like I wanted her to know the rest, especially since the reporters might figure out who I am." She paused. "I didn't sleep very well worrying about that."

"I'm sure. The good news is that I checked the Internet this morning, and there's not all that much about the press conference. But I don't necessarily think that's the end of it. The reporters aren't going to publish anything until they have some more specifics; we just need to keep our eyes open."

"I understand," Sam said. "While I was awake last night, I did a lot of thinking. Is it all right if I ask you some questions?"

Walker put his coffee cup down on the counter. "Of course."

"You told me that they arrested Tom Chambers, right?"

Walker nodded. "Yes."

"So does that mean there's going to have to be a trial? Because I really don't want to have to testify."

"You won't." Walker could see the relief overtake Sam as he continued, "Chambers has agreed to turn state's evidence against his partner from Canada in exchange for a lesser sentence."

"So there definitely won't be a trial?" Sam asked.

"No." Walker debated about how much more he should offer to Sam. Eventually, he decided to go with the whole truth. "Actually, as you heard in the press conference, Homeland Security made the decision to concentrate on the smuggling, so Chambers wasn't even charged with any crime relating to what happened to you."

Sam appeared to take that news in stride. "That's okay. I don't really care about that. It was just the idea of having to talk about it in court... I don't know if I could."

"Well, as I said, it's not something you have to worry about now."

They sat in silence for a few moments, and then Sam asked, "You said something about a lesser sentence. How long will he be in jail?"

Walker couldn't hide his distaste for the answer he was about to give. "Three years."

The blood drained from Sam's face. "Three years, and then he's out free?"

"I'm afraid so."

"But... but once he gets out, what's going to prevent him from coming after me?"

Walker started to formulate some reassuring words, but the truth was that he couldn't come up with any. He hadn't thought about how vulnerable Sam would feel when she found out about the terms of the plea deal. He had just focused on the unfairness of it. Once again, Walker decided to respond truthfully. Anything else felt like a defense of what Broadhurst had negotiated. "I don't have an answer for that, Sam."

Walker watched as tears started to form in Sam's eyes. He thought back to Cheryl's words. "You'll do fine." But he had nothing to offer.

Another moment passed, and then Sam spoke with desperation in her voice. "What if I was willing to speak to somebody now about what he did? If it meant he'd have to spend more time in jail, I think I could do it."

Walker looked into Sam's tear-filled eyes. "I'm afraid it wouldn't matter now. I didn't know it at the time, but the man who was running the investigation—the one who was introduced at the press conference, Jack Broadhurst—was never going to charge Tom Chambers with anything having to do with you. He made the decision to only pursue the smuggling aspect. Chambers has immunity. He can't be charged with any crime related to this going back at least six months, probably longer."

"Then why did he say anything about me at the press conference at all? He didn't need to do that," Sam said.

"No, he didn't. I think he was just trying to make himself look good. The whole thing was wrong from the beginning, Sam. I wish there was something I could have done."

Another moment passed, but the desperation in Sam's voice remained. "I'm going to have to move away, aren't I? I mean, I can finish school here, but then when I go to college... I don't want to be any place near him, where he can find me."

Walker realized that there was little he could say to allay Sam's fears, so he moved in a different direction.

"I can't possibly put myself in your shoes, Sam. And maybe I'd feel the same way, but before you make a decision like that, what about talking to Mrs. Burns? I think she'll be back in tomorrow. I remember her telling me that she worked two weeks after school got out."

Sam hesitated before responding. "It's just so frustrating. Every time I'm starting to feel better, I find out something else." She paused. "I don't know. I'll think about talking to Mrs. Burns." She paused again and then repeated the regret she had expressed the day before. "I wish I had just talked about everything right away. Maybe it would have been different."

Walker shook his head. "If you weren't ready, you weren't ready. You can't blame yourself for any of this."

"In my head I know that's true, but somehow it doesn't feel like it," Sam said and started to get emotional. "There are reporters trying to find me, people probably think I was molested, or worse, and in a few years, Tom Chambers could be coming after me." Sam's tears were coming faster now. She started to say something, but then got up and fled the room. Walker began to call out to her, but thought better of it. His instincts told him to just let her be for the time being.

He stayed in the kitchen for another ten minutes, wondering if he should have said or done something differently. He had no idea. Walker moved into the living room, half-glanced at the Sunday paper, and then decided he needed to go for a run.

By the time Walker finished his shower, it was nearly eleven o'clock. He could tell by the dirty dishes in the kitchen sink that both Maddie and Sam had been down to have breakfast. He checked his e-mail and then searched the Internet again for stories about the press conference and Broadhurst's appointment. He found a number of new ones, but they were all puff pieces.

Around 11:30 a.m., Walker heard someone coming down the stairs. It was Sam. As she sat down across from him in the living room, she said, "I'm sorry about before."

"It's okay. There's no need to apologize."

"I had a really good talk with Maddie. I told her what you told me about Tom Chambers only getting three years. She understood about me wanting to move away, but she thinks I should talk to Mrs. Burns too. I'm going to give her a call tomorrow and make an appointment. I'm going to tell her everything I told you and Maddie. I know you said that it probably wouldn't have made any difference if I had talked about it right away, but I can't help but feel that I should have been stronger. I want to try to be stronger now. I don't want to be afraid anymore."

Walker responded, "That's a good attitude, Sam."

"But I'd still like to stay here for the time being, if that's okay? I don't want to be by myself."

As Sam continued to talk, her words came much more quickly. Walker had often observed the same behavior with Maddie whenever her nerves got the best of her, or she was anxious about something.

"Maybe tomorrow I can go to my apartment to pick up some clothes. I'll have to get the key from Angelo, and I can ask him if anyone has been looking for me, you know reporters..."

As the speed of each sentence accelerated, Walker thought back to the way people had described the teenager sitting across from him, and the way he had thought of her as well: tough and resilient. But at this moment, she seemed anything but that. Instead, she seemed like a frightened little girl who probably felt nothing like an adult, despite what the courts had determined.

Chapter Thirty-Eight

Cheryl got home from her shift late Sunday afternoon. Walker was in the kitchen preparing angel hair spaghetti. No one would ever call him a great cook, but a meal comprised mainly of pasta and Ragu sauce straight out of the jar wasn't all that challenging.

Cheryl came over to the stove, gave her husband a kiss on the cheek, and asked, "How did today go?"

"A little bit of a mixed bag. Sam asked how long Chambers was going to be in jail. She's worried that he might come after her once he gets out."

"That doesn't seem likely, does it?"

"You wouldn't think so, but then it occurred to me that if Chambers heard about the sexual predator remark, he might think Sam told people he did something to her."

"But he's not even being charged with that. Why would he care?"

"He probably wouldn't. I was just trying to put myself in Sam's place and consider what she might be thinking," Walker said. "She's scared. She told me that she's going to finish high school here, but she wants to apply to colleges far away. She doesn't want to be around here when Chambers gets out."

"She's really that frightened?" Cheryl asked.

"Yeah, I think she is. I suggested that she talk with her guidance counselor, Mrs. Burns, before she decides anything. She's going to call tomorrow and try to see her."

"That should help."

"And then on top of that, she's also worried about the reporters looking for her. That one's on me, though. I don't know. Maybe I shouldn't have mentioned it, but I thought she should to be aware that was a real possibility."

"Well it is, isn't it?"

"Yeah, but all it's done is made her more afraid."

"Craig, you've got to remember, you haven't held anything back from her. She trusts you because of that. And she needs to be able to trust somebody right now."

"You're probably right," Walker said. "Evidently, she trusts Maddie too. She told her everything last night."

"I think that's a good thing too. Now she has somebody her own age to talk to as well."

"She brought up again wanting to continue to stay with us. All I could do was repeat what I said before. 'Stay as long as you want,'" Walker said. "She also mentioned that she'd like to pick up some clothes from her apartment. I told her that we'd figure something out."

"It sounds like it was nonstop around here today," Cheryl said.

"Yeah, it got pretty emotional at times." Walker turned away slightly and stirred the contents of the saucepan. "This should be done in about ten minutes."

"Good, I'm starving."

"Oh, I almost forgot. Mark called. I actually kept him on the phone for more than five minutes," Walker said.

"You'll have to tell me your secret."

Walker smiled as he continued. "He said that he's doing fine and looking forward to coming home over the Fourth. I told him Maddie had a friend staying over for a few days, but I didn't go into any other details."

Cheryl nodded. "It'll be good to see him."

They were quiet for a few moments, and then Cheryl said, "I can take Sam to the school tomorrow, if she's able to get an appointment with her guidance counselor. And then either before or afterward, I can take her to her apartment too. Maddie can come with us."

"I appreciate that, but it might be better if I take her to the apartment. I haven't had a chance to tell her that Dave and I searched it when we were first looking for her. She's probably not going to care, but I'd feel better if she knew about it before she went over there. Plus, I'd like to talk to the building superintendent. He knows I'm with the FBI. I want to make sure no reporters have been snooping around." Walker paused. "It would be great if you could take her to the school though." Walker hesitated, and then decided to let his wife in on what he'd been thinking. "While you guys are gone, it'll give me some time to review the case file again. There are a couple of things that are still gnawing at me."

"I thought there was a plea deal in place," Cheryl said.

"There is, but… I don't feel like I can just let this go."

After dinner Maddie suggested that the four of them play some board games, something the Walker family had done at least once a month or so ever since Maddie was a little girl. Walker looked over at Sam, and when she shrugged a sign of approval, he went over to the hall closet and pulled down Uno and Monopoly.

It was a mindless way to spend a Sunday night, and for the first time, Sam seemed somewhat relaxed; it appeared that she had put tunnels, reporters, and plea deals out of her head. A few times Walker stole a glance at her and caught her smiling. He felt as if he could almost read her mind. *This must be how families are supposed to be.*

Sam called over to the high school shortly after nine o'clock on Monday morning. Mrs. Burns told her to come over any time. Cheryl, Sam, and Maddie left the house around 9:30, giving Walker a chance to spread out the case file on the kitchen table and dig in, uninterrupted.

It took him nearly an hour to read the contents of the entire file again. He made a page full of notes, focusing on the two major issues he wanted to talk with Sam about. He decided to wait until after the visit to the apartment before bringing them up.

He was sitting in the living room reading the paper around 11:15 a.m. when he heard the front door open. He looked up and caught Cheryl's eye before Maddie and Sam entered behind her. She nodded slightly, said hello, and then headed up the stairs.

Maddie came in next, said, "Hi, Dad," and went upstairs as well.

Sam closed the front door behind her, saw that Walker was in the living room, and came over to him.

"I'm glad you suggested that I talk with Mrs. Burns. It was really good. I told her all about the ranch; it's actually getting easier to talk about, thank goodness. And I told her about Tom Chambers getting out in three years. It's too early for me to apply to any colleges yet, so she thinks I should wait to see how I feel when the time comes. It makes sense. I guess I wasn't thinking very clearly yesterday. Anyway, I'm just going to try to put it out of my head and not think about it." There was a slight pause, and then Sam shifted topics. "When do you want to go over to the apartment?"

"Whenever you're ready," Walker said.

"I just need a couple of minutes, okay?"

On the way over to Sam's apartment, Walker explained how he and Dave Munoz had persuaded the building superintendent, Angelo Lentini, to let them in when they were first looking for her. As Walker had expected, it didn't seem to faze her.

Once they arrived, Walker took the lead with the superintendent.

"Sam was up in Maine this whole time, but as you can see, she's back now. She's going to be staying with my family and me for a while. She and my daughter are friends; I think you knew that. Anyway, Sam's lost her keys. If you could just let her into the apartment to get some things…"

"No problem," Lentini said.

Although Walker had planned what to say next, he threw it out as if it were an afterthought. "Actually, it's possible that her keys were stolen, so if you could keep an eye out if anybody goes near her apartment, or asks questions about her. I'd appreciate it, if you could let me know."

Walker took out one of his business cards and started to hand it to Lentini, but the building superintendent didn't accept it.

"I still have the one you gave me when you were first here. I'll call you if anybody shows up."

Walker sensed that the building superintendent wasn't necessarily buying the story he was offering, but since Walker was an FBI agent, Lentini probably wasn't going to challenge him.

As Lentini led them toward Sam's apartment, he looked back over his shoulder and said, "In the meantime, I'll have the locks changed." Then he smiled at Sam. "It's good to have you back."

Twenty minutes later, Walker was loading two suitcases into his trunk, and then he and Sam headed back to Danvers. There was silence in the car for the first few minutes, and then Walker said, "After you unpack and get settled, can we talk for a few minutes? I'd just like to get some more details about a couple of things that you told me."

Walker glanced to his right and saw some wariness in Sam's eyes, but it quickly disappeared. "Okay."

Back at home, Walker carried Sam's suitcases upstairs and left them outside the door to the bedroom she was using. Cheryl and Maddie had arranged to go out shopping so Walker and Sam could talk privately.

"Take your time unpacking," said Walker. "When you finish, I'll be in the kitchen."

"It should only take me a few minutes," Sam said.

"That's fine. I'll see you downstairs."

Walker went into his office, gathered up the case file, made sure his notes were on top, and then headed downstairs to the kitchen. He started to put the file on the table when his phone rang. A glance at the screen told him it was Professor Mason.

"Hello, Professor. How are you?"

"I'm not sure exactly."

"Why, what's the matter?"

"I got a phone call last night, and another one just a few minutes ago, both from reporters. I have no idea how they got my number. They wanted to know about the ranch, and if I would comment on what happened there. I wasn't sure what to do, so I just told the first one that I couldn't talk about it and hung up. Then I checked the Internet and found something about a press conference where Redemption Ranch was mentioned. Initially, it didn't seem like much of anything. But then when I got the other call, I figured I better get in touch with you. How did they even know about my connection to the ranch?"

"They probably Googled it. The excerpt from your book is the third or fourth entry. Of course, that doesn't explain how they got your number, but they are reporters; that's what they do."

Walker spent the next few minutes explaining everything that had transpired over the last several days. The professor was appalled at what Broadhurst had done.

"That poor young girl. I'm glad I had the good sense not to talk to the reporters."

"I am too," Walker said. "If anyone else calls, I'd suggest that you do the same thing. Say either 'no comment,' or 'I have nothing to say.'"

The professor started to chuckle. "While I was still lecturing, I'm not sure I would have uttered those words under any circumstances. But I will be sure to do it now."

Walker returned the laugh. "Thank you, Professor."

After he hung up, Walker decided there was no reason to tell Sam about the professor's phone call; it would just raise her anxiety level even further. He opened the case file folder and then got a glass of water. When he looked up, Sam was standing in the doorway.

She eyed the folder on the table and said, "Is that from the investigation?"

"Yes. Are you up to talking about it now?"

"I think so."

"Why don't we sit down?"

Sam pulled out a chair as Walker took a sheet of paper off the top of the pile in the folder. Before he showed it to Sam, he said, "When we searched the main house at the ranch, we found an electronics room with computers, surveillance monitors, and even a hidden safe."

"I didn't see anything like that," Sam said.

"It was behind a fortified door; you wouldn't have had any reason to suspect it was even there. One of our investigators is a tech expert; he was able to get into the computer files, and he found a list of girls' names. Would you take a look and see if you know any of them? They may have been at the ranch the same time that you were there."

Sam extended her hand to take the list from Walker. She took her time initially, and then exclaimed, "I know Tina and Jodi, and Crystal. Crystal was my closest friend at the ranch. When I first went back there, I went to the cabin where I stayed. I found my initials that I had carved into the floor. Crystal's were there too."

Walker remembered that he and Munoz had seen Sam's initials, but he decided not to bring it up; he wanted her to keep talking. Sam looked down at the list again before she continued. "I'm not sure about the other names. A lot of the girls had nicknames; I don't know if I even knew their real names. But I definitely remember Crystal, and Tina and Jodi too."

"Were they all still there when you left?" Walker asked.

"Yes." Sam paused briefly, appearing as if she was trying to recall something, and then she said, "I remember asking the man I thought was JT where the girls were. He told me that they either went home or went to another facility—that the ranch wasn't taking in runaways anymore. That didn't make sense to me, though. Kids who run away aren't just going to go home, or to some other place."

Walker started to speak, but Sam continued, "Do you know what happened to them?"

Walker decided to tread carefully "No, I don't. But I'm going to try to find out."

"What did... Tom Chambers say about it? Did he say the same thing he told me?"

"I don't know; I was never given the opportunity to talk to him."

"What about the other investigator? The one from the press conference. Didn't he ask him?"

"Not that I know of. He was only focused on the drug smuggling."

"But Tom Chambers must know what happened to them. Can't somebody find out from him?" Sam paused and looked intently at Walker. "I can tell you think something bad has happened, don't you?"

Again, Walker chose his words carefully. "I'm not sure what to think, Sam. And I don't have access to Chambers. So at this point, I'm on my own." Walker could see tears starting to form in Sam's eyes, and he was afraid that she might not be able to continue, so he quickly added, "Is there anything you can tell me about the girls—where they were from... Anything at all?"

Sam was still having trouble composing herself. After a few moments she said, "Not really. They were all runaways. They never talked about their real homes, not even Crystal."

"What about e-mails or letters, anything that might have had an address on it? Or photos? Did you guys ever take pictures of each other?"

Sam spoke haltingly. "No. There were no e-mails. We weren't allowed to have phones. And my phone didn't have a camera anyway... Oh, but wait a second. When Jodi first came, she had a phone before they made her give it up. She took a picture of me with Crystal."

Walker was buoyed for a moment, but then he realized the photo was a dead end. There was no way to retrieve it.

"I'm sorry," said Sam. "That doesn't really help, does it?"

"It's all right; I'll figure out another way; I'm not going to give up on this."

Walker could see that Sam was still struggling to keep her emotions in check as she handed the list back to him. He put it in the folder and debated whether to push her to continue. He decided that he had gotten the more difficult conversation out of the way. So he extracted the page of notes he had made earlier and said, "I need to talk to you about something else."

Sam appeared reluctant, but she responded, "Okay."

"Could you tell me again about when you first figured out the man wasn't JT?"

"You mean about Topaz?"

"Yeah. Try to remember as many details as you can."

Sam appeared as if she wanted to ask why, but she didn't. She then recounted the story in a similar manner as the first time Walker had heard it.

When she finished, Walker asked, "Is it possible that he just got confused about which horse it was? Just like he said?"

"I suppose it's possible, but I don't think so. Topaz is a very distinct color. There were only three other horses on the ranch, and they didn't look anything like him." Sam wasn't able to contain her curiosity any longer. "Why are you asking me about that?"

Walker had held back his thoughts concerning what may have happened to the eight girls; he decided to do the same thing here, so he avoided answering Sam's question directly.

"I'm just bothered by the fact that he would lie about something he didn't need to lie about."

Sam looked confused. "Didn't he do it because he didn't want me to know that he wasn't JT?" A moment passed, and then an expression of recognition came across her face. "Oh, I see what you mean; even if JT was the one who was killed in the accident, there was no reason for his brother to lie about how it happened," Sam said. "Do you really think that's important?"

Walker still wasn't ready to explain himself, so he simply said, "Probably not."

Chapter Thirty-Nine

Later Monday afternoon, Walker retreated to his office to contemplate what to do next. The missing girls were obviously the most pressing priority, but without any real details, he was at a loss as to how to proceed. He decided he'd have to enlist Peter Stansky's help if he had any chance of doing what he had ostensibly promised Sam: that he'd find them.

But for the moment, Walker mentally put that on the back burner and moved on to the issue of Tom Chambers. Despite what he had said to Sam, he was reasonably sure that Tom Chambers had lied to cover up something. The question was should he pursue it?

He thought back to the moment when he had first heard about the lie from Sam. His gut had immediately told him something didn't add up. But it was even more substantial than that. Twenty years with the Bureau, not to mention his own life experience, had led him to believe that people rarely lied unless it benefited them in some way. Sure, people exaggerated about all sorts of things. But out-and-out lying when there was no benefit? Unless a person was pathological, that just didn't happen.

But Walker also understood that his desire to investigate Tom Chambers further was motivated by other factors as well. It could lead to getting some justice for Sam and maybe shining some light on Broadhurst's ineptness. But at the end of the day, as corny as it sounded, Walker wanted to know the truth.

As he found himself leaning more and more toward launching an investigation, he also recognized that he'd feel more confident if he had someone to bounce the idea off of. Dave Munoz was the obvious candidate. But since he wanted to pick Peter Stansky's brain about the missing girls, he decided to include him as well. Two minutes later, he punched in Stansky's number.

Stansky answered on the third ring.

"Hi, Craig. So to what do I owe the pleasure of hearing your voice?"

"Wow, I don't think anyone has ever answered one of my phone calls like that. What were you doing, watching Masterpiece Theatre?"

Stansky let out a short laugh, and without missing a beat, he said, "No, actually I was watching cat videos on YouTube."

It was Walker's turn to laugh. "Somehow, I can't envision that."

"I know. Who would have thunk it?" A moment passed and Stansky turned serious. "How's Sam doing?"

"She's getting there, but it's going to take some more time. Actually, she's the reason I'm calling."

"I kind of figured as much."

"Did you hold on to your copy of the case file?"

"Yeah, of course."

"The list of eight girls from the computer files, you know what I'm talking about?"

"Yes, I remember?"

"When I questioned Sam about them, she recognized the names of at least three of the girls. They were still there when she left, but she doesn't know anything more about them. Obviously, Broadhurst isn't going to try to find out where they are. I was hoping you'd be able to give me some direction."

"If I remember correctly, there was some kind of financial transaction in the files that seemed to connect to the list. You thought the girls may have been sold to someone in Canada."

"Yeah, unfortunately I still do. So I feel like I have to do something. I can't just drop it."

"No, I understand. But you don't have anything else to go on but the list of names themselves?"

"No, that's it."

"Well, that's going to make it tough, but let me see what I can do."

"Thanks, Peter, I really appreciate it," Walker said. "Did you see the press conference?"

"No. What press conference?" Stansky asked.

Walker spent the next several minutes recapping the details. He also told Stansky everything else Sam had shared with him. As he was finishing up, he said, "It might be a fool's errand reinvestigating the accident, but it's just like the missing girls. I don't feel right letting it go. I'm going to call Dave right after I hang up with you, but what do you think?"

"I know that if it's eating at you, you're not going to be able to leave it alone. So I'd say you should go for it," Stansky said. "If I find out something about the girls, I'll get back to you. And if you need me for anything else, let me know."

"I will. Thanks," Walker said. "You can go back to your cat videos now."

"I don't think so; the moment's passed."

Walker was smiling as he ended the call. He then scrolled through his list of contacts and tapped Munoz's number.

"Hi, Craig. I didn't expect to hear from you. Is everything all right?"

"Nothing bad. I just wanted to give you an update and run something by you."

"Sure, go ahead."

"I asked Sam if she knew anything about the list of girls that Peter found on Chambers' computer. She said she knew three of them, but didn't remember any details. I just got off the phone with Peter. I asked him to see what he could find out. I still think there's a good chance they're in Canada like we thought. Obviously, I didn't tell Sam that. I just told her that we were going to try to find out where they were."

"Did Peter have any ideas?" Munoz asked.

"He's going to look into it and get back to me," Walker said. "The other thing is, do you remember me telling you about how Sam figured out that it wasn't JT she was talking to at the ranch?"

"Yeah, something about the accident with the horse."

"Right. Well, it's been bothering me that Chambers would lie about that. You know as well as I do that suspects—criminals— almost never lie about things they don't have to."

"I would agree with that," Munoz said.

"So that's what doesn't make sense to me. Why do it? From what Sam told me, she was about to leave, and then Tom Chambers screws up by telling a lie he didn't have to tell."

"There's no chance it was just a simple mistake?"

"Sam says no."

"So let me guess. You want to do some more investigating?"

"I'm seriously considering it, but I wanted to get your take on it first."

"Well, obviously if Chambers really did lie about it, then it's probably worth trying to find out why. But you know that's not going to be easy," Munoz said. "I'm just thinking out loud here. First off, we're going to have to butt heads with Broadhurst, who, I remind you, is the newly appointed *Director* of Northern Border

Enforcement. And I don't think he's going to look kindly on us second-guessing him, especially with a plea deal in place, which also means that he's not going to give us access to the ranch where the accident happened, not to mention that I'm sure Chambers himself will be off-limits." Munoz paused. "So to recap, we won't be allowed access to the possible crime scene, and we won't be able to question the suspect. And the person third in charge at Homeland Security doesn't want us doing this. Wow! Who could resist that?"

Walker chuckled. "Of course, when you put it that way..." Walker's voice trailed off. A moment later he got serious again. "Actually, I did consider all those things before I called you, so hear me out. Here's what I'm thinking. Let's assume we won't be able to interview Chambers."

"Good assumption."

"So what we can do is ask for the 911 tapes. Also, we can interview the first responders who came to the ranch. I think we actually met one of them already. Officer Scanlan. And we should be able to get a copy of JT's autopsy report. Hopefully, something will jump out at us. If it doesn't, we haven't lost anything."

"So I take it you want to head back up to Maine?" Munoz asked.

"Does that mean you're in?"

"I've still got a few vacation days left. What else am I going to do?"

"Great. I'll give Chuck Dalton a call to make sure we can stay at the training facility. I was originally thinking the investigation should be unofficial, but since we're requesting 911 tapes and autopsy reports, I better get clearance from the Bureau. I'll call it in right after I call Chuck."

"So are you talking about tomorrow? What time?"

"We might as well get an early start. How about nine?"

"All right, I'll see you then. I know I was giving you a hard time before, but I actually think that it's worth checking out."

After Walker got the okay from both his supervisor and Chuck Dalton, he told Cheryl what he was planning and then went to tell Sam about his conversation with Peter Stansky. He also told her that he was going back up to Maine but suggested it was simply to ensure that nothing had changed with the plea deal. Sam was very appreciative. And if she was suspicious of the real motivation for Walker's trip to Maine, she didn't show it.

The ride up to Maine on Tuesday morning afforded Walker and Munoz the opportunity to flesh out the steps they needed to take to get the investigation up and running. But before they did that, Walker wanted to fill Munoz in on a couple of things.

"I heard from Professor Mason yesterday. Two reporters called him. He didn't give them anything, but it's got me a little concerned. I'm hoping if they don't find out anything right away they'll just move on to something else."

"How's Sam dealing with it?" Munoz asked.

"It's kind of up and down. I may have made her more anxious by suggesting that the reporters might be looking for her. That's why I decided not to tell her about the professor's phone call."

A few minutes later, Munoz said, "Obviously, you got the okay from the Bureau to go ahead with the investigation, but I'm curious what Chuck Dalton had to say, especially about Broadhurst."

"There's no new training session scheduled until after the next fiscal year starts on July first, so staying at the training facility wasn't an issue. Broadhurst is still there and probably will be for a few more weeks. Nobody seems to know where his new base of operations will be. Dalton hasn't told Broadhurst that we're coming."

"That could work to our advantage. Maybe you'll catch him off guard when you ask if you can talk to Chambers."

"That may be a moot point. Dalton called me last night to tell me that he thinks Chambers is being transferred to the federal facility at Ray Brook in Upstate New York, maybe as early as today. It's medium-level security. Evidently, Broadhurst was considering Danbury, Connecticut, but that facility is only low-level security. At least he used his head on that one. If Chambers hasn't been transferred by the time we get there, I'll ask Broadhurst if I can interview him. I don't think there's a snowball's chance in hell he'll agree, but it's worth a shot. Of course once I do ask, he's going to want to know why, and then he's going to get really pissed off if I tell him."

Walker looked over at Munoz as he continued, "I was thinking about what you said yesterday, and the truth is, I'm not really worried about Broadhurst. He's the one who took short cuts with the investigation just so he could get a promotion. I feel like all we're doing is cleaning up his mess. I guess he could try to stop us, but he's got no authority; this is a separate FBI investigation with no bearing on the plea deal. Chambers doesn't have immunity for crimes he committed nearly a year ago, especially if it involves a homicide."

Munoz returned Walker's gaze. "You're really that convinced that he killed his brother?"

"I am. Maybe we're talking manslaughter rather than murder, but yeah, I think he had something to do with it. That's the only scenario that fits, as far as I'm concerned."

Munoz looked skeptical. "I can't say I'm there yet. Obviously, the fact that Chambers lied when he didn't have to is suspicious. But on the other hand, why call 911? I mean, wouldn't it have made more sense, if he did kill his brother, to just bury him on the property and then take over his identity? Why call for an ambulance and bring in all those people?"

"I know what you're saying. I thought about that too. But I think everything he does is motivated by money. Remember what was in the will? If Tom Chambers predeceased him, JT would get everything. Without proof of death, he wouldn't."

"So... how much was it again? Six hundred thousand, not including the trust fund? And that wasn't enough?"

"I'd say, evidently not," Walker replied.

They went back and forth making various arguments over the next twenty miles before Walker moved onto something else.

"I read over the case file again last night. I found something that ties in with what Sam told me. Sam said that when Tom Chambers was claiming to be JT, he tried to make an excuse about how he mistakenly said the horse that his brother was riding was Topaz. He said that he had sold all the horses and had to tell the new owner about Topaz and just got confused."

Walker paused and glanced to his left. "I looked back through the financials, and there was a check from the Down East Ranch deposited in the church's account last September. I think we should talk to someone at Down East to see if they're the ones who bought the horses and also what they remember about what Chambers said to them."

"Where's the Down East Ranch?" Munoz asked.

"In Gardiner."

"Would you rather go there first? It's almost on the way."

"No, I want to call ahead to make sure we've got the right place. And I'd rather get to the sheriff's office as soon as possible to request the 911 tape and to see if they can help us get the autopsy report."

Chapter Forty

Chuck Dalton had let the front gate know that Walker and Munoz were coming. When they arrived at 11:15 a.m., they showed their IDs and were quickly waved through. As they pulled up to Dalton's office, he was outside waiting to greet them.

They all shook hands, and then Walker said, "Thanks for putting us up again."

"You're in the same rooms you were in before. Another week or so and I'm not sure I could have accommodated you; we've got a new group coming in. Is there anything else you need?"

"Just a way to convince Broadhurst to let us talk to Chambers," Walker said.

Dalton smiled. "I wouldn't even know where to begin with that one. Chambers is gone by the way. They moved him at seven this morning. So even if you can somehow convince Broadhurst, you'd have to travel to Ray Brook to do the interview."

"Did Broadhurst make the trip?"

"No, he's still here."

Ten minutes later, Walker and Munoz dropped off their bags in their rooms and were about to head out, when they ran into Broadhurst. It was obvious from his expression that he was surprised to see them.

"Agent Walker... and Agent..."

Munoz spoke up. "It's actually deputized Agent or Detective Munoz."

"Of course. Detective Munoz…"

Before Broadhurst could say anything else, Walker said, "Congratulations on your promotion by the way. Speaking of titles, which do you prefer now commander or director?"

Broadhurst eyed Walker warily, trying to assess his level of sincerity. "Either one is fine," he said. "I have to say, I didn't expect to see the two of you back here. Is this official FBI business?"

Walker answered carefully. "Yes and no. There are a few things we're looking into."

"Nothing to do with the Chambers case, I trust?"

"We'll see," Walker said.

It appeared to Walker that Broadhurst was trying to decide how he wanted to play out their little confrontation. Eventually, he spoke in a calm voice.

"I don't know what there is to look into. Besides, Chambers was transferred to New York this morning." Broadhurst paused. "Don't tell me you're still fixated on what happened to that girl. I don't know how many times it has to be explained to you. National security takes precedence over everything else. You need to let it go."

Walker couldn't hide his amazement at Broadhurst's mention of "national security." He responded with an edge in his voice.

"I might have been able to let it go, but then I saw your press conference."

Broadhurst stared intently at Walker, but then evidently decided to ignore the dig.

"The plea deal's been accepted, and Chambers is going to start serving his time until he's needed to testify. There's nothing more to investigate; it's over."

"I'm well aware of what the plea deal entails," said Walker. "And you're right, *your* investigation is over."

Broadhurst's nostrils flared, but he kept his tone even. "What could you possibly be looking into relative to Chambers? You mind telling me?"

Walker couldn't help himself. "I'm not comfortable talking about it until we know more."

One of the veins in Broadhurst's neck started to pulsate, but he remained relatively calm as he played his trump card. "I'm sure the FBI wouldn't do anything to compromise an ongoing Homeland Security operation."

Walker responded sarcastically "Of course not... but I'm confused. Which is it exactly? Is the investigation ongoing or is it over? You really should be more clear about that."

Broadhurst was fuming now. "You need to back off."

Walker put on a fake smile. "If you'll excuse us, Commander, we have to be someplace."

They left Broadhurst standing in the hallway.

Once Walker and Munoz were in the car, Munoz said, "What a pompous ass."

"He is that, although I didn't exactly distinguish myself either."

"Given who you were talking to, I'm not sure how else you could have handled it; he was monumentally pissed off, though."

Walker looked over at Munoz with a smirk on his face. "He was, wasn't he? So do you think I should invite him out for coffee and ask him if we can speak to Chambers, or do you think it's too soon?"

Munoz broke up laughing.

The ride to the sheriff's office took twenty minutes. Once they were inside and showed their credentials, Walker spoke to a female officer at the desk whose name tag read Tomasso.

"We're looking to get a copy of the 911 call that came in from Redemption Ranch sometime in late August of last year. Do you know what I'm talking about?"

Officer Tomasso nodded and then responded, "Yes, I do; that was a big deal around here."

Walker decided to offer more of an explanation. He didn't want it to appear that he was calling into question how the sheriff's department had investigated the accident.

"Well then, you're probably aware of what happened with Tom Chambers. We're just trying to go back to the beginning to make sure we didn't miss anything."

Tomasso seemed to accept what Walker had said without giving it a second thought. She moved on to the request.

"Even though you're FBI, I'll still need you to fill out a form. Even next of kin have to do that. Give me a second and I'll get one."

"No problem," said Walker.

She was gone less than five minutes and handed the form to Walker, who started filling it out. He looked up briefly.

"Is it easy to access the 911 calls?"

"Yeah, we used to use the state government server, but now everything's saved to the cloud out in cyberspace somewhere."

Munoz interjected, "We just started doing the same thing in Massachusetts about a year ago."

Tomasso turned toward Munoz. "I guess it's more secure, and it's just as easy to bring up the records. I don't mind it." She turned back to Walker. "As soon as you're finished, I'll just need to find the specific date of the call. I can look it up on the computer, and then it should only be a few minutes."

"Thanks," said Walker. "While we're waiting, is Officer Scanlan available?"

"No, I'm sorry, he's off today. He'll be back in tomorrow though."

A few minutes later, Walker gave Tomasso the completed form. She went behind the counter to a desktop computer and ten minutes after that she was done.

"If you want to give me your phone, I'll download the recording to it, or if you'd prefer I can transfer it."

"Use my phone; that's fine," Walker said.

Walker handed it over, and a minute later he had the 911 recording.

Tomasso then gave him two pieces of paper. "While I was downloading it, I printed up two transcripts of the call. I thought you might like hard copies to refer to. We just had a very sophisticated voice recognition software program installed; it's quite accurate."

Walker offered his thanks as he accepted the transcripts.

"Is there anything else I can do for you?" asked Tomasso.

"Actually, yes. We're looking to get a copy of the autopsy report for JT Chambers."

"I'm sorry. You have to get that from the medical examiner's office in Augusta."

"I suspected that might be the case, but I thought since we were coming here, you might know somebody in the ME's office who could help expedite it."

"Sorry, I don't, but you have to make the request in person or by mail, anyway. They don't even accept faxes, and I should warn you that getting the report could take a couple of days."

"Really?"

"Yeah. Even for law enforcement, they usually make you jump through hoops, although maybe not the FBI. If you're going there now, I could give a call over and let them know you're coming. I don't know if it will do any good, but it might."

"Thank you. I'd appreciate that. What time is Officer Scanlan scheduled to come in tomorrow?" Walker asked.

"By eight."

"Okay, we'll probably see you sometime in the morning; thanks again for your help."

Once they were out in the car, Walker said. "Isn't Augusta right next to Gardiner where the Down East Ranch is?

"Yeah, I think so."

"All right. Let me call the ranch to see if they're the ones who bought the horses. If so, we can go there right after the ME's office."

"Sounds like a plan."

Munoz punched the ME's address into his GPS while Walker placed the call to the Down East Ranch. Five minutes after explaining who he was, Walker had confirmation that the ranch had bought Topaz and the other three horses. The manager, who had negotiated the purchase wasn't sure what he could offer in the way of additional information, but he agreed to see Walker and Munoz later that afternoon.

As soon as Walker hung up, he found the 911 recording on his phone.

"Why don't we listen to the call, at least to get a sense of it?"

A moment later they heard:

"This is the 911 operator. What is your emergency?"

"My brother... There's been an accident."

"What is your location, sir?"

"The ranch... Redemption Ranch."

"In Pendleton, you mean?"

"Yes, that's it."

"What happened?"

"I think my brother must have fallen off his horse. The horse came back to the main house. I tied him up in the barn and then got in my Jeep and went out to check on my brother. I know what trail he usually rides on. I found him, but there was a lot of blood. He must have hit his head. I tried to revive him... but... I think he's... gone."

"What's your name, sir?"

"Tom Chambers... I mean that's my brother. I'm James Chambers... JT Chambers."

"All right, Mr. Chambers. I'm going to put you on hold while I switch over to the other line to dispatch the ambulance. Don't hang up, sir; stay on the line.

"The closest emergency response team is in Eustis. It's probably going to take them at least fifteen minutes to get to you."

"Okay. I'll wait by the front gate to let them in."

"I'll radio that information ahead."

Walker played it two more times before either he or Munoz spoke.

Finally, Walker asked, "So anything strike you?"

"I was trying not to think about the things we already know... as if I was just hearing it without any context. There seemed to be a few hesitations—right at the beginning and then when Chambers was asked his name."

"Yeah, I thought the same thing."

"Of course, if he did just discover his brother's body, you can understand why he wasn't thinking clearly."

"That's one explanation. Anything else?" Walker said.

"Well, when he was asked his name, initially he answered Tom Chambers, but then he quickly added that that was his brother.

Again, that could have just been an honest mistake if he was upset, but…"

"But?"

"If everything happened the way Chambers said it did, and even if for some reason he didn't immediately make the 911 call, how does he come up with the plan to take over his brother's identity so quickly? It just occurs to him all of a sudden? Nobody's that savvy. I have to say, after listening to the recording, I'm a lot closer to believing that the identity switch at least had to be premeditated. And if that's true, it calls into question the whole idea of the accident," Munoz said.

Walker nodded. "I want to play the recording again; something you just said got me thinking."

They listened for the fourth time, and then Walker offered, "No, I didn't hear what I was hoping to."

"What?" asked Munoz.

"I was wondering if Chambers had said anything about where he was calling from, whether he was using his cell phone or the landline."

"What difference does that make?"

"You mentioned the possibility of a delay in making the 911 call. Well, Chambers said he went out to check on his brother after the horse came back and found him where he had supposedly hit his head. That should have been when he called 911. If he waited until he got back to the main house, that suggests something else. Of course it could be as simple as he didn't have his cell phone with him. But that begs the question: Why wouldn't he, if he was going out searching for his brother?"

"I would agree, but let me play devil's advocate again. What if the jamming device was on? He couldn't have used his cell phone if that were the case."

"True. But again, why would he have it turned on when he's concerned about what might have happened to his brother and he's going out looking for him. It doesn't make sense. For me, it comes down to if you've got an emergency on your hands you call for help immediately. If Chambers didn't, I think you have to ask why not. Of course, even if we find out that he did call from the landline, it doesn't prove anything, but it would make me more confident that we were on the right track."

"Don't you think the sheriff's office might be able to tell you where the phone call came from? You can ask tomorrow."

The office of the medical examiner was located in a building that looked like something out of a horror story. So much so that Munoz asked rhetorically, "Doesn't Stephen King live in Maine? He could have designed this place."

Officer Tomasso's phone call saved Walker and Munoz from having to explain what the FBI was doing there. But it didn't save them from having to fill out numerous forms, having to wait until the next day to get a copy of the autopsy report, or having to come back in person to pick it up. The signs on the wall clearly indicated in bold letters, No Faxes.

They thanked the clerk who assisted them and then headed out to the Down East Ranch. Fifteen minutes later, they were talking to the manager, who belied the stoic reputation ascribed to much of Maine's population.

"Andy Gregory," said the manager as he extended his hand. "I don't believe I've ever met an FBI agent before. But that's probably a good thing, right?"

"Probably," said Walker as he shook the man's hand. "I'm Agent Craig Walker, and this is Detective Dave Munoz."

The manager shook Munoz's hand as well and then got right to business. "You said on the phone that you were looking for some information about the horses I bought from Redemption Ranch."

"Yes," said Walker. "Specifically Topaz."

Gregory nodded. "After you called I went on the Internet. The guy I bought them from—Chambers—he's in jail. Right? So I guess I don't understand why..." Gregory didn't complete the sentence, obviously expecting Walker to offer an explanation.

Walker wanted Gregory's cooperation, so he gave him a sanitized version of the story.

"It's possible that Tom Chambers committed additional crimes besides those that he's in jail for. We're trying to determine if that's true."

"So these are federal crimes? They must be if the FBI's involved, right?"

"Actually no, they're not federal. Detective Munoz and I were involved in the original investigation, and we're just doing some follow-up."

Gregory sensed that he wasn't going to get anything more out of Walker, so he left it alone. "Okay, what do you want to know?"

Walker took the lead. "Do you remember the circumstances surrounding the sale?"

"Yeah, pretty much. I got a phone call from this guy right after Labor Day last year. He asked me if I'd be interested in buying four horses. I think he was cold-calling all the ranches in the state, and we're probably second or third alphabetically. I don't think I had ever heard of Redemption Ranch before that.

"I made arrangements to go look at the horses. But before I did that, I called around and one of the managers at another ranch told me about the accident involving the brother. I always figure it's important to have every piece of information you can when you go into negotiations. Anyway, I showed up at Redemption Ranch and the first thing that struck me is that huge gate and the security cameras. Not exactly welcoming. It's not like any ranch I've ever seen. I used the intercom, and the guy I had talked to on the phone let me in. He told me he was JT Chambers, but I guess it was really his brother, although I didn't know that at the time."

"Did he tell you why he was selling the horses?" asked Munoz.

"Something about turning the place into a religious retreat. I didn't say anything, but I was thinking, 'What kind of religion walls itself off from everybody?' I'll tell you something else; he didn't know much about horses."

Walker spoke up this time. "Why do you say that?"

"A couple things. He was very uncomfortable around them. Also, he had no idea what they were worth. I would've gone as high as twelve thousand dollars for the four of them. I ended up paying seven. Of course, that's where doing my research paid off."

"What do you mean?" asked Munoz.

"Obviously, I wanted to keep the price down, so I asked which horse was involved in the accident with his brother. He told me it was Topaz."

Walker and Munoz looked at each other. Walker then said, "You're sure about that?"

"Yeah, he pointed right to him. I then asked him if the horse had a mean streak. I wasn't about to pay full price for a temperamental horse, no matter how beautiful he was.

"He said it wasn't an issue. I said, 'Fine. Then let's go for a ride. I'll get on one of the other horses, and you can ride Topaz.' He didn't like that. That's when he told me that Topaz didn't like to be ridden by men and that may have been the problem with what happened to his brother."

Walker and Munoz looked at each other again. That last piece of information didn't fit as neatly into Walker's theory as Gregory's other statements.

Gregory continued, "Anyway, I told him that I'd take Topaz off his hands for a thousand dollars and two thousand each for the other three. I picked them up two days later."

"Do you still have them here on the ranch?" asked Munoz.

"Sure. That was one of the best deals I ever made, especially for Topaz." Gregory pointed off in the distance. "You can just make him out, out there in the pasture. He's the honey-brown one. When I first got him back here, I tried riding him. That was a big mistake. The owner's wife is a little bit of a thing. She asked to try, and sure enough, there was no problem. Eventually, I figured out what the issue was. The saddle. A man's saddle tends to be bigger. Topaz had some sort of benign growth on his neck covered up by his mane. The big saddles rub against it. It was as simple as that."

Walker and Munoz talked with Andy Gregory for another fifteen minutes and then headed back to the training facility.

They decided that, all in all, the day had been productive. There certainly was no smoking gun, but they were starting to build a case. As they continued to discuss the investigation, Walker made a sobering observation.

"Gregory was prepared to pay Chambers three thousand a piece for the four horses. That's the same amount Chambers got for each of the girls he sold. We've got to find a way to nail the bastard."

Chapter Forty-One

Walker and Munoz spent a few hours Tuesday night reviewing where they were with the investigation, organizing the case file, and outlining what else needed to be done. What became quickly apparent was that they were lacking hard evidence. Hunches, gut feelings, and reasonable assumptions were all in abundance, but those by themselves weren't going to lead to an arrest. They needed more, and they were running out of places to find it.

They got an early start on Wednesday morning and were at the Franklin County Sheriff's office by 8:30. Officer Tomasso was at the front desk again.

"Good morning. I'll let Officer Scanlan know you're here; he's in the back."

Walker responded, "Thanks. But before you do that, I'd like you to check on something, if you could?"

"Sure, what is it?"

"The 911 call. Is there any way to find out where the call originated? Whether it came in on a landline, or from a cell phone?"

"I don't know, but let me see what I can find out."

"Thanks, I'd appreciate that."

As Tomasso was turning around to head into the back, Scanlan appeared.

"Agent Walker and Detective Munoz. Nice to see you again." They all shook hands, and then Scanlan continued,

"Carolyn… Officer Tomasso called me last night and told me that you were coming in today." He gestured behind him. "There's a conference room back here. We can use that."

Before everyone was seated, Scanlan asked, "How's the girl? I checked on her a couple of times, but then I saw that she had been discharged."

"She's doing pretty well," said Walker. "But it's still going to take some time."

"That's to be expected, I guess." He paused. "Are you still involved in investigating something to do with the ranch? I thought I saw that Chambers had been arrested and there was some sort of a plea deal."

"You're right," said Walker. "He was arrested. We're going back further than our original investigation. We're looking into the accident involving his brother."

"The accident? I don't understand."

Walker had decided that he was going to be as straight with Scanlan as possible, but he still eased into it.

"As you probably are aware now, JT Chambers was actually the one who was killed, and then his brother, Tom, took over his identity. We have some new information that suggests that Tom Chambers' version of what happened has some inconsistencies. I remember you telling us that you were one of the first people on the scene; that's why we wanted to talk with you."

"That's true, I was. That was late last summer, I think."

Munoz interjected, "August."

"Let me go get the incident report and my notes," said Scanlan. "Those should help refresh my memory."

Scanlan was gone less than ten minutes; he returned carrying a brown folder.

"Okay, here we are. What is it that you want to know?"

Walker responded, "Why don't you walk us through it, and we'll ask questions as they occur to us." Walker paused. "But before you start, I want to make it clear that we're not suggesting by any stretch of the imagination that you overlooked anything. There would have been no reason to view this as anything but an accident at the time."

Scanlan smiled. "I didn't take it like that. If there's some way I can help with your investigation, I'm happy to do it."

He opened the folder and began. "It looks like we got the call a little after two thirty, and we arrived at the ranch just before three o'clock." Scanlan looked up. "I seem to remember that we met the guy we thought was JT at the front gate. He had it open, and we followed him for a while out into a wooded area. I'm not sure I could describe exactly how to get there. But if it's that important, I could probably find it if we went out there."

Walker glanced over at Munoz before he spoke. "Even if we wanted to, that's not an option. We can't get onto the ranch property."

"Why not?" Scanlan asked.

"Homeland Security has taken it over."

"Really? And they won't let you investigate...?" Scanlan stopped himself. "I guess if you can't, you can't. Okay, let me think. We followed Chambers out to the woods, and then if I remember correctly, he pointed to where his brother was laying on the ground, and then the paramedics rushed over to him. Chambers stayed behind with me.

"I know he didn't say very much initially. I was trying to give him a little space, so I didn't push it. I did ask him a few questions, but then the paramedics came back over to us and confirmed that his brother was dead. Chambers wanted to go in the ambulance, so I wasn't able to speak to him again until we were at the medical center."

"What about forensics?" asked Munoz. "Did anybody do any of that?"

"I think the paramedics did, but that would probably be part of the autopsy report. I took a few pictures with my phone; I'm sure they're in the file here."

Munoz reached out his hand. "Can we see them?"

He and Walker spent several minutes studying the three photographs, but there wasn't much to see: a dead body with an obvious head wound.

As they were looking at the pictures, Scanlan said, "Another deputy and I did come back to the ranch after I spoke to Chambers at the medical center, but we didn't see anything out of the ordinary. It just looked like an accident."

Walker handed the photos back. "I would've done the same thing. There was no reason to think otherwise. As I said, we're only doing this because we've gotten some new information." Walker moved on. "Tell us about your conversation with Chambers at the medical center."

"I took some notes; they should be in here also. Give me a second." Scanlan shuffled through some papers and found what he was looking for. "You know, I just remembered something; I hope I'm not projecting here, but I recall thinking at the time that the story Chambers told me... I don't know... it seemed rehearsed."

"Why do you say that?" asked Walker.

"Because he used the exact same phrases both times I questioned him: once briefly at the ranch and once at the medical center. I didn't save my notes from the ranch because I took a full statement at the medical center. So I can't be certain, but I'm pretty sure he used the exact same words both times."

"Why don't you read us what you wrote down?" said Walker.

"Mr. Chambers indicated that he was at the main house when his brother's horse returned without him. He tied the horse up in the barn, got in his car, and went looking for him. Mr. Chambers said he knew where his brother usually rode, so he started there. He found him shortly after that, tried to revive him, but was unable to and then called 911."

Walker and Munoz shot each other a glance, and then Walker asked, "Did you take that to mean he called from the spot where he had found his brother?"

"Yeah, I thought so. Why?"

"We're trying to figure out where the 911 call originated from. Officer Tomasso's checking on it for us. It doesn't prove anything either way, but it appears Chambers might have given conflicting accounts. We already know that he lied about something else that he didn't need to lie about. Actually, that's what started this whole thing."

Scanlan was quiet for a moment and then offered, "I was going to say, maybe there was no cell service out there, but I remember that the ambulance driver used his cell phone to call the medical center."

Walker responded, "That's why if the call was made from the landline, while it's not definitive proof of anything, it's got to make you wonder." Walker repeated the argument he had made to Munoz. "If you're going out to search for your brother, why wouldn't you have your cell phone with you?"

Scanlan nodded. They talked for a few more minutes, and Scanlan offered to make copies of the incident report and his notes. As they were finishing up, Tomasso found them in the conference room.

"The 911 call came in on the landline, no question," she said.

Once Walker and Munoz were back in the car and on their way to the ME's office, Walker started to compare Scanlan's notes with the transcript of the 911 call.

"I think Scanlan was right on target about it all being rehearsed. I know we don't have his original notes, but Chambers' statement to him and in the 911 recording are almost identical. Listen to this: 'The horse came back to the main house; tied the him up in the barn; then got in my Jeep; I know what trail my brother usually rides on... tried to revive him...' It's almost word for word, and in the exact same order. It's like a script." Walker paused. "I know it doesn't prove anything. Just like the 911 call coming from the landline doesn't prove anything. But I've been doing this long enough to know that when you start adding up one piece of circumstantial evidence after another, eventually, you have to believe where it's leading you."

Munoz looked over at Walker. "You're officially preaching to the choir now. That was enough to push me over the edge," he said. "But as much as I agree with you, Craig, you know we need hard evidence if we're going to make this case stick."

Walker didn't say anything immediately, but then he offered, "I'm hoping the autopsy report is going to give us something. If not, I may have to approach Broadhurst about interviewing Chambers. I certainly hope it doesn't come to that. I hate the taste of humble pie."

Walker was about to say something else when his phone buzzed. He extracted it from his pocket and looked at the screen. Maddie's name appeared.

"Hi, Maddie."

There was a brief period of silence, and then the caller said, "It's me, Sam. Maddie let me use her phone."

"Oh... Hi, Sam. Is everything all right? Reporters didn't show up, did they?"

"No, nothing like that. I called because I was looking through some of the things I brought over from my apartment. I found something I had forgotten about."

"What's that?"

"Jodi, the girl who took my picture with Crystal before they made her give up her phone, she told me that she saved the photo so I could retrieve it when we left the ranch. She gave me her username and password, but I don't remember where it was saved to. I tried

Dropbox and Photosave, but it wasn't in either one of them. I'm wondering if I wrote down the username and password correctly."

"Why don't you give me what you have, and I'll send it along to the agent who's helping us with this? Let him see what he can do with it," Walker said.

As Sam finished dictating the information, she asked, "Were there any changes to the plea deal?"

Walker had forgotten about the white lie he had told Sam, but he was able to recover quickly.

"No, everything's still the same."

"Oh."

Walker could hear the disappointment in Sam's voice; he was tempted to say something about the current investigation, but held back. Instead, he offered a small piece of what he thought might make her feel better.

"They did move Tom Chambers to a federal facility in Upstate New York."

"I guess that's good. But once he gets out, he can still go anywhere he wants, right?"

Walker held steadfast in not revealing too much, but threw out a little hope. "As of now, yes. But a lot can happen in three years."

Sam's tone remained neutral. "I know." She paused and then said, "Do you want to talk to Maddie; she's right here."

"Sure."

Walker spent the next few minutes speaking with his daughter. After he hung up, he filled in Munoz on his conversation with Sam and then phoned Peter Stansky.

"Hi, Craig. If you're calling about the eight girls, I'm sorry; I haven't been able to find out anything yet. I think one of the problems is that they were all minors when they disappeared and probably runaways on top of that. But I'll keep trying. How are you making out?"

"We're making some progress, but nothing definitive. Broadhurst's being his usual charming self, which isn't helping."

"That's not exactly a surprise."

Walker gave Stansky an abbreviated version of what was happening with the investigation. After he finished, he said, "So the real reason I called *is* about the girls; I may have something."

Walker went on to tell Stansky everything Sam had told him. When he finished, Stansky remarked, "I'll give it my best shot. I don't have much else anyway. The only thing is those cloud-based storage sites have multiplied like crazy over the past couple of years. There are probably well over a hundred and fifty of them. It's going to take a while, but I'll give it a go."

"Thanks, Peter."

After Walker hung up, it was quiet in the car for a few moments, and then Munoz observed, "You know, as I was listening to you explain where we were with the investigation to Peter, I began to wonder if we're deluding ourselves. The truth is we really don't have a whole lot to hang our hats on. And even if by some miracle Broadhurst gives the okay to talk to Chambers, he doesn't have to talk to us, and when you think about it, why would he?"

"Yeah, unfortunately, all of that has crossed my mind as well."

Chapter Forty-Two

The clerk at the ME's office had told Walker and Munoz the day before that copies of the autopsy report would be available after eleven o'clock on Wednesday morning. They showed up at five past. The same clerk waited on them again.

"Good morning, gentlemen." She glanced back at the clock on the wall. "You're very prompt. Give me a moment." She went over to her desk and returned with two manila envelopes. "I made an extra copy for you, no charge."

Walker responded with a smile. "Thank you."

"As it so happens, Dr. Michaels, the doctor who did the autopsy, is here today. I think he'd be willing to speak with you, if you'd like."

"That would be terrific, thanks."

"All right, wait here. I'll go see if he's free."

Several minutes later, a tall man who appeared to be in his late forties followed the clerk up to the front counter. He offered his hand to both Walker and Munoz.

"Hello, I'm Dr. Michaels."

"I'm Agent Walker, and this is Detective Munoz."

"Pleased to meet both of you. I understand that you requested a copy of the Chambers's autopsy. I've got a few minutes, if I can answer any questions."

"We'd appreciate that."

"I have an office in the back that I share with a number of other colleagues, but I'm the only one here today. Why don't we go back there?" He turned toward the clerk. "Janice, would you get me the Chambers' autopsy file?"

"I didn't put it away. I figured you might want it."

"You're way ahead of me, as usual."

Dr. Michaels went over to sit behind his desk as he offered the two chairs in front of it to Walker and Munoz.

"Please sit down. As I said, I share the office with other doctors. There are twenty of us statewide who perform autopsies part time. Most of us have our own practice; we do this mainly to help out the state; it doesn't actually pay all that well. I just happen to be here today catching up on some paper work." He paused. "So may I ask why the FBI is interested in the Chambers' autopsy?"

Walker hesitated but decided a moment later to be somewhat direct. "I can't go into a lot of detail at this point, but we're looking into the possibility that it wasn't an accident."

Dr. Michaels appeared surprised. "Really? That was one of my first autopsies; I remember it pretty clearly. As I recall, it was very straightforward. Although, as you'll see, I probably went overboard with all the testing I ordered."

"Speaking as a member of law enforcement, I can say we usually like overboard," Walker said.

Dr. Michaels smiled. "I'm not sure my boss feels the same way, but I'm still here, so I guess I didn't mess up too badly." The doctor paused and looked as though he wanted to ask more questions, but he didn't.

"If you'll open up your envelopes, you'll see what I mean. There are probably fifty pages in total. Most autopsy reports are twenty pages at the most," the doctor said. "So how do you want to proceed?"

"Why don't you take us through the basics of the report, and we'll ask questions if we need clarification."

"That's fine. Let me just skim through the first few pages. Most of it is summary; that should help me recall some of the specifics."

Walker and Munoz opened their copies and read along silently while Dr. Michaels did the same. After several minutes, the doctor said, "As you can see, I determined the cause of death to be blunt force trauma to the head. The trauma was quite evident. There are photos in the back of the file, although your copies may not be as clear. I was told that the victim had fallen off his horse and hit his head on a large rock. His wounds were consistent with that."

Munoz interjected. "Did you say 'wounds,' plural?"

"Yes. Initially, the close proximity of the two of them puzzled me slightly, but then when I saw a picture of the way the rock was shaped, I concluded that when he fell, his head hit the top section first, and then hit the flat portion of the rock below. There were even rock particles in his hair, which I had tested. That's what I mean by going overboard."

"Are the pictures of the rock in here as well?" asked Walker. "I've seen photos of the victim taken by an officer from the sheriff's department, but I don't think the entire rock was visible in them."

"As I said, any copies of the photos may not be very good. Let me see if I can find the originals in the folder." A minute later the doctor produced a photo and handed it to Walker. "See where the top part of the rock juts out and then the ledge below? That's why I think there were two wounds, although, as I said, they were quite close together."

Walker handed the picture back. "Thank you."

Dr. Michaels continued, "Another reason why I didn't question the notion that it was an accident was the toxicology report. The victim had a substantial amount of fentanyl in his system. He would have had trouble standing, never mind riding a horse."

"Fentanyl?" asked Walker.

"Yes and a very large quantity. I assume with all the publicity surrounding opioid abuse that you're familiar with its effects."

Walker nodded and then glanced knowingly over at Munoz as he remembered that fentanyl was one of the drugs found in the tunnel at the ranch.

Dr. Michaels saw the exchange and asked, "Is that significant somehow?"

Walker answered. "I don't know; it might be."

Dr. Michaels didn't pursue it further. He spent the next fifteen minutes going over more of the report and answering questions. As he was finishing up, he said, "I don't think there's much else I can tell you. You can read the rest for yourselves, and if you have any other questions, please feel free to contact me."

With that he extracted two business cards out of a cardholder and handed one each to Walker and Munoz. He then added, "I hope you discover whatever it is you're looking for. As I said, I may have gone overboard, but in this case, it was probably a good thing for you. You can't exhume the body to retest anything. Chambers was cremated two days after the autopsy."

On the ride back to the training facility, Walker and Munoz were more frustrated than hopeful.

"I think it's more of the same," said Walker. "There's no doubt that everything points to premeditation, but I don't think we have enough to convince a prosecutor to move forward, never mind a jury."

Walker held up the envelope containing the autopsy report.

"But at least we have some light reading for tonight."

Shortly before they got back to the complex, Walker's phone rang; it was Peter Stansky. Walker didn't even say hello.

"Don't tell me you found something already."

"I did. I just got lucky. It was about the tenth storage site I tried; it's called Shoebox. There are only three pictures in the girl's account. I'll send them to you as soon as I hang up. I assume you want me to run them through our database using the facial recognition software. I can also pass them along to the BEST units so they can do the same. We think the girls are in Canada anyway, right?"

"Yeah, do both of those things, please. That's amazing work, Peter. Thank you."

"Glad to help. Any progress on your end?" Stansky asked.

Walker recapped what was happening and closed by saying, "If the autopsy report doesn't give us something, I'm not sure what else we can do. We've pretty much decided that interviewing Chambers is a nonstarter. Broadhurst's probably not going to give us access, but even if he did, there's no incentive for Chambers to cooperate. We'd just be wasting our time driving to New York"

Stansky commiserated, indicated he would continue to follow up on the photos, and ended the call.

Once they were back at the training complex, Walker touched base with Cheryl and forwarded the photos Peter Stansky had discovered to her phone.

Cheryl asked, "Don't you want to tell Sam about them?"

"No, you can do that. And why don't you print out copies of them for her as well? Just tell her that we're still working on trying to find the girls and that finding the pictures was a big help. I'm hesitant to talk to her; I'm afraid I'll slip about what we're really doing up here. I almost did that yesterday."

Walker and Munoz spent the next several hours evaluating where they were with the case. What did they know for certain?

What did they surmise? What could they prove, even circumstantially? It was not a pretty picture.

After dinner, Walker went for a run, while Munoz read the entire autopsy report cover to cover. In Walker's case, the run cleared his head; in Munoz's case, reviewing the autopsy report did the opposite.

There was more discussion in the early evening, and then they both went off to their rooms just before nine o'clock. The two of them spent the rest of the night reading about the weight of JT Chambers' liver and kidneys postmortem, the contents of his stomach, detailed toxicology reports, blood screening results, mineral analysis, signs of disease in Chambers' vital organs, etc., etc.

Munoz finished reading the report for the sixth time just before midnight and decided to go to bed.

At 5:30 in the morning, he found himself in a semiconscious state: half-awake and half-asleep. An idea that had begun to form in the back of his brain started to gain momentum. Initially, his subconscious dismissed it as part of a dream fantasy with no basis in reality. But as his body began to adjust to waking up, it became clear that he had come up with something significant.

Two minutes later, his eyes opened wide, and he shot up into a sitting position. He moved his head from side to side, trying to shake the thought from its foundation, testing whether it was as substantial as he hoped it was. It remained intact.

He then threw the covers off, went over to his laptop and powered it up. As it was coming to life, he grabbed the autopsy report, found the section he was looking for, and reread it. He then typed a few words into the search engine, looked at the choices offered, and clicked on the first one. Five minutes later, Munoz closed it out and clicked on the second offering; then he looked at the third option.

Each time he became more and more excited. They all said the same thing. He then went to the case file and began searching for some additional corroboration, but what he was looking for wasn't there. He was convinced, however, that it was simply that he hadn't written it down, not that he was mistaken.

He glanced at the clock. It was only 6:20. But Munoz didn't hesitate. Now that he was sure, Walker needed to know immediately.

Chapter Forty-Three

Walker's phone buzzed at 6:21 a.m. Before he even looked at the screen, he concluded it had to be Munoz, and it had to be important. The first words out of Munoz's mouth confirmed it.

"I found something; I'll be right there." Munoz gathered everything he needed, left his room, and headed several yards down the hallway.

Walker already had his door open.

"What did you find?"

"The mineral analysis of the rock particles."

"What about it?" Walker asked.

"The report says that they're limestone fragments. The rock that Chambers supposedly hit his head on is granite. The whole ranch is surrounded by granite." Munoz's words quickened. "I checked the Internet; there are no limestone deposits in that part of Maine, none." He paused. "But you know what *is* made of limestone?"

The realization came to Walker even before Munoz could supply the answer to his own question. "The rock the professor told us about. The one in the picture—the one that disappeared."

"Exactly," Munoz said.

Walker was quiet for a few moments as he tried to process all the ramifications of what he had just learned.

"Wow; that was a great catch, Dave. This is just what we needed."

"At the very least, it proves his brother's death couldn't have happened the way Tom Chambers said it did."

"Okay, why don't we try to put together a theory of what we think *did* happen? We should use the outline we made yesterday—what we know for sure, what we assume, and what we can now prove." Walker found the outline among a stack of papers, and they went to work. There was no large whiteboard in Walker's room, so everything had to be written down on a pad of paper. They started with the basics: motive, means, and opportunity.

The motive seemed obvious. Tom Chambers killed his brother to assume his identity and get his hands on the inheritance. And as they had agreed before, Tom Chambers most likely staged the accident in order to confirm proof of death and to cash in on another four hundred thousand dollars.

And thanks to the mineral analysis, they now knew the means: two blows to the head with the limestone rock depicted in the portrait in the main house. And while they didn't have the actual murder weapon, the conclusion that it was that particular rock now seemed unassailable.

As they began to consider the idea of "opportunity," they realized that creating a reasonable theory of what had transpired had some uncertainty. Had the murder been committed in a fit of rage after an argument, or was it done methodically with premeditation? There was no way to know for sure, but then Walker remembered the fentanyl. If Tom Chambers had somehow gotten his bother to ingest the drug, his brother would have been relatively incapacitated, and killing him would have been much easier.

The scenario involving the fentanyl seemed the most likely to both Walker and Munoz, but they acknowledged that the "opportunity" phase of their theory was much less definitive than the motive and the means.

Shortly after they concluded their discussion on that topic, Walker made a suggestion.

"I think we should contact Professor Mason and confirm about the limestone, and also ask whether there was any chance JT Chambers was involved in drug use. I think I know the answer, but I'd like to hear it from the professor." Walker looked over at his phone to check the time. "It's too early to call now. Why don't we plan to meet in the dining hall for breakfast in an hour or so, and then I'll give him a call?"

"I think that's a good idea, but it probably means you're going to have to tell him why you're asking those questions," Munoz said.

"Yeah, it probably does. But given everything else he's recently found out about Tom Chambers, I'm not sure it's going to come as a complete shock."

When they finished eating, it was nearly 8:30. Walker waited a few minutes more and then placed the call to the professor. He answered on the third ring. After Walker heard "Hello," he said, "I hope I'm not calling too early. It's Agent Walker."

"No, it's not too early at all; I've been up for a couple of hours. I suspect this isn't a social call, is it?"

"I'm afraid not." Walker got right to the point. "We have reason to believe that JT's death wasn't an accident. We think that Tom Chambers was responsible."

"This just keeps getting more and more disturbing. Thank God Lemuel isn't alive to see this. What do you think happened?"

Walker explained the theory he and Munoz had developed and then asked the two primary questions he wanted answers to.

"I was hoping to confirm what you told us about the rock that was in the portrait—the one that came from England. That was limestone, correct?"

"Yes, as I told you, it came from the White Cliffs of Dover according to Lemuel. Why do you ask?"

"We think that was the murder weapon. Fragments of limestone were found in JT's head wound. As far as we can determine, there's no natural limestone formations on the ranch property. And the fact that the rock disappeared…" Walker didn't finish the sentence.

"This is just awful," the professor said.

Walker waited a moment and then posed the next question. "Do you think there's any possibility that JT was into drugs, specifically opioids?"

"After all that's happened, I'm reluctant to answer definitively, but that would be totally out of character for him."

"That's what we thought too. I'm sorry if I've put a further damper on your memories of the Chambers family."

"As difficult as all this is, I appreciate you keeping me informed. So what's going to happen now?"

"We're still sorting that through. We may not have an answer for a while." Walker paused and then said, "Take care, Professor, and thanks for your help."

As Walker hung up, he looked over at Munoz. "I assume you got all that."

"Yeah, I'm glad he was able to confirm what we thought," Munoz said. "So where *do* we go from here?"

"The problem as I see it now," said Walker, "is that if we're hoping to charge Chambers with murder… or even manslaughter, it has to be done through the state. I don't see how it can be considered a federal crime. So I don't know exactly who we bring it to. I would assume it's the local D.A., but I don't know for sure. I was thinking that we should talk to Chuck Dalton to see if he has any local connections."

They waited until nine o'clock and then headed over to Dalton's office. He was able to see them right away.

"What's up?" Dalton said.

"We just got a major break in the investigation." Walker looked over toward Munoz. "Thanks to Dave."

For the next several minutes, he and Munoz took turns laying out the case against Tom Chambers. As they finished up, Walker said, "We're not exactly sure who has jurisdiction. We were hoping you might know one of the local prosecutors."

"I'm sorry, I don't. But I do know Sharon Wentworth. She's the US attorney for this district, and she's as sharp as they come. She might hand it off to one of her assistants, but I would think somebody in her office would be able to give you some direction. And as an added bonus, there's no love lost between Sharon Wentworth and Broadhurst. In fact, he pulled rank on her concerning the Chambers plea deal. She was none too thrilled."

"That sounds like a place to start," offered Walker. "Do you think she'd be willing to talk with us?"

"I can give her a call and find out," Dalton said.

An hour later, Walker's phone rang. "Agent Walker, this is Sharon Wentworth, United States attorney for Maine. Chuck Dalton asked me to contact you. Can you tell me what it is you're looking to do?"

Walker was surprised at how quickly everything had developed, but he was able to outline his dilemma coherently.

When he finished, Sharon Wentworth said, "Are you available tomorrow morning?"

"Uh... Yes."

"Okay, bring everything related to the case, including the initial investigation. I'll see you at nine o'clock."

Before Walker could say anything else, the line went dead.

Walker and Munoz spent the bulk of Thursday reviewing their notes, organizing the case files, and making an additional copy for Sharon Wentworth.

They left the training facility at 7:30 a.m. and were in Portland by 8:45. They were seated outside the US attorney's office for no more than five minutes when she invited them in.

Sharon Wentworth was a stunningly attractive woman, about five seven with an athletic figure and a generous smile. There was also an aura surrounding her that exuded confidence.

After formal introductions and handshakes she said, "Gentlemen, come in and sit down, please. So after your phone call yesterday, I gave a lot of thought as to how you ought to proceed. And frankly, I think the best approach is to go the federal route."

Walker and Munoz looked at each other, as she continued, "I can see that that surprises you. But here's my thinking. Any local prosecutor is going to have to try this case in a vacuum. He or she won't be able to bring in any of Chambers' prior bad acts. But depending on what's in those documents you brought me, the federal government might be able to. At the very least, I'm thinking we would charge Tom Chambers with first-degree murder, and since I would declare that the crime was committed in order to further possible terrorist activity, that makes it a federal offense and gives us a lot more leeway. We can thank Commander—or should I say Director Broadhurst for that little wrinkle. I assume you saw the press conference."

Both Walker Munoz nodded and said, "Yes."

"All right, now that you know what I'm thinking," said the US attorney, "Talk me through everything and be as thorough as possible. I've set aside two hours."

Munoz handed Sharon Wentworth a copy of both case files, and he and Walker began. They started with the most recent development: the discovery of the particle analysis. And for the next half hour, they outlined everything they had against Chambers, including statements by Professor Mason, the autopsy reports, and the possible motive.

They then turned to the initial investigation and how they became involved. Sharon Wentworth asked, "So, you two were the ones who found the girl?"

"Yes," said Walker.

The US attorney shook her head. "I had no idea. Broadhurst never mentioned any of that. He made it seem as if his men had found her. Unbelievable. Okay, what else?"

Walker and Munoz explained about the computer files, the cash, the diary, and then gave additional details about the will to put their theory about the motive in context. Eventually, assuming Wentworth knew all about it, Walker mentioned the eight girls.

The US attorney appeared stunned. "What are you talking about? What girls?"

Walker delineated everything: the $24,000 in Canadian currency, as well as the shorthand notations and the conclusion he had reached.

When he finished, Wentworth asked, "And Broadhurst knew all about this?"

"Absolutely, but he said we couldn't prove it, so he was going with what he could prove."

"Yeah, that sounds like him, especially given that he had to move so quickly to make sure he got his promotion. I'm sure that's one of the reasons I got pushed out of the way; he knew I would have fought him on dropping that part of the plea deal if I had known about it. Eight girls disappear and Chambers gets immunity? I knew Broadhurst was an arrogant ass, but this is unconscionable. But he won't be able to force me out this time; there's no potential terrorist threat, and that's the only time he has authority over me. Do you have any idea what happened to the girls?"

"We have our suspicions." Walker shared the theory he and Munoz had developed and also told Wentworth about the photos and what Peter Stansky was doing.

The next hour seemed to go by very quickly, and then Sharon Wentworth said, "I need to study the case files further, but I'm beginning to see the strategy I can use. I'm going to call you tomorrow and let you know what's happening. Are you still going to be around?"

"We can be," said Walker.

"I'm not sure it'll be necessary, but just in case I need to talk to you in person. Okay, you'll hear from me tomorrow."

True to her word, the US attorney contacted Walker early Saturday morning. She asked him to have Peter Stansky send her everything he had on the photos, including who he had forwarded them to. She closed by saying, "I hope you understand, Agent Walker, I tend not to do anything halfway. So I'm going to take over from here. I'm putting four full-time investigators on this. And I promise you, I'll figure out a way to make it right."

It was ironic, thought Walker. *Broadhurst had spoken nearly the exact same words to him as Sharon Wentworth just had. The difference was he believed her.*

Chapter Forty-Four

JULY

Sam had decided to return to her apartment for good just prior to the July Fourth weekend when Maddie's brother Mark was due to come home for a visit and to reclaim his room. Maddie, Cheryl, and Craig had urged Sam to stay, but she said it was time. Walker still hadn't told her about the investigation into the circumstances surrounding JT Chambers' death. If for some reason Sharon Wentworth wasn't able to get an indictment, he didn't want to see Sam disappointed again.

Walker was able to help Sam with another matter, however: a new phone. And this time it wasn't a disposable. His FBI badge convinced the clerk at the wireless store that despite her age, Sam was considered an adult and could enter into a contract. Sam expressed her gratitude and wrote down her new phone number and her new e-mail address for him to give to Maddie.

Two weeks after Sam's departure, Walker got a call from Professor Mason.

"Hello, Agent Walker."

"Hi, Professor. How are you?"

"I'm doing well, thank you. I think this is a bit of a role reversal. I actually have some news for you that I don't believe you're aware of."

"What's that?" Walker asked.

"I received a call from the head of the Ohio branch of the Church of Universal Redemption. In light of Tom Chambers' incarceration and the scandal surrounding it, the church has decided to sever all ties with the Maine property—and they didn't even know about the possible additional charges. You haven't heard anything, have you?"

"No, not as of yet."

"Anyway, the church is selling the property to the state of Maine for one dollar. The only condition is that a portion of the property has to be set aside as a museum focusing on the church's early years in America. The main house will be turned into a visitor's center.

"They want the rest of the property to be a memorial to the Underground Railroad movement. That's where I come in. They want me to oversee that part of the project. Evidently, Lemuel told them about my interest and vouched for me. So they're trusting that I'll be fair in my depiction of the church's role."

"That's wonderful, Professor, congratulations."

"Thank you. As part of the sale, the church petitioned the court to allow me to take possession of the diary immediately. That way I can begin to plan the exhibits and make sure they're historically accurate. Also, I'm seriously considering writing another book based on the contents of the diary. But, we'll see... one thing at a time."

"I don't think they could have chosen anybody better," Walker said.

"You're very kind," the professor replied. "Oh, I almost forgot. The head of the church also confided in me that another reason they sold the property was to negate the provision allowing Tom Chambers to live there in perpetuity once he's released. That provision was only valid if the property continued to be church owned."

"I think they did the right thing."

"I agree."

The professor started to say good-bye, when Walker interrupted him. "Professor, do you mind if I ask you something?"

"Of course not. What?"

"I've been wondering about this, and every time I was speaking with you I forgot to bring it up. When I was in the tunnel, there were these metal rings. In fact, Sam was chained to one of them. If the tunnel was meant to help the slaves escape to Canada, why were they chained to the wall?"

"Actually, they weren't. There was usually a rope threaded through those rings, and the slaves held on to the rope to maintain their footing. It was obviously dark in the tunnel, but they rarely used torches. First of all, as the slaves were entering and exiting the tunnel, the torches would have easily been spotted. And secondly, the torches used up too much oxygen in the tunnels." The professor paused. "I'm glad you pointed that out. I'll have to make sure we post information about that once the exhibit opens."

"Glad to be of assistance, even if it was out of ignorance."

Shortly after he hung up, Walker called Munoz and Stansky and told them about his conversation with the professor. He also indicated that he hadn't heard anything from Sharon Wentworth as of yet.

But that changed two days later.

"Agent Walker, Sharon Wentworth here. I'm sorry I haven't gotten back to you sooner, but I've been at this nonstop. I was able to finalize a deal this morning. It'll be formally announced in the next day or two. But I assure you, there won't be any press conference. Chambers will be pleading guilty to involuntary manslaughter. He's going away for ten years."

"In addition to the three he's already going to serve?" Walker asked.

"Yes, the sentences are not concurrent."

"If he's pleading to involuntary manslaughter, how did you get him to agree to a ten-year sentence? I've never heard of that."

"To quote the Godfather, 'I made him an offer he couldn't refuse,' although it took a bit of doing to get there. Even when I told Chambers and his lawyer what we had on him, they said they'd rather take their chances with a trial… if we could even get an indictment.

"I told them that Chambers had better waive the indictment and settle for a plea deal, or he'd be charged with human trafficking. Of course, his lawyer reminded me that he had immunity on those charges. And then I reminded him that that was true, at least as far as the United States was concerned, but not with our Canadian friends. I could make one phone call and he'd be extradited in a heartbeat. And the law in Canada is a lot tougher when it comes to human trafficking. Life sentences are not uncommon, especially if the victims are under eighteen.

"As an added incentive, I told him that I had talked with Eli Peters, who, in exchange for a reduced sentence, was more than willing to testify about the deal he had brokered for Chambers to sell the eight girls. After that revelation, Chambers and his lawyer came to their senses and tentatively accepted the deal. Chambers was adamant, however, that his brother's death was an accident, which I'm still not buying. But that was his last condition. He wanted the charge to be involuntary manslaughter. That way, he said, people would believe it was an accident. I didn't care if we called it jaywalking, as long as he went away for an additional ten years. I suppose I might have gotten more if I pushed, but I wasn't willing to take that chance. It could have fallen apart. Plus, I wanted to put this to bed and let everybody get on with their lives, particularly Sam."

"Well, it's no reflection on you, but it's more than I expected we were going to get, especially when we started the investigation," said Walker. "Thank you."

"You're welcome. But we should all be thanking you for being so persistent. You and your partner are the ones who really made this happen."

"It's nice of you to say that, even if it is an exaggeration."

There was a short period of time when nobody spoke, and then Sharon Wentworth said, "I do have some news on the girls; I'm afraid it's not as positive as we'd like. We got a hit on two of them through facial recognition. They were picked up for prostitution in Edmonton; that's why they were in the system. It appears they weren't selling themselves by choice. The guy responsible has evidently taken off. The Canadian authorities are trying to track him down.

"They did find one more girl in an apartment where the girls stayed, but at this point, they have no idea what happened to the other five. The three girls they did find are being returned to their families in the States; any charges against them have been dropped."

"Do you know the names of the girls they found?"

"I don't remember off the top my head, but I'll get them and send them to you. Come to think of it, I do remember one name. It was Crystal something."

"She was Sam's best friend at the ranch," Walker said.

"Well, at least you can tell Sam that she's safe. I wish we knew where the other girls were. But, hopefully, now that the Canadian authorities are aware of what happened, they'll be able to find them."

Walker decided to call Sam before he let Munoz and Stansky know what Sharon Wentworth had shared with him. Sam answered on the second ring.

"Mr. Walker?"

"Hello, Sam."

"Hi."

"I… just got some news that I think you'll want to hear."

Walker outlined much of what Sharon Wentworth had told him about the Chambers' plea deal, leaving out some of the more unseemly parts.

When he finished, Sam said, "Thank you for everything you did. You and your wife, and Maddie... I don't know how..." She was unable to continue.

A few moments passed and Sam was able to speak again. "I'm glad that he'll be in prison for that much longer... but I don't know what it is... the last couple of weeks I felt like it didn't matter as much; I was going to be okay. I wasn't going to allow him to have that power over me. Does that make sense?" she asked.

"Yeah, it does. Despite your age, you're one of the strongest people I know, Sam."

"Thanks for saying that." She paused. "I had even decided that I was going to apply to the University of Maine and major in veterinarian studies. It didn't matter that he could be coming back there."

"That's great, Sam," Walker said. "There's something else I need to tell you."

"What?"

"They found Crystal."

"Oh my God! Is she all right?"

Walker didn't think it was his place to talk about the circumstances, so he just said, "She was in Canada, but she's back in the States now. You won't be able to contact her directly, but if you give me permission, I know somebody who can get your e-mail address to her. Would that be all right?"

"Of course." Emotion began to creep into Sam's voice. "What about Jodi... and the other girls?"

"They found two more of them, but I don't have their names yet. I'll let you know as soon as I do. But the other girls... we don't have any information on them."

Sam had trouble speaking. "That could have been me," she said.

There was nothing Walker felt he could say. A moment passed and then he offered, "You and Maddie have Habitat this Saturday, right?"

"Yes."

"Afterward, why don't you come over for dinner? We haven't seen you in a while," Walker said.

Sam hesitated and then said, "I'd like that. That would be nice, thank you." She paused and seemed to get her equilibrium back. "But only on one condition. We have to play Uno and Monopoly."

The End

❧About the Author❧

Thomas Hall is a former English teacher and middle school and high school principal. Two of the schools where he was the principal received national recognition for their academic excellence. He and his wife Marcia live in Central Massachusetts. They have three adult children.

Mr. Hall was born on Long Island, New York and lived there for the first seventeen years of his life before his family moved to Massachusetts. After graduating from high school he received a full athletic scholarship to Northeastern University for track. He received his Bachelor's and Master's degrees from Northeastern.

Although writing has always been a passion, he limited his efforts to short stories and non-fiction articles until after he retired and had sufficient time to tackle a novel.

His first book *"Hidden"* was published in 2013, and after receiving much acclaim in the literary industry, established Tom as a recognized professional author.

His second published work *"Nothing as it Seems"* was released in 2015 continuing his success.

"No Loose Ends" is Tom's third work in the Walker-Munoz Series.

When Mr. Hall is not writing, he enjoys reading, going to the movies, jogging, and playing softball. Over the past several years he has participated in numerous Senior Softball tournaments throughout the United States and Canada. Mr. Hall can be contacted at:

tomhallauthor@aol.com.

CPSIA information can be obtained
at www.ICGtesting.com
Printed in the USA
FFOW03n0304140317
33317FF